Meïr Aaron Goldschmidt

and the Poetics of Jewish Fiction

Judaic Traditions in Literature, Music, and Art

Harold Bloom *and* Ken Frieden, *Series Editors*

Select titles from Judaic Traditions in Literature, Music, and Art

Bridging the Divide: The Selected Poems of Hava Pinhas-Cohen
Sharon Hart-Green, ed. and trans.

Lingering Bilingualism: Modern Hebrew and Yiddish Literatures in Contact
Naomi Brenner

Literary Hasidism: The Life and Works of Michael Levi Rodkinson
Jonatan Meir; Jeffrey G. Amshalem, trans.

My Blue Piano
Else Lasker-Schüler; Brooks Haxton, trans.

Social Concern and Left Politics in Jewish American Art: 1880–1940
Matthew Baigell

Travels in Translation: Sea Tales at the Source of Jewish Fiction
Ken Frieden

The Travels of Benjamin Zuskin
Ala Zuskin Perelman

Vilna My Vilna: Stories by Abraham Karpinowitz
Helen Mintz, trans.

Meïr Aaron Goldschmidt and the Poetics of Jewish Fiction

◆ ◆ ◆

DAVID GANTT GURLEY

Syracuse University Press

Syracuse, New York 13244-5290

First Edition 2016
16 17 18 19 20 21 6 5 4 3 2 1

∞ The paper used in this publication meets the minimum requirements of the American National Standard for Information Sciences—Permanence of Paper for Printed Library Materials, ANSI Z39.48-1992.

For a listing of books published and distributed by Syracuse University Press, visit www.SyracuseUniversityPress.syr.edu.

ISBN: 978-0-8156-3486-7 (hardcover) 978-0-8156-3472-0 (paperback)
978-0-8156-5384-4 (e-book)

Library of Congress Cataloging-in-Publication Data
Available from publisher upon request.

Manufactured in the United States of America

This book is dedicated to all the Fontenots, but especially my mother, Janice Marie.
Without her undying love and unwavering support for my education,
none of this would have been possible: you taught me
my first words and how to love language.

◆ ◆ ◆

Contents

◆ ◆ ◆

Acknowledgments

Many people over the course of my education and life have contributed to this work in various ways. My days at Bard College were seminal in my formation as a writer and thinker, and I would like to begin by thanking Richard C. Wiles. Dick, as I called him, was an amazing and gifted teacher yet treated me like a colleague. More than any other he was the scholar who introduced me to the life of the mind, and I will always be grateful for the many penetrative and engaging discussions I had under his tutelage. In the acknowledgments to my BA thesis, I wrote how everything I would write after Bard would always bear his name, so I am more than proud to mention him here; I am beholden. While at the University of California at Berkeley, I was fortunate to work with many outstanding scholars in Near Eastern Studies and Scandinavian. I would like to thank my dissertation advisor, Karin Sanders, who saw early iterations of this work and offered many productive thoughts on Meïr Goldschmidt and Golden Age Denmark. I am especially indebted to Joseph Duggan and Carol Clover. I became more invested in Goldschmidt while I was at Brandes Skolen in Copenhagen under the direction of Pil Dahlerup. Pil's thoughts and insights were invaluable to my progress as a scholar of Danish, and she brilliantly encouraged me to look deeper into Goldschmidt's English stories. I spent many hours in the manuscript collection of the Royal Library in Copenhagen thanks to the generosity of Ivan Boserup. Over the years I have had many great discussions with Poul Behrendt and Mads Bunch concerning Goldschmidt, and I am grateful for their enthusiasm and expertise. My time at the Center for Jewish Studies at Harvard allowed me to refocus and refine my thinking on Goldschmidt in a very productive environment. I would like to thank Bernard Septimus and Shaye Cohen for all their early support in this endeavor. I would also like to thank my colleagues in the Department of German and Scandinavian at the University of Oregon, especially Michael Stern, who has from the beginning believed in this project, and Jeffrey Librett, who advised me during the manuscript's publication. My good friend Martin Klebes was also instrumental in his support and always unstinting with his time. My colleagues in Judaic Studies—Deborah Green, David Wacks, Judith Baskin, and Daniel Falk—also offered many valuable perspectives during the book's composition. I would like to thank my longtime friend and collaborator Edan Dekel, whose spirit of ethics and whose love of poetry have guided me past many a windmill. I would also thank all the students who have sat in my Scandinavian and Jewish literature classes over the years and who, after being assigned to do so, diligently read and discussed Goldschmidt with me. Many thanks to the Oregon Humanities Center for their generous support. Last but not least, I am also incredibly grateful for my family, friends, and community. My mother and sister have been such special influences in my life, and I owe them much more than could ever be said. I will show this book to my grandfather, Pervis Fontenot, and I suspect that his pride will mean the most of all. It has been a great pleasure sharing Goldschmidt with you all.

Meïr Aaron Goldschmidt

and the Poetics of Jewish Fiction

Prologue

"In the Spirit of 'Num"

The Jewish writer Meïr Aaron Goldschmidt (1819–1887) was born during the Golden Age of Danish culture (1800–1850).[1] Though not as well known to a modern audience as his elder contemporaries Hans Christian Andersen (1805–1875) and Søren Kierkegaard (1813–1855), the two titans of Golden Age Copenhagen, Goldschmidt was, by his own account, destined to be a major figure in the halcyon days of Danish letters. The Danish Golden Age was an era of mental radiance, poetry, fine arts, and choreography, coupled with great scientific and social achievement.[2]

Reforms that had been set in motion in the late eighteenth century brought about in the early nineteenth century an era of cultural change in Danish life, culminating in a sudden and new constitution in May 1849 that limited the power of the monarchy and gave freedom and full rights to all of its citizens. In an age of popular government, Golden Age Denmark was an enigmatic

> period of literary and artistic splendor, of a cultural blossoming in which intellectual, artistic, and ecclesiastical life was dominated by the brilliant writers, artists, and clerics. . . . The Golden Age was the collective product of the scions and servants of an elite which was a very narrow and highly urban social stratum. This brilliant elite shone all the more brightly in the first half of the nineteenth century. . . . The members of the generation of urban aristocrats which produced the Golden Age were the last representatives of their class who could pretend to speak for Denmark as a whole.[3]

This passage, as beautifully as it describes the age, does not make room for such a writer as Meïr Goldschmidt, whose work despite being in a national, European vernacular is already a translation of a deeper linguistic matrix of Jewish thought. Goldschmidt was neither an aristocrat nor a member of the elite, but he was a brilliant writer whose art radiated out of little Denmark to the streets of London, the salons of Paris, and the enclaves of Vienna and Berlin. That a single Jewish writer came to be a dominant force in the conservative, elitist aesthetics and bellicose politics of Denmark is a remarkable feat. That he accomplished this without being a citizen until the very last years of the Golden Age is a testimony to his extraordinary voice. His should be a triumphant story in the history of European letters, but somehow Goldschmidt remains virtually unknown to our modern disciplines.

With so much recent development in the study of European narrative and secular Jewish letters in the wake of the Haskalah, the Jewish Enlightenment of the eighteenth and nineteenth centuries, one might reasonably expect Goldschmidt to have been hailed as canonical.[4] But in a recent collection edited by Jonathan Hess, Maurice Samuels, and Nadia Valman that, to my mind, defines the health and vigor of our field, there is only one mention of Goldschmidt, and it is incorrect: "The Danish-Jewish writer Meir Aaron Goldschmidt earned international recognition for his 1846 novel *En Jøde* (*A Jew*), which was translated into any number of European languages in the nineteenth century."[5]

A Jew was actually published in 1845 under the pseudonym Adolph Meyer and was translated into two other languages in the nineteenth century, German and English.[6] This absence of any substantial discussion concerning Goldschmidt's role in the broader conversation of European Jewish literary trends illustrates some of the potential benefits of the present work. I hope that scholars of European literature will be able to use it as a reference through which to navigate the existing scholarship and key debates on Goldschmidt as well as Danish Jewry. Finally, my work paints a diverse portrait of a writer who was as complex as the times in which he lived. Goldschmidt's reintegration into the annals of nineteenth-century Jewish thought provides a rich context for the discussion of European Jewry, without which we have but a foggy picture at best of Europe's northern boundary.

Here is one of the most important and most innovative Jewish writers of the nineteenth century, a Danish national heirloom, a pioneer of the European liberal press, a radical freedom fighter and convicted dissident, the progenitor of the Jewish bildungsroman, and an early innovator of ghetto fiction. Yet it is hard to find a mention of him in the literary history or criticism of our day that gives any hint of the richness of his authorship.[7] His absence in the scholarship might reasonably be explained as a function of the peripherality of Denmark in European literary history more broadly, but in fact the situation is more complicated.

Goldschmidt stands on a double boundary, so to speak: the cartographic line that has been drawn between continental Europe and Scandinavia since medieval times, and the ethnographic line that runs between the dream of a homogenous, Protestant Europe and an enlightened minority's rational call for freedom and equality. To complicate matters, Goldschmidt did not belong in or to any mainstream Jewish community, as his radicalness positioned him at the very edges of Jewish culture as well. In his fiction and memoirs, Goldschmidt often attempted to use this peripherality to his advantage, but it was also something beyond his control, something that haunted him and propelled him to action, to pen. He stands on the periphery by standing right in the middle, which in turn lies on the periphery. In this way, Goldschmidt was, as Jan Schwarz has elegantly offered, "the quintessential marginal Jew."[8]

With an international career that spanned some fifty years as a professional writer and journalist, it might be expected that Goldschmidt would have crossed into the twentieth century as an icon of world fiction.[9] Writing for the mainstream from the margin is a trait that Goldschmidt shared with some of the nineteenth century's greatest Jewish writers, for example, Heinrich Heine (1797–1856) and Berthold Auerbach (1812–1882).[10] Perhaps, if he had been born in Vienna or Bohemia and had written in German, Goldschmidt would have a much stronger presence in contemporary European and Jewish literature. But therein resides the double and disconcerting discordancy of Goldschmidt: it is exactly his Jewishness that sets him apart from other Danish writers of the nineteenth century and allows him to be marginalized in the Danish national movement that began to strengthen in the 1840s. Likewise, it is his Danishness that has complicated his voice within the Jewish canon, as very few scholars have focused on Danish as a Jewish language, especially in nineteenth-century literature.[11]

The lack of broader familiarity with Goldschmidt partly has to do with Goldschmidt's historical reception in Danish criticism, where his Jewishness is often seen as a political construction of his identity.[12] To many who do know his name, Goldschmidt is but a footnote in the illustrious life of Søren Kierkegaard. As a recent monograph on Kierkegaard has discussed, this shadow cast over Goldschmidt has marks of anti-Semitism, and we must not lose track of the fact that Golden Age Denmark was not unique in this sense; it had currents and undercurrents of anti-Semitism.[13] Goldschmidt was subject to these mentalities for the majority of his life, but we cannot allow his reception under our watch to be bound by these same diminished and antiquated attitudes. We can read his work as both the possibility of the rehabilitation of knowledge and the revolt against national oppression.

When Goldschmidt expressed his opposition to the nationalistic incorporation of Schleswig in the 1840s, he spoke for the Jutlanders, he spoke for Danes, and he spoke for Jews.[14] N. F. S. Grundtvig (1783–1872), the great Danish educator, minister, and hymnist, attacked him then on the grounds that he was a foreigner, a mere guest of the Danish Crown, and thus had no right to engage in political discourse.[15] In response to such rhetoric, Goldschmidt could be quite ironic about his ethnic peripherality. Take, for instance, his famous opening line at Skamlingsbanken in July 1844, in front of Grundtvig and thousands of others who had come to discuss the Schleswig-Holstein matter: "I am a Jew, what do I want among you?"[16]

Goldschmidt turned this question, which had plagued his memories of a lost home, in his favor by predicting the very thing many in the audience would have been thinking: "Why is this Jew speaking?" Goldschmidt also teased Grundtvig in a later retort. Because, by Grundtvig's own admission, Goldschmidt wrote Danish better than most Danish writers, Goldschmidt mockingly replied that if Grundtvig had learned to write Hebrew, he would surely write Hebrew better than most Jews. The joke pointed to Grundtvig's own inability to read the "writings of Moses and the prophets,"[17] as well as to the backhandedness of Grundtvig's previous comment. As much as it must have plagued him personally and politically, such racist banter never seemed to stifle Goldschmidt's professional career.[18]

Even after the new constitution of 1849, which granted full citizenship to Danish Jews, Goldschmidt was frequently reminded "of the anti-Semitism still prevalent in certain circles of Danish society."[19] For example, in the 1860s Goldschmidt was not allowed to have full brotherhood in the Danish Freemasons because he was a Jew.[20] He was addressed as "stepbrother" instead of brother, and certain members told Goldschmidt directly that "Israel still wanders with the mark of Cain on its cheek, homeless, friendless, kinless."[21] Another brother, Brestrup, said that "as long as he lived, there should never be any Jews recognized as Freemasons in Denmark."[22]

During the last two decades of his life, Goldschmidt became more and more devoted to his nemesis project.[23] The aim of the project was twofold: protoreligious and protolinguistic. The first was to give a historical account of the notion of nemesis, usually understood to come from the ancient Greek concept of divine retribution. For Goldschmidt, however, nemesis was a mystical force that created a certain counterweight to one's privilege and achievement in life. Not only was nemesis a historical force at work in the world, but it had roots in Ancient Egypt and the god 'Num, who was for Goldschmidt the spirit of the world. It was a protoreligion that Goldschmidt could trace over the course of his life time and time again, and the narrative section of the memoirs is driven by this notion.

The other point of the project was to map out a superfamily language based on ancient hieroglyphics and comparative Semitics. Goldschmidt had spent extensive energy learning ancient Egyptian hieroglyphics in the sixties and seventies. This mystical, ideogrammatic protolanguage was for him the root of all Indo-European languages, the seed corn of all European thought.[24] Combined with his lifelong studies of rabbinical languages, hieroglyphics excited the poetical imagination of Goldschmidt, and although he had integrated the notion of nemesis in his earlier fiction, the notion becomes perfected in his work during the 1870s. The Greek word *nemesis* he derived from the Egyptian hieroglyphic root *nm*, which meant for him something like "to divinely appropriate."[25] Nemesis was for Goldschmidt a force revealed in ancient Egyptian by conducting a series of lexical permeations through which one can verify the presence of a divine force in one's life. This was for Goldschmidt 'Num, the spirit of the universe that penetrated his destiny and defined his Jewishness, strangely enough, both as something Egyptian and somehow Danish.

Today, in Denmark, Goldschmidt is widely accepted as a Danish author and even one of the great national writers of the nineteenth century. Indeed, the statement is often made in Danish literary criticism that the 1860s were dominated by the prose writings of Meïr Aaron Goldschmidt.[26] These are quite extraordinary claims about a man who did not enjoy the right of citizenship for nearly the first three decades of his life simply because he was a Jew. He was without a doubt, as Hans Kyrre once described him, destined to bear the burden and the banner of being Denmark's last Jewish writer: "Goldschmidt is the last Jew in Danish literature, but he continues also to bear the mark of it his whole life."[27]

The other important Jewish writer of Danish letters, Georg Brandes (1842–1927), wrote the earliest important study of Goldschmidt in 1869.[28] Though exceedingly harsh and dismissive of Goldschmidt's role in configuring the parameters of the "Modern Breakthrough,"[29] Brandes was generously clear concerning the quality of Goldschmidt's craft: "The essential feature in Goldschmidt's authorial work is that, to a higher degree than in any other Danish author's . . . he is a stylist."[30] Despite such praise, Brandes's critique is often quite brutal, attacking Goldschmidt for his Jewish stories and tales, which often featured magical and superstitious beliefs. Brandes despised the mysticism inherent in Goldschmidt's vision of a protoreligion, viewing it as a Romantic ideal.[31] He called Goldschmidt a "Nazarene" and likened the nemesis project to "a poor doctoral dissertation."[32] But it was Goldschmidt's Jewish stories that bore the greatest offense for Brandes.

Brandes accused Goldschmidt of representing Jews with an archaic and tribal demeanor instead of as enlightened universal humans.[33] He thought Goldschmidt corrupted the image of the modern Jew by his Jewish characters' use of Yiddish and Hebrew alongside Danish.[34] Goldschmidt was also fond of using Jewish stereotypes and discussing Jewish rituals and holidays in his fiction. On this feature of his writing, Brandes haughtily remarked, "Goldschmidt ought not to, as I have heard an eloquent Jew say, serve his grandmother up with a sharp sauce."[35]

Danish critics, following Brandes's lead, have mostly agreed that Goldschmidt was the quintessential stylist in the Danish tongue and that he was seminal in the development of a language of realism. This praise, however, comes at the expense of suppressing an equally expressive part of his authorship, his Jewishness. Since Brandes's essay, the native response to Goldschmidt's uniqueness has tended to delimit his relationship to Judaism, often by overestimating his relationship with Christianity. It is also not entirely clear what Brandes meant by *stil* (style) or *stilist* (stylist). As Kenneth Ober has pointed out, the term "stylist" has been applied to Goldschmidt in almost every published scholarly context; scholars, however, have found it quite elusive to formulate exactly what Goldschmidt's style is.[36] Some, such as the reformist Frederik Dreier, have even slandered Goldschmidt for being too stylistic, a technique used "to mask a lack of ideas."[37]

The most critical example of Goldschmidt scholarship concerning this matter of stylistics is Mogens Brøndsted's 1967 book *Goldschmidts Fortællekunst* (Goldschmidt's Narrative Art).[38] Although the book is extremely valuable for its summaries, sober structural analysis, and insightful, if not sensitive, readings of Goldschmidt's major works, it still falls short of solving Brandes's ubiquitous notion of style. It is, however, the only full study of Goldschmidt's literary art in the twentieth century and serves as a useful starting point for inquiry into Goldschmidt's authorship.[39]

The American scholar Kenneth Ober succinctly summed up Goldschmidt's role in Danish literary history: "Although some of his Jewish stories are among his most popular works, it seems clear that Goldschmidt's fame has achieved the synthesis of the Danish and the Jewish that was never attained in his life. To the modern Danish reader he is only incidentally—by virtue of his superb Jewish stories—thought of as Jewish; he is acclaimed as one of the greatest Danish national writers."[40] Ober's works on Goldschmidt represent the majority of Goldschmidt's reception in the United States. Ober has done more than any other critic to create a contemporary audience for Goldschmidt. His translation of *A Jew* and his short biographical survey have made the study of Goldschmidt possible for Anglophone readers, although both books are now regrettably out of print.[41]

Questions of Goldschmidt's place in Danish literary history have settled quite comfortably into the position that Goldschmidt was indeed "one of the greatest Danish national writers" of the nineteenth century. To date, there has not been a single systematic investigation of this claim of stylistic domination of the 1860s (carefully situated, I might add, between the death of Kierkegaard in the 1850s and the rise of the Brandes brothers in the 1870s), which leads me to think that it is but empty praise. It is empty not in the sense that it is false—Goldschmidt was truly a force to be reckoned with, however, not just in the 1860s but also the 1840s and 1850s—but rather because it rests uncontested, that it is true by default, or worse, that it is true by concession. This statement concerning the national value of Goldschmidt cannot be used to mask the even greater truth that Goldschmidt was one of the great Jewish writers of the modern era.[42] Which claim is more important should be spoken by Goldschmidt himself.

The Mother Tongue

This book focuses on Meïr Aaron Goldschmidt as first and foremost a Jewish writer, one who was well versed in Jewish textual and storytelling traditions, and whose reading habits had a great effect on his fiction. Goldschmidt identified as Jewish in a much more multifarious and complex way than most scholars have realized, despite his own words being extremely clear on this matter. The title of Danish stylist, after all, does not explain his textual and cultural intimacy with the Hebrew Bible, the Talmud, or the midrash. I do point out, however, that Goldschmidt had a superb sense of humor and irony, especially when it came to depicting the everyday panorama of Jewishness in his fiction. Perhaps it is this latter point, his deeply sarcastic and biting humor, that some scholars feel precludes him from any contiguousness with Jewish literature at large. Reading Goldschmidt as a Jewish writer opens up new questions of interpretation and the possibility of reading outside of a monocanonical Europe, beyond a monolingual Denmark. We can then see Goldschmidt as part of a larger, global continuum of Jewish culture and storytelling, and this perspective, in turn, reveals even more clearly the richness of his poetical art.

Although Goldschmidt wrote predominately in Danish and was very much a product of the Jewish Enlightenment, he still retained a deep connection with the textual and linguistic traditions of Judaism. Writing in a period when modern Jewish fiction was still in its infancy, Goldschmidt represents a radical voice from within the literary mist that stretches between the Haskalah of Moses Mendelssohn (1729–1786) and the Modernism of Franz Kafka (1883–1924). Now that literary scholars have begun to describe a canon of early nineteenth-century Jewish fiction, it is useful to point out what is unique about Goldschmidt's fiction in relation to that of his Jewish contemporaries. To that end, I would like to begin by offering a brief summary of the state of Jewish fiction in the wake of the Enlightenment.

The early nineteenth century saw the rise of a new Jewish fiction that began to gain momentum across the European continent. By the end of the century, this embryonic literary movement would transform into a literary renaissance in both Hebrew and Yiddish. Modern Jewish fiction attained megalithic status in the 1880s through the writings of Sholem Yankev Abramovitsh (1835–1917), Scholem Aleichem (1859–1916), and Isaac Lieb Peretz (1852–1915), but earlier nineteenth-century fiction written in German, French, English, and Danish is just as paramount to our understanding of the Jewish encounter with the modern. Goldschmidt created for us a world very much contiguous with the portrait of quotidian Jewish life that is depicted in the oeuvre of classical Yiddish fiction. He is a beacon at the very edge of our notion of both Europe and Ashkenazi Jewry, shedding light on the very possibility of what Dan Miron has called "positive contiguity" of the Jewish literary complex.[43] Miron writes,

> The concepts of contiguity and tangentiality should help us to understand the modalities of mobility with that space, the Jewish literary complex; a mobility, which often enough brings those or some of those who happen to share it—synchronically or diachronically—into some kind of contact, which can be strong and deeply experienced but also slight and non-penetrative. . . . As such, they must enable us in reifying institutions that have not been detected yet. They must help us in reifying intuitions that have told us that within the space of literary *Judesein*, strange and wonderful encounters are discreetly and even unconsciously taking place, which the conventional critical imagination would never have dreamt were possible.[44]

In the wake of the French Revolution, there was great social and cultural change in Jewish communities in central and western Europe. Acculturation had great impact on the languages spoken and read by European Jews. This shift in cultural identity meant, for many Jews, learning the local vernacular language, albeit often at the price of losing the native tongue: "For Jews in central and western Europe, however, acculturation typically meant linguistic assimilation, and by the mid-nineteenth century Jews in these countries tended no longer to be versant in Jewish vernaculars."[45]

This linguistic assimilation had a profound impact on Jewish reading habits, which in turn shaped and contoured the nature of early Jewish fiction. Considering the rich and diversified nature of early nineteenth-century Jewish reading in contrast to premodern reading habits, Hess, Samuels, and Valman state, "Jews during this period, of course, did not confine their reading to Jewish literature, and historians and literary critics alike have long since pointed out the importance that reading played in Jewish encounters with the non-Jewish world."[46] Given the adoption of this new literary matrix as part of an integration into Western models of Bildung, secular Jewish fiction is born. That fiction, however, at least early on, does not face the future and the contemporary literature that will emerge in the 1880s, but looks backward into the past, toward Golden Age Spain.[47]

In France, Eugénie Foa's work marks the emergence of modern Jewish fiction, although none of her early work went through more than one printing.[48] During the early 1830s, Foa published seven novels and short story collections. Her first novel was published in 1830 and was called *La Kidoushim* (The Betrothal). Her novel *La Juive* (The Jewess, from 1835) appeared in German that same year.[49]

Phöbus Philippson (1807–1870), a country physician, and his younger brother Rabbi Ludwig Philippson (1811–1889) created a more stable readership in Germany in the thirties. The collaboration between the two brothers yielded a compelling fiction that played into the religious nostalgia of a newly calibrated young Jewish reading public. *Die Marannen* (The Marranos), which appeared serially in 1837 in Ludwig Philippson's *Allgemeine Zeitung des Judentums*, was another early publication of vernacular Jewish fiction. Eighteen thirty-seven also marks the publication of Berthold Auerbach's wildly popular *Spinoza: Ein Denkerleben* (Spinoza: A Thinker's Life). In 1838 Ludwig Philippson published in his *Allgemeine Zeitung des Judentums* his novella called *Die Gegensätze* (The Opposites), which he referred to as a "Jewish-religious novella."[50] Eighteen forty saw the publication of Heinrich Heine's fragmentary novel *Der Rabbi von Bacherach* (The Rabbi of Bacherach), although it was written some twenty years previously.[51] Ludwig Philippson also published a longer novel in 1842 entitled *Förderung und Hemmniß* (Challenge and Hindrance).[52]

Grace Aguilar's historical romance, *The Vale of Cedars; or, The Martyr* was written in English in 1834, though not published until 1852. Her writings became more oriented toward Jewish themes with the publication of her novella *The Perez Family* in a new series called the Cheap Jewish Library in 1843.[53]

The Jewish historical novels and novellas from this era have one thing in common: they are encumbered with a nostalgia for the past, therefore ceasing to be contemporary, and they offer no direct commentary on or conception of the nature of the reader's awareness of the modern Jew. The domestic fictions are essentially contemporary English-style works with a dressing or veneer of something Jewish, usually focused on Jews falling in love and finding eternal domestic bliss. Instead of forcing the reader to establish a position vis-à-vis the politic of European Jewry, these sets of writing establish a sentimental connection with the world of idealized Jewish family life. The reader is potentially swept away in these narratives, envisioning an allegorized Europe in either an idealized past or an assimilated present.

On the other hand, Goldschmidt's fiction constantly forces the question of assimilation to the foreground: how do Jews belong in a modern Europe? This requires that there be a self-reflexivity in the narrating voice, a mobility of presence that calls attention to the friction inherent in Jewish identity in a Europe that is trying to define its borders and therefore its national character. Nowhere is this attention to the friction of dissimilarity more pointed than in the northern margins of Germanic culture.

This book is ultimately an attempt to rehabilitate Goldschmidt as a father of modern Jewish fiction, as a writer contiguous to the more substantial literary complex that unfolds at the end of the century. I will closely examine the material in Goldschmidt's oeuvre in which a modern Jewish fiction is created through a poetics that is deeply influenced by tradition. This is, however, a secular fiction, contemporary in setting, hauntingly visionary, and very much unlike the other Jewish literature that began to trickle across Europe in the early nineteenth century. The fact that his novels take place in a contemporary world demarcates Goldschmidt from the major trend in early nineteenth-century Jewish fiction, expressed in the sentimental novels that are set in an idealized past or a contemporary fantasy in concert with Sephardic myth.

Throughout my study, I have chosen to use the term "dissimilarity" in my discussions of Goldschmidt's relationship both to mainstream Danish Protestant culture and to European Jewish identity, rather than "dissimilation," which has its own problematic history and connotations. My views on these terms are influenced by the arguments in Jonathan Skolnik's 2014 monograph *Jewish Pasts, German Fictions*, where he teases out certain historical nuances of the notion of dissimilation.[54] Particularly insightful is Skolnik's reading of the architecture of Berlin's Neue Synagogue as an idealization of the Sephardic past. His arguments make a substantial contribution to our understanding of the way cultural memory engages with the birth of German-Jewish fiction, creating a type of mythological platform of collective achievement.

In pointing to a journal entry by Franz Rosenzweig, Skolnik clarifies how dissimilation could be read in the works of fathers of early German Jewish fiction: "For Rosenzweig, dissimilation is a countermovement that accompanies assimilation. The crucial distinction is that it is a conscious step in the affirmation of a Jewish identity."[55] Skolnik's discussion of Heinrich Heine is relevant to an understanding of Goldschmidt's dissimilarity from the main body of early Jewish fiction. It would seem appropriate to apply the term "dissimilation" in some respect to Goldschmidt as well. Heine's late career overlapped with Goldschmidt's emergence in the 1840s, and both were pioneers of early Jewish fiction. Goldschmidt knew Heine's poems intimately, quoting a verse in his memoirs (*Livs Erindringer og Resultater* [*LER*]) and mentioning him several times as a model of poetic quality. In the second volume of his memoirs, he references Heine writing his *Confessions* and the *Hebrew Melodies* from his "deathbed" as a confirmation of the grandeur and power of Moses.[56] For Goldschmidt, Heine helped define his sense of religious authority. Goldschmidt found in Heine's words a type of "racial consciousness"[57] that became a hallmark of Goldschmidt's career. "Moses created Jehovah because Jehovah's *Akhu*, breath, was in him and all religion is a subjective sensation; but the subjectivity does not float in the air without having its deepest basis in the spirit of '*Num*.'"[58]

In his search for identity Goldschmidt does not turn back to the Sephardic ideal so popular with Jewish writers in the early nineteenth century. Rather Goldschmidt pushes even further back, to the Egyptian, although not to the Egypt of Joseph and the years of Pharaonic slavery, but to the numinous protoreligion of the earliest dynasties. Goldschmidt was radically dissimilar to Heine (and by extension to European Jewry) in several key ways. 'Num was Goldschmidt's primordial god, "Egypt's living, personal god," meaning "the spirit or breath over the water."[59] Goldschmidt traced his history back to three thousand years before the Common Era. 'Num was the creator God, "'Num was not, but is. . . . that with each sunrise and with each birth of a child a world becomes created. . . . whose right eye is the sun, and whose left eye is the moon."[60] It should be clear from this passage that it was not the Sephardic past that Goldschmidt mythologized, nor was it the pre-Reformation Rhineland as in Heine's *Der Rabbi von Bacherach*; it was the ancient Egyptian past that verified and actualized a sense of the mythological in the modern world. Egypt formed something much more spiritual than a mythologized past for fiction: it was the birth of language itself.

Through the ideograms and iconology of Egypt, Goldschmidt formulated an Afro-Semitic protoreligion that he sought to reveal and resubstantiate in the modern world. From this position, Goldschmidt could not only deliver a superior sense of cultural achievement but also a rhetoric of supersessionism. Rather than fictionalize assimilation, Goldschmidt dismantled the very myth of European hegemony by placing Europe's origin in the ancient Afro-Semitic culture of the Nile Valley. The Indo-European language family was for Goldschmidt a daughter of an ancient Egyptian superfamily, and by the strangest laws of reciprocity he believed that when he wrote Danish he was writing in a language whose origin was just as the origin of all things, the god 'Num. Even Moses and the Hebrew God were derivatives, or what Goldschmidt called results, of this supreme power.

Dissimilarity in my analysis has to do with the confluence of sources that swell in Goldschmidt, forming a poetical identity that constantly detaches itself from any predefined sense of the European experience. Through these poetics, Goldschmidt is revealing the hidden mechanisms by which Jewish thought and religion survive in

European thought and letters. He wrote fiction in a mostly contemporary, unidealized world in which conflict is built upon the choice between either "Jewish" or "X" (where X = Christian, Protestant, Danish, European, Romantic, and so forth) in all its iterations of impossibility. The double sense of dissimilarity arrives in Goldschmidt's unique solution to the choice: that the Egyptian, or more specifically the Afro-Semitic, reintegrates the two positions into a singular linguistic and religious origin. Much of Goldschmidt's thinking in *LER* seems contiguous with Sigmund Freud's *Moses and Monotheism*: "A strange fact in the history of the Egyptian religion, which was recognized and appraised relatively late, opens up another point of view. It is still possible that the religion Moses gave to his Jewish people was yet his own, *an* Egyptian religion though not *the* Egyptian one."[61] For Goldschmidt, to be Jewish was to understand that Moses was both a Levite,[62] like himself, and an Egyptian.[63]

This book contains four main chapters, each elaborating on a particular facet of Goldschmidt's poetics. The first chapter is focused on contextualizing Goldschmidt's life in Golden Age Denmark until he writes his first novel, *A Jew* (*En Jøde*, published in 1845 under the pseudonym Adolph Meyer). This was an intense period of growth for Goldschmidt as a thinker and a writer. Parallel to his career as a writer of fiction, we see him evolve from a savvy provincial journalist to a radical political figure on the national and international stage. Goldschmidt's editorial presence in Danish politics is usually seen as an endeavor separate from his literary career. I argue that his first novel is a natural outgrowth of the radicalness that manifests during the *Corsair* affair and reaches a sophisticated, national influence in his journal *Nord og Syd* (North and South).[64] By examining his life through the lens of his own memoirs, I hope to present a more informed perspective on the many tributaries that form Goldschmidt's writings as dissimilar to both Protestant and Jewish milieux. I give specific attention to the episodes of his life that have bearing on his narrative art and trace his relationship to the shifting world around him.

The same struggles with artistic formation found in the pages of *LER* also inform Goldschmidt's sense of the poetics of the novel.

The second chapter offers a close reading of Goldschmidt's novel *A Jew*. This novel presents a dissonant world, hostile to Jews but figured through Jewish reading habits. I examine Goldschmidt's poetics through the lens of midrash, the ancient rabbinical practice of interpretation. Here I explore Goldschmidt's various glosses on Yiddish and Hebrew dialogue as well as his cultural explanations of the Jewish holidays and customs as a form of poetics, in order to tease out the contemporary politics in Goldschmidt's cultural criticism, and in particular, his attack on the Romantic dream of assimilation.

The third chapter investigates the category of allusion in Goldschmidt's writings. Allusion is the essence and emotional center of Goldschmidt's poetics, and I draw material from many corners of Goldschmidt's corpus including some of his most beloved short stories. The chapter is divided into two parts: biblical allusions and Talmudic allusions. Here I am particularly interested in the ways Goldschmidt demands to be read first and foremost as a Jewish author by paradoxically essentializing his own Jewishness. By examining the specific points of intersection and connectivity among Goldschmidt's works and both the Hebrew Bible and later rabbinical tradition, Goldschmidt's unique and radical participation in the secularization of sacred scripture becomes evident.

Chapter 4 is centered around Goldschmidt's use of the figure of the rabbi. In this chapter I pay particular attention to some of Goldschmidt's English tales and his significant, but little-known, role in the promulgation of the Jewish tale and the Jewish anthology. The material in this chapter shows Goldschmidt's deep and intimate knowledge of rabbinic tales, some of them quite obscure and scholarly. Contrary to the tradition of form, Goldschmidt sees fit to recast some of these tales in ways that make them iconoclastic to their original meaning. When Goldschmidt does participate in the appropriation of "the myth of Sephardic supremacy," for example in his two tales "Rabbi Meïr's Wife" and "Rabbi Raschi," it is in a protomodernist way, in which disruption is brought to both the contemporary allegorical situation and to the received tradition of narrative itself.

Finally, in a brief epilogue, I present a reevaluation of Brandes's reading of Goldschmidt and offer a reading of Goldschmidt's English tale "The Wandering Jew" as a master-tale for Goldschmidt's oeuvre, a tale that demonstrates his great mobility and contiguity with the later masters of the Jewish literary complex. I end with the suggestion that Goldschmidt, an iconoclastic figure writing from the margins of Europe, should be read as a protomodernist, anticipating Franz Kafka and the history of twentieth-century Jewish vernacular fiction. Goldschmidt thus emerges as one of the seminal figures in Jewish fiction, helping to define the shape of modern fiction vis-à-vis the paradigms of tradition and refining the expressive capabilities of his native Danish tongue.

The question, however, remains: why should we read Goldschmidt today? The extant scholarship might have us believe that, as a Jew, Goldschmidt was a minor political figure in Danish politics and that, although he wrote fiction, it was of no importance to the broader discourse of Jewish letters. As Danes, we are supposed to read Goldschmidt as a reformer of the Danish language in the 1860s (only in the 1860s, that fissure in Danish literary history between the death of Kierkegaard and the Modern Breakthrough) and therefore one of the great national writers of the nineteenth century. Furthermore, although he was Jewish, we should not read him as so, given that he only attended orthodox schooling less than one year of his life. As I will show, neither of these readings is adequate and they are the result of a constraint of knowledge.

Ramón Grosfoguel has labeled this institutional suppression by academic discourse "epistemic racism," and I can think of no writer in the nineteenth century that has borne the brunt of this truncation more than Goldschmidt.[65] As I have shown above, the terms "stylist" or "nationalist" offer no real reading of Goldschmidt as a Jewish artist.[66] Furthermore, such titles require a concession to the very categories of knowledge that excluded Goldschmidt in the first place. Grosfoguel calls for "epistemic diversity in the canon of thought," and by rehabilitating Goldschmidt into the Western and Jewish canons, an exciting and stimulating artist is allowed to express the many worlds around him and the many rivers of thought inside him.[67] Before turning to the first chapter, in which I explore some of the social, political, and personal contexts in which Goldschmidt lived and worked up until the writing and publication of his first novel in 1845, I begin here with a short overview of his life.

A Short Biography

Goldschmidt was born in Vordingborg, Denmark, and grew up in a modern, middle-class Jewish family.[68] His father, Aaron, was an austere man caught between his desire to be an urban merchant and his love for horses and Danish farming. His free-spirited mother, Leah, was a strong support for Goldschmidt, and she had a very intimate connection with her son throughout her life. The household was a mix of Jewish tradition and Danish values. There were Jewish languages, stories, and rituals, but there was also a strong and current Danish style to the Goldschmidts' household, particularly when it came to education. The young Goldschmidt spent close to a year in an uncle's house, where he learned about Orthodox Judaism, but he was formally educated in Denmark's best parochial or Latin schools. The boy excelled at academics and, even early on, seemed to have a knack for literature and language. It was while studying at the University of Copenhagen that Goldschmidt took up both journalism and fiction writing.

Goldschmidt's literary career can only be described in superlative terms. He was an acclaimed journalist and editor at the age of seventeen,[69] and during the course of his career he founded and edited two of the most important Danish periodicals of the nineteenth century, *Corsaren* (The Corsair)[70] and *Nord og Syd* (North and South).[71] In June 1843 he was sentenced to twenty-four days of incarceration in Copenhagen's "Water and Bread House"[72] for his blatant and continual disregard for the censorship laws while serving as editor of *The Corsair*.[73] Freedom of speech and a free press were inalienable human rights in Goldschmidt's view, and he fought for and provoked change in many aspects of Danish law.[74]

From the beginning, the journals Goldschmidt edited were also platforms for his career in fiction writing. Goldschmidt was a prominent novelist and short-story writer, even making significant contributions to the literary history of the Jewish tale in English literature. His work was translated into German, English, and French during his lifetime. Between 1845 and 1867 Goldschmidt wrote four novels and is widely considered the master of the *dannelsesroman*, the Danish version of the bildungsroman or "novel of artistic formation."[75]

Goldschmidt's first novel, *A Jew*, published in 1845, was an international sensation and is one of the very finest pieces of Golden Age Danish literature. There had been Jewish novels published in Europe before *A Jew* but they were mostly sentimental in nature and were usually set in an idealized Sephardic past. *A Jew* was set in contemporary Europe and around contemporary Jewish issues and as such was also remarkably the first Jewish bildungsroman to be published in any language. In 1849 Denmark suddenly adopted a new constitution, and Goldschmidt, who had fought for freedom and citizenship more than any other major journalist, realized his dream of finally becoming a Dane. Despite his readership in Denmark and his enduring love for the country, Goldschmidt had a tense relationship with his homeland, and he left and returned several times.

This radicalness in the political and literary facets of his life mirrors in some way his amorous relationships as well. Very early on Goldschmidt held some very modern and controversial views on women and family. These themes echoed through all phases of his writings. His only two children, Adolf and Theodora, were born out of wedlock from his affair with Johanne Marie Sonne, the daughter of a Copenhagen shipping mogul whom Goldschmidt had met during his days at *The Corsair*.

Goldschmidt had several other affairs that spread through the gossip mills of Golden Age Copenhagen. In 1844 he began a relationship with Pauline Seidelin, whom he had met in Jutland. The heat of their affair seemed, like many of his liaisons, to have burned ardently and dissipated quickly. While visiting Rome for the first time in 1847, he fell in love with Charlotte Munch, and this set the tone for the ambiguous relationships Goldschmidt would have with several married women.[76] In 1848 Goldschmidt finally married Johanne Sonne in order to legitimize his son Adolf, but the couple never lived together and the marriage was later annulled in 1852. Goldschmidt expressed doubts that Theodora was his actual daughter.[77]

The most important relationship Goldschmidt had with a woman outside of his immediate family was with Hester Rothschild, the wife of his English maternal cousin Louis Meyer, who had made a millionaire's fortune in the diamond trade. It is clear from their correspondence and Hester's nurturing of Goldschmidt's love of the English language that they were not only lovers, but that she was the love of his life or as close to such a thing as was possible for Goldschmidt.[78] Benjamin, as her husband, Louis, was known to his friends and family, most likely had no idea of the relationship, as he was on good terms with Goldschmidt and expended quite a sum of money supporting him in his literary endeavors in England and his travels abroad.

In 1851 Goldschmidt had moved to England with the hope of reformulating his career in the English language. Through Hester, Goldschmidt became increasingly involved in the London Jewish community, but his radical views proved to be too much for the English Jews and several influential rabbis forced his cousin Benjamin to turn him out. Back home in Denmark, Goldschmidt committed himself to the pages of *North and South* and the composition of his second novel, *Hjemløs* (*Homeless*). In 1858 he fell ill with typhus and traveled southward to Italy to find a better climate. During his travels he met the important Jewish writers Berthold Auerbach, Leopold Kompert (1822–1886), and Ludwig August Frankl (1810–1894).[79]

After returning from his trip, Goldschmidt decided to end publication of *North and South* and again moved to England in the summer of 1861 (no doubt to be close to Hester again), this time supposedly for good. He was forty-two years old. During this time in London, Goldschmidt published in English many quality stories in such venues as *Chambers's Journal*, *Cornhill Magazine*, *Macmillan's Magazine*, and *Victoria Magazine*. He also worked on an English version of his Danish novel *Hjemløs* (*Homeless*). In London he renewed his interest in the theater, and he would end up writing several dramatic works of note in Danish: *Rabbi Eliezer: Dramatisk Digtning* (Rabbi Eliezer: Dramatic Poem [1861]); *Svedenborgs Ungdom: Dramatiseret Skildring* (Swedenborg's Youth: Dramatized Portrait [1863]); and *En Skavank: Skuespil i tre Acter og med et Forspil* (A Flaw: Play in Three Acts with a Prelude [1867]). In 1869 he published *Rabbi'en og Ridderen: Drama i tre Acter* (The Rabbi and the Knight: Drama in Three Acts), a liberal reworking of his 1861 play, alongside his Aristophanic comedy *I den anden Verden: Komedie i to Acter* (In the Other World: A Comedy in Two Acts [1869]). Goldschmidt was a publishing tour de force in the sixties and seventies. His last two novels were finished, *Arvingen* (The Heir [1865]) and *Ravnen* (The Raven [1867]), and two highly acclaimed collections of shorter works appeared, *Kjærlighedshistorier fra mange lande* (Love Stories from Many Lands [1867]) and *Smaa fortællinger* (Small Stories [1868]). The independently published story "Avromche Nattergal" ("Avromche Nightingale" [1871]) deserves special mention as it is one of Goldschmidt's most popular and most often published stories, having been reprinted multiple times in Danish, German, English, and Russian. It was in these decades, free from editorial duties, that Goldschmidt perfected the notion of style for which he became renowned, changing how the Danish language was used to express the modern world.

The year 1867 was a real turning point in Goldschmidt's Jewish writings. Goldschmidt read an article on the Talmud by the noted scholar Immanuel Deutsch (1819–1873), which he quickly translated and published anonymously in 1868.[80] Several of his best Jewish pieces postdate the appearance of this translation. Goldschmidt had found in Deutsch a kindred spirit and became more markedly invested in Jewish mysticism until his own death.

During the last two decades of his life, Goldschmidt became more and more fixated on ancient Egypt. Goldschmidt had taken up the study of hieroglyphics quite seriously. In 1875 he was given the title of Professor of the University of Copenhagen by Christian IX (1818–1906), a fitting honor for a man who had done so much for his nation. It was, however, not clear to scholars of his day of what subject he was a professor, but Goldschmidt saw himself as an Egyptologist, a Semitic linguist, and a professor of religion.[81] During the seventies he also completed the two volumes of his memoirs. These texts, if not actually the first modernist Jewish texts, certainly gesture toward the movement that will be marked by its "paradoxical amalgam of iconoclasm and hypertraditionalism."[82] The second volume is extensively devoted to Goldschmidt's concept of nemesis. Goldschmidt became obsessed with the philosophical notion of nemesis and devoted much of his later energy to a visionary type of "superfamily" linguistics based on his comparative study of Egyptian hieroglyphics and classical philology.[83]

Goldschmidt was to publish two collections in the 1880s. The first, *Fortællinger og virkelighedsbilleder: Ny Samling* (Stories and Pictures of Reality: New Collection), came out in 1883 and contains two of his most cherished Jewish tales, "Mendel Hertz" and "Levi and Ibald." The second collection was called *Smaa skildringer fra fantasi og fra virkelighed* (Small Descriptions from Fantasy and Reality). It had been assembled by Goldschmidt to commemorate his fiftieth year as a published writer since the very first number of *Næstved Weekly* had appeared on October 3, 1837.

Unfortunately, Goldschmidt never got to see this last collection in print or celebrate his fifty years as a Danish writer and journalist. He died somewhat suddenly on August 15, 1887, in Frederiksberg and was buried in Vestre Kirkegård in Copenhagen. The collection was published later that year by Goldschmidt's son, Adolf, as a tribute to his father's memory. Adolf, who was a successful medical doctor, also edited an eight-volume edition of his father's *Poetiske skrifter* (Poetical Works) in the late 1890s. This was an important work that shows that Goldschmidt's popularity extended until the turn of the century.

After Goldschmidt's death, his sister Ragnhild, who was an excellent storyteller in her own right, was distraught that no one had cared to write an elegy for her beloved brother, a tradition usually afforded to Denmark's great poets.[84] She wrote twice to the poet Carl Ploug and pleaded with him. After a second emotional plea, Ploug, who had been a close colleague of Goldschmidt, finally agreed to write the elegy.

A beautiful obituary followed by the poem appeared in the Danish newspaper *Dagbladet* on August 28, 1887.[85] The last stanza of Ploug's elegy seems particularly apt in highlighting the many boundaries of Goldschmidt's career:

> He loved Denmark so highly and fully and truly
> as ever a son has loved his mother;
> even though foreign blood ran through his veins,
> to us he was still a true and steadfast brother.
> Never the cross did dare to ornate the Levite's grave,
> but Denmark's crossed-flag over his shall wave;
> because this his daily work and his art he gave,
> and he has augmented our people's most precious gift.[86]

The tension or split between Jew and Christian and Jew and Dane is presented in fascinating images: the mother tongue superseding the foreign blood, the Danish flag overruling the Christian cross, the Levite resting under its pennant, as Danish as the ground in which he is buried. The correlation that Ploug has mapped out here between the mastery of Danish prose and the rigidity of Jewish blood, I will argue, is all part of Goldschmidt's dissimilarity and the confluence of streams of influence that mark his unique style. Ploug, one of the last Danish Romantics, saw the richness of Goldschmidt's fiction and yet seems to distance himself from Goldschmidt in the last line, which should read "his people" in order for it to include the "he" that is the subject. Instead the line reads "our people" and, intentionally or not, separates itself from the "he" of the subject, which is, of course, Goldschmidt himself.

Neither Rome nor the Ghetto

The image of the Danish flag is nowhere more problematic than seen flying over the Levite's grave, marking him as Jewish and Danish, and as dissimilar from both. A scene from one of Goldschmidt's later essays affords a strong example of the myriad of confluences through which Goldschmidt establishes his dissimilarity and disrupts the myth of European identity as something static and immutable.

Goldschmidt visited the Roman ghetto on two occasions, once in 1847 after he had published *A Jew* and then again in 1863.[87] After his second trip Goldschmidt wrote an essay entitled "Ghetto," which appeared in his 1865 collection *Fortællinger og skildringer* (Stories and Descriptions).[88] The story begins with an account of his earlier visit to the ghetto and continues with a historical outline of the ghetto as an archeological site of clashing ideals and identities. Upon completion of his survey, Goldschmidt marks out a distinct relationship between Rome (the metaphorical center of all imperial Bildung and culture) and the ghetto (an alternative site of culture that forces perspective onto the former).

> Rome is History, Poetry and Art's heathen-Christian city, and whether it is a blessing or a curse to be moved by this Civilization, one must accept in return the consequences. There is a strange comfort in rabbinical Judaism—especially for him who has his childhood memories bound to it. One is as in a family, separated from the whole world, with his own family-god, one whose relationship with other people is uncertain and undefined. But for this exact reason, there is a lack of symbols within Judaism, against which the fate of Rome is symbolic and expansive. Rome is meaningful for the entire world and evokes human sympathy, despite all the cruelty and all the demoralization that appears within it. And, so, Rome has also produced works of art, whose sympathetic nature touches mankind and attracts us to itself. But, the ghetto too operates in such a manner that when one leaves it, the study of Rome's monuments awake far less devotion than they do resentment. Either Rome or the Ghetto.[89]

Standing in a place in 1863 where he could see simultaneously both the ancient Pantheon and the Roman ghetto, Goldschmidt uttered these sobering words that seem to capture his own position in both Danish society and European letters: "Either Rome or the ghetto." These two metonyms for Europe and Judaism respectively define the boundaries of Western civilization, both geographically and culturally. Goldschmidt portrays the insularity of the Jewish minority as something separated from the very notion of Europe, but the text itself is written in the Danish tongue, very much a European language, albeit one on the margin. Goldschmidt is forcing the question of the status of Jewish art, here Jewish writing, in the European consciousness. The solutions to the passage are mutually exclusive. One is either the former or one is the latter. However, the passage is framed in terms that demand the ethical consideration of the reader. Civilization has consequences and, as we shall see, this postulates a third possibility.

The religious experience of Judaism for Goldschmidt is completely intimate, tethered to the past through childhood and memory, rooted in the notion of family. Importantly, the fate and status of other religions and peoples are not circumscribed within his religious doctrine. They are only "uncertain and undefined." Instead symbology, iconology, and archeology, all marks and totems of expansiveness, become the defining counterweights to the ethical. Rome, Goldschmidt demands, is to be weighed against the feather, not according to its achievements but to its crimes and cruelty. He peels back the curtain of civilization and invites us to step inside, into the ghetto. There we might divorce ourselves, if only momentarily, from the national myths of unity and oneness. There, through the lens of the ghetto, the glory of Rome becomes opaque; its glamor uncovered by centuries of human suffering and resentment alone is enough to cast it aside. Upon leaving, the operation is clear: there is no longer a singular Rome; there is also the Jew.

This passage, just as much as any in Goldschmidt, helps frame the position of the Jew in a contemporary Europe: he is either a European or he is something else, a Jew. This is the concept of dissimilation that Rosenzweig has in mind and that is so elegantly discussed by Jonathan Skolnik,[90] but Goldschmidt stands dissimilar from the collective of dissimilation. His words pierce through the illusion of both a homogenous and heterogenic Europe and a monocultural Jewish experience; they speak to a segregated, culturally dissimilar matrix of language, symbols, and ethnic origins.

Standing between, and thus already apart from, two architectural sites of human culture and memory, Goldschmidt reminds us that he was never comfortable in, or a pure product of, either place. He belonged no more in Danish society than he did in Jewish society, but he had the right to be in both places, solidifying his position as something fractured from the framework of European identity. Although he problematizes the etymology of the word *ghetto* as being derived from Hebrew *ghet* (divorce between married couples), the 1865 essay as a whole describes the ghetto as a cultural prison, adjacent to European civilization but laterally inaccessible.[91] This position amounts to an alternative reading of European culture. As we shall see, this solution developed steadily during Goldschmidt's life, but it only became complete in his notion of philology and with the ethnogenetic posture that Afro-Semitic culture and religion are the origin of all European thought and language.[92] As Goldschmidt stood looking over the Parthenon, a temple that is commonly understood to be for all gods, his thought was that it was his people, Semitic people, that seeded the classical world, yet the family-god of the Jews had been superseded by the heathen-Christian notion of cultural violence. As he looked over to the ghetto, he saw a people separated not only from their homeland, but divorced from the seminal role they played in the construction of a modern Europe. This vantage point had the effect of alienating him from both.

This marginalized shadow stands now as a proleptic monument to a Europe marked by classical cultivation yet marred by human suffering. This now-ossified worldview stands in contrast to the myth of one nation, one people, one language.[93] Through its Egyptian optic it cites the spirit of 'Num to be the source of all European thought in an attempt to define Europe as Afro-Semitic. With that in mind, let us turn to a more detailed examination of how this figure, dissimilar to both Danish and Jewish cultures, became such a disruption to a conservative Denmark on the brink of change.

1

"I Am of the Tribe of Levi"

The moniker "Golden Age" invokes an idyllic and opulent past, but a complicated nation emerged during this half-century, a more modern nation no doubt, but one laden with problems. Although the very beginning of the Golden Age was a bustling age of arts and letters, Denmark also underwent radical social, demographic, and economic change.[1] The Golden Age had emerged in tandem with the Napoleonic Wars and saw the rise of one of the nation's greatest periods of economic success, 1801–7.[2] Napoleon had shut down most other major continental ports, and as a result Denmark's neutral harbors faced little competition. As the war progressed, however, Denmark became more and more entwined in France and England's respective maritime war policies.

Despite Denmark's blind policy of neutrality, a situation from which it had profited greatly since the middle of the eighteenth century, England feared that Denmark would hand over its coveted navy to the French, whose own had been substantially diminished at Trafalgar in 1805. In September 1807 the English fleet, for the second time in five years, bombarded Copenhagen. Unlike the events in 1802, there was no armistice this time. The city was seized and the English sailed off with the remainder of Denmark's warships.[3] The so-called Gunboat Wars would continue, occupying most of Denmark's naval efforts until 1814 and the signing of the Treaty of Kiel. It would, however, take the nation decades to recover from the hardships that would follow.

The "cultural efflorescence" of the Golden Age would forever be intertwined not with the boom of its very beginning but with the economic collapse and commercial bankruptcy that would mark the next decade. The Golden Horns of Gallehus seem a fitting metaphor for the complexity of this time.[4] These ancient horns, which would be so hauntingly figured by Adam Oehlenschläger in his 1803 anthem "The Golden Horns," announcing the dawn of Danish Romanticism, would be stolen and destroyed in May 1802.[5] Their tenure as a link between Danish prosperity and the notion of a Scandinavian past quickly dissolved into a temporal and tenuous memory, much like the golden opulence that came in the early years of the Napoleonic Wars.

As the decade progressed, the Danish Crown became increasingly weaker, its currency reaching one-fourteenth of its face value by 1812. Within a year of the currency falling, the nation underwent complete bankruptcy.[6] In 1814 Denmark's foreign policy began to wane as Norway was lost to Sweden. The decreasing price in grain and a strong British mercantilist policy, including the Importation Act of 1815, often referred to as the Corn Laws, made Denmark even more susceptible to the impending global economic crisis of 1819. By the end of the decade Copenhagen's status as one of the North Sea's most profitable trade centers was wiped away and the social fabric of the nation was being eroded.

In particular, the period from 1807 to 1830 was devastating to an increasingly educated, ever-growing, and powerful rural class.[7] The rise of the price of grain in the late 1820s helped Denmark's economy improve, although it was the rural population that benefited, as Copenhagen, financially dependent on finished goods, lagged behind.[8] By the middle of the century this shadow class would total one-third of Denmark's total population.

The conservative production of culture and elitist politics that defined the Golden Age came to a definitive halt with the new constitution of 1849. The power of the monarchy became limited and full freedom was extended to all citizens. After some sixty years of reform, the age of the common man emerged in Denmark.[9] One of the groups that benefited from all this social change was Denmark's Jews, but they too had struggled to earn their pathway to citizenship.

Goldschmidt the Jew

The first Jew to be registered in Denmark was one Jochim Jøde ("Jochim the Jew") in Elsinore in 1592.[10] The Jews under the Danish king Christian IV (1588–1648) enjoyed some favor and position, but their presence was minimal before the seventeenth century.[11] Glückstadt had a temporary and small Jewish population in the early part of the seventeenth century, and certain towns in Schleswig-Holstein, such as Hamburg, Altona, and Wandsbek, were the first to host Jewish congregations.[12] By the eighteenth century the majority of Jews in Denmark began to reside in Copenhagen. In 1711 there were thirty-six adults and forty-eight children living in the capital city.[13] Fifty years later, there were some seven hundred Jews living in Copenhagen.[14] By the end of the century, there were around four hundred families living in Copenhagen, some sixteen hundred Jews.[15] For a short time, the notion of establishing a ghetto in the center of Copenhagen on Teglgårdsstræde was brought up, but it never had much support and was primarily a reaction to the rumor that Jews had started the great fire of 1728.[16] Despite the anti-Semitism that existed in Denmark in the early eighteenth century, it never materialized into any coherent policy of the Crown. The Jews of Denmark grew slowly and steadily in both number and political power, although the majority of them still lived below the poverty line.[17]

The treatment of the rural and marginal communities of Denmark became a basic philosophical keystone in the discourse of Scandinavian Enlightenment. Rousseau himself had given some privilege to Judaism owing to its ethical nature and pointed in his novel *Emile* to the tyranny and inequality that Jews faced in Europe.[18] It may seem somewhat paradoxical that the Golden Age's call for the freedom of mankind was issued by the same elitist culture that expected to control Denmark, presumably on the basis of tradition, after setting it free.

> No conspiracy theory is necessary to understand that enlightened and public-spirited men deriving from the old elite should consider themselves the natural leaders of a society whose great majority were

> only beginning to acquire some rudiments of prosperity, literacy, and awareness of a wider world. They meanwhile strove, as circumstances allowed, to improve the lot of the least favored inhabitants of the state—the Jew, the farm laborer, the pauper, the convict, eventually the West Indian slave—as well as of the peasant cultivator. In sum, ideal motives combined with practical needs to lay the bases of a new way of life.[19]

H. Arnold Barton's words here suggest a homegrown colonialism where minorities are tolerated because they represent an exploitable practicality to the nation.

With visceral ties to the nebula of Jewish life in German-speaking lands through the porous boundaries of Schleswig-Holstein, the dream of equality spread to the Jews of Denmark as the Haskalah movement of Moses Mendelssohn reached northward. This notion of equality for the Jews of Denmark first emerges during the Struensee period in the early 1770s in what is a very odd strand of Denmark's history.

While traveling through France and England in 1768, King Christian VII (1749–1808) was introduced to a German doctor from Halle named John Frederich von Struensee (1737–1772).[20] The next year Struensee became the king's physician-in-waiting and had great influence with the king when he collapsed from a mental illness. Subsequently, Struensee became the lover of the queen, Caroline Matilda.[21] His influence in the royal house was so great that he was appointed prime minister by the ailing king. For thirteen months, Struensee, a radical Rousseauean and Spinozist, controlled Denmark, and one of the things he called for was equality for the Jews. Struensee's execution by the state in the spring of 1772 ensured that none of his reforms would come to pass.

It was a momentary flicker of hope for Denmark's Jews, but Struensee's demand for equality was enough to start a debate in both Christian and Jewish communities about the role of Jews in an emerging Danish nation. However, all was not lost at Struensee's death. In September 1770 one of Europe's earliest and most revolutionary edicts became inaugurated in Denmark under his direction: the unlimited freedom of the press.[22] This edict also laid the groundwork for Jews to become professional writers, editors, and publishers in the upcoming emergence of a Danish liberal press.

In 1784 Crown Prince Frederik (1768–1839) was appointed regent at the age of sixteen because of his father's mental illness; he held this position until his ascension in 1808. Prince Regent Frederik had a strong sympathy for the Jews of Denmark, mostly based on his adherence to Rousseau. Through his reforming and restructuring of Denmark's medieval system of law and land tenure, the Jews benefited from the crown prince's endeavor to rule Denmark under a model of Natural Law. Although Prince Regent Frederik was instrumental in the emancipation of Denmark's Jews, he also used them to his advantage, for example to break up certain monopolies in Danish trade. There was quite an uproar in the guilds when, in 1788, Prince Regent Frederik allowed Jews to apprentice for skilled trades. Furthermore, in that same year, he removed the language in the constitution that denied Jewish students (on account of their "false knowledge") the right to earn university degrees.[23]

By the end of the eighteenth century, Jews had the right to marry those of other faiths and the freedom to live and travel anywhere in the country. In 1809, after barely a year on the throne, King Frederik VI (reigned 1808–39) gave Jews the right to serve in the army and formally attend university.[24] Bent Blüdnikow sums up our picture of Danish Jewish life on the brink of enlightenment: "The picture emerges of a community marked by a deep religiosity, fairly isolated from the rest of the community, whose attitude to Jews was characterized by the traditional anti-Semitism. Many Jews lived in close proximity to each other in central Copenhagen, and they spoke to each other in Yiddish or Hebrew. Links with the communities in Fredericia and Hamburg-Altona were strong, not least on account of family ties."[25]

This traditional image of Jewish life in Denmark is typical of Jewish life all over Northern Europe in that period, but it is at odds with the more complicated picture that emerges. At the turn of the nineteenth century, the Jews of Denmark did not occupy any extraordinary status among European Jewry. There were around twelve hundred registered Jews in a Copenhagen of ninety thousand residents. The majority of these families belonged to the lower class.[26] They were small in number and gaining some ground politically, especially with regard to the guilds, but cohesive reform was only a gesture at this point. They still lacked the one thing that would mark the difference between the eighteenth- and nineteenth-century Jewish experience in Denmark: the Danish language.

Goldschmidt's authorship in several European vernaculars, his international lifestyle and popularity, and his radical religiosity suggest a strong counterpoise to a now more antiquated notion of Scandinavian Jewry as a state within a state. Besides a religiosity that could be characterized as something more dynamic than "deep," the greatest change in the picture of nineteenth-century Jewry is indicated by the expanding use of and fluency in vernacular language. Yiddish and Hebrew begin to become increasingly secondary in the Jewish experience in Denmark.[27] A good example of the movement away from Yiddish is given to us by Goldschmidt in his reflections on Yiddish and Hebrew in his novel *A Jew*. Goldschmidt claimed that he had to consult his father for the correct usage of the Yiddish in that text. Goldschmidt, already twenty-six when he wrote the novel, is expressing a lack of fluency and pointing to a tipping point in traditional language use between himself and his father's generation.[28] In other words, Goldschmidt is saying that he has a real understanding of Yiddish and Hebrew, but they are not to him as Danish was, a mother tongue. This reading also suggests that the mother tongue becomes something already translated in the *Judesein* of the nineteenth century, a vessel for something born beyond experience itself.

Although there are very few secular documents of Jewish life in Denmark in the eighteenth century, we do have the writings of Mendel Levin Nathanson (1780–1868), a mercantilist and economic historian from Altona who was an indefatigable figure in the Jewish cause for equality.[29] Many of the reforms and the ensuing emancipation rested on the shoulders of Nathanson. He had strong relationships with the Crown and the royal advisors, and he was most certainly one of the instrumental forces in the creation of modern Danish Jewry.[30] He established the first parochial school for Jewish boys, Den Mosaiske Friskole for Drenge, in Copenhagen in 1805, and in 1810 a corresponding girls' school, Karoline-Skolen.[31] The importance of these schools and the Flour and Bread Society that helped to offset tuition costs was that they promulgated the Danish language to the effect that Yiddish would rapidly become a relic, a language of the older generations.[32] It is telling of his assimilative strategy that Nathanson made the patron of his girls' school Crown Princess Caroline (1793–1881) herself. Between 1805 and 1814 Nathanson initiated key reforms that helped root out class discrepancies within the Jewish community and solidify community finances.

Many of these reforms laid the groundwork for the modernization of Danish Jewry, such as abolishing taxes on kosher meat, the adoption of a progressive income tax, the systematizing of bookkeeping and official records, and the assimilation of burial customs. These types of policies effectively made the Danish Jewish community not only more modern, but because many of Nathanson's ideas were in concert with Protestant practices, the face of Danish Jewry also began to appear more Danish.[33] In 1855 Nathanson became a Knight of the White Ribbon; he was inducted into the Dannebrogorden, an elite chivalric order that was instituted by Christian V (1646–1699) and was historically only open to the nobility.

Like Goldschmidt, Nathanson was natively comfortable in the Danish language, marking the linguistic leap that is paramount for understanding differences between the Jews living in Denmark in and before the eighteenth century and the rise of Danish Jewry at the turn of the century. Through a literary career spanning half a century, Nathanson illustrated to many young Jewish writers, including Goldschmidt and his close family friend the playwright Henrik Hertz (1797–1870), that a Jew could have a successful career writing in the Danish tongue. Nathanson exemplified how a Jew could raise a certain amount of literary capital in the inner circle of Golden Age politics. From 1838 to 1858 and again from 1865 to 1866, Nathanson was the editor of the *Berlingske Tidende*, and under his direction the paper became a dominant voice in Danish politics.[34] His 1860 book *Historisk Fremstilling af Jødernes Forhold og Stilling i Danmark, navnlig i Kjøbenhavn* (Historical Account of the Jews' Conditions and Position in Denmark, Especially in Copenhagen) provides a rare perspective into the transition in Jewish culture from the occupational ghetto of commerce to the skilled trades of the nineteenth century. Nathanson even published an instructional book of reformed Judaism modeled on the catechisms taught in Danish confirmation classes.[35]

Nathanson's agenda of equality and co-religion began to take root in the early nineteenth century. Although there was an internal debate in the Jewish community concerning change, turn-of-the-century Danish Jewry was feeling the cultural impact of the Haskalah, and modernization was inevitable.[36] Emblematic of this opposition between conservatives and reformists was the conflict around the building of the new temple. The land for a new synagogue in Krystalgade in Copenhagen was purchased in 1799, but because of the friction in the Jewish community, construction wasn't begun until 1830. The synagogue was completed in 1833.[37]

For Denmark's Jews, the Decree of March 29, 1814, also included their equal right to conduct business. This right had been previously established by Prince Regent Frederik decades earlier, but the Decree was monumental in that it formally articulated the Crown's position on Jews: "Those of the followers of the Mosaic religion, who are born into Our kingdom of Denmark, or have received permission to settle therein, shall be permitted to enjoy the same rights as Our other subjects to support themselves in every lawful way."[38] In reality, the Decree of 1814 represented more a paper citizenship for Denmark's Jews, stopping short of full equality. However, the tireless work of Nathanson and the liberal Jewish community saw that a new generation of Jews would continue to demand that full equality.

Although the Decree was a tangible achievement for modern Jewish Danish identity and deserves to be celebrated, it granted only one exclusive right, that of employment, and it should be noted that the right to employment had already been in practice since 1788.[39] The fact that Jews were given the right to vote but could not hold political office illustrates the inadequacy of the document. Furthermore, there is evidence that bias still extended into state and parish job culture after the issuing of the Decree.[40] "In 1837, for example, not a single Jew held a position as teacher at a Danish Latin school, as a clerk in a government ministry, as an officer in the army, or as an official in the customs service."[41]

In fact, if one carefully examines the Decree's twenty paragraphs, the majority of them do not concern equal rights for Jews at all. They effectively and efficiently dismantled the authority and ritual autonomy of the Jewish community.[42] The Decree removed most of the partitions that allowed for a so-called state within a state. Danish law now trumped Jewish law. This moment was transformational for Danish Jewry; it carved out an actual identity for the Jews, one in which they ceased to be the Jews of Denmark and became Danish Jews, allowing us to speak of Danish Jewry as something definitive and reactive, as a political entity. Nathanson had a very large role to play in the language and composition of the Decree. One of the mandated provisions was that all children must be taught the national religion and become confirmed. Of course, it was Nathanson's reformed catechism that became the state-issued textbook.

The real power of the Decree of 1814 is that it brought the question of Denmark's Jews into the discussion of nationhood and thus Scandinavianism. A national debate thus arose concerning the Danish Jews and their role in Danish society. The ugly side of this debate became known as *Den litterære jødefejde* (The Literary Pogrom).[43] It began in print in 1813, spurred by the Copenhagen poet Thomas Thaarup's (1749–1821) translation of Friedrich Buchholz's 1803 *Moses and Jesus*. This publication sparked much debate and no doubt had a great impact on not only the issuing of the Decree but its role in determining the possibility of citizenship in the future.[44] When Denmark's economic problems worsened after its national bankruptcy in 1813, the Jews became an increasingly popular scapegoat as Europe moved closer to an economic crisis.[45] Nathanson himself had to go in hiding as his firm was accused of purposely creating the collapse.[46] By 1819 this sentiment had even targeted King Frederik, as mobs scribbled graffiti on several houses in Copenhagen that mocked the king as "The King of the Jews" and "Jew King."[47]

On the 3rd of September 1819, an anonymous author pinned an anti-Semitic pamphlet up on Børsen[48] that raised the issue of the Jews as "this culture's plague" and called for all "good Christian citizens" to help drive them from the nation.[49] Violence against Jews (the so-called Hep-Hep riots) quickly spread from the south out of cities like Bayern, Frankfurt, and Hamburg in July and August 1819.[50] The violence reached Denmark in the first weeks of September. When the riots began they were not contained only in urban Copenhagen but were spread out across the country. On September 12 there were violent uprisings in Odense, resulting in the conviction of twenty-eight men.[51] In the provincial town of Vordingborg, where Goldschmidt was born, there was a mob-like atmosphere as private property was destroyed. Luckily casualties were averted because of the intervention of the local constable and two other officers.

Bent Blüdnikow points out that tensions between Jews and Christians at this time in Denmark were particularly hostile. There was an increase in conversions after 1820, presumably out of fear. But there was also revolt; Blüdnikow gives as an example a startling report of a Jewish man throwing "a bucket of water over people in the street, shouting 'Christian dogs.'"[52] By the time Goldschmidt was born, the Danish pogrom was waning, although it would remain discernably active for the better part of another year.[53] The young Goldschmidt would have been too young to remember any of the acute excitement and anxiety that the Jewish community in his native Vordingborg would have experienced during that first year of his life, but it nonetheless would make a deep impression on both his identity and his artistic formation. Years later, in his first novel, the protagonist Jacob Bendixen would also be born into such a commotion. Goldschmidt tells the story of the Vordingborg pogrom in his memoirs as well.[54]

Goldschmidt the Dane

I offer now a more in-depth look at Goldschmidt's life up until he published his first novel, *A Jew*, in 1845. I will use Goldschmidt's own memoirs, *LER*, as an optic through which to examine Goldschmidt's increasing radicalness as a writer. *LER* is such an important text for understanding Goldschmidt's narrative art because it is an admixture of fictive memory and mantic autobiography, a narrative that is in conversation with both Bildung as a cultural phenomenon and nemesis as a protoreligious memory. The memoirs also give a deeply intimate voice to Goldschmidt's life and career. With the amount of epistemic misinformation that surrounds his reception in the twentieth and twenty-first centuries, he should be allowed to speak for himself.

On October 26, 1819, Meyer Aaron Goldschmidt was born to Aaron (1792–1848) and Lene (or Lea) Levin (Roskilde) Goldschmidt. He was the firstborn of five children and his father's eldest, a privileged position in Judaism and for Goldschmidt a profound destiny.[55] Later he would change the spelling of his name to Meïr because it meant "light" in Hebrew whereas Meyer, he claimed, was "without meaning."[56] This semantic cluster of light and narrative comes together on many different levels in Goldschmidt's writing, and a picture unfolds of an author who saw in his own writings an image of illumination.

The opening chapter of Goldschmidt's memoirs, *LER*, illustrates many fascinating moments of Goldschmidt's life story. Because it is told through such a specific and retroactive lens, it gives us a unique window into his narrative art. In fact, the opening words of the text give us the greatest insight into how we should read Goldschmidt's authorship: "I am of the tribe of Levi."[57] This statement is more than just biographical; it is a hermeneutic key for understanding the literary life of Meïr Goldschmidt. Although these words are often quoted by scholars writing on Goldschmidt, they are seldom taken seriously enough.[58]

Goldschmidt was intrigued by the hidden path his family took to get to Denmark, and his reading of this movement is already a critique of the Epicurean view of the past that stressed the merger of memory and historiography.[59] He could trace the family's origin from Canaan because of his father's name, but the thought that his family just appeared obliquely in the eighteenth century is marked by a sense of anxiety. Contrasted with the text's opening lucidity on his Jewish identity, the journey from homeland to Europe is shrouded in fog, an archive negated by an imagined wandering that suddenly surfaces in family lore, distant and already detached from its origin. Goldschmidt also paints a dark cloud over this emergence: "What pictures would be unfolded, if I could trace my family from Canaan's land to here! But we did not wander under the conditions which allowed for archives or produced historical writings! We tread out as if from a fog and the earliest family that I, in my childhood, heard referred to was that we were family with the famous London banker Abraham Goldschmidt or Goldsmid, who shot himself in 1808."[60] By recalling the suicide of an uncle, Goldschmidt's tainted fog accurately captures the modern Jewish relationship to history. Yosef Hayim Yerushalmi writes, "Only in the modern era do we really find, for the first time, Jewish historiography divorced from Jewish collective memory and, in crucial respects, thoroughly at odds with it."[61]

Goldschmidt's lament for Jewish history is very stark here. It is an obscured landscape of time from which families would emerge, homeless and storyless, in a new frontier that restricted their value both commercially and humanly. The language and tone here are reminiscent of the phrase Heine used to describe Jewish historiography as "Egyptian darkness."[62] For Goldschmidt, narrative was a way of creating memorial connections through the dark fog that existed between the spirituality of the past and the modern Jewish experience.[63] Names might be preserved from biblical times and hold value within Jewish tradition, but they only become emphatic because there are no other records to account for history as it splinters and splices through Europe. History becomes a broken looking glass for Goldschmidt: "The historic view was mainly reliant on the religious and for that reason became unhistorical, because one forgets the perspective and past experience in temporality's moods, and when one otherwise in times of rest occupies oneself with memories anecdotal material concerning Jewish families' strife, suffering or remarkable salvation springs up."[64]

The plight of the Ashkenazi Jew for Goldschmidt is replaced by a repeatedly fragmented historical existence marked by movement and migration and thus unable to establish a centrifuge of knowledge outside of the religious realm. The force of Goldschmidt's passage is reminiscent of what Harold Bloom says of the diaspora, namely that Jews are the most ahistorical of peoples and that the historical archive is the most alien of Jewish knowledge.[65] "Nothing could be more un-Jewish, and one sees again why the great rabbis used 'Epicurean' as a term of the greatest abuse."[66] As they emerge from the fog, it is Goldschmidt's own life story that casts light onto his people, pulling them from the shadows of history into the modern. For Goldschmidt, it was his mother's family that first tread out of the emptiness of the past: "That was my mother's kin, whom I—because I was born in the country or 'in the province' and because they also lived in the country—first came into contact with, and therefore I shall begin with them."[67]

Lene's family had left Poland to come to Fredericia, a town on the east coast of Jutland. From there the family moved to Nakskov, which lies on the western shore of Lolland, and then finally settled in Roskilde. Goldschmidt considers this wandering as a search for religious freedom.[68] Goldschmidt then recalls a second story told to him as a boy, and later corroborated by Baroness Rothschild, about the further migration of his mother's family. The baroness told him "that in her husband's kin was a memory or a tale about somebody coming from the city 'Rothschild' in Denmark."[69]

> A trivial and indeed curious circumstance was told to me once in passing by an old Uncle, my mother's brother, namely that his mother had remembered a kinsman who in her youth had left Roskilde for Frankfurt am Main. Baroness Lionel Rothschild in London told me later, that in among her husband's kin was a memory or a tale about somebody coming from the city "Rothschild" in Denmark. Others understood that the family's name simply came from a house in Frankfurt's ghetto, which was called "to the red shield." I have not found myself prompted to research the issue more broadly and I put more weight on the fact that the oldest thing I can remember about my family on my mother's side [is that they] spoke remarkably clean Danish.[70]

The account above and the surrounding passages in *LER* mark out a powerful point about Goldschmidt's childhood that is often overlooked. First, it establishes Goldschmidt's intimacy with Jewish storytelling. Within his family there was a living story tradition, as is evident when he states, "the earliest thing I heard mentioned in my childhood."[71] He goes on telling about his mother's family, "A piece of family history that was remembered." Goldschmidt laments in his old age that as a younger man he should have "sat and talked with the elders" so that he might have "heard a tradition." Another story "was told to him by an old uncle." Likewise, his mother also had a role as family storyteller, "My mother had earlier told." Words such as *Minde* (recollection), *Sagn* (legend), and *Erindring* (memory) also point to the oral nature of his early childhood.

This passage also suggests something culturally significant about Goldschmidt's youth. It is usually assumed that he did not come into contact with traditional Judaism before he left the provinces for his uncle's house in Copenhagen. However, this assumption cannot be true, because the young Goldschmidt had a rich social and storytelling community around him. It is not necessary, and in fact rather shortsighted, to assume that only contact with Orthodox Judaism is exposure to a "real" Judaism. Storytelling and oral family history are just as much Jewish as the *Schul*. For the young Goldschmidt the vehicle of all these stories and tales was the Danish language, which to Goldschmidt was just as much a Jewish language as Yiddish.

The most remarkable thing about Lene and the Roskildes was their native tongue. Compared to the ephemerality of human memory, native language, vernacular language, asserted lucidity in the contemporary Jewish experience. Goldschmidt constructs a relationship here that extends over the entirety of his oeuvre: his linguistic genealogy with "clean Danish" (*rent Dansk*). These words carry much weight in Goldschmidt's poetics of identity. For Goldschmidt it meant something different from indistinguishable; it marked the way a Jew claimed a nationality. "Clean" is the mark of a native tongue, something that navigates otherwise impassable ethnic and national boundaries. He used the phrase twice in talking about his mother's family.[72]

Goldschmidt tells a contrasting story about his father's family: "They [the Roskildes] could throw themselves down in the grass in the forest and sing a song with a glass of wine, whereas my family on my father's side would search out a nice hill in the woods. They were not the types to sing out of pure exuberance with wine (except my father, he was happy in his youth)."[73] The Goldschmidts were Copenhageners, unlike the Roskildes, who seem to have enjoyed the simpler ways of provincial life. Goldschmidt's father's family had deeper roots in Denmark, and Goldschmidt especially dwells on their mercantilist nature. Aaron's great-grandfather, who was also named Meyer, had come to Denmark in 1684 from Hamburg, Germany.[74]

Aaron's family had, like dozens of Jewish families in the late seventeenth and early eighteenth centuries, migrated to Copenhagen from Hamburg. Christian IV had acquired Hamburg from the counts of Schaumburg in 1640, and many Jews from Hamburg and the surrounding areas, such as Altona, were free to travel throughout Denmark.[75] Goldschmidt asserted that his great-grandfather Meyer had received an invitation to settle in Copenhagen in 1684.[76] For Goldschmidt there is a certain irony to this migration into Scandinavia. He mentions that after the expulsion from Canaan and the Fall of Granada, his family was somehow invited to settle in Denmark.

Aaron and Lene married in January 1819 and purchased a country estate in Vordingborg, some one hundred kilometers south of Copenhagen. The property was quite large, with a panoramic view that stretched out over a broad street into the Danish countryside. Goldschmidt described the property as "a square, which was missing one side."[77] There were stables for animals as well as a brewery and distillery on site. Whatever agrarian dreams Aaron Goldschmidt had of running a farm-based business and raising a family, this was the perfect place to bring them to completion.

Goldschmidt's idealization of it, however, is fraught with looming secrets, something chthonic in his mythic reminiscence: "Instantly, whenever I think back to my childhood the first notion attached to it is a wide, bright outlook and something hidden, concealing itself under a hill."[78] This polarization is reverified with two subsequent images. The first is of the deep ruts and holes in the run where the bulls would take exercise. Goldschmidt's sense of this place was something disturbed and wild as the bulls would make depressions by goring at the ground with their horns. This image is contrasted with "the little garden gate" adjacent, which had on each side of it "a beautiful Goldrain or Goldchain" tree.[79] This gate opened up into a secret garden for the young boy. Throughout his writings this image of the estate in Vordingborg establishes itself as home and homeland, however uncannily remembered.

Goldschmidt recounts that his father's love of animals, especially horses, was the source of Aaron's pastoral desires in the face of his mercantilist nature.[80] Perhaps the desolation that Goldschmidt sensed on the estate was owing to the complex of tensions in his father as a figure stuck between the traditional and the modern of two different cultures. On the one hand, Aaron fluctuated between the old ways of Northern European Jewry and the contemporariness of the new urban Jewish middle class. And on the other, he seemed conflicted between the Romanticization of traditional ways of Danish land-use and the promise of a new suburban affluence.

It is not surprising, given Aaron's emphasis on the values of tradition, that the young Goldschmidt was sent to Copenhagen to live with his father's sister Jette and her husband, Heyman Joseph Levin. For Aaron, there were simply not enough Jews in Vordingborg to support the type of immersion a young boy needed in daily Jewish life. The aunt's house was Orthodox and here the young Goldschmidt was exposed to a more traditional way of life; he attended synagogue and participated in a wider array of rituals and festivals than he did back home (69). During the school day Goldschmidt studied natural history, human anatomy, and Latin, but he relates that the value of this year away was his new relationship with Judaism and his ancestry (76). He asks, "But what was then the Judaism that I learned? Yes, what was it? It was the house, the people and their practices, a wonderful atmosphere which did not reach from us down to the street, but away out to distant times colored by fantasy" (63).

The simple everyday life is emphasized by Goldschmidt. His aunt's house defines this new Judaism for him, as well as the people in it and the rituals and customs that were a part of their daily life.

This was a house of love (63). Goldschmidt began to learn Hebrew at this time and participated in a more complete set of Jewish rituals. In the aunt's house the Jewish storytelling arena of his later fiction would begin to take shape, a narrative hand reaching back to times long past. Describing the Passover Seder he attended, Goldschmidt writes, "There was the Haggadah, the book on the liberation from Egypt, recited in Hebrew" (69). This scene gives an image of the first time Goldschmidt realized the power language had over narrative. We see in Goldschmidt's memory the birth of an inner scriptural life that would shape the very fabric of modern Jewish fiction. It was during this time with the Levins that Goldschmidt also learned that Moses was a Levite like him, and the hidden world of Jewish spirituality was opened for him (69–70).

After the family distillery burned (75), Goldschmidt returned to his family in September 1827. Aaron bought a farm in Valby, a small community to the southwest of Copenhagen (73). Although they only lived on the farm for a few years, Goldschmidt remarks that he was connected to that place and at least once a year he recalled the red gateposts of the farm. Some time after moving, Goldschmidt tells that he traveled back to the farm, where he was first met by a girl who looked at him strangely and asked, "What do you want here?" This question presents Goldschmidt with a "painful unreliability" of existence: "time and time again, one is ripped up like a plant that was close to having its roots deep in the earth" (86). To his mind, the historical narrative of the Jewish people was not to be rootless, but rather to have been in a state of deep rootedness and then suddenly to be deracinated and forced again to start as from seed. The very question itself, "What do you want here?" marks the questioned as foreign and arrogantly assumes no memory of what it was to once belong. This phrase echoes throughout his memoirs and his career, constantly defining him as dissimilar.

Peripherality in the memoirs is also constructed through the tension between the Danish and the Jewish. "That is mystical in the same way as the sayings of Philo and the Gnostics: that every people have their Logos, or, as the French say with a lighter swing, their raison d'être. Each individual of our people's blood receives something of this raison in his soul, and my whole lot in life has been marked by the two factors, my Danish birth and my Jewish blood, which fight over my domestic rights" (87). For Goldschmidt the metaphor of blood was a figure of great mystical and paradoxical thought. It was the figure that gave him great connectivity with his Jewishness and yet defined his dissimilarity in Danish society. The passage also marks the metonymic value blood had in his writings.

Rural Denmark in the early 1820s was a trying time to begin farming. Although grain prices had surged early in the decade, rye and barley prices began to plummet, and by the end of the decade rapeseed, which had remained steady, also began to fall (85). After three years, in 1829, Aaron decided to cut his losses on the farm and enter the shipping business in the capital. The export business was regaining its strength and he was keen to take advantage of the trade routes. The family moved to Nørrebro, a neighborhood beyond the northern gate of Copenhagen city center. Their ship was docked in Christianshavn, and the Goldschmidt children loved exploring the docks. The urban environment seemed a wonder to the boy who had grown up on the farms and distilleries of the parishes, although this opportunistic time is matched once again with an ambient darkness, a "biting night frost" (88).

For the Goldschmidt family, and especially the children, the ship was a magnificent site of adventure. Goldschmidt saw his father's ship as the emblem of his own fate, his father's fate, his family's fate, and his people's fate. Goldschmidt relates a story about how his father's ship was detained in Norway because Jews did not have the right to stay in the country without permission. Aaron escaped any charges but lost much profit on this particular expedition (89–90). This event seems to foreshadow the catastrophe that looms. The family was heart-struck to learn that the ship went down in the North Sea. To make matter worse, Aaron was cheated out of the insurance money by an English agent. This streak of bad luck and mismanagement had a devastating effect on Aaron's relationship with his brothers. Goldschmidt reports that later that year he witnessed an uncle in whose lumberyard he had played curse and banish his father from the family (95). The catastrophe of the sinking ship is one that plagued Goldschmidt throughout his career, showing up in two of his novels, *Homeless* and *The Raven*. The ship is also alluded to in the memoirs. Giving another example of nemesis, Goldschmidt claimed that years later he received the exact amount that the ship was worth from his English author royalties.[81]

This curse is brilliantly narrated with a ritualistic and darkly magical figuring in *LER* (95–96). It is described as "evil" and "sorcerous." The portrait is one of immense and enduring power, as he describes it, "God himself bound the words" (95). Yet this passage is bound to the act of writing itself. Not only is it embedded in a larger storytelling scene about his father and the ship, but the passage builds to another episode, some twenty-five years after the curse, during his editorship of *North and South*. He had stayed up one night waiting for the journal to be printed and feverishly wrote a poem called "Rabbi Eliezer's Curse," which he subsequently turned into his 1861 drama *Rabbi Eliezer*. The result of this creative reckoning of the curse is that, two days later, Goldschmidt had to go to the hospital because of a possible bout of typhus. The curse was a poison of the mind that could cause physical damage—as in the case of his uncle, who a short time after issuing the curse over Aaron died painfully of kidney stones—but also gave one the power to fictionalize experience. For Goldschmidt, the prophet and the prophecy were one, a concatenating poetics of ontology. He concludes that it is a source of his poetics, further pointing to the real nature of his nemesis project, storytelling and fiction: "I drove fantasy away, but the thought of the curse pushing quietude aside and breaking from joy and fear and becoming poetry" (96).

This period in Nørrebro became a sound harbor for the later writer. It was the ship's coxswain, a former navy man, who taught Goldschmidt how "to fish, row, and tell stories," and these scenes in the early part of chapter 4 of *LER* illustrate the link between Goldschmidt's storytelling style and the rich storytelling tradition of his youth (88). From the navy man's stories of the Napoleonic Wars as they rowed together around the city's shores and harbors, Goldschmidt discovered the realistic elements of narrative. He encounters or feels the "*historisk Plet*" (historical spot). It was in autumn 1830 that he also became aware of European politics, reading about the July Revolution and the November Uprising in local periodicals (98–99). This seems to be the birth of his fascination with Poland and with the figure of the Pole who wanders through his writings. This sense of location and storytelling becomes a fixture of his realistic aesthetic. It was also during this time that he experienced for the first time the vividness of physical attraction. While visiting his uncle's house, he met his first crush, "*den blaaøjede Pige*" (the blue-eyed girl) (92–93).[82]

Not only did oral storytelling and Hebrew language fascinate the young writer, he also took to classical languages and European literature, reading plays, medieval heroic literature, and contemporary fiction. Goldschmidt attended det Schouboeske Institut during the family's time in Nørrebro and seemed especially fond of his French teacher, Ole Christian Borch.[83] Borch told the young Goldschmidt that he resembled Napoleon and was fond of Goldschmidt posing with folded arms, impersonating the emperor. For Goldschmidt, this reinforced his Danish identity and proved that his physiognomy was not immediately identifiable as foreign or Jewish, and he notes that up to this period of his life he was never plagued by racism by his schoolmates.[84]

It was, however, during this time on Blegdamsvejen that Goldschmidt was finally confronted for his Jewishness. "One day, as I walked to school, three well-dressed boys—they looked like brothers—eight to twelve years old came down Blegdamsvejen after me. They yelled 'Jew, kike!' and made gestures."[85] As the boys chased Goldschmidt, throwing a potato at him and shouting at him, he experienced a metonymic moment of identity. He carried the fate of his people and in that moment became "with his person his entire people."[86] This caused the young boy to gather his hidden saber and attack the boys, but at that moment his mother intervened and stopped the brawl. Goldschmidt remarks that at that moment she might have been remembering the uprisings when he "had lain under her heart, while there was talk of killing."[87] Deflecting the anxious memory to his pregnant mother when it is clear that Goldschmidt is the one doing the remembering allows the scene with the saber to resonate with the potential for nemesis, creating a prenatal pattern in the life of the author.

The sinister elements from his childhood days became distilled in the uncle's curse and had a spiritual effect on Goldschmidt's life. After his bar mitzvah the young Goldschmidt seemed to be full of religious energy, "a kind of wild enthusiasm for the Lord."[88] Goldschmidt's description of the coming-of-age ritual has ecstatic elements to it. However, it is the mystical and hidden nature of the religious that was revealed to him that day. He felt something beyond himself and this trepidation compelled him to answer a resounding "No!" when afterward his father asked if he wanted to be a rabbi.[89]

Finally Aaron retired the family to Næstved, where he opened yet another distillery.[90] Aaron's career as a merchant was riddled with failure but also resolve.[91] But as much of a speculator as he was, he refused to gamble on the education of his children and especially the eldest son. The young Goldschmidt resumed his Danish education and in April 1833 he matriculated at the Westenske Institut, which was directed at that time by Vilhelm August Borgen (1801–1884).[92]

Goldschmidt excelled under the much-admired Borgen.[93] During the three years he spent under his tutelage, Goldschmidt consistently received the second highest marks in the class. He also credits Borgen with his sense of deep engagement with poetry. For the young Goldschmidt, Borgen represented a humanistic education, a complete and entrancing Bildung, what he called a "lively, radiant humanism."[94] Rector Borgen had also inadvertently inspired him to temporarily discard the physical signs of his Judaism, the *tefillin* and the *arbakanfos*.[95] A certain pantheism seems to have developed in the mind of the young Goldschmidt under Borgen's tutorship. His search for meaning in the world brought him to conclude one night that all physicality and spirituality were simultaneously god, a position that Borgen later accused him of having stolen from Empedocles.[96] The paradox of this time is that the humanistic curriculum of the school brought him closer to Christianity, yet it was the image of Christianity that shadowed his memories as a schoolboy.

As Goldschmidt walked one fine sunny day in 1836 to his first entrance examination at the university, a darkness fell over his path, the shadow cast from Frue Kirke.[97] It was expected that Goldschmidt would receive the highest honors on the examination and be accepted into the university with prestige. However, he received a low mark in Religion, which disqualified him for this distinction. His average marks in Latin and Latin style and especially Danish would have also been upsetting to Goldschmidt.[98] Nemesis had once again presented itself in a living figuration (the shadow of Denmark's holiest church) that had already predetermined a critical failure in his life. Ober points out that the question must have been on the New Testament and "was a devastating blow to his father."[99]

Around the time of the exam, Goldschmidt fell in love for the first time. He does not name the young woman but we are told that they had supposedly talked about eloping. After his exams it appeared as if she was only playing with the young student. Between this and the next mention of his unnamed betrothed a few pages later, Goldschmidt tells another story about a girl he met while visiting the home of his old tutor, Thomsen. She did not have the blue eyes of Esther from his uncle's lumberyard, but when he first saw her, "The sunshine illuminated her hair, and I looked with shy admiration upon this glory."[100] She lived in the front apartment of Thomsen's residence and was the daughter of a famous actor. After she left the parlor, Thomsen, noting Goldschmidt's awe of the girl, related to him that "You tread where you do not belong. There is more power in a young girl than in ten students!" He remarks quickly after this meeting that he never saw the girl again, but that he used "the color from that Sunday" in portraying Ellinor in his last novel, *The Raven*.[101]

It seems possible that these girls could either be the same girl or that they are both manifestations of the same erotic fiction. Regardless, it is love-sickness and jealousy that jump-start Goldschmidt's fictive creativity. One night while pining, staring over a marble statue in the courtyard below, he wrote his first short story. Goldschmidt seemed to have been quite proud of the story and its compositional art, and he brought it to the famous publisher Andreas Peter Liunge.[102]

Liunge apparently disagreed with Goldschmidt's reading of the piece and called it "swill" when he handed it back to him.[103]

Goldschmidt does not reveal the name of the story either, but he was so haunted by this episode that he thought he had been cast down literature's stairs. He resumed his studies and passed his *philologicum* exams, acing the Greek portion of the exam. During the holidays that year, he visited for the last time his uncle's place in Kallundborg in the west of Sealand. Practicing his target shooting with an old rifle, he accidently shot the sail of one of Uncle Kaufmann's ships. The uncle threw him out of the house, calling him a "nitwit" (Danish *Døgenigt*) and swearing that he would never be called on again.[104] This casting-out along with the harsh wounds from Liunge's words propelled Goldschmidt to a new creativity. He would sell subscriptions around Næstved and publish his own weekly paper, remarking that if his stories were not good enough for Copenhagen perhaps they would be for the commune of Præstø, his "native heath."[105] While still a student at the University of Copenhagen, Goldschmidt published the first issue of the *Næstved Ugeblad eller Præstø Amts Tidende* (Næstved Weekly or Prestø District News) in October 1837.[106] He was a few days from his eighteenth birthday. He mentions that it included a short story of the sort he had written earlier, a clear reference to the one he had shown Liunge.[107]

The weekly was soon so successful that a piece of Goldschmidt's, "an ironic-comical article on the excellence of small marketplaces," was picked up by the very paper that Liunge had founded and edited, the *Berlingske Tidende*.[108] This brought Goldschmidt so much pleasure that he wanted to continue in this vein of writing: "However, I did not have the stuff and could not find the source in me."[109] Goldschmidt's writing during this time is primarily focused on contemporary politics and rural culture as well as fiction and criticism, the latter of which can be found in almost every issue he published over four literary journals. He mentions that it was the July Revolution that inspired him to start writing about the demographic and cultural changes that were taking place in the parishes in the late 1830s.

The point has been made that the leniency under which the rural papers and journals operated was important in the rise of the Danish liberal free press.[110] Given that the material in the provincial papers was exclusively of a local nature, it was not subject to the censorship that the international publications in Copenhagen were.[111] They were only examined after they appeared in print. Because these weeklies were so popular and more numerous than the capital's offerings, the officials were less likely to interfere with their content. The result was that more people started reading these provincial publications because they could find information and political thought in them that would never have passed censor officials in the capital and thus never have been printed in the first place.[112]

Eighteen thirty-nine was a profound year in the career of the young editor. By the time he sold his weekly at the end of December of that year, he had become a well-known liberal voice in the press. Goldschmidt writes that, shortly after King Frederik VI's death in December 1839, he published a cheeky question among some paid advertisements: "Can a city councilman, who is called a liar in the city council, continue to be a city councilman of the city?"[113] Apparently a shopkeeper in Næstved believed the question was directed at him and he initiated a case against Goldschmidt. Subsequently, Goldschmidt was fined and censored for an entire year. In the meantime he had already sold the weekly, although he would remain its editor until April 1840.

Goldschmidt's last article for *Sjællandsposten* (no. 59) was entitled "The Young Denmark." It was an amplification of the sentiments announced earlier in Hertz's *Stemninger og Tilstande*.[114] Goldschmidt was far more radical than Hertz and felt that Hertz's vision for Denmark was too vested in the traditional social and cultural structures of the past. This would continue to be Goldschmidt's position vis-à-vis his fellow Danish Jews, including Hertz and later the Brandes brothers. However, of all the freethinking and liberal writers of the period, Goldschmidt was also the one most steeped in Denmark's literary past.

"The Young Denmark" demarcated an aesthetic line among liberal parties. Goldschmidt separated himself from those liberals such as Hertz who idealized the new government as a servant of the people. Goldschmidt was inspired by the July Revolution to take real action.

Freedom was no longer aligned with the goals of the government. The desire of the people had become more powerful than traditional social structures, and in this want there was the potential for freedom and thus equality.[115] The world was on the brink of change. Frederik VI had died, and for the young writer "[t]here was electricity in the air."[116]

After selling the weekly paper, Goldschmidt took an editorial position at the Copenhagen paper *Dagen*. Despite its reputation as an organ for conservative Copenhagen, the paper hired Goldschmidt because of his rapidly growing popularity. This position allowed Goldschmidt to be more socially mobile. During his short time at *Dagen*, he met many other writers interested in a new Denmark. With revolution in the air, a new monarch, Christian VIII, took the throne, and a new Denmark was truly on the horizon. The calls for a liberal constitution rang loudly.

While at *Dagen*, Goldschmidt became involved with a liberal organization called the Academic Reading Union. There he became acquainted with radical writers and journalists who shared some of his beliefs about the role of the press in the movement. It was the writer Poul Chievitz (1817–1854) whom Goldschmidt credits for suggesting the need for a satirical paper to antagonize the conservatives. Though Chievitz had many good ideas, in Goldschmidt's opinion he lacked action, and it was Goldschmidt who took the plan for a satirical journal seriously. Chievitz would contribute only one article to the journal. It was suggested by a young clockmaker who called himself Danton that the paper be named after the French satirical journal *Le Corsair–Satan*.[117]

The goal was to create a publication that would parody and attempt to permute the political situation in Denmark.[118] This spirit of change was fueled by *The Corsair*'s "poetical or fanciful desire for freedom and instinctual fondness for the people."[119] With its roots in the revolutionary spirit of France, the paper's aim was to light a fire in the Danish public by calling loudly for the formation of a young Denmark.

Goldschmidt had the energy and courage to see the project into completion. He had already experienced censorship and was not as fearful of the government censor officials as his cohort. Along with his old friend and tutor Thomsen, Goldschmidt conceived of a plan to use the latter's errand man, Lind, as a fake editor. In order to hide his identity, Goldschmidt would set up thirteen of these "straw-men" while running *The Corsair*.[120] This must have been somewhat for appearance as it was Goldschmidt himself who had to present the first edition to the justice administration for approval. Even though he was still under censorship, the paper was approved, but it was clear to Goldschmidt that despite the "strange and wild name" on record, all fingers pointed to him.[121] *The Corsair* was off and running and would be for the next six years the talk of the town—"Satan's paper."[122]

The first number of *The Corsair* appeared on October 8, 1840. Its motto was "His hand against all, the hand of all against him."[123] The agenda of the paper was clear in its citation of Genesis: Goldschmidt was calling for the "abolition of the absolute monarch," and nobody would be spared.[124] The paper had a strong socialist ideology, calling for equal rights for all citizens, a fairer distribution of wealth, and better treatment for small farmers and workers.[125] The paper quickly had more than a thousand subscribers and would grow to five thousand in five years, becoming famous for its caricatures and scathing satire of the old Denmark.[126] Despite its reputation "for vicious, malicious character assassination that has endured to the present," even the king was rumored to be a subscriber.[127]

When King Christian took the throne in December 1839, the Danish people demanded by deputation that there be a free constitution. King Christian had by then been swayed from his Rousseauvian roots, turning into a more strict and conservative ruler in order to keep hold of his authority. He rejected all calls for a new constitution, a free press, and more lenient tax reform.[128] Goldschmidt's and the Academic Reading Union's timing was paramount. October 1840 was the perfect time for a radical demand in print that a new Denmark be formed. Goldschmidt's innovative strategy of selling subscriptions, his increasing popularity as a journalist, and a public eager for an intelligent liberal media created the perfect opportunity for the radical politics of an emerging minority writer. As Uffe Andreasen has made clear, *The Corsair* did not have a true revolutionary agenda; it was a political tool used to upset the elitist and unjust normativity of the Danish Crown and its public subsidiaries.[129]

To be fair, however, some are right to see *The Corsair* as a sensational and combative journal. It became by its third issue a target of the censor's office, which confiscated the journals. In all, forty-three of the 342 Goldschmidt publications were censored.[130] During his six-year tenure as editor, the paper was involved in twenty-nine litigations. Goldschmidt had set up an elaborate network of strawmen editors, thirteen in all, in order to deflect the legal penalties.[131] The anti-Crown and pro-republican publication had become quite a thorn in the side of the conservatives, and the game of shadow editors came to a head in June 1843 when Goldschmidt was sentenced to jail for twenty-four days. He was also heavily fined and received a lifelong personal censorship, although this particular sentence was pro forma and did not have much effect on Goldschmidt's ability to serve as publisher or to write and edit under a matrix of various pseudonyms.[132]

During this time in jail, Goldschmidt handed over the editorship of *The Corsair* to his mentor Peder Ludvig Møller (1814–1865).[133] He had met Møller in the fall of 1842, and this meeting, and indeed their resulting collaborations, gave Goldschmidt a feeling of youth and an eagerness to learn again. As Goldschmidt remarks in his memoirs, "Then P. L. Møller loomed."[134] The first thing Møller told Goldschmidt was that he brought tidings from Norway and especially from the poet Henrik Wergeland (1808–1845), who was a fan of *The Corsair*. Wergeland thought it so good that he deemed it fit to be a Norwegian journal. This encounter brought about a new poetical spirit in Goldschmidt. He wrote of this meeting that "all aesthetic and poetic instincts awoke in me, but I was on thin ice. Møller seemed to me to have the key to them, the key to myself. I needed him as a redeemer."[135]

Møller was an important writer during this time. In 1841 he had published his *Lyrical Poems*, which was well received. He had won the university's gold medal for an essay on French poetry in 1841 and was thought to be a strong candidate for the university's chair of aesthetics after Oehlenschläger retired. His relationship with Goldschmidt was complicated. The two men worked together for some time and certainly shared many common ideas about aesthetics, but Møller asserted a certain superiority over Goldschmidt. It is clear that Goldschmidt represents Møller as someone who supported his writing. According to Goldschmidt, Møller had read his "Cooper-esque Roman" in *The Corsair* no. 125 at his barber's, and he told Goldschmidt that his storytelling style had made "a hop and springs right into comic composition." For Goldschmidt this was quite a marvelous review.[136]

Møller was well versed in European literature of the day; he read Byron, Heine, Hugo, Stendhal, and even Pushkin. Inspired by the French critic Sainte-Beave's notion of historical method, he brought a cosmopolitan aesthetic to Danish criticism.[137] Møller saw in Goldschmidt's writing the strong psychological composition that he demanded of a contemporary literature.[138] Later in his own journal, *Arena*, Møller defended Goldschmidt when he was sentenced to jail.[139]

In June 1843 the Danish poet Carl Ploug invited Goldschmidt to attend a student union trip to Uppsala. These union trips were a chance to discuss Scandinavianism with colleagues across national lines. It is certain that Goldschmidt felt a rare sense of inclusion in the larger discussion of the Danish national movement at Ploug's invitation, but again his politics of a future Denmark were markedly different from those of his fellow liberals.

The question that defined the mid-nineteenth-century notion of Scandinavia centered on the incorporation of Schleswig-Holstein. Goldschmidt came to the conclusion in the late 1840s that there could be a federation of states under one free constitution.[140] Goldschmidt had a vision of Denmark as a nation not unified by historical dominion or incorporation but by the will of the people.[141] Even though his radical ideas of a new Denmark clearly demarcated him from associates like Ploug and the Danish nationalists, he found some sense of camaraderie in the student union. Despite all of their differences, Ploug remained one of Goldschmidt's closest colleagues. It was, however, Møller who met Goldschmidt at the docks in Malmö on his way back from Uppsala to tell him that the high court had overturned his acquittal and that he would have to spend twenty-four days on "bread and water."[142] He was sentenced on June 7, 1843. For Goldschmidt this was retribution for his speaking out, not based on the quality of his words but based on his Jewishness. He concludes, "I consider it one of the conditions of luck in being Jewish: namely that one feels under the gaze of a suspicious majority."[143]

While in prison, Goldschmidt recalls that one time "a young woman brought strawberries. The jailor, who escorted the little party, said, 'Naa, the lady brings some flowers.' She did not understand the wink and answered him so proudly, 'No, it's strawberries!'"[144] The woman in question was most likely Johanne Marie Sonne (1825–1900). Johanne was the daughter of a wealthy shipowner and must have begun her relationship with Goldschmidt in the early 1840s. Goldschmidt had two children together with Johanne. The first was Adolf (1845–1912) in 1845. Later, in 1848, the two had a daughter, Theodora (1848–1914). They did not marry until 1848, but only to legitimize Goldschmidt's son, Adolf, who lived with him. Goldschmidt never lived with Theodora or Johanne.[145]

During his days in prison, Goldschmidt decided that once he was free, he would escape the eye of the public and travel to Paris. This would be the first of a long series of trips for Goldschmidt, and these experiences and impressions abroad would invigorate the writer for the rest of his life.[146] Ober has pointed out how his first three novels all have deep reflections of his many travels, and this first voyage seems to be inaugural on many fronts. In a letter he wrote to Møller from Paris on November 4, 1843, Goldschmidt brags quite comically about his rendezvous with a *grisette*.

Ober, who had an excellent knowledge of Goldschmidt's letters, mentions the sexual nature of the encounter in his biography, but he does not capture the sense that this is truly one of the most humorous moments with language in Goldschmidt's archive. While in prison he had written to Møller three times, and the tone of those letters is dark and sarcastic. In the letter from Paris, there is a more lively and free tone. He wants to play with language in the letter. The French word *grisette* is indicative of his folly as the somewhat mythical figure of the Parisian Latin Quarter was a radical emblem of human sexuality that sought to subvert the hetero-normativity of bourgeois life.[147] For Goldschmidt, she represented not only sexual freedom but an escape from the stale conservatism he had faced at home. The dramatics of the letter are highlighted in the two actresses to whom he reveals the details of this encounter. In his memoirs he recalls that these two actresses, to whom he was introduced through the actor Adalbert and his wife, took him in and "coddled him like a baby."[148] He quickly switches between French and Danish and ends the opening paragraph of the letter with an idiomatic climax of sorts. "And the girls are pretty and beautiful, charming, ravishing! O! O! O!"[149]

These two encounters, the one with Johanne in the prison cell and the one here with the French women, paint a very liberal, almost bohemian, picture of the young Goldschmidt. The girl with strawberries and the folly of the letter to Møller show a playful side of Goldschmidt. The fairy-tale style of the scenes and the infantilizing tone help underscore the magnitude of his sexual awakening. The prison sentence seems transformational in the memoirs. The man that emerges from the cell is more virile and free. His sexuality, like that of the grisette and Johanne, is a subversion of bourgeois social norms: the sexual Jew.[150]

This coming of age for Goldschmidt stimulates a new chapter in his life, although he returned home to Copenhagen in the fall of 1843 and resumed his place as editor of *The Corsair*, which was his "one and proper place."[151] It is sensible to see another change in Goldschmidt's reflections after his travels to Paris. He begins to create a bifurcation in his identity, what he called "a mixing of Jewish and Danish."[152] This is not the first time Goldschmidt had this feeling, of course, but it announces how this dissimilarity becomes political for him.

The censorship did not prevent him from appearing as *The Corsair*'s publisher. As before, most of the articles were still written by Goldschmidt. His political ambitions were not curtailed either, and in July 1844 he spoke at the second language rally at Skamlingsbanke in Jutland.[153] The speech's opening words have become canonical among

Goldschmidt scholars: "I am a Jew, what do I want among you?" However, the entire speech is worthy of comment. Goldschmidt continued addressing the festival with the little-known following words, "Ah yes, that is certainly correct, that I am among you, because you all are likewise Jews, indeed you are more Jew than I!—Because the Jews were insulted and oppressed in foreign lands, but you are oppressed in your own."[154] The rhetoric here is sublime. By emotionally charging his audience by aligning their plight with the Jews' plight in Egypt, he asserts a charge against the Danish Crown. Namely, because Jews are foreigners and oppressed in foreign lands, Denmark's Jews live in a land of oppression. He goes on to talk about his mother tongue, as if to remind the thousands of people listening that this speech, a Jewish speech, is all happening in perfect and clean Danish.

The speech then turns to a saying from the New Testament about turning the other cheek and compares it to one from the Hebrew Bible, about an eye for an eye. The punch line here is that in the case of Schleswig-Holstein it is once again better to go with the Jewish rule, "If you will so strike the head of Schleswig-Holstein, then likewise shall I strike at your head." Goldschmidt stopped just short of calling for war, something he later thought was imprudent, but ended the speech with a toast to Jewishness: "Therefore a hurrah for a merry feast with the Schleswig-Holsteiners in old Jewish fashion."

The speech here is evocative on several fronts. It is for Goldschmidt the first time he articulates a quasi-ethnic call to arms. The mere intention of mapping regional folk and language onto the ahistorical diaspora of the Jewish people seems quite hyperbolic, but Goldschmidt is morally obligated to fight for the liberty of a people not able to choose their own future. It is also a way of acknowledging and legitimizing the social and political status of Denmark's Jews. Suffering became for him in this speech a rhetoric of commonality. He stated, "In the pain am I your brother. Here is my hand. If it can write for you, if it can kill for you, so command: It is a brother-hand." Comparing the Danish folk to Jews and suggesting that the Hebrew God supersede the Christian one must have seemed inflammatory to some of the thousands that were present at the gathering.[155] To make the Schleswig-Holstein question one of minority suffering focused the conversation about Denmark's borders into a conversation about human rights. For Goldschmidt, this coloring of the Jutland folk was an attempt to bring a commonality to their suffering by relocating and realigning them in the Protestant Bible. In doing so, the Jew was also reshaped not as the figure who murdered Christ but as original suffering.

Among those present at the meeting was N. F. S. Grundtvig, the great Danish educator. When Goldschmidt exercised his opinion against the nationalistic incorporation of Schleswig, Grundtvig attacked him with outright bigotry and xenophobia. The speech at Skamlingsbanke and the anti-Semitic rhetoric that spilled forth in response were crystalizing moments for Goldschmidt. The empowerment he felt from giving this monumental speech and the "fever and disharmony" he internalized from being made peripheral to the very movement he helped to create collided in the young writer and awoke the novelist.[156] He related to Møller all that had transpired, and Goldschmidt notes that for the first time in their relationship they actually talked together "about deeply personal things."[157] The conversation was inspiring for Goldschmidt. As Møller grabbed his hat to take his leave he remarked, in his philosophical hot-bloodedness, "Those are the feelings with which one writes a novel."[158]

That night Goldschmidt tells us he wrote the first draft to the last chapter of his first novel, *A Jew*. This novel would become an international success and Goldschmidt would become a different caliber of writer from what he was while writing for the two journals.[159] He was now an artist, a novelist, a poet. Through this journalistic lens we see that his experience at *Næstved* and *The Corsair* was a training ground for Goldschmidt's fiction. There is a continuum of Goldschmidt's narrative art from the very first short story he showed Liunge to the very first novel he wrote. There is a transfer of both his short, semipolitical realism in the journals and his radical politics of identity into the vehicle of the novel. In particular, the speech given at Skamlingsbanke opened the door to the possibility of a radical novel.

In Danish *En Jøde* has two possible meanings. Though the novel is usually translated as *A Jew*, it could just as likely be *One Jew*, given that *En* lacks the diacritic to distinguish the two possibilities. The title is a palimpsest of his dissimilarity. The underlying depths of the simple title point to a blank space that is completely full. Goldschmidt was a complexly dissimilar man in those years: Danish nationalist, scion of the Golden Age press, social activist. When it came time, however, to write the book, he identifies it as just "a Jew," which is what he was first and last.

2

Midrash and Metaphor

In this chapter, I will show that Goldschmidt's groundbreaking bildungsroman, *A Jew*, is completely consistent with the radical trajectory of his journalistic career. This work, the first novel from the double margin of Scandinavian and Jewish letters, codifies the expression of Goldschmidt's uniqueness and dissimilarity. In its pages was the "sharp sauce" that Brandes and other Jews accused Goldschmidt of serving up in betraying his heritage. It is indeed a rather sharp sauce that Goldschmidt serves. The novel was radical because it presented an alternative canon to voice its support for a constitutional democracy and a call for freedom. If we read this work in context of not only the Modern Breakthrough, but Modernism itself, then we can begin to see how Goldschmidt's radical use of sacred texts forms a system of poetics and gestures toward the iconoclasm that becomes so predominate in modern fiction. The most important of these interpretive traditions was the midrash: "the typical midrashic predilection for multiple interpretations rather than for a single truth behind the text; its irresistible desire to tease out the nuances of Scripture rather than use interpretation to close them off; and, most of all, the way midrashic discourse mixes text and commentary, violating the boundaries between them and intentionally blurring their differences, flourishing precisely in the grayish no-man's-land between exegesis and literature."[1]

Midrash is the tradition of rabbinical commentary and interpretation of the Hebrew Bible.[2] The recording of midrash in manuscript form began in the second century CE, with many of the earliest classical texts being recorded in the third and fourth centuries. Originally composed to explain the legal intricacies of the Hebrew Bible (*halakhah*), it evolved primarily to contain homiletic readings (*aggadah*) often interlaced with parables (*mashal*), liturgical poetry (*piyyut*), and folkloric anecdotes.[3] It is essentially a generative text that operates through interpreting, translating, and (re)telling the Hebrew Bible. The narrative nature of these interlinear commentaries constitutes a mode of reading in which interpretation is always left open, with the resulting harmony lying in its multiplicities. Attached to this aesthetic of infinite interpretation is the paradox of reading itself. Meaning is not absolutely free; it is negotiated through the lens of scripture. It is always constrained either directly by the Hebrew Bible or indirectly by the tradition of midrash itself.

This narrative obfuscation of the boundary between text and commentary has produced some of the most capricious styles in ancient and medieval literature, and has inspired in more modern writers a dislocation of genre, a disregard for tradition, and often a radical secularization of scripture.[4] As Rabbi Ben Bag-Bag says in the Talmudic tractate *Pirke Avot* (Teachings of the Fathers), "Turn it and turn it, for everything is in it."[5] Meaning is free as long as it is centered in the biblical tradition. As such, midrash is both a secondary and a parallel literature: secondary, because synchronically it is under the control of the prime text, the Hebrew Bible; parallel, because it moves diachronically alongside the Hebrew Bible, attempting to fill in the gaps of biblical narrative. This dynamic relation to Holy Writ is what I define as parabiblical.[6]

Robert Alter's brief but enlightening study of Franz Kafka explores what midrash looks like in the hands of a Jewish writer in the twentieth century.[7] Through his discussion of canonicity and the Bible, Alter is able to find in the fiction of Kafka a fusion of the vernacular with the classical, the secular with the orthodox. Alter sees this iconoclasm, or ab-use of scripture, as seminal to Modernism, what he calls the "paradoxical amalgam of iconoclasm and hypertraditionalism."[8] Kafka embodies this point because of "the midrashic adroitness with which he fleshes out the meanings of the text" and his proposal for "heretical midrash" or "radical midrash."[9] In discussing Kafka's ab-use of the Tower of Babel episode in Genesis 11, Alter writes, "But it also reads the biblical texts against the grain, teasing out of it an idea that contradicts the explicit condemnation in Genesis of the effort of the builders as an act of overweening presumption. . . . a precise rotation of the biblical story from up to down, but it also accords a certain respect of the biblical text, seeking, as the classical midrash does, to bridge the yawning gap between the interpreter and the text."[10]

This reading against the grain is exactly what I am interested in examining in Goldschmidt. There is a systemic quality consistent in his work that allows one to speak of a poetics.[11] Often this poetics is based in Jewish textual communities and at the same time is often at play with both the text and the canonicity of the Hebrew Bible. This pervasive poetical style works "against the grain" of tradition in much the same way as the midrashim used it, by turning scripture. The full point of Alter's reading, however, is to reestablish the philological word-craft of the ancient in medieval rabbis in a vernacular and secular setting. Goldschmidt expresses his awareness of these traditions as a modern storyteller and not as a rabbinic authority. It is a fictionalization of what he already acknowledges as canonical. Let us take an example from Goldschmidt's writing so that I might demonstrate my point more clearly. The following is the opening scene from Goldschmidt's novel *Hjemløs* (*Homeless* [1853–57]).

> In the garden was a large green place and in the middle of this stood a lonesome little apple tree, abounding with dense leaves and half-ripened apples. Emilie had found an apple that had ripened too early and fallen from the tree; suddenly the band of playing children gathered around, but commanding as a queen the eight-year-old girl said, as she held the apple high, "Please, be quiet, you shall all get a piece." She added with a sidelong glance, "Whoever cares for me the most and gladly waits to the last, shall have the largest piece." Next to her stood a boy of the same age with yellow hair and hazel eyes; he immediately stepped out of the circle and waited in the distance while she carved the apple into pieces and handed it out. All of a sudden she cried, "So, now there is no more!" and while laughing held out her

> empty hands in the air. The little boy had tears in his eyes, and his lips quivered as if it was difficult to keep himself from bursting out in loud tears, while the other children began to laugh at him because he was so fond of sweets and had been tricked. He wanted to go away quietly, when she came closer to him and whispered as she passed him, "I didn't get to taste the apple either, Otto; we two were the only ones who didn't get any." With these words an immeasurable joy broke over the boy's face; without even looking at her he sprang back among the others and led the wild, jubilant game through his father's orchard between the currant and gooseberry bushes and down into a grove of poplars that belonged to the garden.[12]

The scene is easily recognizable as being at play with the garden story from the book of Genesis (2:8–3:24).[13] By "at play" I mean to emphasize that it is both an allusion and an inversion. On the one hand, the scene means to reference the Book of Genesis and construct a contextual notion of original sin: God strictly forbade Adam and Eve to eat from the tree of knowledge of good and evil in the middle of Eden (Gen. 2:16–17; 3:2–3). Therefore, there is something rather mischievous about Goldschmidt's placing an apple tree in the middle of Otto's father's orchard.[14] The band of children "suddenly" being called together by the fallen fruit at its base recreates the idealized innocence of the primeval existence.

On the other hand, the scene in *Homeless* does not unfold quite like the scene in Genesis. Besides the fact that other people, in this case the children, are around, the two protagonists of the story are the only ones not to eat the prematurely ripe apple. This process of inversion creates an interesting twist and is typical of Goldschmidt's exegetic strategy with the Hebrew Bible. Inadvertently following the command in Genesis, Otto chooses to abstain from the first pieces of apple Emilie is to hand out so that he might receive a larger piece later, as well as her affection. When the apple has been divided and there are no more pieces, both the reader and Otto are shocked at how the pastoral intimacy of the scene has been interrupted by Emilie's cruelty. She is a fairy-tale figure in this moment, but the emotionally devastated Otto, who can barely hold back his tears, is suddenly jubilant when Emilie reveals to him that she too has abstained from eating the apple.

On a linguistic level, the passage is framed by the phrases *i Haven* (in the garden), *til Haven* (to the garden), and *i hans Faders Haven* (in his father's garden), all of which, besides setting the Edenic tone of the passage, create an intimate movement inward, as if the reader himself is entering. Once inside, the reader is lured into the lushness and innocence of a secret garden. The first image encountered is *et ensomt lille Æbletræ* (a lone little apple tree), no doubt the emotional center of the passage as well as the garden. The figure of the tree is set apart by the fact that it has produced what no other tree in the garden has yet been able to produce so early in the season, a ripe apple.

It is, of course, Emilie who finds the ripe apple and, like her allegorical counterpart Eve, offers the apple to others. Although still young and innocent, she is depicted as an evil queen type, *bydende som en Dronning* (commanding like a queen) and stipulating rules as to how the apple might be divided. When Otto realizes that there is no prize for his abstinence and patience, Emilie, as if to show her emotional superiority over the boy, is described as *leende* (laughing) as she stretches her empty hands toward him. As in the garden story, Otto, like Adam, is characterized by his obsequiousness to the female figure. As soon as Emilie announces the stipulation for receiving the largest portion of the apple, Otto *øjeblikkelig* (instantly) forfeits his place among the circle to wait for his prize. The scene emotionally resolves from a stark moment of betrayal to a wonderful elision of young affection; "[de] To var de Eneste, der ikke fik Noget" (the two of them were the only ones not to get any). Just as the reader was introduced to the green and growing garden, and then tricked in the barren deserts of an empty hand, so now has it returned to fruition. The children resume their games among the red current and gooseberry bushes, the poplar grove, and the lone little apple tree, all of which *hørte til Havnen* (belonged to the garden).

There is, however, another force at play in the scene that helps explain the depiction of Emilie as the commanding queen. The passage returns Otto to that idyllic sensation that occurred before the fall of the apple. After all, these are only children, and Otto is quick to rejoin the games at hand, although he is, of course, unaware that a dark foreshadowing has been set in motion by the commanding actions of Emilie. If one reads the story from Genesis as an allegory of sexual awakening, then a certain innuendo of forbidden love between young Emilie and Otto also manifests itself. In fact, the notion of forbidden love is one of the central themes throughout the novel, and the fallen fruit motif is again revisited when, toward the novel's end, Otto and Emilie try to arrange a secret affair while her husband is away.

To sum up, the poetics of the passage are midrashic. It relies on the constraint of the biblical text, its images and emotions, to process its literary setting into a contrast of meaning. The novel opens with a similar scene as the Book of Genesis, although the author has inverted or "played" with the exact details and descriptions of the primary scene. The poetics not only frame the allusion with respect to setting, they reduplicate certain characteristics, such as Eve's mischievous innocence and Adam's obsequious charm. The passage builds an imagistic relationship with the garden story in the placement of the little apple tree and the lushness of its surroundings. Yet Goldschmidt has also ab-used the scene from Genesis. Whereas in Genesis the whole of Adam's lineage—the trajectory of mankind—will suffer for his sin, Otto's plight seems to be metaphorically conjoined to the lone little apple tree itself. Unbeknown to him, this is as close (in this world) as he will come to paradise. His journey will be one of displacement and disillusion. This of course must unfold over the course of the novel, which, despite its vastness, never abolishes this primal scene. Otto's life will be constrained by this childhood sin that he will mistake for destiny. This Edenic moment *var blevet for tidlig modent* (became ripe too early).

Although Goldschmidt certainly does not exhibit all of the hypermodern features of Kafka, what both writers do share is an affinity for parabiblical narrative, a deep sense of iconoclasm, and specific Jewish reading habits.[15] But what is most extraordinary about Goldschmidt is that he adopted this radical interpretive mode at a much earlier date than Kafka. This establishes Goldschmidt as a protomodernist.[16]

Goldschmidt's Jewish reading habits infiltrate his Danishness, and his study of the texts of Rabbinic tradition has left in his literary works a midrashic sweetness that is both baffling and intoxicating, something found only among the most sophisticated and sensitive writers of the nineteenth and twentieth centuries fascinated with the double canonicity of biblical narrative. From this point of view, it might be more fruitful, as Wentzel and others have suggested, to read Goldschmidt in a world literature setting rather than through the limited lens of Danish and Scandinavian literary history. In terms of the sheer creativity expressed through the constraint of biblical narrative in fiction, Goldschmidt, in my opinion, reads better against Herman Melville and William Faulkner than he does against Brandes and Kierkegaard. Furthermore, Goldschmidt, unlike all of his Golden Age contemporaries, has a working knowledge of the languages of rabbinical scholarship and is able to access traditional sources unavailable to Protestant authors. The Protestant tradition of reading the Bible is Luther's, that is, the Greco-Roman tradition adopted from the vernacular translations of the Septuagint and later the Vulgate of St. Jerome.[17] As a reader of Hebrew and Aramaic, Goldschmidt forces us to explore an alternate mode of *dannelse*, or education, that is influencing the nineteenth-century Danish novel.[18]

In this chapter I argue that Goldschmidt's style is predominately midrashic. Nowhere in his oeuvre is this more evident than in his first novel, *A Jew* (*En Jøde*), published in 1845.[19] I will demonstrate in the remainder of this chapter how, by means of interlinear glosses, storytelling, and parabiblical play—all functions of his Jewish reading habits—Goldschmidt is able to turn and turn, simultaneously reading into and against the grain of biblical tradition in the generating of "new" narrative, a modern Jewish fiction.

The Notion of Bildung

The German term *Bildung* (education, culture) or in Danish *dannelse* defines a very productive motif in Goldschmidt's writings. As I mentioned earlier, his second novel, *Homeless*, is generally considered to be the classic nineteenth-century *dannelsesroman*, the Danish version of the bildungsroman.[20] But it is really in Goldschmidt's first novel, *A Jew*, where the issues of education and artistic formation are richest in terms of the politics of the narrative.[21] Indicative of this, even at the editorial level, Goldschmidt chose to publish the novel under the pseudonym Adolf Meyer. In 1845 Goldschmidt was still under censorship and still the "publisher" of *The Corsair*. It is interesting to point out that the editorial games that Goldschmidt used in his journalistic career to evade authority are also practiced in the production of his novels, further connecting *A Jew* with the timbre and politics found in *The Corsair*. Another striking characteristic is gestured in the thinness of the disguise. The pseudonym Goldschmidt used for *A Jew*, Adolf Meyer, is a construction of his name and that of his only son, pointing right back to Goldschmidt himself, just as Lind, his first straw man at *The Corsair*, led right back to him.

A Jew is an anomaly in nineteenth-century fiction. It was the first Jewish novel in Scandinavia; it was one of the first Jewish novels in northern Europe not written in Hebrew or Yiddish; and it was the first Jewish bildungsroman. The novel depicts the birth, life, travels, and death of the hero, Jacob Bendixen, following his life from his youth in the Danish provinces to his university days in Copenhagen, his coming-of-age in Paris, and subsequently to the battlefields of Algeria and Poland, and back home to Denmark. It is an attempt to highlight the particular among the universal, and although it is in concert with the general trajectory and peculiarities of the genre, Goldschmidt's novel ultimately represents a rupture from "subjective partialness transfigured, the apotheosis of the Individual."[22]

A Jew also indicated a new direction in Danish literature, pushing the boundaries of Realism and the psychology of the novel. Jacob's formation into the world is one of constant alienation, a trait so embedded and calculated that the novel adopts the trope of *alienus in aliena* as a new pathology. Traditionally, the novel has been read as Jacob's struggle for assimilation into a Protestant milieu, but, as I have pointed out, the notion of assimilation was never idealized by Goldschmidt. Mogens Brøndsted wrote that *A Jew* was "the first important Danish novel which consciously has a fate develop according to the seed established in the youngest years of childhood."[23] It is precisely this germ of alienation that forms the architecture of the novel, but it is through the notion of constraint that meaning becomes mediated.

Immediately, as the novel opens, the reader is faced with two interlaced texts. By reader I mean a mid-nineteenth-century, contemporary, Protestant reader with little knowledge of Judaism and no academic knowledge of Yiddish or Hebrew. The first text is straightforward and concerns the birth of Jacob Bendixen, which ominously coincides with the Spanish deserting Napoleonic Denmark in order to fight the emperor's brother Joseph back home. Jacob is born to Philip and Jette Bendixen in a little provincial town on the island of Fynn, presumably sometime in the spring of 1808. After the desertion, the civil guard parades past the houses of the village Jews, shouting racial slurs as they retire to the local inn to celebrate the Spanish withdrawal. During this commotion the hero is born and his maternal uncle, Isak, utters the first of several prophecies that will shape the boy's future: "Isak drank a glass of wine and announced: 'Well, it's good enough, but I'll continue to claim that it was not a sensible time to give birth. If the boy had only been a Christian, then the din under which he was born would have meant that he was to be a great hero. But as a Jew it will only give him a double aversion for war and unrest; he will be labeled such a coward that even the Jews will call him cowardly.'"[24]

Along with the mother and father, Uncle Isak takes it upon himself to educate young Jacob. This tripartite education becomes the germ for most of the conflict and friction in Jacob's life. Philip takes charge of teaching Jacob the religious and textual aspects of Judaism, how to read Hebrew, say his prayers, and study the old rabbis. Uncle Isak, an ex-soldier who is described as "what is rarely the case among Jews—a tall and very strong man" (11), teaches Jacob stories about "soldiers and about knights and about foreign lands or biblical stories of Jewish heroes so that the child in later years would not remember having learned these stories, but almost imagine that he was born with them" (13). Jette, his mother, takes charge of teaching Jacob Danish ballads; "she bestowed on him the most beautiful gift he brought with him from his paternal home out into the world, a mother tongue, as pure and clear, as it rang through the rhythms of the poets" (37). The seeds of conflict, thus, are the rabbinical (or learned), the heroic (or martial), and the romantic (or balladic), and over the course of the novel these will manifest in the lurid possibility of a Byronic Jew.[25]

The second text, and here I use the term more stylistically, concerns the glosses at the foot of the page. Throughout the novel there are some 210 glosses for various Yiddish and Hebrew words and phrases; there are glosses for Hebrew prayers and longer expository passages on Jewish cultural history and holidays. For the typical reader these glosses become necessary on page 1 of the novel in order to translate the three Yiddish words that Philip uses to chastise his clerk, Benjamin: *Hramor* (idiot), *Ohs* (carcass; wicked person), and *Beheimo* (moron). Although for the most part Goldschmidt's Jewish characters speak Danish, they do like to pepper their everyday speech with a little Yiddish—albeit, I contend, at the expense of the reader.

This confrontation and constant disrupting of the novel's main narrative is something the reader experiences throughout the course of the book, forced (out of ignorance or interest) to stop reading the text proper and to glance down at the foot of the page. The reader must translate the reading experience across the bifurcation of the page to have any sense of continuity. Why these glosses interest me so much is the way in which they engage the reader by constraining meaning particular to one's reading habits. They not only invoke a certain type of authenticity of speech and cultural knowledge, but the typical reader comes to rely on their existence to understand the many expressions of Jewishness in the novel. In fact, without even being aware, the reader has entrusted his becoming a Jew to the all-telling, all-knowing narrator. As we all know, narrators are often the most unreliable of educators.[26]

At first glance, the glosses in *A Jew* are a part of an exposé of contemporary Jewish culture. In fact, scholars have pointed to the reliability of Goldschmidt and his narrators to provide historically accurate information about nineteenth-century Scandinavian Jewry. On the other hand, we also know that Goldschmidt was highly criticized from within the Jewish community for secularizing the religious aspects of Judaism and demystifying Jewish ritual life. This is what led that other, more famous of Danish Jews, the critic Georg Brandes, to write that Goldschmidt served "his Grandmother up with a sharp sauce."[27] My contention is, however, that Goldschmidt was far more radical and cryptic than critics have realized. Goldschmidt's narrator forces the readership into the subtext through the bait in the glosses below. This specific technique influenced Leopold Kompert as well.[28] This reading out of and through the foot of the page simulates Goldschmidt's finest narratological innovation, the second-person (or reader-simulated) bildungsroman.[29]

My understanding is that the glosses themselves operate as a type of Bildung for the reader. For as Jacob Bendixen grows up in his increasingly incubated community and learns to become a Jewish man, so the reader side by side with Jacob engages in learning (probably for the first time) actual customs and mannerisms of the Jews that live within his own country. As a bonus, for the particularly astute reader, a fair amount of Yiddish can also be learned. Indeed, this reliance on the gloss is something shared between the reader and Jacob and helps build an emotional connection between them. When Jacob learns about Passover, so does the reader; when Jacob learns about Hanukkah[30] and Rosh-hashana,[31] so does the reader, and so forth. As this pattern develops, a certain complacency overcomes the reader, that all things Jewish and every bit of Jewishness will be translated for him. All one needs to do in order to understand the strange language and unfamiliar customs is to stop reading the text proper and look down into the glosses where an intimacy has developed between reader and narrator. This is of course blind faith; there is no benevolent Jewish narrator behind the textual curtain. For example, the narrator produces no expository footnote for Yom Kippur, suspicious for a novel that seems so unforgiving to its characters and readers.[32]

As it stands, much happens between these many gestures and glances toward the foot of the page, and it does not take long for an epistemological gap to manifest between Jacob and the reader. As early as chapter 5, we are told, "Thus, Jacob steeped himself in his people's mysterious erudition" (35). Likewise, when he leaves the provinces to go to Latin school in Copenhagen, days after his bar mitzvah, he takes with him an acute understanding of the Talmud.

> At first, Jacob swam in ecstasy. Since he, with his intellect formed by Talmudic sharpness and with his memory filled with fragments from so many sides of human knowledge, came to the school without knowing a schoolbook, he was like a person who can play an instrument but cannot read music. He was examined like any of the other boys, and yet he could not answer a word. But when he began to take part in the instruction and the interstices, so to speak, between the fragments began to fill up and he himself came to an awareness of his own knowledge, he made dizzyingly rapid progress in the judgment of his teachers. (81)

In this passage, knowledge for Jacob is initially specifically Jewish, a Talmudic wit or sharpness. All of this learning has happened away from the reader, in the background of the novel. There are no glosses that explain the Talmud or expose Jacob's Talmudic erudition. These gaps also exist in the reader's knowledge of the Jewish, and as these "interstices" (Danish *mellemrummene*) of knowledge become filled, there should be an epistemological convergence between Jacob and the reader. But Goldschmidt's narrator has slowly and steadily over the course of the novel withdrawn his end of the bargain for a package deal.[33] The vice of the glosses is one of semblance, that while seducing the reader's want for knowledge of things Jewish, it is allowed to mechanize the illusion of harmony through very subtle sins of omission.

The sins of the narrator accrue and accelerate over the course of the novel as Jacob's eruditeness seeps over into the normative paradigm of dannelse. Jacob becomes just as gifted a student of nineteenth-century humanism as he does of the Talmud, the only difference being that one is and will always remain prior. The situation at the end of part 1 finds a battered and disheartened Jacob sailing away from the island of Fynn toward Copenhagen. His uncle has beaten him, his father forsaken him; he will never speak to his mother again. The impetus for this conflict is the distance his humanist education has forced between himself and Judaism. Although this has been predicted in the narrative by means of the many storytelling scenes, the actual unfolding of the events has happened away from the narrative lens. My point is that although Jacob appropriates the humanist ethos into his Bildung or dannelse as a Latin schoolboy, the reader does not likewise gain the equivalent insight, one that explains the Talmudic knowledge at play in both the character and the narration itself. It is as if the discourse of humanism obfuscates Jacob from the narrative eye. And here we may speak of Goldschmidt and the poetics of the veil; for the reader will continue to believe for some time that the didactic element of the novel, the coming to Bildung, is a shared or holistic experience. The reader becomes almost arrogant in his conception of Judaism, given that the text empowers a reading that Jacob is being too sensitive to the world around him. This creates an overconfident understanding that what the reader is seeing is not Jewish. It is at best a thin projection of some things Jewish. Yet the eagerness of the reader coupled with the seductive sleight of hand of the glosses themselves produce a contract of shared harmony that diminishes the anxiety of the unknown by simulating it. This obfuscation is a political maneuver that accelerates during the course of the novel, increasing the epistemological gap between Jacob and the reader until the two are completely disparate and estranged from each other. (Un)reliability is one of many performative masks that the narrator wears throughout the novel.

In the context of the Latin school, Jacob's aptitude is presented as virtuosic yet rough around the edges. He is likened to a musician with no formal training, innately playing by ear while not being able to read a note. The ironic maneuver here is that to the Protestant ear Jewish Bildung sounds primal, lacking the foundation and fundamentals of a more literate culture. These interstices or gaps in Jacob's knowledge represent his lack of a traditional Danish (that is, Protestant) upbringing, although his mother's songs (the aforementioned Danish ballads) have prepared his emotional facilities for the more accepted model of humanism and ultimately for the Romantic ethos: what becomes in his days as a medical student, his undying devotion to "eternal poetry and eternal life" (131). This potential, Jacob's propensity for the Byronic, lurks below the surface of his being. The director of the Latin school senses this when he compares Jacob to a wild panther cub surrounded by domestic animals. "If only the other whelps will treat the panther cub well so that its nature is not aroused" (81). I find the feline metaphor in this scene quite fascinating, and because it is rather easy to predict that the panther cub's nature will become aroused, I will use it to steer the discussion into the notion of prophecy.

The Notion of Prophecy

I would like now to turn to a scene in chapter 5 of part 1 in which Jacob's playtime fantasies drive him to torture and disembowel the family cat. It is a very brutal yet innocent scene that seems to be mostly a comic play on the stereotype of the Jewish father insisting that his son will be a famous doctor.[34] But the narrator reveals the act more as transgression, a product of Jacob's psychological isolation to the family garden amplified by the heroic legends and lore taught by Uncle Isak. "This loneliness caused an occurrence, which became an overwhelming influence over his entire future" (31). Jacob is confined to the little fenced-in garden because Uncle Isak thrashed some of Jacob's classmates for calling him *jødesmaus* (kike). The garden functions here not as the place that man tries to regain, the *locus amoenus* of many a Romantic novel, but a place from which man cannot escape. Jacob is like a wild animal, caged. Like young Otto in Goldschmidt's second novel, *Homeless*, Jacob's future will be driven by the notion of a paradise constrained. Here, Goldschmidt seems to understand the etymological meaning of the word *paradise* (Danish *paradis*) as a "walled enclosure."[35] This incubated landscape of Jacob's youth becomes a cage from which his future actions are constrained as the scene itself is constrained by its biblical source.

The severity of his solitude materializes itself through Jacob's mixed imagination, a product of his tripartite educational program. In this beautiful passage, the narrator describes one of the boy's favorite games, war, and how he battled his most worthy adversary, the family cat. The game, however, comes to a head when once again Uncle

Isak's influence interferes with the outcome. He has passed down to Jacob a favorite token of war.

> But finally Jacob realized that for one thing, it wasn't fair in that the cat was far better armed than he, and that for another thing, the whole war was unnatural in that nobody fell on the side of either the attackers or the attacked. Perhaps mixed in with this was also a secret grudge against the cat over the fact that he always had to be the one to sue for peace, and although he was bleeding everywhere, he had to propitiate the cat with a good meal to boot, something which incidentally is usually incumbent upon the defeated power at the conclusion of peace. So much is certain that Jacob did not rest until his uncle had given him a small dagger, a war souvenir, and armed with it he renewed the war. The cat undoubtedly remarked, like Hector of old, that its adversary, in some way or other, had come into the possession of an invincible weapon, but nonetheless it did not give way and fought to the last drop of blood. (32–33)

On this particular day, Jacob's father walks into the garden and witnesses the boy completing his dissection of the cat with Uncle Isak's dagger. Now a normal father might be deeply disturbed by such actions, maybe concerned for the psychology behind the violent tendencies of such a young boy. A proper father might scrutinize where such a young boy might have gotten his hands on such a weapon. He might be tempted to take the weapon away from the boy! But not Philip. His first impulse is to read this act as "a sign from heaven," interpreting that Jacob "is called to be a doctor just like der Rambám who also was driven by his nature to dissect animals and plants in order to acquire knowledge" (33).[36] This comparison with Maimonides is the only real moment of harmony offered by the novel. The narrator uses the opportunity to tell a story about Maimonides's stellar medical career, and for that idyllic moment (the exact length of the story) there is a possibility that Jacob will be as his father (and many a reader) wishes: "My son! Become a great a sage like der Rambám and be just as humble as he" (34).

These are, of course, requests that Jacob will fail to fulfill. The truth is that Uncle Isak's stories and curses have more impact on Jacob's life than Philip's blessings. Philip's ecstatic reading of Jacob torturing the house cat as prolepsis of Jacob becoming a great physician does not take into consideration that the dagger is originally Isak's. Nor is Philip aware of the actual game Jacob is playing with the cat. It turns out not to be just any war he is acting out but *The Iliad*, and specifically the final battle between Hektor and Achilles.

Jacob is trapped between two modes of reading, indicative of Goldschmidt's play with the notion of Bildung. First there is the Torah and all the rabbinical methodology of the father's lessons. Second there is the heroic code taught by the uncle. Isak's dagger, as a trope, reads back against the binding-of-Isaac scene in the Book of Genesis (Gen. 22). The difference here is that now the cleaver is in the hands of the son of the son, Goldschmidt's midrash on the history of Abraham's knife. When Isak gives the dagger to his nephew, it allows him to enact a type of sacrifice. Of course, Jacob is not Isak's son, but according to Genesis he should be. And if one reads the text closely with this allegory in mind, there is more evidence suggesting at least a partial father-son relation in the novel. Regardless, Isak is a surrogate father to Jacob and at the very least represents one-third of the parental influence during Jacob's childhood. So, what is sacrificed in the scene above? The answer, at least metaphorically, lies in the feline. This reading against the grain is typical of Goldschmidt's use of the Hebrew Bible in his storytelling art.

Jacob's slaying of the cat can be read as a mirrored moment, a sacrifice of the self. The feline is the symbol of the house of David, the lion of Judah, and in stabbing it to death Jacob has transgressed the ethical boundaries of his self. I do not doubt that Maimonides dissected animals for purposes of science when he was a boy, but I cannot believe that while doing so he was pretending to defile the corpse of Hektor out of rage. Both these stories, the binding of Isaac and the defilement of Hektor, address the tension inherent in one's ethical responsibility. There is, I believe, a pointed allusion here to

Kierkegaard's 1843 book *Fear and Trembling*. In Goldschmidt's critique, what Jacob has in common with Kierkegaard's Abraham and Homer's Achilles is the failure to properly negotiate the boundaries of the self. Somewhere caught in the juxtaposition of these two readings, Jacob begrudgingly enters into a martial frenzy, brutally stabbing the son, the enemy, the panther cub,[37] the Jew, and the self, not to mention the poor, seemingly brave cat.

The narration specifically calls the dagger "a token of war," and it will become in Jacob's hands the weapon with which he wages his greatest wars, the war with his family and the war with the world that manifests during the pogrom of 1819. The radicalness of the midrash lies in Abraham's knife as a cursed object that has been passed down from son to father across the twisted naming-game of the novel. The generations of biblical and familiar past become crisscrossed in the narrative history of the Bendixen family, much as the Trask family radically reenacts the story of Cain and Abel between Charlie and Adam in Steinbeck's *East of Eden* (1952). Here, the treachery of human sacrifice, although avoided in the biblical story of the binding of Isaac, becomes reverified through the one constant object, the knife.[38] For Jacob it is that very same dagger with which he stabs a farmhand who is leading an angry mob into the Bendixen's home by attempting to enter secretly through the cellar.

> There sat the boy on a stone, and in his hand he was holding his dagger. It was bloody up to the hilt. The weak lighting falling in the passageway revealed to the father and the uncle the boy's pale face and the bloody weapon. With one glance they guessed what had happened.
>
> With a strange feeling of fear and admiration the father bent over his child, who fell unconscious into his arms.
>
> The uncle said, "Now there is blood between him and the Christians." (72–73)

Both of Isak's prophecies, the one spoken at Jacob's birth saying that he will be such a coward that even the Jews will call him cowardly and this one, articulate Jacob's future activities in the world. He fails to become a great soldier on the battlefields of Algeria because he cannot shoot the enemy; and he is nearly killed in Warsaw during the commencement of the Polish revolution, relegated to being a "half-conscious witness to the raging battle" (266). Likewise, his life will be a conflict of personalities with the various Christians he comes into contact with. When Jacob is sent to Copenhagen to live with his Orthodox uncle, Marcus, so that he might attend a Latin school, the realization of the father's dream of Jacob becoming a great rabbi is initiated. However, Phillip's misreading of the fate of his own son acts more as a curse than any revelation of his greatness. The boys at the Latin school will call him Moses, making gestures with their hands down over their chins, and end all their words with *-øde* and *-aus*, mocking sublimations of the words *jøde* and *jødesmaus.* This would be the equivalent of ending words in English with *-ew* and *-ike*, for Jew and Kike. Later Jacob drops out of medical school because he cannot bear the tag of the Jew, the Jew Bendixen, the epithet itself suggesting a complication of the particular and the universal. Jacob even severs ties with his family when he comes home for break during his Latin school days.

Armed with his newly learned humanism, symbolized by his patronage to the Golden Age poet Adam Oehlenschläger, Jacob admits to his uncle that he has stopped wearing the tefillin and arbakanfos (two important articles of dress in Orthodox Judaism) and that he has eaten chaser "pork."[39] Uncle Isak strikes the boy violently until he almost loses consciousness. From this point on there is blood between Jacob and his family. He never sees them again. His mother mysteriously dies in the background of the novel, and his father passes away while Jacob is in Algeria, never fulfilling his father's lifelong wish for his son to say kaddish over his grave.[40]

And indeed there is no son to say kaddish over Jacob's grave; he dies never having taken a wife. The novel shoves aside the generational aspects of the Abraham narrative for the fragility of romantic love; the novel is also tragic as Jacob falls in love with and is briefly betrothed to a girl he can never have, a girl from the other side of the tracks, a Christian girl. The psychology of this predicament is, of course, framed by the *shiksa*'s name.[41] Her name is Thora, which in Danish looks like the word for the Hebrew Bible and simultaneously like a feminization of the Norse god Thor. It is in this name that Jacob becomes split between his Jewish heritage and the Nordic identity of his homeland that he has learned through three venues: oral ballads, sagas, and poetry, specifically the *universalpoesi* (universal poetry) or *organismetanken* (organic thought) of Oehlenschläger, all rich expressions of cultural capital in the Golden Age.

Oehlenschläger's Tear

When the rector of the Latin school gives Jacob his first volume of Oehlenschläger, he says, "Read these, then there will also come a bird and gather you, though not exactly back to your parents; however, it is good for one to travel around a bit in the world" (86).[42] The rector's seduction stresses its own attempt to break Jacob away from his familial roots. By reading this poetry, the rector promises that Jacob will be able to travel beyond his wildest dreams, beyond the fenced-in garden of his youth, into the life of the mind, although if we closely consider the metaphor that will supposedly free Jacob from his stasis in the world, something more sinister appears at play. As I shall demonstrate shortly in an upcoming section, the avian trope is already a metaphor for Jacob's constraint.

The figure of the seductive rector establishes itself in opposition to Jacob's pious uncle Marcus's Talmudic ponderings and the authority of the rabbi, who later sees through Jacob's fascination with Christianity and even taunts his aching by offering him the apple on his desk.[43] The allegory of sexual awakening, the desire for the forbidden, has already written itself across Jacob's future and the rabbi is there to verify the seductive power of the Romantic ethos that is offered by the rector.[44] Both the rabbi and Uncle Marcus realize (as did Jacob's father and Uncle Isak, as well as the storyteller in chapter 6 known only as Polaken [the Pole]) that it is the delicate notion of Jacob's faith that hangs in the balance.

The rector's introduction of Oehlenschläger—here the premium metonym for Danish Romanticism and the humanist mind—into

Jacob's curriculum is presented as an avian rebirth outside of genetic patterning, "though not exactly back to your parents." The text again becomes the medium that will supposedly harmonize Jacob into the world, but the rector's offer is less experiential than it is existential. For Jacob, it will require that he doubt the very religion of his father. "Faith, whether it is made up of ceremonies and superstition or it is purely spiritual, is not to be likened with a house from which one can remove a single stone and set another in its place. As soon as doubt seeps in, the whole house wobbles, it caves in, and one cannot reuse the materials to construct a new one. Doubt does not stick to faith like a rust spot, slowly corroding; it is rather like that poison that needs only graze a man's tongue before instantaneously spreading throughout his entire system" (89).

The house metaphor describes this doubt as something systemic, something that infects the entire foundation of life. Even though Jacob's faith was mostly made up of wearing meaningless amulets and "half-thoughtlessly reciting long, almost incomprehensible Hebrew prayers," it was nonetheless a stable foundation for Jacob. Once his flirtation with the rector's worldview commences, Jacob's Judaism, that is, his father's Judaism, becomes irrecoverable, and this spiritual and experiential foundation must be built from scratch. The first stone recast no doubt belongs to the realm of dannelse. Note the following sentence, which begins the very next paragraph: "Jacob had immersed himself in Oehlenschläger and engrossed himself in the Nordic heroic age and the pagan era" (89). Through this immersion into the national literatures of the Nordic countries, Jacob attempts to seduce himself from his Jewish faith. But as the reader will see, it is this posturing to the world that strangulates Jacob throughout his adult life, forcing him back, perhaps grudgingly, to the fixed roots of family and tribe.

There is a term in Romanticism that describes the power of the imagination. This is the Coleridgean term *esemplastic*. I would argue that this notion is integral to the very nature of Romanticism.[45] Coleridge defined esemplastic as "Having the capability of moulding diverse ideas or things into unity" (from Greek *es-* [into] + *en*, neuter of *eis* [one] + *plastic*, adjectival of *plasma* [image] apparently after the German term *Ineinsbildung* [forming into one]). The dream of assimilation, here objectified in the poetry of Oehlenschläger, falls subject to this supposed power of the imagination, that the mind is its own place, its own sentience, its own complete subjectivity. Through his discourse on Oehlenschläger, Goldschmidt is able to destabilize the tenets of Romanticism by producing the one thing that cannot be imagined: the ethnic.

Oehlenschläger's poetics become the central topic of a heated debate during a dinner party at the very wealthy wholesaler Bernbaum's house, a place "open to all scholars, young and old." In this parlor scene (itself a parody of Biedermeier slumber), Goldschmidt's narrator starts to rebuild upon his agenda of language politics by having the wholesaler's office clerk read aloud from *Aladdin*.[46] Whereas in the glosses this politic of speaking is addressed by varying degrees of access, here the tension concerns sophistication and Bildung. The vernacular or ethnic is featured closer to its own element, yet even among a roomful of Jews any timbre of the ethnic violates the poetical aesthetic. This is a function of Goldschmidt's developing naturalistic gesture: a tendency toward an organic classification of languages.[47]

> The office clerk read *Aladdin* with the same tone as if it had been his boss's ledger, and with a strong Jewish accent. But Jacob was so completely moved by his feelings as a guest and in awe for the welcoming house that he automatically sought to find all things beautiful. Soon he followed the reading with the same interest with which one might listen to a beautiful melody even though poorly performed. The students by the window leaned their heads together and laughed.
>
> The reading went along undisturbed, until the place where Noureddin cries out with new copper lamps to trade for old ones. Here the reader wanted to introduce something innovative to his monotonous delivery and the words:
>
> "Who will trade old copper lamps for new?"
>
> He tried to the best of his ability to impersonate that voice which called out "peat" in the street.

> At this noise the wholesaler awoke, rubbed his eyes and said, "That was quite a barter! What kind of demented book have you gotten your hands on?" (115–16)

The provincial storytelling scene of Jacob's childhood has been translated into the idyllic savvy of the nineteenth-century reading circle, the culture of dannelse. The office clerk's reading is marked by his strong accent, a feature that would be undoubtedly unmarked in a provincial storytelling setting. We are told that despite this affectation, Jacob and a few of the others are transfixed in "æsthetiske Nydelse" (aesthetic delight), an apparent testimony to the musicality of the poetry able to transcend performance.[48] It also suggests that, congruent to Oxfeldt's reading that the Orient was something reconceptualized in terms of Denmark's relationship to other Western nations, there is a Jewish perspective that sees itself as the invisible "Oriental counterpart."[49]

Despite this aesthetic incongruity of Oehlenschläger in a strong Yiddish accent, the office clerk goes on *uforstyrret* (undisturbed) for some time until he reaches a scene in the text that calls for improvisation into the vernacular. When Noureddin poses as a peddler in an attempt to bring out the lamp, the office clerk takes it upon himself to call the text out in a particular accent, that of the poor peat peddlers he has witnessed in the streets. From the reaction in the room, one can almost imagine the shrieking disparity of the moment. Somehow T. S. Eliot's mercurial words "You are the music while the music lasts" (the mantra for the unity of performance) become entangled in themselves, already unable to reconcile the text and the performance, the Danish and the Jewish.[50]

This incongruity, or rather this dissimilarity, startles wholesaler Bernbaum out of his parlor doze: "That was quite a barter! What kind of demented book have you gotten your hands on?" It is comical that the noise (Danish *Larm*) that awakens the wholesaler happens in this moment of subterfuge and commerce. In fact, if one thinks back to all the scenes in *Aladdin* that might insult a roomful of Jews, this is certainly not the one. Perhaps the vernacular tone of the office clerk's reading would have been more successful if the words were spoken by a Jewish character in the ghetto streets—or is there somewhere in the background of the dream, here hidden in the wholesaler's slumber, a crafted pointing to a more lurid portrayal of the Jewish figure?

There is such a street scene in the first part of the play when Aladdin is accosted by a Jewish peddler. This should be the scene under discussion; my argument is that it is this scene somewhat asleep in the background that startles the wholesaler. The metonymic device for this recalling is the voice of the office clerk. Did he not read that scene in the same way? Or is it that exact scene he is recalling into the performance? This earlier scene fits more aptly with the pogrom mentality the book outlined in part 1. I would argue that the expected scene would have contained something of the following.

> ALADDIN: (trashes him)
> Get on home, you pallid dirty dog!
> Say that you have swindled a Muslim.
> THE JEW: What Muslim? Who brought up religion?
> When push comes to shove,
> I'd swindle any man, even if it was
> the Lord himself.[51]

The Jew has swindled Aladdin in their transaction. This historical figuring is to be expected in Oehlenschläger, and in all Protestant literature of the North before and after Goldschmidt. But here again there is a tear in the fabric of the poem. The Jew even asks, "Who brought up religion?" Aladdin here does not speak as a Persian or a Muslim; he speaks as a Protestant. He is the deliberator and demander of an old debate. In bringing up religion, he has turned the Jewish peddler into the premier figure of Christian anxiety and disdain for Jews, the Wandering Jew.[52] By offering the evidence that he would double-cross even "the Lord himself," the Jew walks into the hole that justifies his victimization.

In response to the office clerk's ethnic reading of some of the passages in Oehlenschläger's *Aladdin*, a law student proclaims that the work is epistemologically faulty because of all the linguistic errors latent in the characters' dialogue. He asserts, "What I first and foremost demand of a poet is truth and naturalness" (117). He is arguing for the vernacular as something specific to place, namely that sailors should speak like sailors and shepherds should speak like shepherds; neither should speak like poets or professors, or "with a strong Jewish accent" (115). The law student becomes Goldschmidt's mouthpiece for an attack upon the Romantic imagination.

> Well, then I also demand that Orientals speak like Orientals and have Oriental practices. He should not . . . oh, may I see the book. . . . Aladdin should not talk about "ripping his trousers at the knee," which is not Eastern, since in the Orient they do not wear long pants. . . . That is beastly. In particular there is a place which I was debating with a friend of mine, it is on page 48. The poet has the Spirit of the Lamp say:
>
> "A new Prometheus will again restore
> The noble light to humanity today;
> Another Odin, through the mountain's stones,
> Will steal the drink and Gunnlöd betray."
>
> This intimacy of the Spirit of the Lamp with Greek and Nordic mythology can certainly be juridically defended: for the Spirit of the Lamp, no branch of knowledge need be unfamiliar. But poetically taken, the Lamp's spirit is Eastern, an Eastern spirit and scent should be diffused over the fairy tale of the Lamp. This is Oehlenschläger who is flaunting his mythological knowledge here and again tears us clean out of the illusion. . . . what say you, Mr. Bendixen? Am I not right? (117–18)

The critique is essentially one of universalpoesi, which is characterized by its synthetic infusion of varying elements from world literature and mythology. Such a production, by definition, cannot be accurate in any realistic terms. These ahistorical and anachronistic elements prevent any suspension of disbelief, a force absolutely necessary to the poetic mode, the instinct "to find everything beautiful" (115). The law student's claim is basically that this technique, a stone soup of allusion, fashion, and fake vernacular, is inorganic and interrupts the illusionary quality of the text. They "rip us clean out of the illusion." This tearing is amplified by the pitch of the clerk's rendition of the Jewish hawker, itself a type of affectation or appropriation of the vernacular, albeit through the medium of appropriation of the Orient.

This ripping is precisely Goldschmidt's agenda. The fact is that Goldschmidt's "Orientals" talk like "Orientals," because, after all, Jews themselves are from the Orient. He remarks in his memoirs how he went out of his way to preserve the historicity of the Yiddish passages in the novel, and it is this very historical accuracy and actuality that has drawn scholars to Goldschmidt's narrative style. This accuracy, in turn, fuels the poetic "spirit" of the novel. The problem with this realism is, of course, that it requires glosses for a "real world" reader to understand. And as this dependency on the commentator becomes more and more expected, the more reading (and to some degree meaning) becomes mediated by the commentary. In direct contrast to the Jews in Holberg, Oehlenschläger, Blicher, Andersen, and Gyllembourg, Goldschmidt's Jews are accurately portrayed, right down to their speech patterns, which is enough to awake the slumberer dreaming of assimilation and embourgeoisement.

Likewise, for Jacob to be considered the new Maimonides he must speak like a Jew, which for the most part he does not and the novel must do for him.[53] All the light of the lamp reveals is that cultural imagination is bound by reading habits. As a mechanism, this commentary prevents any semblance of the esemplastic. The problem for Oehlenschläger's text under such scrutiny is that to create the dream of a new Prometheus, Aladdin must speak and act like a Persian, that is, in the Persian tongue. In Goldschmidt, it is language that verifies nationality, and here he points to the limits of the esemplastic to create a sufficient fictional reality. The fact that Oehlenschläger's Aladdin speaks like a Copenhagener only serves as a constant reminder to the reader that the power of the imagination is interminably limited by boundaries of human knowledge, which are specifically represented here as language.

Walking away from the party with his friend Levy, Jacob seems to realize his own dissimilarity to the world around him. Soon after, he cries out in frustration to Levy, "My blood loves the Jews, but my intellect cannot live amongst them. It is a Christian intellect, and it seeks its like with instinctual impetuosity" (124).[54] This is again a slight of narrative hand. It is very tempting to read the scene as Jacob's and perhaps Goldschmidt's yearning to have a Christian soul, as if they are mermaids or some other beast, but the discussion here is one of refinement and dannelse. These are metaphors for Jewish tradition and for Protestant aesthetics, respectively, and since Jacob is already so familiar with the Talmud and Jewish tradition he yearns to broaden his education by immersing himself in the discourse of European aesthetics. This is not a plea for conversion. Levy even makes this mistake, calling for Jacob to "Be baptized!" Jacob then goes on a tirade about human rights and establishes definitively his relationship to Christianity and Christian spirituality. He does not want Jews to convert to Christianity but he sees the value and the danger of Christian dannelse.

> When we, who in education [Danish *dannelse*] have advanced ahead of our people, abandon them, so that finally only the scum was left, the superiority of the Christian would be complete, then their persecution would be justified. . . . besides, I do not acknowledge the Christian religion. Judaism is well on its way to decaying from its contact with civilization, and this decaying is plaguing the disposition of those stepping forward. A worm gnaws on our existence and we, who stand in the middle of the transition, are being torn asunder. (124–25)

Jacob is Goldschmidt's mouthpiece for the cultural danger of assimilation and conversion. For Jacob, Christianity is not compelling because of its religious authority, but only because of its aesthetic production. Judaism's dissolution affects both unrefined and refined Jews alike. As I showed in the quote from "Ghetto" above, the mythology of European civilization cannot survive without the dismantling of the Jewish, and it can only be validated if it erases the history of oppression for its cultural minorities. The phrase "Neither Rome, nor the Ghetto!" rings true in this passage as well. The gnawing worm of cultural imagination is particularly brutal to the Jews like Jacob, who stand in between the Jewish and the Christian worldview. But as Jacob goes on he shows that there is no real recourse for the Christians either. They, like Aladdin, seek a new age, a new Christianity. Christian Europe too staggers from the very myths of unity that it promulgates. This relationship for Goldschmidt is anxious and desperate, producing a painful secret behind "their most joyous hymns." The veneer of achievement does not correct the violation of human rights. The worm gnaws at the Christian as well; in fact, "The worm gnaws at the whole race, despair broods over it."

Tribe as Trope: Metaphors of Constraint

As Ploug's elegy, which I discussed in my prologue, correctly identifies, ethnicity for Goldschmidt is the trope of immutability; Goldschmidt's Jewishness (specifically his Jewish reading habits) trumps his identity as a Dane. This does not disqualify him as also a Dane, but it certainly problematizes that status. This ethnic reading of the self is precisely his point of departure from other writers of the mid-nineteenth century perfecting the Danish dannelsesroman, such as H. C. Andersen and Thomasine Gyllembourg, as well as from the earlier German bildungsroman of Goethe. Unlike these authors, Goldschmidt's relation to the figure of the outsider is both poetic in the Coleridgean sense, which is to say imagined, and it is actual or, more accurately, ethnic: "I am of the tribe of Levi."[55] This latter relationship, the tribal, is animated outside the framework of the formal text; it is extra-textual. But let us make no mistake, it exerts a kind of pressure on the narrative experience, stretching the boundaries of what the text is toward itself. It reassembles the readability of the text, expanding the narrative experience. As a poetical figure, ethnicity almost always mechanizes first in Goldschmidt, and it is produced by a representation of constraint that surrounds the figuration of Jacob Bendixen. This next section of my argument traces this phenomenon as an extension of the readings above. In the metaphorical fabric of the novel, this rigidity of the ethnic is synonymous with a conflicted psychological complex as long as constraint is resisted. This boundness becomes for Jacob a personal motif, the fixed notion of tribe.

The Tethered Bird

The second part of *A Jew* is focused on Jacob's life during his medical studies and his courting of a Christian girl, two products of his experimentation with assimilation. His fatal attraction to a Christian girl does not seem entirely unexpected for Jacob. The narrator has offered several suggestions that Jacob's mother, Jette, had preconditioned him for such a "mixed" lifestyle. Her songs are "a lively alien melody. . . . from another country and another breed; gold locks and blue eyes rode these swells of sound" (35–36). Jette teaches Jacob the traditional ballads of the Danish people, Danish comedies (presumably Holberg's), collections of drinking songs, travel narratives, and so forth. These are the strange melodic waves that pierce through the Jewish legends and folktales taught by Uncle Isak and the Talmudic erudition taught by his father, Philip. There is no doubt that, in Jacob's didactic family triangle, Jette is the voice of assimilation; she is after all literally the mother tongue. Unfortunately for Jacob, there is no confluence of these three rivers of thought, and while the teachings of his father and Isak can be grouped together owing to their ethnic nature, Jette's teachings reflect the more humanist education of the Copenhagen literati and are a failed promise of the esemplastic power of language.

Jette teaches Jacob "a mother tongue, so clean and clear like the tone through the rhythms of the poets" (37). This purity of language is doubled in Goldschmidt's own language and is synonymous with the poetic style of the novel. In fact, the notion of "*rent Dansk*" (clean Danish) will occupy much of Goldschmidt's thinking about his own ability with the Danish tongue.[56] As Jacob enters his humanist education in Copenhagen, it is this clean language that allows him access to the eternal poetry of Romanticism, specifically that of Oehlenschläger. But the Latin school will also be the place where he learns the oppression of his ethnicity. "Just as the Negro slave is and always will be black, even if they 'emancipate' him," so "Jew" is "branded on our forehead" (123). He can dream of the gold locks and the blue eyes, just as he can flirt with assimilation, but this dream (of eternal poetry) has no realization, and this is the failure of the imagination to create any experiential understanding across ethnic bounds. The notion of wearing a mark "branded on the forehead" brings to mind the mark of Cain.[57] The problem Goldschmidt mechanizes through the slave metaphor is Jacob's fixedness to his tribe. He wears it like the African slave wears his skin, and this skin, because it cannot hide behind the power of language, cannot dream of assimilation. The very act of language always marks the Jew as dissimilar, no matter how clean or fluent the speaker. How can the esemplastic and the Jewish coexist when one serves as constant reminder to the other that assimilation is never possible?

This complex is crystallized through the metaphor of the tethered bird. As Jacob is departing his family for the last time, the narrator likens him to the seagulls that gather around the boats in a storm. Then the constraint was invisible: he was still enamored with the possibility that the world would afford him a place without alienation. But once the pressures of this exploration begin to press on Jacob's mind, he becomes chained to the mast of the ship—ethnicity, his albatross.

Through his university friends, Jacob begins to enter Danish society with some promise as a young medical student, and this affords him many adventures, introductions, and balls. When Jacob's love turns out to be Thora Fangel, the sister of one of his friends, the clash of the Romantic and the Jewish is finally named.[58] Danish *Thora* means "Torah," but, as mentioned before, *Thora* also looks like a feminization of Old Norse Thor, the name of the god of war. This duplicitous semantics is a game the narrator will repeat several times. These two etymologies represent the two forces tugging on Jacob's conscience, the notion of tribe versus the Romantic dream of assimilation and amelioration, or rather the "apotheosis of the Individual."[59]

In his relationship with Thora, the closer Jacob comes to being intimate with Protestant culture, the more fastened he becomes to his Jewishness. The interactions Jacob has when he is with his fiancée's family are not unlike those he had while at home. There are elements in both environments attempting to control his future. Instead of the pressure to become a great scholar and physician like Maimonides, the Fangels want Jacob to convert to Christianity. This highlights my earlier argument about the difference between Goldschmidt's religion and his idea of Christianity as a public dogma. The Dane is allowed to represent himself and all that is good about being Danish outward and eastward into the Persian orient, but the Oriental, the Jew, is not allowed to see himself as Danish. It would seem, concerning the esemplastic power of the imagination, that it only works from the Christian outward. The mixed engagement is fraught with tension, and the scenes in which Jacob joins the Fangels for dinner are exceptionally excruciating, suggesting that any union between himself and Thora would be emotionally if not physically impossible.

Out of the blue Jacob receives a letter from his father acknowledging the engagement. The letter has an intoxicating rhythm of Danish and Yiddish with the latter tending to occur at the end of clauses or sentences. This produces an incantatory effect. Of the twenty-two glosses in the text of the letter, fifteen occur in this final position with the entire last four lines of the letter written in Hebrew. "[T]he Father's letter had made the Jews and everything, which belonged to the Jews, precious for Jacob" (182). Goldschmidt does not exactly draw attention to the myth that "the nation was conceived in language, not in blood." For Goldschmidt, language was blood. The letter is for Jacob a partial reconciliation with his father and with his ethnicity. It is the Jewish tongue, the patterns of communication, resonating through the Danish at the end of the lines that move Jacob to remember compassion for his family and the Jewish way. This negotiates a split with the reader's sense of heroics; for now, as Jacob is spiritually returning to his roots in an almost ecstatic moment of nostalgia, the Protestant reader is again forced to break illusion and decipher the commentator's translations at the foot of the page. The mysterious language charms Jacob while simultaneously marking the reader as different.

At the height of his flirtation with Christianity, Jacob longs for home. He has surrounded himself with Christian friends and a surrogate Christian family, but still there is no easing of his suffering and loneliness. Immediately following Philip's resonating letter, an aged Jew knocks on Jacob's door begging for alms. Jacob sees in the pain of this figure one of his own, "one of his nearest kin," and he gives him a generous donation (182). As the old Jew leaves the house he blesses Jacob in Yiddish, "med Ordene: Gott soll Euch benschen" (with the words: God bless you!) (183). As in the father's letter, the Yiddish of the old Jew ignites Jacob's feelings of home. The narrator says that Jacob envied the poor Jew because he "was now on his way to the Jews" (183). Jacob the stranger yearns for home and his father's embrace, desiring to be once again a Jew among Jews.

This reconciliatory spirit, however, only splits Jacob more and more between the twin semantics of Danish *Thora*. She is the metaphorical mirror reflecting his constraint and the figure that binds him.

> Torah?
>
> Like the bird, who is bound with a tether flying lively in the air, but suddenly is held back and must move in a circle around the fixed point, so stopped Jacob's feelings at that name and took off in another direction.
>
> Thora. (183)

It is in this passage of the novel where the reader now fathoms that Jacob's struggle is not with religion, that is, Christian versus Jew; it is ethnic, Scandinavian versus Jew. The rigidity of tribe preanimates Jacob's experience in the world. Like the American slave, he can be emancipated, liberated, assimilated, but he will continue to be black (wear the mark of Cain). Although it is possible to read both instances of *Thora* as either Torah or Thora, it seems most sensible to read the first as Torah and the second as Thora. It is the Torah that is associated, at least in Jacob's mind, with home and his family, and especially with his father's teachings. And it is the girl Thora who has interrupted this *retning* (direction), causing his affection to awake "with doubled strength" (183).

"The fixed point" in the metaphor is his ethnicity, that which constrains Jacob as he attempts to move away from its teachings, the teachings of his father, the teachings of his people. The Torah is a metonym for the fixedness of his own ethnicity. The rector's Romantic image of the limitless songbird is here transformed into an inescapable binding, and the name of the beloved might be enough to disrupt the centrifugal edge of Jacob's Jewishness, but it cannot free him from it. The more a Christian life and wife become a possible reality, the more Jacob's Jewishness becomes reactivated and reels in his dream of assimilation through marriage.

The fixedness of the trope promotes the idea that Jews cannot assimilate under any condition; however, there are other Jews in the novel that seem to have succeeded in assimilating. Jacob's mother, although the daughter of a rabbi, can be said to have had, at the very least, an assimilated worldview. Although he is a Christian, the rector too demonstrates a continuation of Jette's insistence on a humanist education as being the path to Jacob's identity as a Dane. The blindness they share is the failure to read the tether, the tribal umbilical cord. But there is one Jewish figure who stands in contrast to this idea of fixedness and through whom the metaphor of tribe is able to drift through boundaries of social coding.

The Amphibian

At the graduation celebration, Jacob meets a young Jewish man named Martin Levy.[60] The two quickly become friends, and Levy becomes Jacob's confidant and doctor. Levy embodies the very dream of assimilation that Jacob's mother had wished for him. The reader learns through the dinner conversation when the two first meet that Jacob's mother is already dead. There is no explanation given for her death, nor are there any scenes in which Jacob is informed of his mother's death. We are even spared a mourning scene such as we have in Algeria when Jacob finds out his father has died. Jette's death in the background of the novel is announced as his friendship with Levy begins. This points to the emergence of Levy as a projection of Jette's dream of assimilation. Throughout the rest of the novel, the reader is forced to compare Jacob and his melancholic persecution complex with the paragon of assimilation, Martin Levy.

The difference between these two characters is expressed metaphorically when Levy suggests that Jews are amphibians, equally at home in the company of both Jews and Christians. For Levy, the amphibian is a liminal metaphor, navigating the boundaries between Protestant and Jewish culture at will, untethered. Levy is at home among both Jews and Protestants, although he cannot stand mixed company. "What do such Jews want with the Christians in their homes? In this state Jewishness is altogether incommensurate with Christianity" (110). Levy is functional in either mode of discourse as long as there is a clear boundary between them. In this sense, Levy is less a figure of assimilation than he is a figure of functional segregation. In fact, Levy is such a thin character that he only appears once in the narrative without Jacob, and that is at Jacob's death. What Levy lacks is any emotional identification with his ethnicity, and therefore the boundary between these two codes of culture, Jewish and Christian, is simply a matter of behavior and poise. For Jacob, this boundary is impassable, a suffocating wall enclosing him from the inside yet trapping him from his natural environment. "Amphibians, you say, that we Jewish students are? It seems to me that we are exactly the opposite of amphibians, that we have abandoned that element, to which we originally belong, and have been transplanted into one which does not fit our nature" (110).

In very scientific language, Jacob pulls the metaphor from the abstract world of social barriers to the world of elements and nature. The element of water here can be identified as the super motif of creation. In Genesis 1:2, before creation even begins, there is only God's breath hovering over the primordial waters. The fixed point of Jacob's worldview and his existential crisis is his ethnic roots. The element that he and the other Jewish students have abandoned (or been forced to abandon) is their own Jewishness. Jacob cannot escape the memory of his origins. For Jacob, the metaphor specifically points to a failed evolution: the water creature leaving his original environment without having developed in full the means to survive on land.

This metaphor of origins was important to Golden Age thought. The amphibian was used earlier by H. C. Andersen in his 1835 novel *Improvisatoren*. There, in a similar discussion between the protagonist, Antonio, and his friend and confidant Bernardo, the metaphor is aimed at chastising Antonio's hyper-Romanticization of the world and his transparency of emotions. "How grave and solemn!" exclaimed Bernardo, laughing. "You are not in love! Now, that is actually true, you are also one of these spiritual amphibians, not knowing if you actually belong to the corporal or the dream world!"[61]

The difference between the two attestations of the metaphor is indicative of the relationship each author had to the other and the representative authors' aesthetic for appropriating the Romantic mode. Antonio is of two worlds, but these are not Goldschmidt's two world-historical elements. One is a spiritual realm, the world of dreams and forms, which secures Antonio's function in the novel as a poetic genius. (There is no doubt that Goldschmidt was aware of Andersen's metaphor, and Goldschmidt's amphibian or failed amphibian metaphor is a commentary against Andersen's.) In contrast, Goldschmidt's amphibian is by nature not a fully evolved creature. Antonio's struggle with the poetic is measured in the Christian (or Catholic) iconography and ethos of the novel. Jacob's struggle is not being split between two realms of thought as is Antonio's, nor is it being split between two codes of culture as is Levy's. Jacob's struggle is at the level of basic genetic survival; he is a fish out of water.

With no more options in Copenhagen, and on the brink of a complete paranoid breakdown, Jacob ends part 2 by leaving Thora and running away to France to join the Foreign Legion (French Légion étrangère). Jacob feels responsible for testing his uncle's prophecy spoken during his infancy that he would have an aversion to war. Consequently, the metaphor of tribe emerges from the North African deserts and confirms Isak's vision of Jacob being a great coward. Jacob is again forced to look into the mirror and recall his tribal origin.

The Bedouin

Chapter 4 of part 3 opens with Jacob arriving in port in Algiers. Instead of immediately being thrown into the fray of battle, Jacob is forced to confront a strong sense of belonging and kind; he sees men dressed in turbans, Turks, and "Jews in black robes and with long, tangled beards" (227). As he disembarks, Jacob feels a new possibility. The figure of the Dark Continent, usually in the hands of Europeans a motif of the exotic other, is for Jacob superseded by his ethnic profile. Northern Africa is the land of Moses and the Exodus; it stands at the origin of the Torah. For Jacob, it is nothing less than a homecoming. "'So, now I am in Africa,' said Jacob, when he set his foot on the ground; 'now this is my fatherland!'" (227).

This is possibly the most radical moment of the text in terms of Goldschmidt's "midrashic adroitness."[62] By calling Africa his homeland, Jacob is either stating that he was born into slavery (that is, born before the Exodus, before the Torah), or he is saying that this blood son of Shem (from whom the Israelites are descendants) is figuratively a son of Ham (whose descendants inhabit Africa), or both. At least one son of Ham, Canaan, is cursed to be a slave, so that brings the figuration back to slavery, but Canaan and his lineage are doomed specifically to be slaves to the descendants of Shem.[63] No matter how the metaphor of setting foot on the African continent is read, it emphasizes Jacob's enslavement. It points to Jacob's estrangement from his clan (namely, it is Mosaic), to his predicament with curses (or his predilection for accruing them), and to his enslavement to his own Jewishness (the fixed metaphor of tribe), and, perhaps most important, it posits the reasoning and rationale of Jacob's persecution complex in the novel (that is, it substantiates all the riches in the novel as actual and not psychological). Furthermore, this startling homecoming also reveals Goldschmidt's natal bond with Egypt and Afro-Semitic culture, suggesting again that from the Jewish perspective, Africa and the Orient are not mediated through

European models of appropriation but through the constraint of the Hebrew Bible.

The battlefields of Africa are not unlike the one in the scene elaborated upon earlier in which Jacob slays the family cat. Jacob has made great effort to refute the prophetic words of his uncle by joining a real war, but instead of finding the worthy adversary upon which to assert his heroism, he is again forced to deal with the projection of the self onto the battlefield. Whereas in the scene above his actions were constructed biblically through a radical reading of the binding of Isaac, here it is illusory within the land of mirage. What should transpire as a *fata morgana* is again the constraining force that causes all Jacob's actions to overcome his uncle's curse to be in vain. How is Jacob to subvert his (un)heroic destiny to be a coward by killing off his own kind in the fatherland?[64]

> Suddenly in front of this a line of Bedouins appeared, who shielded by a trench and a wild hedge, supposedly in order to stop the French cavalry, aimed their long flintlocks at them. More and more heads appeared in the long line, the white burnooses flapping in the morning wind, the white hoods contrasted queerly with the brown faces and black beards. Now the front rows stood tall in their white robes. Jacob reined in his horse. At synagogue during the great Day of Atonement, the Jews dressed in the same manner, just as when they were laid in their coffins. It was as if his father was there, dressed in his shroud, as if all holy Jews were there, newly risen from the grave. At that moment the signal to attack sounded, but even if it had meant his soul's salvation, he could not have opened fire on these figures. The trumpets blared, rifles and pistols popped, his subordinates ran to the right and the left around him into the smoke clouds of battle; Jacob stood still and motionless. (232)

Jacob freezes in the line of fire as the heads of Bedouin soldiers circle around him. The figure of the Bedouin reminds him of his father on Yom Kippur, the Day of Atonement. This image of the father recalls the Hamitic metaphorics I laid out above. This recognition of the father in the Bedouin is the birth of the Afro-Semitic continuum in

Goldschmidt's oeuvre. In Genesis 9:22, Ham sees "his father's nakedness" and his family is therefore cursed by Noah, "Cursed be Canaan, / the lowliest slave shall he be / to his brothers."[65] Jacob, here, experiences the Hamitic *mise en abyme* by figuratively seeing the nakedness of his father. But Jacob sees deeper than the naked flesh or skin of his father. He sees into the genetic code of an entire cursed race. The curse here and the curse that is the novel's epigram both have an askew target. It is an odd thing that the son is cursed for the father's sins. It is likewise odd that the soil is cursed for Adam's sins. Perhaps it is no wonder Jacob produces no offspring, seeing as though both the textual world and the world of the novel offer no recourse from a sin inherited. Furthermore, the curse too becomes evidence (although perhaps previously announced) that Jacob is trapped in the abyss of his own ethnicity. The naked flesh is a metaphor for the genetic code exposed, but perhaps not exposed in the sense of revealed, but in the sense of ruined or tainted. The undead father in his shroud haunts, as all Holy Jews do, the lives of their offspring.

Jacob emerges as a Jew, albeit a failed Jew, through this reading of the Bedouin soldiers as the devout Jews in attendance at his father's burial. In this moment, the Afro-Semitic conscience is pulling Jacob toward identifying with the Bedouin soldiers over his allegiance to the French, as if for once blood were thicker than water. He even imagines that his father and all the pious Jews rise out of the ground to participate in the battle. For the first time, the conflict for Jacob has proven itself real. Face to face in battle, just within the reach of glory, Jacob realizes there is no poetry, no heroic code, no call to arms greater than his tribal roots.

The notion of kinship in this passage, however fictive, is important here as it belongs to Goldschmidt's overall strategy of promulgating an Afro-Semitic continuum, something of which he is the early forerunner. I discuss this topic in the final chapter of the book. Suffice it to say here that Jacob's psychological experience during the Algeria episode is enhanced by his father's death. Jacob is forced to realize his failure as a Jewish man when he is unable to be at his father's burial, by not saying kaddish over his grave. But it is also in this experience where we begin to see Jacob's loyalty moving toward his identity as a Jew. As he stares into the Hamitic abyss, the father too stares back: "Then his thoughts heavy with regret turned back to his father's deathbed and to his long deceased mother. He saw her again so kind, so pale! He saw his father as the end approached, and he was alone! What was being alone in a strange city to being alone on one's deathbed! With infinite longing his dying eyes searched for his only son, and maybe his last thought lingered with the suffocating certainty that his son would not even say kaddish over him when he lay in the grave" (230–31).

He testifies to his dead father and the apparition of his mother, "Let them hear outside that I am a Jew! Yes, I am a Jew" (231). It is the articulation that he has tried to suppress throughout the novel but it is also the confession he dared not to make. His sin is not that he could not articulate that he was a Jew, but his sin is that he is simply "a Jew." The elegy is too late, unable to reverse the hopelessness his future will contain. The deepest wound that cuts Jacob is the image of his father gazing at the door as he dies, never giving up hope even in his last living moment that his son will come bursting through to honor his death. In Jacob's memory, he takes with him to the grave this shame and disgust, his last earthly memory. This reflexivity comes to a head when Jacob finally enters the battlefield, his one chance to defy Isak's binding words. But here, too, he is surrounded by his own Jewishness, and is forced to see the inescapability of his ethnicity. From Algeria, he will move to the battlefields of Poland to join the fray of the November Uprising, but here too he will find his heroic destiny subverted by a near-fatal wound.[66] Like the Wandering Jew, Jacob is not able to find release even from death.

The Padlock

After coming back home from Poland and recuperating from his battle wounds, Jacob learns that his Christian love, Thora, has conveniently married his boyhood nemesis, the suave and debonair Lieutenant Engberg. To add insult to injury, Jacob returns one night (which just happens to be Thora's birthday) to the secret country garden where he and Thora would escape during their courtship. Here again the garden becomes a tainted metaphor as he secretly sees his Thora in the arms of a third man, Grabow. What is even worse is that this Grabow bears a striking resemblance to Jacob himself.

This is more than Jacob can bear. But when Grabow, who has replaced Jacob in his circle of medical school friends, comes to him asking for money to pay for a picture of his beloved Thora, Jacob "just like the other Jews" does not hesitate to lend him the money, at least not after a few days (284). Several days later Thora learns (from a note attached to the portrait) that Jacob caught sight of her illicit affair with Grabow in the garden, and in high Romantic fashion, she dies of an inflammatory fever. In order to attend the funeral in style, Grabow asks Jacob to borrow another twenty rix-dollars on top of the money for the portrait. Jacob is furious at Grabow's assumptive pleas for financial aid because, after all, as a Jew Jacob has financial power over the Protestants: "'Do I?' cried Jacob, springing up. 'Do I? . . . Then write down the promissory note! I will dictate'" (289).

These words ring ominous at the closing of the novel's penultimate chapter. In the end, Jacob becomes that which the reader could have never predicted: the stereotypical Jewish moneylender. As the novel progresses, the reader is coaxed into a sense of a shared subjectivity with Jacob. Likewise, the reader has invested a great deal of his own psychology in Jacob's success. Not only do we want to see him become a great and successful doctor like der Rambám, but who among us does not want him to become assimilated, at least to the point where he is not haunted by his ethnicity and the specters of the past? No doubt in Goldschmidt's day there were also those readers who (like Thora's old aunt) even wanted Jacob to convert to Christianity. Instead he has become the most rigid and fixed trope of all, the Shylock, the ghetto voice that pierces through the bourgeois culture of the Danish Golden Age. The imaginative experience of the novel becomes disrupted and imagination itself dismantled in the novel's final chapter.

The deepest moment of background narrative in the novel, the darkest interstice the reader experiences, happens between the penultimate and ultimate chapters. An indefinite amount of time has elapsed and an overwhelming amount of narrative has unfolded. The reader has been shut out of Jacob's life completely. What transpires in the space between those two chapters is a negation of the novel. And in this move, the imaginative mode has become once and for all subverted. After Jacob abandons the Romantic ideal, there is little use in continuing his story.

The best example of the critique of the esemplastic in Goldschmidt's novel is the discussion of Oehlenschläger's *Aladdin* that occurs in the Bernbaum salon. The conversation concerns whether it is realistic for Oehlenschläger's "Orientals" to dress in trousers and speak like Danes, or have any knowledge of the Nordic gods. Although Oehlenschläger had never been to the Near East, his imagination gave him license to visit those tales and lands and even further to conflate them with both a European and a Nordic past. This is the modus operandi of Coleridge's "Kubla Khan," his "Rime of the Ancient Mariner," and other classics of high Romanticism such as Byron's *Cain* or *Childe Harold*. More appropriately, we might even think of H. C. Andersen's flirtation with the Jewish figure in *Only a Fiddler* (1837) or Thomasine Gyllembourg's "The Jew" (1836).

For Goldschmidt, however, the idea of the Byronic Jew is antithetical to the identity of the Jewish people. When he opens his memoirs with the statement "I am of the tribe of Levi" he is in essence distancing himself from the mainstream Protestant culture but also, and perhaps more important, he is stamping his authority on the Jewish figure. A Jew stands in sharp contrast to the Protestant representation of Jews and the Jewish figure that is inherited from medieval comedy. In fact, one can read the novel as a parody of the Christian imagination. There can be no further play with the Jewish figure after Goldschmidt; it is forbidden to imagine such things. It is Goldschmidt's own ethnicity that creates a fatal difference between his project and the project at large, Romanticism.

The final chapter opens with "The Jew's closed black hearse" (289), but this is not just any funeral procession; it is described specifically as "an Orthodox Jewish funeral" (289). The reader finds out that Jacob Bendixen has died. And furthermore, that he has become the Jew not even his father could have imagined. As a moneylender, he was known to have charged 200 percent interest! The disruptive atmosphere of the funeral plants little doubt that Jacob was despised as a man. The streets outside the little Jewish cemetery on Møllegade swarm with Jacob's former customers. "A mob of riffraff pursued the hearse, howling, whooping, and throwing stones; policeman dashed around in the crowd dealing out blows to those who were throwing stones and to those who were not throwing stones" (289). For readers, this scene is confusing. When did Jacob, the sensitive boy we grew up with, become so hated? When did he become an Orthodox Jew? How did he die? The questions are limitless and the text provides few answers. There are even questions from within the Jewish community, as the scene shifts from the mob on the streets to the inside of one of the coaches in which seven elderly Jews sit and talk.

The conversation concerns Jacob and his role in the Jewish community, which none of the elders seems to know much about. But a mysterious figure emerges, Schaie Jisroel, claiming to have known Jacob intimately and testifies that "[h]e was a pious man!" On Yom Kippur, for the whole of the day, they had regularly sat next to one another in Schul. The dialogue between the elders is fraught with disruption. All the elders speak Yiddish except for Jisroel (a speech pattern suspiciously reminiscent of Jacob's own), and the glosses at this point in the novel have become relatively sparse if not absent altogether. Yiddish words and phrases occurring in the earlier parts of the novel are no longer glossed, forcing the non-astute reader to backpedal into the novel to find their meaning. And what once was retrojected into the end of sentences in an effect of cadence now occupies the entirety of the spoken sentence and paragraph. Few of the new Yiddish words are even glossed, renegotiating the earlier illusion of Bildung. The dialogue as a whole is inaccessible, further interrupted by the racist shouts of the outside mob that filter through the coach window. Finally, we learn secondhand through Jisroel of Jacob's final moments: "'He was not at all pious in his youth. He had even been engaged with a Christian girl. But so came the Lord's spirit over him, and he left her and became an Orthodox Jew. . . . The last night he did not speak a word. Then as death came, he sat up and gazed around himself and cried out for Moses' law, the blessed Thora[h]'"(293).[67]

Is this, "blessed Thorah," the inversion of the name that she, Thora Fangel, never bore, Thora Bendixen? Interestingly, in the moment when Jacob appears most stereotypical, the moment when his attempted assimilation or esemplasticism (and perhaps the reader's) appears to have completely failed, he emits one final utterance that attempts to assimilate Thora (and by extension Danish culture) to his own world, the ultimate attempt to bridge the ethnic and the esemplastic. Either this or all duality has been abandoned, and Thora is now specifically and uniquely the Hebrew Bible. This too dies with Jacob.

Jacob Bendixen leaves the world as he entered it, surrounded by the ugly cries of anti-Semitism. Amid shouts of "Blood-sucker" and "Kike," a locked padlock is thrown on top of the casket as Jacob's Orthodox uncle, Marcus, steps forward and casts the first shovels of dirt, a final act of Orthodoxy burying the Romantic dream.

Martin Levy, Jacob's closest friend from his medical student days in Copenhagen, remains after everybody else has departed. Looking out over the woods of their youth, Levy recites a final kaddish or benediction over Jacob's grave: "He once believed in eternal poetry and eternal life!" (295).

Levy (namely, Goldschmidt of the tribe of Levi) makes one last attempt to bridge the divide: the traditional kaddish, the most solemn of all the Jewish rituals described throughout the book, is subverted into a Romantic epitaph, different in meaning but somehow strongly reminiscent of Keats's: "Here Lies One / Whose Name was writ in Water."[68] But again, is this the Jewish yearning to be Romantic or the Jewish yearning for the Romantic to be assimilated back to the Jewish? Can esemplasticism overcome the rigidity of ethnicity? Can eternal life be padlocked together with eternal poetry? Or have Romanticism and the Romantic dream been locked away forever?

The death of Jacob Bendixen is a tragedy based on the impossibility of assimilation. The underlying tensions are not so much the conflict between the Christian and the Jewish, as scholars have tried to convince us for 150 years, or even, as Kierkegaard thought, in the notion of conversion itself.[69] The fatal disease of Jacob Bendixen, one that Martin Levy was never able to cure him of, was Romanticism itself, the power of the imagination. Jacob's character is a site of disparate notions that refuse to occupy the same space: the ethnic and the esemplastic, the Jewish and the Byronic. His death marks the fatal disruption of the Romantic mode and buried with him is the ominous padlock that once again binds mortality to that great Promethean stone, trapping eternal life and eternal poetry in a metaphorical iron heart that was metonymically missing throughout the novel. One can only imagine it is the hand of Goldschmidt, the Realist extraordinaire, himself not allowed into the little cemetery on Møllegade, that casts the padlock over the stone walls and into the grave of Jacob Bendixen. One can imagine, but one can never know.

3

The World of Allusion

By now I hope it has become clear that Goldschmidt has used the novel as a vehicle for his reflections on biblical stories and motifs, and that this transformative process is harmonized not by any singular interpretative strategy but in the multiplicity of readings posed or possible. This is activated on several levels, from literal glosses at the foot of the page to metaphorical commentary that is woven through the images and dialogue of the text. It is also vital to note that the Hebrew Bible and subsequent parabiblical texts and storytelling traditions provide the foundation not only for Goldschmidt's narrative art but also for his very imagination. In this third chapter, I would like to turn our attention to how the dynamic process of alluding to the Hebrew Bible and the Talmud form literary expression in Goldschmidt's poetics. I will pay particular attention to some of Goldschmidt's shorter works.

Literary allusion is a game of triggers, whether semantic or pictorial, in one text that activates a narrative element or pattern either in itself or in another text.[1] It is an unloosening of the boundaries between artistic imaginations. Wordsworth describes this navigation in an almost perfect series of images:

> One summer evening (led by her) I found
> A little boat tied to a willow tree
> Within a rocky cave, its usual home.
> Straight I unloosed her chain, and stepping in
> Pushed from the shore. It was an act of stealth
> And troubled pleasure, nor without the voice
> Of mountain-echoes did my boat move on;

Leaving behind her still, on either side,
Small circles glittering idly in the moon,
Until they melted all into one track
Of sparkling light.[2]

The game is cryptic in nature, requiring stealth to produce a pleasure that is "troubled"; however, the quality of allusiveness is flexible. That is to say, some allusions are overt and deliberate while others are so obscure that their sources become more and more soluble over time until they vanish, like the "small circles" of *The Prelude.* The dissolution of source into text again testifies to the esemplastic power of unifying all into one. The kind of allusion I am interested in, in this chapter, is global allusion, an allusion or more likely a series of allusions that activates a series of metaphors that substantiate meaning in the current text. Regardless of its transparency, how an allusion operates in a text, that is, what it activates in terms of the narrative depth of the text, is what determines its importance to that text. For example, I illustrated in chapter 2 how Goldschmidt alluded to the garden story from Genesis to activate a metaphor for forbidden love and primal sin in his second novel, *Homeless.* The apple tree established a prehistory for his young characters, Emilie and Otto, and also constrained the possibility of their future selves. The apple tree is not mere embellishment but stands on the opening page of the novel as a tutelary image that controls the dynamic of the characters' relationship vis-à-vis the opening chapters of Genesis. The biblical story forms the metaphorical fabric from which the narrative is cast. It activates the motif of forbidden and troubled love that will follow the young lovers Otto and Emilie throughout their lives; the allusion to the Genesis story provides the "sparkling light" that radiates our reading of the scene.

Let us examine another literary allusion from twentieth-century American literature in order to illustrate this point more clearly. Steinbeck's 1939 novel *The Grapes of Wrath* is a text famously laden with allusions. Many of the allusions are biblical in nature and activate parallels between the California migration of the Joad family and the plight of the Hebrew people.[3] There is a provocative scene at the end of chapter 10 when the Joads are packing up their truck to escape Oklahoma for a new beginning in California. The imaginative power of the scene is driven by the allusion to Noah and the Ark in Genesis.[4] "Pa said, 'Ma, you an' Granma set in with Al for a while. We'll change aroun' so it's easier, but you start out that way.' They got into the cab, and then the rest swarmed up on top of the load, Connie and Rose of Sharon, Pa and Uncle John, Ruthie and Winfield, Tom and the preacher. Noah stood on the ground, looking up at the great load of them sitting on top of the truck."[5]

Steinbeck here is scintillating. The trigger is not that Noah Joad is looking up at the fully loaded truck as Noah did the ark, but rather how Steinbeck loads his ark.[6] The allusion is not limited to the biblical names of some of the characters—at least not at this point in the narrative, some ten chapters in. The reader has already digested the names of Noah and the Rose of Sharon from the Hebrew Bible. The real trigger is placing the Joads on the truck two by two: Ma and Granma, Connie and Rose of Sharon, Pa and Uncle John, Ruthie and Winfield, Tom and the preacher. This alludes to Genesis 7:15, "They came to Noah into the ark, two by two of all flesh that has the breath of life within it." The allusion is dynamic. It points to the cleansing process of transformation that the Joads hope to accomplish by heading west. It signifies the hope of transformation for a nation as the Joads are just one family of thousands that made the journey during the Dust Bowl of the 1930s. Steinbeck has a great power of inversion invested in his narrative art. He trades the floodwaters of Genesis for the barren deserts of Oklahoma to also create the layering of allusions that the Joads are a people in exile and they journey for a new land.[7] Instead of loading animals and birds two by two, the narrator loads the Joads in a spectacle of sequence. Steinbeck even crafts humor from it when Noah asks, "How about the dogs, Pa?" and Pa says, "Take them chickens, too. . . ."[8]

Despite the dynamic nature of literary allusion, the reader always remains grounded in the current text. During the departure episode in *The Grapes of Wrath*, the reader never forgets that he is reading a novel, and that is precisely why *drawing on* and *pointing to* miss the mark: texts themselves do not distinguish from one another. The reader does not have to leave Steinbeck to access the ark narrative, but neither does he extract the ark narrative from Genesis. The two exist in a momentary conjunction, almost in the astronomical sense, as when two planets or stars are in the same (or nearly the same) position when viewed from earth. They are not really in the same place, but they appear to be from the earth's vantage point. This configuration is called "syzygy." The ark narrative and the Joads' loading in the car two by two appear to be in complete alignment from the vantage point of the reader, but they both retain their actual textual locations with all that entails. If the reader does not have the right vantage point (namely, he does not know the Genesis text), then the Joad story still has the imaginative ingredients to stand by itself; however, even if the allusion goes undetected, as many do, the poetics of the text is still dependent on the antecedent text. The notion of canon is critical here. We can also see that allusion thrives on canonicity. Modern fiction thrives on the syzygy of concatenating texts to create a series of dissipating rings in the wake of the reader.

The pervasiveness of allusion in all literatures of the world testifies to this truth: allusion is indispensable to the very act of human narration. This is perhaps worrisome to think about, this standing on the shoulders of giants to look at literature and the literary imagination. The Romantic vision of the demiurge poet extemporaneously producing perfect verse from nothing or the genius whose creativity cannot be extinguished are myths of the literary world. Yet literary influence is treated as a pathology, an anxiety of the imagination.[9] In a 1359 letter to Boccaccio, Petrarch sheds light on the intricacy of borrowing and the pursuit of style.

> But sometimes I may forget the author, since through long usage and continual possession I may adopt them [from Virgil, Horace, Livy, Cicero] and for some time regard them as my own; and besieged by the mass of such writings [*turba talium obsessus*], forget whose they are and whether they are mine or others'. . . . I much prefer that my style [*stilus*] be my own, uncultivated and rude, but

> made to fit, as a garment, to the measure of my mind, rather than to someone else's . . . each [writer] must develop and keep his own [style] lest . . . by dressing grotesquely in others' clothes . . . we may be ridiculed like the crow.[10]

The game of allusion is like Wordsworth's commandeering of his small boat in the beginning of the *Preludes*, "an act of stealth and troubled pleasure." When a writer adopts or adapts something from an antecedent text, there is a twofold pleasure. One is of course that it will be discovered and understood to enhance the text; the other is that it will not be discovered and lie in obscurity as the author's own invention. Allusion often hides in the shadows and folds of a text, obfuscated from its origin; however, the little rings of its wake are constantly moving outward, yet by doing so constantly point to their source. Any time one of these rings crests over the narrative of the text, there is a game to try and unlock the syzygy. This projection of textual intercourse is tied to the artist's notion of style, to borrow Petrarch's terminology.

But biblical allusion is even more complicated not only because it requires a great deal of literary culture but because it deals with the authority of canon and often the deepest contours of Western civilization. Goldschmidt is one of those modern authors whose work displays a "remarkable density" of biblical allusions.[11] For writers such as these, and one could again add the likes of Faulkner, Melville, and Steinbeck, the world of allusion is a foundational act indistinguishable from imagination and the impetus to narrate. In speaking of the Hebrew Bible's own propensity for alluding to earlier Syro-Palestinian poetry, more ancient Mesopotamian literatures, and indigenous Hebrew traditions, Robert Alter states, "Such promiscuous borrowing occurs again and again in literary history not because of any poverty of imagination but rather because the language in which the literary imagination speaks is constituted by all the antecedent literary works available to the writer."[12]

The potential imagination for Alter is rich because of tradition, but it is critical to understand that allusion as a poetical device only works because of works read or heard. For modern writers it is similar: literary imagination is articulated through access or reading. The one point I would clarify is the difference between midrashic and global allusion.[13] Midrash, as I used it in the first chapter, is commentary spun from gaps in the narrative of a controlling text. Particular to Goldschmidt, we examined the special case of using interlinear glosses and gaps to goad the readership into a semblance of authority. Allusion, or more specifically global allusion, is by nature much more externalized. It is not dependent on the shadowy material of a text; it is an attempt to produce a shadow of an antecedent text in the current narrative. This is important for writers like Goldschmidt and Steinbeck, writers consumed with the genealogy of the text. "Allusion, then, is not an embellishment but a fundamental necessity of literary expression: the writer, scarcely able to ignore the texts that have anticipated him and in some sense given him the very idea of writing, appropriates fragments of them, qualifies or transforms them, uses them to give his own work both a genealogy and a resonant background."[14]

For Goldschmidt—and we cannot claim this for Steinbeck—the written word is genetic, and this is tied to his frequent use of the term "blood." I believe this word for Goldschmidt does create a sense of essentialism to his notion of Jewishness, but it is an attempt to define the linguistic and genealogical elements of Jewish writing as prior to European thought and culture. Given the pervasiveness of his alluding to the Torah, especially Genesis, we must ask to what degree literary expression is already anticipated for him. I mean to ask, how is Moses as writer of canon a figuration of Goldschmidt's own authorship? To what extent is Goldschmidt's authorship an "unswerving line" straight back into the Mosaic? I would like now to explore what I see as the most provocative and active allusion in all of Goldschmidt's work, the death of Moses. Through this examination I will show how allusion is a mode of Goldschmidt's poetics and how the Mosaic trope dominates the tragedy of certain memorable characters. In this episode from his memoirs, itself set within a storytelling arena, Goldschmidt narrates the genesis of this ecology.[15]

The Death of Moses

> God came and talked to Moses—this was a tale so straightforward and natural as if it was some everyday occurrence and yet so breathtaking; because God was Jehovah and he to whom he talked was my kinsman. You are a Levite, said uncle suddenly to me. You are of the same tribe as Moses. —Was he a Levite? asked one of my small cousins amazed. —Lord God, how I was proud! What noble child has felt the way I did, so distinguished in blood from head to toe, while I without doubt knew at the same time, that that honor would not count as a step up the ladder.[16]

Goldschmidt's fascination with the figure of Moses was extratextual; for him it existed outside the boundary of the physical text and was affirmed by the relationship formed with texts. It was a genealogical exploration through which he elucidates a blending of the past with the present and the present with the past.[17] Goldschmidt's relation to the figure of Moses is both poetic, which is to say engaged through the notion of being *alienus in terra aliena* (a stranger in a strange land), and it is actual or, more accurately, genealogical, "I am of the tribe of Levi."[18] This latter relationship is animated outside the framework of the formal text. However, it exerts a kind of pressure on the narrative experience, stretching the boundaries of what the text is toward the narrator, allowing him a privileged position of authority from behind the veil of the written page. It reassembles the readability of the text by expanding the narrative experience. In this case, writing becomes an attribute of kinship, a connective poetics established through the written word.

What interests me most about this passage is how this revelation undoubtedly plays a role in the narrative experience. For, even as a young listener of the Talmud, Goldschmidt's engagement with the text is significantly marked after his kinship with Moses is revealed. The drama of the passage lies in the middle when his uncle proclaims, "You are a Levite. . . . You are of the same tribe as Moses." Again we see the word *tribe* (Danish *stamme*) used to ascertain authority over the narrative experience. This is, of course, a reamplification of the opening words of *LER* and as such reinforces both the genetic metonymy of the Moses narrative and the narrative authority to trump any fictive or Romantic association with a purely literary or Christian Moses. In the memoirs the term "tribe" (Danish stamme) ascribes the binding authority of the author's credibility to tell his life's story, the story of a Jew. Here, it is the authority to unlock the storytelling experience from a Jewish perspective, no doubt in Goldschmidt's mind a position of authority.[19] Because Goldschmidt's family is descended from Aaron, the brother of Moses, he is allowed to celebrate intimately the trials and tribulations of Moses. The cycle of Moses moves beyond sacred scripture and secular source; it becomes revelation of family history, legacy, and genetics, and as such it becomes a resonant background from which Goldschmidt spins his experience into written word.

What this passage illuminates, underneath this lifelong pride for his ancestry, is a genetic determination haunting Goldschmidt's young psyche. As a kinsman of Moses he is entitled to certain laurels, and I would contend that writing and authorship for Goldschmidt become an inherently Mosaic task.[20] The passage continues, "The story suddenly went deeper and attracted, to use a modern word, something dramatic and piquant."[21] This is an exciting narratological moment describing the Jewish imagination awakening in the young Goldschmidt's creative hold with the world around him. Not only is it cast around the figure of Moses, but it is amplified by the phenomenon of genealogy. Storytelling becomes a Mosaic act of revelation. Both the words "dramatic" and "piquant" invoke a provocative tone, the moment of excitement when the reader lures the listener into the story. This moment is experienced simultaneously as Goldschmidt learns he is Moses's kin. Upon hearing of this relationship, Goldschmidt is provoked to tell stories. Experience becomes more dramatic in the narrative sense and adoptive in the personal sense. I suggest this seminal passage is an origin story: a foundational myth of the birth of writing in the author. It is a way of textualizing the world by writing one's self into it, a figural type of ecology.

There is no doubt that what preoccupied Goldschmidt the most about the figure of Moses was his death. It was, in Goldschmidt's worldview, the perfect example of nemesis.[22] Now, there is perhaps no more haunting moment in the Hebrew Bible than the death of Moses in Deuteronomy 34:1–12. His fate was to deliver his people to the Promised Land and to be able to see into its borders, but never to set foot therein himself. This gaze into the promised unknown is a comment on the punitive nature of God, but also on the fragility of man—what becomes in Modernism the disillusion of mankind, "for heroic fulfillment is more a teasing dream than a realizable destiny in [t]his world."[23] Biblically, this fate is compounded by the final description of Moses's grave, "And he was buried in the glen in the land of Moab opposite Beth-Peor, and no man has known his burial place to this day."[24] Through this allusion to the death of Moses, Goldschmidt is able to tease out the disillusive nature of the individual and posit it before us all. The figure of Moses becomes the metaphor par excellence for Goldschmidt to create a modern fiction by lacing it to the past. The stranger in a strange land complex will be a high mark of twentieth-century fiction, but it is already gestured to in the biblical-resonant fiction of Meïr Goldschmidt. Let us look more closely at this allusion in one of Goldschmidt's most memorable texts, "Mendel Hertz."

"Mendel Hertz"

Considered one of Goldschmidt's finest short stories and his last Jewish story,[25] "Mendel Hertz" is about a poor, slightly deformed, middle-aged Jewish cobbler who lives with his mother and never married.[26] It is a prime example of Goldschmidt's use of allusion, because it encapsulates so many different narrative combinations of antecedent texts in such a limited narrative space. In the first part of the text, the narrator, who remembers Mendel from his boyhood, gives the reader brief insight into Mendel's life and psychology and then reports a short segment of his life in which Mendel falls in love with his aunt's teenage stepdaughter, Salome.[27] Like many of Goldschmidt's Jewish stories, and as the name of the beloved here suggests, it is romantic in nature, a tragic story of broken love. Despite its compactness, a mere seven pages, the story is a vessel of allusions. The most interesting thing about the text, and something that has never been noted in the scholarship, is how these allusions jockey for the position of centralizing metaphor.[28]

The narrator portrays Mendel as a dedicated and hard-working man who has a rather healthy opinion of himself. For example, Mendel considers himself "the world's, or at the very least Denmark's, best shoemaker."[29] The narrator suggests that when Mendel looks in the mirror it is possible he sees "a handsome man."[30] This vainglory seems limited, as it is possible only because Mendel has spent his whole life in the company of "the poor and weak."[31]

> His quiet, level complacency however did not hinder in the least the fact that he was also extremely depressing, mostly in matters that did not really concern him. In regard to Moses, Mendel had, what could be said in passing, thought much about religion and as a result had become freethinking. He found it completely absurd that there should have walked a pair of all living things, of livestock and fowl, up into the ark. While he nimbly let the waxed threads glide though the holes already made by the awl, or hammered out a sole, he could sternly prove that it would have been impossible for there to have been food for them in the ark.[32]

Despite his even temper concerning himself, we are also told that Mendel has a tendency to comment on the world around him with a melancholic tone. Goldschmidt's final posturing of his character here is very crafted. He has, in a short five paragraphs, without any dialogue, created the perfect Jewish stereotype: a small, poor, disfigured shoemaker who has a high opinion of himself although he speaks to others in a depressing and critical manner. He is the quintessential Jewish shopkeeper with strong tones of The Wandering Jew, or Jerusalem's Shoemaker as he is also known in Danish,[33] although Mendel seems somewhat casually constrained to his immediate Jewish environment. His wanderings are only figural.

The narrator then presents a sharp image of Mendel's personality by abruptly signaling away from him, "In regard to Moses." The fragmentary nature of the sentence jams itself between the smooth portrait of the Jewish shoemaker and the religious notions that occupy Mendel's thought. Mendel, as a figure, moves from being understood by the reader through his physicality as the traditional Jewish shopkeeper, to a posture that focuses on his intellectual and interpretive capability. He "thought much about religion." We see the clash between the traditional, medieval Jew and the emancipated, freethinking Jew, which counterpose one another along the dividing line of appearance and thought. It is strange, however, that this bifurcation is couched in regard to Moses, the strongest metonymic figure for law and tradition. It is an awkward statement because it comes out of the blue, turning a quaint and simple genre portrait based on a medieval stereotype into a puzzling biblical rationale.

As I pointed to above, the name Moses always signals a claim of identity in Goldschmidt. Commonly used by Goldschmidt's Christian characters, it stands for the Jewish stereotype, the (medieval) Jew. This is evident in *A Jew* when Jacob is among his peers: "Although he was named Jacob, they called him Moses, and whenever he approached they made signs with their hands under their chins as if to mock his beard."[34] A variant of the slur is also used by the parish administrator during the *jødefejden*, "I am not intolerant, but I frankly admit, that I do not like Moses's people. This loathing of Jews must also have a deeper reason; it's in our blood."[35] But the name's value functions differently when used by Goldschmidt's Jewish characters, and we must assume that the narrator of "Mendel Hertz" is a Jew.[36] So, although Mendel is one of Moses's people, as a rational being he is skeptical of a historical Moses. Mendel goes so far as to criticize Moses (as writer of the Torah) for asking the Jews to take such stories as truth, but admits he would never have his mother learn of his skepticism. "One is really not a child, he said; how can Moses demand this of one's intellect!"[37]

However, despite his skepticism, he still uses biblical allegory to frame his conversations about religion. His rationalization of allegory is illustrated through the allusion to the ark. Unlike the Steinbeck allusion quoted above, the rhythmic poetics of the loading of the ark is replaced by its practical impossibility: there would have been no way to store forty days worth of food on the ark for all the living creatures on board. In fact, the narrator tells us that Mendel can make this argument while stitching a shoe, "While he nimbly let the waxed threads glide though the holes already made by the awl." This allusion to the flood story in Genesis becomes layered here against another tradition, the rabbinical commentary on how evil survives the flood. The midrashic text known as the *Pirke de-Rabbi Eliezer* tells that Noah made a deal with Og of Bashan.[38] In exchange for his survival, Og would then be a servant to Noah and his family. In order to feed the giant, Noah drilled a hole in the ark so that he could pass food to him. As Mendel races through his argument against a biblical realism, the narration uses another type of biblical resonance to define the contours of the story. The rhythm of the story kept to the beat of passing the needle through the hole. In denying the Mosaic law, Mendel replicates the forty days and forty nights of the feeding of Og through the narrative act of stitching. Goldschmidt and his narrator are not only activating the legend of the Wandering Jew with the figure of the Jewish shoemaker, they are stitching literary imagination into the character of Mendel Hertz. Here we see a strong parallel with the Steinbeck passage as both narrators use the ark story as an allegory of change and rebirth but marked by an imminent tragedy, the Noachic curse.[39]

Despite the narrator's establishing Mendel as opposite to the lawgiver Moses, the layering of allusion is much more complex. Mendel is distinctly critical of the legal portion of the Torah but seems quite fond of the storytelling aspect of Jewish textual tradition. Goldschmidt is, to say the least, intrigued by a tragic casting of the figure.[40] Moses is the one prophet whom God knew face to face; he is a hero chosen by God to lead his people to the Promised Land; however, he is taken down off the mountaintop and buried in the earth. Moses is not a metonym for the Jews; Moses was like every man, flawed, guilty, mortal.

> A wholly different tone was used when he talked about Moses's death. "God," he said, "took him up to the mountain Nebo on

> account of an error and said to him: Here shall you sit and look over the Promised Land with your eyes! Therein you will not come! And so Moses sat there and stared and died from longing," —Mendel's bleak face became even bleaker as if he himself should die from it. "Clearly," he continued in order to comfort himself and me, "as my blessed father used to say, to God we all owe a death."[41]

Here, the narrator's misdirection becomes transparent. The point of Moses in the story is not to differentiate Mendel from the faithful, but to introduce a certain model of the tragic. Moses is a man, and he too must die. Although he is favored by the Lord and given a great destiny, he does not get to escape mortality in Enochian fashion.[42] Moses committed an error and the price for this mistake was to be denied the Promised Land of his people. But just what is the transgression with which Moses affronts God? The Hebrew Bible leaves this answer in the same gauzy light as the grave of Moses. In Numbers 20, the Israelites are in the Wilderness of Zin and are without water. They assemble against Moses and Aaron, demanding to know why the Lord would take them to such an evil place to die. The Lord speaks to Moses saying, "Take the staff and assemble the community, you and Aaron your brother, and you shall speak to the rock before their eyes, and it will yield its water, and I shall bring forth water for them from the rock and give drink to the community and to its beasts."[43]

As Moses takes the staff he addresses the people as rebels, something contrary to the Lord's wish for community. He also uses "we" when the Lord was clear that it was He who was bringing forth the water. Finally, Moses strikes the rock twice instead of speaking to it as commanded.[44] Despite these errors water is abundant, but the Lord confronts Moses and Aaron: "Inasmuch as you did not trust Me to sanctify Me before the eyes of the Israelites, even so you shall not bring this assembly to the land that I have given to them."[45] A sensible reading is that Moses has tried to project himself as an arch-magician in the eyes of the Israelites and thus accrued the wrath of the Lord. It also seems plausible, however, that Moses was confused by the directions, thinking that he was already doing God's will as a type of medium. As Alter points out, however, Numbers 20:13 reads that the abundant water was a confirmation of God's power and that God was, despite Moses's antics, "sanctified" by his people.[46]

The answer is further tensioned by the explanation given at Deuteronomy 1:37–38. In his address to the Israelites on the eastern shores of the Jordan, after forty years of wandering, Moses proclaims, "Against me, too, the Lord was incensed because of you, saying, 'You, too, shall not come there.'"[47] This explanation is an error of accession. When the Israelites planned to send out spies, Moses did nothing to stop them, and in the eyes of the Lord he is implicated through their guilt. This act of blaming the Israelites in the incident of the spies is echoed throughout Deuteronomy.[48] Whatever the Mosaic error, it points in the background of the text to something inevitable and transferable yet intangible.

There are (at least) two different traditions represented in the Masoretic text, but neither is fully adequate to explain the haunting tension and lyrical fragility produced by the death of Moses: "'This is the land that I swore to Abraham, to Isaac, and to Jacob, saying, "To your seed I will give it." I have let you see it with your own eyes, but you shall not cross over there.' And Moses, the Lord's servant, died there in the land of Moab by the word of the Lord. And he was buried in the glen in the land of Moab opposite Beth-Peor, and no man has known his burial place to this day."[49] The emotional conviction of this passage seems to be driven from the backgrounding of the crime. In the final sentencing of Moses there is given no accountable charge. The composers of Deuteronomy have gone out of their way several times to blame the Israelites for Moses's error while never mentioning the earlier story in the Wilderness of Zin. This is the perfect narrative moment to announce with finality the charge against Moses. Instead, the charge and crime at hand slip into the background. The facts are loosened under the lyrical cadence of the passage, so that all that remains is the semivisible image of the lost grave and for the reader to become inundated with a great sadness. This tragedy has a profound effect on Mendel; he becomes pale, perhaps recognizing in the story of Moses's death some impending, proleptic vision of his own human flaw: desire. The lesson of his father is clear: if Moses himself is not immune to human flaw, then the shoemakers of the world stand little chance.

Although these words have a tone of finality to them, they are not the closing to the first part of the story. The narrator goes on to tell more of Mendel's character and in a semi-synesthesia of literary traditions throws out two more allusions that will vie for the right to control the text and thus Mendel's future. "Despite Mendel's free-thinking there was to him no possible comparison between Moses and Napoleon. He could hardly think of them both at the same time. But when his thoughts lingered on Napoleon on St. Helena, he almost felt the same deep sorrow and sadness he felt for Moses on Nebo."[50]

There is a similar abruptness couched in this allusion as well. Like the earlier Mosaic allusion, this opposition between Moses and Napoleon is stated as if there is some way to identify the two together. Or is it instigated to signify a common clash of ideals in Goldschmidt, the Romantic versus the Jewish? Even though Mendel does not buy into any real analogy between the two men, he sees in Napoleon's death something that reminds him of the painful thought of Moses's grave. The narrator, playing along, observes that this pain manifested itself the most when Mendel sang his favorite song, "General Bertrands Afskedssang" (General Bertrand's Farewell Song).[51] While singing, Mendel's countenance takes on the same "bleak face" as when he contemplated Moses's death.[52] The sorrowful tone of the song overwhelmed Mendel so much that he even interjected himself into the fealties of the loyal General Bertrand so that the last line reads, "I was, my Kaiser, loyal until *my* death."[53] The narrator lets the reader know that the song should end "his death."

It is pertinent to understand Goldschmidt's take on the figure of Napoleon. The best source to shed light on the possible meaning of the song's attestation in "Mendel Hertz" is his 1846 story "Emperor Napoleon: A Fairytale for Children."[54] In this story the young Napoleon makes an oath to a once powerful fairy that should she make him the strongest knight in the world and kaiser of Europe, he would marry her daughter to reinstate their lost nobility. She gives him an eagle that would always show him the path to honor and glory; a standard that would bring courage to his supporters and cause his enemies to quiver; and a horse that knew no boundaries. Napoleon has many adventures slaying dragons and defeating various kings of Europe. The fairy's final gift is a star that shone over his head, illuminating the world and warding off enmity. Napoleon wants to make good on his contract with the fairy. He announces that he wishes to call upon the fairy's daughter for marriage. Contrarily, his advisers convince him to marry a more suitable woman, an Austrian princess. The fairy's daughter is heartbroken so the fairy flies to Napoleon's castle and extinguishes the star. One by one his heroes die and desert him and his gifts fail him. Finally, he is betrayed by his closest ally, bound, and chained to a cliff, where he bemoans the loss of his wife and little son. The fairy sees his sorrow and brings him to his throne to die, relighting the star that favored him. The story ends where it started, in a great storm: "On this night Emperor Napoleon surely dies."[55]

Reading this story against "Mendel Hertz," we see that the Napoleonic death is for Goldschmidt—as it ultimately is for Mendel—different from the Mosaic death. Napoleon is cast into a fantastic world of fairies and magic where his transgression is to break an oath to a magical being. It is within Napoleon's power to keep the oath and only at the last moment is he swayed from keeping it. As a result he is slowly stripped of power and companions, betrayed, and subsequently serves a Promethean exile until he is allowed to die.

This is hubris, pure and simple, completely different from the contemplative nature of the Mosaic death. The allusion to the chains of Prometheus makes that crystal clear. Mendel does not betray God. Although he considers himself the best shoemaker in Denmark, his hubris is in check. We know he thinks beyond himself when he expresses that there are many things that he would not say in front of her, "so long as Mother lives, and God let her live until my death, I'll say nothing to upset her."[56] Furthermore, the sorrow sparked when he sings "General Bertrand's Farewell Song" shows a deeper side of Mendel, the possibility of devotion. When Mendel sings the song he is able to project his own potential into the lyrics; he feels "as if he himself was dying of fidelity."[57]

The template for suffering then moves into Danish poetry, for "Mendel also felt for another great fate, in particular the tragic."[58] Mendel had not frequented the theater, but he did happen to see a performance of Oehlenschläger's 1810 *Axel og Valborg.*[59] Although he had no "literary manners"[60] to fully appreciate the piece, he was able to sing the parts from memory while he worked. "It was without a doubt, comical; but, as it stands in my memory, it startled something inside me and had a hint of noble human suffering."[61] The chain of allusion closes in unrequited love, something Mendel too feels deeply. This comical portrait of Mendel singing "with as much as possible a women's voice," Valborg's departing words to Axel, shows the depth of Mendel's ability to feel the suffering of others. But lurking in the shadows underneath the allusion to the doomed lovers is the transgression of incest. As the narrator shifts gears away from the portrait of Mendel Hertz, the trope of forbidden love looms over the building drama of the text. No matter, the confluence of allusions here is staggering and is indicative of a wide and hyper-canonical array of reading habits: biblical, rabbinical, legendary, historical, folkloric, patriotic, and tragic.

In the second part of the story, the narrator shifts from his reflection on the character of Mendel to an actual reporting from Mendel's life. The story relates Mendel's affection and affinity for his aunt's stepdaughter, Salome. The two are presented as kindred spirits. Mendel insisted on naming the girl Salome when she was an infant and took an interest in her education. Although he was not too keen on her attending Karoline-Skolen, a private school for Jewish girls, he was amazed at her sewing skills, and she often danced in his workshop while he worked and sang.[62]

In the meantime, Mendel has an upcoming birthday and Salome asks him if he would like something from her other than the silk handkerchief that is her usual gift to him. He admits that he has been skeptical of all her learning and writing in school, but because he has never in his life received a letter, he would like to know what it feels like to get one on his birthday. Salome with great enthusiasm responds that she will send him a letter as he requests and it will still be a surprise because he does not yet know what will be in the letter. When his birthday comes around, falling on the first day of Purim, Mendel receives the letter. It reads: "May you get a kiss from the one you most desire." With these words, Mendel falls in love with Salome and begins to dream of a new life with her. He even contemplates opening up a boutique and having his own apprentices and journeymen.

When the Sabbath comes, Mendel gets dressed up and goes to his aunt's house to propose to Salome but interrupts an important conversation between the young woman and his aunt. "She, Salome, had received a kiss from the one she most wanted, namely Isak Davidsen, who worked for a draper but was now looking to settle down and start a business dealing with all things to do with tailoring and dressmaking. 'Like Jacob his Rachel, I woo you!' said Mendel Hertz with opened arms."[63]

The world of allusion here becomes grotesquely congested. The Mosaic shoemaker proposes to a girl ominously named Salome by referencing the biblical patriarch Jakob and his complicated betrothal to Rachel, daughter of Laban. Of course the girl's reaction is to "turn blood-red and recoil."[64] The tragedy is marked by the sanguine embarrassment of Salome against the absent bleak face of Mendel. He has marked her as the femme fatale who shares her name.[65] All that is left is for his aunt to step forward and reprimand his lack of judgment.

> The Mother measured him surprised from head to toe and snapped: "Alive and healthy and a dolt![66] Mendel, are you a man for marrying? —And is she not engaged to Isak Davidsen? What were we just standing and talking about? —What's that paper? You know I cannot read letters."
>
> Mendel mechanically read out loud: "May you get a kiss from the one you most desire."
>
> "Nah," said the mother mildly, "that is another matter! You are putting on an act.[67] —The kiss she will likely get is from Isak Davidsen. —Will you eat a piece of meat and a pickle?"[68]

Within this sweeping mixing of metaphors, Mendel is unraveled into the alienated figure of Moses on Mount Nebo, a figure that had haunted Mendel's workshop sermons. He is no longer the typical Jewish shoemaker; he is the alienated fixture of the modern world, *alienus in terra aliena*. This is also a transformation of the Jewish figure and the Mosaic trend in the text, from the rigid stereotype to a Jewish perspective on origins. This latter phenomenon is signaled by the first Yiddish words in the text: "*Frisch und gesund und meschugge*" (Alive and healthy and a dolt!). The paradisiacal vision of the trophy bride and all the opulence it would bring cascades into the quotidian world of coarse Yiddish and meat and pickles.

As many scholars, Brøndsted foremost, have contended, Mendel's mistake is to confuse his place in the world and overstate his worth. "Mendel's very human error is that he overestimates himself; he actually believes himself to be both beautiful and intelligent, until his aunt's outburst tears the veil from his eyes."[69] The error Mendel makes is not that he falls in love with an eighteen-year-old girl that he has no chance of wooing, but that he fails to understand language itself. What is obviously a common convention among birthday wishes (especially in the teenage locution of Salome) becomes eroticized or somehow eroticizes the self through misunderstanding. What Mendel fails to realize is the difference between oath and aphorism. Just as Jacob Bendixen was bound to the oaths of his uncle and the reverse-oaths of his father, Mendel is bound by his father's words, the very words he repeats throughout his life: "To God we all owe a death."

What Mendel finally realizes once the veil is lifted from his eyes is that these words do not bind him to some tragedy he can avoid. He is as biblical allegory suggests, guilty. They do not focus on the committing of some heinous act. Even if Salome were to have had him, it would only be symbolic incest; she is but the stepdaughter of his aunt.[70] As I mentioned above, Goldschmidt is attracted to the Mosaic error not because it is a discernible action, but because it is obfuscated in background, something almost intangible and unseen. The words to which Mendel is bound prohibit entrance to the Promised Land—in this case a vision of owning his own shop with boys to apprentice and the lovely Salome by his side. His error was to believe that the fire sparked by Salome's words was anything but a vision of perfection, a fragile, lyrical moment. There is also an irony in the fact that Mendel cannot differentiate the way words are coded when they become written. Like his skill with music and song, his skill with language is predominately "by ear."[71] He, like so many of Goldschmidt's Jews, displays a certain vernacular wisdom with words and sayings, a skill in Goldschmidt found only in being a "disciple of the Talmud."[72] When he reads Salome's words out loud he suddenly makes sense of his mistake. Enunciated, they become the clearest of conventional sayings and cease to be erotic on any level. Like all convention they are mechanical in nature, the everyday, the meat and pickles of conversational niceties. "Without answering a word Mendel went home. 'Mother,' he said, 'you shall come to see that now I am mad, and before the year is up, they will bring me to that good place.'"[73]

Here the Mosaic allusion opens up and asserts its position in the text. No longer is there a game of allusive opposites: Mendel to Moses, Moses to Napoleon, Salome to Valborg, Salome to biblical Salome. Upon understanding his complete misreading of the simplicity of Salome's letter, Mendel leaves abruptly for home. He now sees his affliction and the guilt has driven him to madness (*fra Forstanden*). The Yiddish euphemism for cemetery, *den guten Ort*, literally "the good place," places Mendel back into the quotidian world of vernacular sayings and expressions, and shadows the anonymity of the Mosaic death. The phrase is itself a local allusion to Leopold Kompert's 1855 novel *Am Pflug* (At the Plow), where it occurs seven times in a narrative about Rebb Schlome and Anschel driving a corpse by wagon to be buried in the good place.[74] There the tone of the story is macabre, whereas Mendel's contrition and madness open up into a midrash on the death of Moses.

When Moses died, we are told that it was "by the word of the Lord."[75] This phrase, literally "by the mouth of the Lord," is quite common in Torah; however, as Alter notes, "the use of 'mouth' encouraged the Midrash to imagine here a 'death by a kiss' (Hebrew *mitat neshiqah*), the ultimate favor granted to the righteous leader."[76] It is hard to imagine that Goldschmidt is not creating a sly irony by playing the rabbinical tradition of the kiss of death off of Salome's birthday wish that Mendel gets the kiss he wants most. The irony rests in the fact that Mendel's kiss of death came not as divine favor but from the love between the young couple, Isak Davidsen and Salome. For Goldschmidt the midrash is nested in the moment. Whereas the Hebrew Bible skips over any narrative between the point at which Moses hears for the final time that he is not to enter the Promised Land and the time of his death, Goldschmidt elucidates a kind of mechanical madness in which the hero is frozen in a fatal lyricism, awaiting death alone. If we think back to Mendel's depiction of Moses on Mount Nebo, we see the allusion opening the door into midrash. Goldschmidt's use of parataxis to paint a Moses staring into the despair of a promised land is sublime, "And so Moses sat there and stared and died from longing . . ."[77] It is from within this stare that the narrator concludes, "This did not happen exactly, but almost, as he had said. Now ever since he has understood that which his father and he himself had said: To God we all owe a death."[78]

The narrator ends with the repetition of the saying that is at the heart of the story. The use of the adverb *nu* (now) suggests that Mendel lives past the end of the year and has time to turn over the contrition in his mind. Perhaps it suggests that he is haunted by his guilt, or that the narrator himself is somehow bound by the Hertz family saying. There is also the possibility that the narrator is speaking for us all: here is the genealogy of alienation. The final image and allusion hanging over the text is the unknown grave of Moses, somehow visible to the mind's eye as a thin shadow while forever hidden from the eyes of men. It is an allusion into the modern.

The Poetics of Talmudic Allusion

I would now like to turn the discussion of literary allusion in Goldschmidt from being centered in the Hebrew Bible to one centered on the Talmud.[79] As my reading of "Mendel Hertz" showed, Goldschmidt tends to activate scenes or episodes from the Hebrew Bible in his writings to produce a genealogy of reading, a double canonicity alongside a double dissimilarity. This coding takes place at the extradiegetic level; it is a coded narrative embedded in an already external narration.[80] Although characters are in no way privy to this coding, it nevertheless marks them as tragic and a product of a genealogy of transgression. Mendel Hertz, in his rationality, is blinded by the constraint of scripture and cannot see what we the readers see, that biblical allusion (often in contest with allusions to the European cannon) produces the code by which the narrator activates the tragic flaw. The emotion in "Mendel Hertz" is nowhere in Goldschmidt better narrated on so many levels of reading.

Like Jacob Bendixen, Mendel misreads the world around him. For Goldschmidt, writing was hereditary. It was a Mosaic act. Goldschmidt speaks of the Talmud as a body of literature complementary but prior to the discourse of European national culture. However, it is not merely an alternative model of Bildung in Goldschmidt's thinking. Goldschmidt also speaks of the Talmud as a mystical entity, using very specific metaphors to conjure a poetical subjectivity that is again genetically bound. The two metaphors that I am most concerned with in the following analysis are blood and the eternal, as these comprise for Goldschmidt the metonymical framework of the Talmud, that which looks inward and that which looks outward, the Janus of subjectivity.

There is an inherent problem in discussing the Talmud with respect to a Reformed Jewish writer such as Goldschmidt. Reformed Judaism in the nineteenth century was a rather new movement in European Jewry, a direct product of the Jewish Enlightenment that spread forth out of Germany in the eighteenth century. This secular movement to loosen the cultural and religious restraints of rabbinical orthodoxy plays a large role in the identity of the Jews in Northern Europe, a major theme in Goldschmidt's writings. But as a result of this cultural revolution, intimate knowledge of traditional texts such as the Talmud became increasingly remote, as did the fluency required in Semitic languages to comprehend it, namely Hebrew and Aramaic. The Talmud also did not have a strong non-Jewish readership in Europe during the nineteenth century as it was not completely available in German or English before the beginning of the twentieth century.[81]

Because his work is rooted in the new politics and culture of reformed European Jewry, one might ask just how important such a traditional topic as the Talmud might be to Goldschmidt's writings. Perhaps even more perplexing is my suggestion that these texts (or this textual community) would present any source of poetics for Goldschmidt, yet this is one of the poetical features that lends Goldschmidt his complex and extraordinarily rich imagination. On the one hand, it is Goldschmidt's intimacy with and use of the Talmud that make him exceptional in the nineteenth-century Danish literary landscape; on the other, it is his secularization of the Talmud at such an early date that positions him on the verge of modernity.

In a letter to the critic Clemens Petersen dated December 8, 1867, concerning the final proofs of Goldschmidt's translation of Emanuel Deutsch's monograph entitled "The Talmud,"[82] Goldschmidt writes, "[the Talmud] contains the key to what one amicably calls my poetry, and to what you call my culture or education. This is not merely an individual product, but essentially a legacy of blood and it is the exciting joy or happiness I have had in translating the work as if I have been personally present with my own past, before I was born, as if I have undergone a type of soul migration, except in the opposite direction, from the present to the origin instead of from the end to a new beginning."[83]

Goldschmidt is here constructing a poetics contingent upon two metaphors: blood and the notion of the eternal. For him these are the two basic elements of the Talmud. This claim authorizes his stylistic notion of allusion and supersedes any non-Jewish attempts to control Jewish sources. It is also critical of a Jewish education solely based on dannelse. Despite all the political ramifications of the letter's tone, it is lyrical because it is based upon the naked gesture required to recognize a presence beyond the self.

There are three assertions in this passage worth pointing out. First, that the Talmud is the foundation or "key" to his poetry and his "dannelse." This implies that assimilation always rests on a substrate of origin. There is no doubt that Goldschmidt becomes quite educated in matters external to the Talmud or Talmudic discipline during the course of his life, but this later cultural and literary knowledge is additive. Second, Goldschmidt asserts that the Talmud is a tradition that he is bound to by blood, bound by his ethnicity as a Jew, as a Levite. This notion of a "legacy of blood" also authorizes the literary imagination much in the same way as the young Goldschmidt's finding out that he was a descendant of Moses. Jewish tradition says that Moses passed down the Talmud orally to Joshua; Joshua to the seventy Elders; the Elders to the Prophets, and the Prophets to the Great Synagogue. Although the image conveyed in the memoirs is more a myth of origins, here it seems to assert a genetic chain of poetics. Goldschmidt wants us to believe that his poetics is part of this legacy of blood. Lastly, for Goldschmidt the Talmud is the connective tissue with the past and prehistory of the Jewish people. It is a mystical eye through which he experiences the subjectivity of an entire body of people. This last point is crucial because it allows Goldschmidt himself to undergo a transformative process, a soul migration, and gives him authoritative access to an important body of stories if not to the art of storytelling itself.

These claims concerning the Talmud are rather peculiar and at the same time rather extraordinary coming from a Reformed Jew who spent less than one year of his childhood undergoing rabbinical schooling and wrote natively in the Danish language. The 1867 letter is quite intriguing and rather emotionally revealing, a rarity, in my opinion, among Goldschmidt's correspondence. As I mentioned earlier, it concerned Goldschmidt's translation of Emanuel Deutsch's "The Talmud." In the letter, Goldschmidt begins by humbly asking Pedersen for a favorable review of his latest translation project, but quickly slips into a poetical exegesis on the nature of the Talmud itself and its importance to Goldschmidt as a writer. As the letter continues, the notion of blood ignites the eliding subjectivity that forms the heart of Goldschmidt's poetics. Goldschmidt even admits that he may be partial as to the quality of the work: "I confess to being extremely curious to learn what impression the book will have on you, little, lukewarm, or nothing at all? For it is possible that I can be completely mistaken, that I am prejudiced in 'the most tender confusion of the subject with the object.'"[84] The interesting question here is just what is the object of Goldschmidt's blindness? Although the letter at first concerns Goldschmidt's recent translation of Emanuel Deutch's essay "The Talmud," it is the Talmud in general with which Goldschmidt becomes increasingly concerned. The connective tissue between himself and the Talmud becomes confusing for Goldschmidt in these lyrical self-portraits. He is like Petrarch and cannot tell the difference between his own thoughts and the thoughts of the source. For Goldschmidt, the boundary between himself and the Talmud does not exist, just as the boundary between Moses and himself does not exist; they are all related to him by blood and, by a transformative equation, so is the act of writing.

After this intimate proclamation of conflated subjectivity, the narrative shifts into an autofictive mode of delivery. I say this because there are several references in the letter that either mimic or allude to scenes in Goldschmidt's novel *A Jew*. Let me summarize this narrative portion of the letter. First, Goldschmidt moves into an autobiographical account of his relation to the Talmud. It begins rather nostalgically: "The more I think about it, the more curiously I feel my relation to the Talmud."[85] This nostalgic meditation goes on for 130 lines or about four full pages of Morton Borup's edition of Goldschmidt's letters. Goldschmidt writes about his schooling in both rabbinical and Christian schools, highlighting some of the anti-Semitism he encountered while growing up. He comments that "Judaism was for me during this time a pain, a misfortune I was born with, like a hump."[86] Goldschmidt narrates how it was he came to rid himself of wearing the tefillin and arbakanfos, two important articles of dress in Orthodox Judaism.[87] Inspired by witnessing the morning prayers of his school rector, V. A. Borgen, Goldschmidt writes, "After this visit with Borgen, I let the tefillin lie unused and cast off the arbakanfos, with the conviction that in doing so I separated myself from something superstitious or from a soulless symbol."[88]

It is shortly after this moment that Goldschmidt narrates how he began to develop a new worldview. Released from the laborious rites of Judaism, he was eager to explore a new subjectivity or what he calls "self administration."[89] What unfolds is not a turning away from his Jewishness but a freedom from Jewish rites and rituals by which Goldschmidt feels more connected to the mystical nature of the divine. "During this search there was an evening that rose up before me, when I, at Kongens Nytorv, looked into the night sky, with passionate zeal and enthusiasm that all this beautiful world, the earth, the stars, the sun, were God's body, and that the soul which moved therein and held the whole together was God himself."[90] This new worldview, or what Goldschmidt refers to as "my new theory," produces a passion in him that is expressed at this time mainly through poetry. With the night sky impinging on a delicate astrothesia, the second metaphor, the eternal, is awakened in the schoolboy Goldschmidt.

He stresses that he was writing a fair amount of verse during this period and was eager to show his teacher Borgen his work. However, upon doing so, Borgen accused Goldschmidt of having stolen from Empedocles, the pre-Socratic philosopher. Goldschmidt adamantly denies that he plagiarized from Empedocles this "new theory" that God was the universe and that man was a part of him. Instead these notions were to be traced "from my great kin-in-faith or more correctly my blood-kin, Spinoza, who also had it or could have had it from the Talmud."[91] This is a very fine moment of Goldschmidt pointing to the epistemic racism that has narrowed the reception of his work. Borgen's first and only frame of reference for reading Goldschmidt's verse is the European canon and is thereby incompatible with the notion of Jewish source.

Once again we see Goldschmidt's deep concern for the heritage of knowledge. The chain of authority is passed on to Goldschmidt through his blood, this time with another Jewish figure, Spinoza, mitigating the connective skin. This notion of blood kin supersedes any notion based on strictly European origin or classical source, in this case early Hellenistic philosophy. Also important to note is how the Talmud as a whole begins to assume a quality of the divine and infinite in Goldschmidt's thinking.

The autobiographical portion of the letter is complemented by short anecdotes of two other great contemporary Jewish artists, but these are counter-examples, Jews who in Goldschmidt's opinion have misused their blood, namely Jacques Offenbach (1819–1880) and Georg Brandes. Goldschmidt never embraces the phenomenon without also revealing its negative or inimical nature. What is interesting here is that the failures of these men, according to Goldschmidt, are ascribed to the way they handled their respective assimilations into Christian European society. He says of Offenbach, "Personally, I want greatly to believe that Offenbach is sincerely good friends with the Parisians; but when he sits alone and composes, it is his Jewish blood which writes the notes, the Jewish blood which has lost awe, which denies everything, even his own origin, and gladly sees everything dancing forth out of Hell."[92]

Goldschmidt is very critical of Offenbach's use of the demonic to subvert the ethical, but does not pass the blame on to bad company or Parisian fashion. He maintains that Offenbach himself and his Jewish blood are held accountable for the error of his denial. The metaphor of his blood weakening is quite callous: Jewish blood turned from its origin becomes disconnected from true Jewish artistry. Concerning Brandes, it is his atheistic notions of reason and freedom over belief and faith from which Goldschmidt wishes to separate himself. It seems Goldschmidt's idea of the ethical imagination is self-replenishing. He writes, "But I could never understand why a man is not cautious of speaking such denial. There are so many people, well the majority: they could neither live nor die in Freedom, if they were not allowed to believe [something] more than they know. Therefore, it should follow, in my opinion, that for each denial of a tenet of faith something new and positive, a cleaner tenet for faith, be created."[93]

Goldschmidt admonishes those who have abandoned their Jewish heritage to such a degree that they would ask of themselves and of others to give up their faith and deny the legacy he holds so honorably. Nested in this comment is also Goldschmidt's repeated critique of the Reformed Jew who has slighted the textual traditions of Judaism. He is quick to separate himself from this certain "class of people."[94] This class of people seems to be on the one hand, the Reformed Jew who has either, like Offenbach, embraced the demonical "joie de vivre," or who, like Brandes, has abandoned faith and tradition altogether. Goldschmidt by appealing to the basic human right of freedom evokes the individual's right to believe in something eternal. What Brandes labeled as a socialist nature in Goldschmidt's work is the very nature that is in turn critical of Brandes's efforts to govern human expression.[95]

The earlier, autobiographical portion of the letter narrated several instances in which Goldschmidt was confronted by anti-Semitism. In fact, the denial of Jewish blood, hatred against one's fellow man, anti-Semitism, and its ugly vestige the pogrom are all, in Goldschmidt's worldview, seen to be collectively unethical. For Goldschmidt, always the Dane, this hatred of one's roots and disregard for one's fellow man "has emerged in individuals as a result of brutal times, but does not exist as a principle of the nation."[96]

Earlier I had mentioned that there is something problematic about Goldschmidt, a reformed Jew, having an intimate knowledge of rabbinical traditions such as the Talmud. He makes a convincing point that the Talmud is his by birthright, by the very nature of his Jewish blood. However, owing to its religious nature, the Talmud might seem out of place in the secular writings of a Reformed Jew. Although Goldschmidt must be read as a Jewish writer, it is difficult to think of him as a religious or devotional writer. One might see his criticism of Brandes's atheism as teetering on hypocrisy. Here we see the Talmud not just as a vessel of faith but as a mode of subjectivity that moves beyond the self. This is something that dannelse alone cannot produce for Goldschmidt. At the end of the 1867 letter, Goldschmidt explains the logistics of his Talmudic influence:

> No, I do not belong to the Talmud; I have not yet restored Jehovah. . . . But on the other hand, you will also see that the Talmud is extremely tolerant and holds heaven's door open ajar, even after the bell has sounded for its closing. If the soul of the Talmud serves as

> St. Peter, according to the theory, it will still open for him who can simply say as his justification: I have at every day's end brought forth out of myself an unending, remote standing and yet present, the highest, glorified, idealized picture of my self, and to this unending magnified yet related figure, who looks upon me with my own deepest seriousness and concern, and in whom I recognize my father in heaven, have I entrusted everything, have I accounted for all my frailness, and have I beseeched him to be graceful to me and help me, with my whole being becoming nearer to him.[97]

This idealized picture of the self is quite lyrical, an exquisite positioning of the individual's ethical delivery of the self into the eternal. Goldschmidt suggests that in some ways he has no business discussing the Talmud as he has not personally "restored" God. His faith, however, in something beyond himself is not so much directed at the religion of the rabbis as to their devotion to conceptual thought through writing. Still, Goldschmidt's Talmud nevertheless echoes rabbinical thought because only through it is heaven's door left ajar.

In his writings, certain characters as well as Goldschmidt himself (indeed, he seems to be his own model here) exhibit knowledge of the Talmud. This feature is a trademark of Goldschmidt's narrative art. Talmudic knowledge is not constructed within the walls of the European university, but it is characterized as a native discourse prior to and outside of such university learning. He writes of his introduction to rabbinical discourse in his memoirs with a great sense of heroics, one that trickles down into the quotidian Jew in many of his stories.

> Now the time drew near when I, in my thirteenth year, should be confirmed in the Jewish manner, to come of age, bar mitzvah. Actually that should be indeed a kind of closing to a purely Jewish upbringing, and in Poland and southern Romania, where life is still so closed, and where children virtually do not learn without the Law and the Talmud, it's also customary for boys of thirteen years to stand in front of the synagogue and make a speech, a *drosho*, a thinning out of one place or another in the Talmud, often of the

most marginal kind, but summoning extraordinary readership, penetrating or meticulous. Such a droscho is rare here in Denmark. In my time there the object for my admiration pointed out only one, who had recently accomplished it, a real tender-hearted, calm person whom I, from time to time, still have the pleasure to meet on the street. He is a grocer; but how a Christian professor of Hebrew would be surprised if he got into a dispute with this grocer![98]

The report shows some familiar elements the reader will recognize from my discussion of *A Jew*: the role of Polish Jewry (and here, southeastern European Jewry) in upholding storytelling traditions; the bar mitzvah scene; and the role of the Talmud as a specific type of education. When Jacob Bendixen first came to the Latin school, he was described as an untrained musician who played only by ear, ascribing any brilliance and potential to his native "Talmudic sharpness."[99] In *LER* Goldschmidt essentially uses his own bar mitzvah to disclose a more closed Jewish practice of boys interpreting the Talmud in front of the synagogue. Throughout his life and his work, Goldschmidt will hold the Talmud as the highest mark of a man's creativity, cognition, and devotion, perhaps because the meticulousness needed to thin the text out is a rarity in Scandinavian Jewish circles. Here enters the harmless grocer.

This figure appears in Jacob Bendixen and in the various rabbis that populate Goldschmidt's writings. Mendel Hertz is also a version of this figure, but it is this unnamed grocer who seems to be the model for this homage to the Talmudic underdog. For Goldschmidt, the Talmud is a mode of thinking that is attached to experience and a way of life more than mere learning or education. For Goldschmidt, Talmudic knowledge is not based on appearance or context. It is something purely abstract, the result of a closed environment of study. Because of this experiential requirement, it too defies the esemplastic power of the mind: Christians can become professors of Hebrew (at Christian universities), but they cannot hold their own in debate with a Jewish grocer. Goldschmidt wants to put this grocer from his youth up against any Christian scholar of Hebrew to demonstrate that

Talmudic sharpness is a worthy epistemological category beyond the university professor's expertise, and that it supersedes the European notion of Bildung. It is, of course, also a way of announcing his own genius among the literary Copenhagen elite.

The most beloved example of this increasingly rare genius comes from Goldschmidt's novel *Ravnen* (The Raven), first published in 1867.[100] In the very beginning we meet Simon Levi, another slightly deformed Jew who exhibits the trait of Talmudic sharpness. After portraying the mysterious and powerful Abraham Krog in the novel's opening scene, the narrator goes on to tell us that there was only one person seen on a daily basis at Herr Krog's. This was Simon Levi, whom Krog employed to run business errands and mediate small commissions. In the beginning of the novel, the narration insinuates that Krog overpowers and outclasses Simon Levi.

> But Simon Levi was not put off by that affected indifference or nonchalance. He was the kind of Jew that is now beginning to disappear: brought up under a certain victimization by the Christian's side and therefore humble and apprehensive, educated in the peculiar double mode, to be good with money and to be able to interpret the wisdom which lay in the Talmud. He could think deeper and more brilliantly than someone who first saw him might believe; but one could say on the other hand that he was a disciple of the Talmud; when he thought and talked on his own behalf, it was in a mixed mode, more after experience than learning, cautious and clever, often fine, almost always intricate.[101]

Simon Levi is considered Goldschmidt's "triumph of characterization."[102] In my view this is true not because of perfect temperament or psychology, but because he is the best manifestation of Goldschmidt's idea of double canonicity and the mixed mode of dissimilarity. This *figura*, a sort of modern Jew with an Old World feel and an innate Talmudic wisdom, is Goldschmidt's trademark. Simon Levi here demonstrates, as did the grocer of Goldschmidt's youth, that looks can be deceiving. What this character looks like is the medieval Jew, the

Shylock, but as Krog finds out in the end, this little hunchbacked Jew bites back. Mendel Hertz too had this physicality that masked the depth and profundity of his desire. Jacob Bendixen's dark, brooding lyricism is also rooted in this characterization. Possessing an ironic moodiness and bearing a Talmudic sharpness, these characters, while perhaps not successful in their narratological lives, all play a concrete role in dismantling the stereotype of the medieval Jew. This mixed mode of Simon Levi is a vocalization of Goldschmidt's poetics. On the one hand, Simon Levi is easily recognizable as the Jew of the medieval stage, but his amazing powers of interpretation, another kind of anagrammatic poetics, are too cryptic and profound for his Christian adversaries to handle.[103] In the end, because he underestimates him and mistreats him, Krog meets his demise at the hands of Simon Levi.

An excellent example of Goldschmidt's assertion of Talmudic authority and poetics concerns a story that is directly lifted from the Talmud. In the postscript to *Love Stories from Many Lands* (1867), Goldschmidt comments on the origin of one of his stories, "The Bird that Sang."

> There is a Talmudic story or parable about two friends, who had promised one another that whichever of them was the first to die, that one would give the still-living friend an announcement of eternity. And the announcement took place through a bird who sang; but he who had listened to the bird was transformed by listening into an old man. This [tale] I have used for story number eight, which also, perhaps more correctly, could have the title "The highest." —This parable, which in the easterly mode intends to present the notion of eternity, and in the Hebraic or Aramaic form was written down ca. 1,500 years ago. Since there are hardly any older legends of this type known, it [the Aramaic] should be considered to be the source of the tale, which is nowadays found here and there, such as in Christiern Pedersen's "Miracle of the bird, who sang for a monk" (ca. 300 years old from the German).[104]

Story number 8 in *Love Stories* is Goldschmidt's "The Bird that Sang" and what is most interesting about this story is Goldschmidt's use of the Talmud to claim authority and origin for this particular tale. He is claiming authority over the tale because the Talmud is his "legacy of blood," and this claim extends from the present into the past following a metonymic chain of discourse and storytelling written down by rabbis since the sixth century CE.[105] To legitimate his claim that the tale is Jewish and more specifically Talmudic, he evokes the names Aramaic and Hebrew, two of the languages in which Goldschmidt exhibits extraordinary ability.

In its Germanic manifestations, Goldschmidt considers the tale to be much younger, and therefore dependent on a Talmudic source. The fact that Goldschmidt mentions that the Germanic version occurs "here and there" suggests that it circulated within the Danish literary circle. Hans Christen Andersen's "Dynd Kongens Datter" ("The Bog King's Daughter") (1858), as well as his tale "Urbanus" (written before 1858) and Frederik Paludan-Müller's *Tithon* (1844), all illustrate familiarity with the tale, not to mention works like Henry Wadsworth Longfellow's *The Golden Legend*, which appeared in 1852. All of these manifestations, by Goldschmidt's standards, are inferior to the Talmudic source. To clarify, Goldschmidt is here asserting that only Jews, but not every Jew, as we saw in the reference to both Brandes and Offenbach, have access to these types of sources, which really are the doorway to Goldschmidt's imagination. One could make the argument that it matters not in the game of borrowing whence one borrows. Yet Goldschmidt is adamant that there is a mystical quality that is contained exclusively in the original form. His tone resonates as if he is bound to remind these and other Danish writers that the depth of their source or tradition is shallow compared to the Hebraic thought that supersedes them.

This mystical tone manifests in the more technical discussions of *LER* as well. Specifically in *LER*, he uses the Talmud as a commentary on the philosophical alignments of historical persons. These allusions are also indispensable for achieving an understanding of Goldschmidt's narrative art. Goldschmidt's entire concept of nemesis, in my opinion, rests within a convention of narration and takes on a much more complex ideology than the traditional classical understanding of nemesis as divine retribution. Take for instance his discussion of Linnaeus and his 1848 notes on and examples of nemesis *divina*.[106] Goldschmidt writes,

> The long predominant impression of all the notes is dark and mystical—a mysticism in the meaning, that there is an inclination to the dark, different from the mysticism of thought that seeks light, and in the end cannot escape encountering difficulty. And yet all these experiments, all these exempla, so well [steeped in] mystical profundity as poetic highness, are inferior to a single similar comment in the Talmud (Tract. Sabbath 5th Book), where certainly the word *Nemesis* is not used: When Salomon married a heathen princess, the angel Gabriel soared down to earth and planted a bush in the sea; this bush grew into an island and firm land, and on this land the city Rome was built, wherefrom the torches were issued against Jerusalem and the Temple.[107]

As Goldschmidt tries to establish a context and a history of the idea of nemesis in European thought, he again positions the Talmud as the antecedent source for all such discussions. Although never named in the Talmud, for Goldschmidt the concept of nemesis is laid out to a greater degree and with a more valid worldview than can be found in European thinking. Although beyond the immediate scope of this book, the concept of nemesis is ordered in his memoirs as a specifically Afro-Semitic concept, which Goldschmidt derives from ancient Egypt and the hieroglyphics of the Middle Kingdom.[108]

Because all doors are held ajar, Goldschmidt has been able to slip into many rooms. His success as a Danish author should be regarded as one of the greatest literary and linguistic achievements of nineteenth-century Scandinavian literature. Yet Goldschmidt's secular use of the Talmud in a literary context (that is, written in Danish for a Danish audience) distances him from contemporary Jewish writers.[109] In this matter, we must place him beside writers such as Kafka, masters of modern midrash and disciples of the Talmud.

There is something prophetic, something proleptic, about Goldschmidt as a student of rabbinical tradition, as a reader of Aramaic, as blood kin of the Talmud. It is paramount that we not forget, however Danish we might now consider him, that he was first and foremost, at the origin of things, a Jew, as was his gift of language and storytelling Jewish. Goldschmidt's own words and works express the intimacy he feels with this rabbinical, textual community, the Talmud. Despite how "Danish" and "Scandinavian" we now accept Goldschmidt and his writings to be, this rabbinical tradition is pervasive in his writings and poses an alternative to the nationalistic discourse so prevalent in the scholarship. The Talmud, like Wordsworth's "little boat," can too unlock the firmament and its canopy of sparkling light.

4

The Figure of the Rabbi

The figure of the rabbi is a high mark of Goldschmidt's poetics. Like the Talmudic grocer, the rabbi establishes himself above and beyond the medieval, and by now stereotypical, Jew of European literature and stands contrary to European models of learnedness and canon. While preserving the Talmudic adroitness of the Orthodox Jew, the figure of the rabbi projects forward into the future, and has about him a proclivity for the eternal. The complexities of the characterization in Goldschmidt are stable. The rabbi is pious; he is the subject of Christian persecution; he speaks with Talmudic sharpness, often displaying amazing powers of interpretation; he is a mediator between the laws of Moses, this world, and the eternal. This figure is the embodiment of Goldschmidt's most reverent idealizations of Jewishness. In this chapter, I focus my discussion on the rabbi in some of Goldschmidt's lesser known Hebrew and Jewish legends, a figure that shows the doubling of dissimilarity. In this doubling there is both a preservation and a reverence of the past as well as a renewal of the figure of the rabbi in the present, modern age. Let me illustrate my point with a traditional narrative that speaks to it.

> Rav Judah said in the name of Rav: When Moses ascended on high he found the Holy One of Blessing, engaged in affixing coronets to the letters. Said Moses, "Lord of the Universe, Who stays your hand?" He answered, "There will arise a man, at the end of many generations, Akiba b. Joseph by name, who will expound upon each tittle heaps and heaps of laws." "Lord of the Universe," said Moses, "permit me to see him." He replied, "Turn around." Moses went

> and sat down behind eight rows [and listened to the discourses upon the law]. Not being able to follow their arguments he was ill at ease, but when they came to a certain subject and the disciples said to the master, "Whence do you know it?" and the latter replied, "It is a law given to Moses at Sinai" he was comforted. Thereupon he returned to the Holy One of Blessing, and said, "Lord of the Universe, you have such a man and you give the Torah by me!" He replied, "Be silent, for such is my decree." Then said Moses, "Lord of the Universe, you have shown me his Torah, show me his reward." "Turn around," said He; and Moses turned around and saw them weighing out his flesh at the market-stalls. "Lord of the Universe," cried Moses, "such Torah, and such a reward!" He replied, "Be silent, for such is my decree."[1]

The Talmudic story above in which Moses visits the classroom of Rabbi Akiba (ca. 50–135 CE) illustrates how oral tradition was authorized alongside the Torah. It is essentially an argument for continuity, interpretation, and the power of language. But it also shows a rupture in rabbinical thinking, a self-conscious reflection of how far the rabbinical mode has strayed from the original teachings of Moses. The purpose of the story is not to limit or criticize rabbinical discourse. On the contrary, it authorizes the role of creativity in rabbinical thought. Moses does not rebuke Akiba even though he cannot follow his teachings. He tells God, "Lord of the Universe, you have such a man and you give the Torah by me!" The point here is that although everything that is to be known was already revealed to Moses on Sinai, there is a living force of creativity and play in what lies between Akiba's and Moses's thinking. The role of the rabbi is a posturing between the rigid Mosaic past and the shifting contours of the future. Always facing two positions at once, they are the embodiment of this Janus of subjectivity. Although this particular tale is not used by Goldschmidt, it is a touchstone for him, providing the narrative license for creative interpretation and radical midrash.

The most relevant aspect of this famous rabbi tale is that it highlights the state of intermediation that marks the figure of the rabbi in

Goldschmidt. The rabbi, like Moses, and like Goldschmidt himself, in order to perform these creative discourses is always forced to "turn around" while simultaneously gazing into the eternal, constantly blurring the line between revelation and interpretation, prophecy and midrash, scripture and play. It is this very turning, this carousel-like nature, that gives Goldschmidt his often noted "religious mysticism."[2] It must, however, be made clear that this mystical quality is not, as Brandes has claimed, owing to his Judaism, nor is it an overt, simplistic Romanticism like we see in early Oehlenschläger and Grundtvig. Rather, Goldschmidt's mysticism is based on his reading habits in ancient and medieval Jewish literature. In his canon the writings and tales of the great rabbis are the foundation of textual community.

I have mentioned at length in this book that Goldschmidt establishes a genealogy of reading through a genetic projection of identity. In *LER* this genealogy is clearly announced in the opening line, "I am of the tribe of Levi." The first volume of *LER* is the story of Goldschmidt's life, fashioned with its many anecdotes, colorful biographical material, and astute references to the writers and artists who are canonical to Goldschmidt. The name of a rabbi is rare there among the likes of Frederik VI, Goethe, Plato, and Georg Zoëga, the great Danish numismatist and Egyptologist.[3] The majority of Jewish names in that work belong to Goldschmidt's family. In the opening pages, Goldschmidt gives a detailed history of his Levite family tree and the immigration into Denmark by his "great-great-grandfather, who was named like me, Meïr Goldschmidt."[4] When talking about his mother's side of the family, Goldschmidt narrates a sweet yet profound discussion he had with his grandmother before she died,

> A remark that I in my fifteenth or sixteenth year heard from my grandmother, shortly before her death, contributed for a while to maintaining the mysterious feeling that my kin through my grandparents directly touched the oldest of times, especially the Egyptian. She talked with conviction about soul-migration. It was said pithily with quiet authority, like something she knew on her own. How this notion of soul-migration is handed down, or what points of contact

it has in an earlier more distant past, is otherwise not difficult to demonstrate. This exists in Maimonides (12th cent.), in Albo (15th cent.), and in other Jewish scholars.[5]

It is vital to understand Goldschmidt's narrative maneuvers here. Goldschmidt replays a conversation through which he learned that his kin were enslaved in Egypt, reveals the seed of his thinking on soul-migration, and establishes the phenomenon as a specifically Jewish or rabbinical mode of discourse. Although the grandmother's comments are not explicitly revealed, this episode serves as a more specific version of the origin myth discussed in chapter 3. The grandmother and her tenets on the projection of the soul are the foundation of Goldschmidt's experiments in soul-migration. He is citing her as the source for his diverse subjectivity, the mystical eye into the future that by looking back accesses knowledge of the past. He is drawing a straight genetic line from the Levites in Egypt to the medieval rabbis to his grandmother and finally to himself. This ability to experience a textual sentience through a genetic lens is a remarkable concept, considering that it predates Mallarmé and Rimbaud by at least a decade. As we saw in the last chapter, this concept of soul-migration is a powerful extratextual subjectivity that Goldschmidt uses to induce a poetical genealogy. Like Moses, Goldschmidt remembers building pyramids.

Goldschmidt goes on to say that his grandmother's thinking on the topic could be traced to G. E. Lessing's 1780 work *Die Erziehung des Menschengeschlects* (*The Education of Humankind*), but again stipulates that it could also be found earlier in the work of Lessing's friend Moses Mendelssohn, once again trumping the European notion of source and learnedness. It is not important for Goldschmidt to try to prove to us that this phenomenon of soul-migration exists because it has already been written, and thus substantiated, in the words of the great rabbis, the Rambam and Josef Albo.[6] He believed he was reading truth into his interpretation of contemporary life. The point I want to stress here is that during the genealogical exposition that opens *LER*, the figure of the rabbi clusters against the supersessionism of European thought. Goldschmidt sees the rabbi as a figure lost on the horizon. The rabbi, who was once a centralizing force in the foundation of European thought, by Goldschmidt's time had been marginalized and ghettoized, placed on the periphery of European intellectual achievement.[7] He, like Goldschmidt, is a victim of epistemic racism, and reading Goldschmidt demands a rehabilitation of the rabbi. For Goldschmidt, the rabbi is a figure of access, inducing a seer-like state, an eliding subjectivity through which narrative simulates experiences in between persons, places, and times. Like Moses stepping forward to meet Rabbi Akiva, Goldschmidt slides along this genealogy of rabbinic figures, wrestling them and their stories off the periphery so that they may once again interpret for future generations the great mysteries of this world and the world to come.

Hebrew Legends

In 1862 Goldschmidt published a set of English stories in *Chambers's Journal of Popular Literature Science and Arts* under the title *Hebrew Legends: In Two Parts.* The stories in the first part consist of five rabbi tales, "Rabbi Meir's Wife," "Rabbi Joschuah and the Princess," "A Greek Philosopher and a Rabbi," an untitled story that is clearly "Rabbi Jochanni," and "Rabbi Raschi."[8] These were printed along with a sixth story, a more generic sage tale concerning the wisdom of Aristotle, "Alexander and the Skull." The second part consists mostly of Talmudic retellings of biblical stories and moralistic tales, but does include a longer tale entitled "The Kamzan" and two innovative versions of the Ahasverus legend, "The Wandering Jew."[9] Per the scope of this chapter, I am mainly concerned with the five rabbi tales of part 1, but the collection as a whole and the fact that they appear printed in English raise questions of genre and audience, and once again show the many confluences of Goldschmidt's authorship.[10]

In the introduction to his *Hebrew Legends*, Goldschmidt writes,

> The following legends are the result of a reading extending over years, but as they claim only a poetic value, it would be superfluous to quote all the works which have given rise to them. Suffice it to say, that *the spirit* of the old Hebrew tales is scrupulously maintained,

> whilst *the form* is often new. As they now appear, they are in many instances a recasting; in some, an old idea serves only as the basis to a new tale.
>
> About forty years ago, some Hebrew legends, collected by Mr. Horwitz, were published in English, but the collection has but a few lines in common with the following.[11]

It is clear that Goldschmidt does not claim these tales to be his own.[12] Instead, he attributes them to the process of "reading extending over years." This is a very elastic moment in Goldschmidt's authorship because it shows how indebted he is to the storytelling tradition of the rabbis and how involved he is in continuing and contributing to this textual community. Jewish tradition is a living tradition in Goldschmidt's mind. Words such as "maintained" and "recasting" offer little in favor of the creative process of the Romantic genius. Instead the "poetic value" of his legends is determined by their relation to "all the works" whose "*spirit*" they embody. Poetics here means not the product of the demiurge poet, but rather refers to the genealogy of the text. Poetical value or *spirit* can be relayed regardless of narrative shape or *form*. This opening paragraph is Goldschmidt's authorization for a new Jewish literature, whose *form*, and here we can include style, may be entirely innovative (for example, the novel, the novella, the fashionable folktale, the dramatic play) but whose poetics is valued by the tradition it "scrupulously" embraces. Before I look at Goldschmidt's collection more closely, it might be constructive to linger on the publication history of these rabbinic tales in the English language, as they have quite an unusual story.

Goldschmidt's mention of Hyman Hurwitz's *Hebrew Tales* (1826) is both understated and loaded, and so demands attention.[13] Goldschmidt undoubtedly respected Hurwitz and the collection in question, although he is ironically inexplicit, suggesting that Hyman's work "has but a few lines in common with" his own. This could not be farther from the truth and must be untangled.

Hyman Hurwitz (1770–1844) was a renowned Hebrew scholar of his day.[14] The author of several Hebrew grammar standards and a philological and syntactic examination of the Hebrew language, Hurwitz also wrote numerous songs and hymns in both Hebrew and English. Hurwitz also had the honor of overseeing the printing of the first Hebrew Bible in America in 1814, and in 1835 published a specimen of a newly revised Hebrew text of the Torah.[15] Hurwitz was also a close friend of Coleridge, who supposedly translated three tales for the collection.[16] Coleridge is also given credit for translating a Hebrew dirge of Hurwitz's into English.[17] Hurwitz had the distinction of being the first Jew to hold any chair at University College London, when in 1828 he was appointed Professor of Hebrew.[18] Hurwitz was a steadfast political speaker and a defender of the Jewish religion and people. He displayed a remarkable aptitude for rabbinical studies and Semitic lexicology, and was, perhaps above all else, one of the great English stylists of the first half of the nineteenth century.[19]

Hurwitz's collection exemplifies, along with Emanuel Deutsch's 1867 *Talmud*, the important efforts of the Jewish press in England during the early to mid-nineteenth century to make traditional and oral texts accessible to a non-Jewish-language reading public.[20] Hurwitz's book has the distinction of being the "the first rabbinic anthology in English,"[21] and is the most prodigal attempt at the rehabilitation of the figure of the rabbi.[22] The book is aimed at elegantly presenting "a positive image of the rabbis, their moral leadership, and their literary creativity."[23] Written six years after his monumental curriculum reform, *Vindiciae Hebraicae* (1920), the book also aimed to become the "aqueduct" by which Christian students could taste the "invigorating waters" of rabbinical thought.[24] Because Christian students of Hebrew found the language of the rabbis unapproachable, Hurwitz sought to bring the ancient rabbis of the Talmudic age to life, figures like Maimonides, Rabbi Meir, and Rabbi Eliezer. He was fully devoted to defending their "beautiful allegory,"[25] and like Deutsch would argue that they be placed among the classics of European thought, ancient philosophy, poetry, and mythology.[26] "When *Esop*, in answer to the question put to him by *Chilo*, What God was doing? said, 'That he was depressing the proud, and exalting the humble,'—the reply is considered as most admirable. But when a poor Rabbi says the same thing, only differently expressed, then it is treated with ridicule."[27]

One can detect in Hurwitz's writing a certain tone that surely resonated with Goldschmidt and his insistence on the priority of Jewish culture and his war against epistemic racism. The real force of Hurwitz's dilemma is posed by the words "only differently expressed." Because they were expressed in an alternative Bildung than that which serves as the foundation for canonicity, they are the subject of ridicule. They are dismissed as being tribal, uncouth, or both. The rabbinic, Hurwitz maintained, was seen as "perverted and distorted,"[28] and deserved to be rescued from the prejudices that obscure their merit.[29] Although Hurwitz's ideas were noble, and he should be considered the father of this rehabilitation, there was a compromise inherent in his plan. In English, he could make his rabbis sound right to the English ear, but he did so to the detriment of "their unique idiom and cultural perspective."[30] Here we have the opposite phenomenon that I discussed in chapter 2 in the parlor-reading of Oehlenschläger's *Aladdin.* Instead of the critique of the esemplastic, with Hurwitz's tales we see the critique of too little distinction, a sort of whitewashing of Jewish affectation and mannerism.

As I fully discussed in chapter 3, Goldschmidt was inexorably involved in bringing Deutsch's monograph on the Talmud to the Danish reading public. So it should not come as any surprise to see that Goldschmidt was also paramount in the redistribution of Hurwitz's work as well, not to mention a successor to the tactic of rehabilitating the rabbi in English literature. The advantage Goldschmidt had over Hurwitz, in my opinion, was a developed sense of literary creativity. Hurwitz was surely the master Hebraist, but Goldschmidt was undoubtedly the master narrator. Goldschmidt's own project of rehabilitating the Jew begins much earlier than his assumed contact with Hurwitz's *Hebrew Tales.* The figure of the rabbi and the rabbi tale occupy a central role in *A Jew.* We need not read any further than the tale of "der Rambám," the tale of the journeying Pole, and the story of the rabbi and the golem in that novel to establish the origins of Goldschmidt's interest. But the drive to anthologize them clearly has a stouter agenda.

Goldschmidt's remarks concerning Hurwitz's collection have proved difficult for scholars.[31] He admits that the two authors do share some narrative sequencing but insists that any textual overlapping is minor: "but the collection has but a few lines in common with the following."[32] Suffice it to say, there is a great deal of intended irony in such a statement, especially when one considers that the entirety of part 1, that is "Rabbi Meir's Wife," "Alexander and the Skull," "Rabbi Joschuar and the Princess," "A Greek Philosopher and a Rabbi," and "Rabbi Jochanni," all appear in Hurwitz's collection.[33] It is crucial to note that "Rabbi Meir's Wife" and "A Greek Philosopher and a Rabbi" appeared even earlier, when in 1810 Coleridge published them in his weekly, *The Friend*.[34] Curiously, these are exactly the tales that Goldschmidt takes liberty in recasting. The question here becomes one of authority and authorship versus innovation. The fact that Coleridge's name is somehow attached to the tales Goldschmidt sees fit to innovate also informs the disruptive tension between these two authors and again dismantles the esemplastic in Goldschmidt's favor. Goldschmidt's recasting of Coleridge's translations direct their authority back to the proper and prior source, in this case Mendelssohn. From him, the tradition seeps back into the rabbinical tradition. Coleridge as an esemplastic Jewish source is greatly disfigured in Goldschmidt's text, pointing to the veil of Coleridge's scholarship. Once again we see how the Romantic vision of the world is greatly limited by the Jewish perspective.

Goldschmidt never claims these tales to be his own. Like most of the material in *Chambers's*, his name was withheld in lieu of the *Chambers's* brand. In fact, by publishing them under the generic title of *Hebrew Legends*, we can assume that he is attributing them to tradition. He states clearly in his introduction that these tales "are the result of a reading extending over years. . . ." and he admits to "recasting" certain elements of the original tales in a new "form."[35] But if these tales or legends belong to tradition, why does Goldschmidt feel

Table 1
Distribution of Goldschmidt's *Hebrew Legends*

Goldschmidt's English (1862)	Goldschmidt's Danish (1860)	Hurwitz (1826)	Source Notes
Part 1			
Introduction			*Original*
"Rabbi Meir's Wife"	"Kongens Hjerneskal"	The Value of a Good Wife (supplied by Coleridge)	Yalkut to Proverbs 31, 964, Midrash Proverbs 31:10
"Alexander and the Skull"	*"Rabbi Meirs Hustru"[1]	Ambition Humbled and Reproved or Alexander and the Human Skull	Tamid 32b
"Rabbi Joschuah and the Princess"	*"Rabbi Joschuah og Prindsessen"	The Princess and Rabi Joshua	Ta'anit 7a; Nedarim 50b.
"A Greek Philosopher and a Rabbi"	*"En græsk Philosoph og en Rabbi"	"Conversation of a Philosopher with a Rabbi" (supplied by Coleridge)	'Abodah Zarah 54b
Untitled ["Rabbi Jochanni"]	*["Rabbi Jochanni"]	"Mercy in Judgment—A Parable of Rabi Jochanan"	Megillah 10b
	*"Maimonides"	"The Climax of Benevolence; or, the Golden Ladder of Charity." From Maimonides, after the Talmud	Maimonides, Yad ga-Hazakah, Mattenot 'Aniyyim 10, 7–13; cf. Kohler, *Jewish Encyclopedia*, 3:670a
"Rabbi Raschi"	"Rabbi Raschi"		Medieval (possibly, *Galerie der Sippurim*, published in 1847 by Wolf Pascheles of Prague)
Part 2			
"The Kamzan"	"Den Gjerrige"		Medieval (possibly, *Galerie der Sippurim*, published in 1847 by Wolf Pascheles of Prague)

Table 1
Distribution of Goldschmidt's *Hebrew Legends* (continued)

Goldschmidt's English (1862)	Goldschmidt's Danish (1860)	Hurwitz (1826)	Source Notes
"The Bird that Sang to a Bridegroom"	Originally written in English, it later appears in *Kjærlighedshistorier* (1867)		Despite Goldschmidt's claim, this is not a Talmudic tale. See note 105 in chapter 3 (possibly, *Galerie der Sippurim*, published in 1847 by Wolf Pascheles of Prague)
"David's Death"			Shabbat 30a–b, Ruth Rabbah 1.17, Eccl. Rabbah 5.10 but none has the Bathsheba ending
"The Witnesses"			Rashi on Ta'anit 8a (but it may go back to a lost source from the Talmudic age)
"The Drunkard and His Sons"		"The Wilful Drunkard"	Leviticus Rabbah, 12; Yalkut to Proverbs 23, 960
"Our Pledges"			Song of Songs Rabbah 1.4; Midrash on Psalms 8, 76–77
"The Ram"			Mostly Yashar Wa-Yera 46b; Pirke de-Rabbi Eliezer 31; the ram stretching itself out to touch Abraham's garment is innovative
"Isaac"			Genesis Rabbah 65.4–10
"Ambition"			Sanhedrin 102a
"Reward-Chastity"			Genesis Rabbah 90.3, Leviticus Rabbah 23.9, Numbers Rabbah 14.6, Tanhuma Genesis 12, Zohar 1.19b

Table 1
Distribution of Goldschmidt's *Hebrew Legends* (continued)

Goldschmidt's English (1862)	Goldschmidt's Danish (1860)	Hurwitz (1826)	Source Notes
"The Wandering Jew"			Innovative[2]
"Tolerance"			The tale is not at all rabbinical. Traditionally, it is accredited to Benjamin Franklin.[3]
"Solidarity of Sin"			Leviticus Rabbah 4.6
"Martyrs"			Gittin 57b; Lamentations Rabbah 1.16

1. The five tales with asterisks appeared in Danish in Meïr Goldschmidt, "Jødiske Sagn," *Nord og Syd* 2 (1852): 80–85.

2. Note that this is the first Jewish appropriation of the medieval Christian legend in a folkloric collection.

3. See George Alexander Kohut, "Abraham's Lesson in Tolerance," *Jewish Quarterly Review* 15 (1902): 105, who ascribes it to Milman, who, in his *History of the Jews* (New York, 1877), 3:459n, ascribes it to George Gentius (died 1667), who quotes it in the dedication of his Latin version of Solomon Ibn Verga's *Shebet Yehbida*; cf. Fürst, *Bibl. Judaica*, 3, 474; Steinschneider, *Catal. Bodl.*, 1009, published in Amsterdam, in 1651, 1654, and 1680.

the need to do any recasting at all? What exactly is the nature of this recasting? And why does he publish some of them in Danish first and then redistribute them in English? In order to fathom this process more clearly, let me examine the innovations between the tales in question. Table 1 shows the complex relationship and concordance between the distribution and attestation of these tales. Its purpose is not to bewilder the reader with obscure sources but rather to illustrate the traditional fabric of Goldschmidt's craft.

Table 1 is a testimony to the depth of Goldschmidt's knowledge concerning rabbinical story from difficult Talmudic texts to the most recent German language anthologies.[36] These tales are set amid his own fictive creations and recastings. The table is actually an astounding picture of an artist and his philological and narrative promise, but it is a graphic that is dissimilar to a European notion of Bildung and it exposes an increasing dissimilarity to an ever more prominent and modern European Jewry. It is a list in which neither the names Coleridge nor Brandes belong.

"Rabbi Meir's Wife"

This tale appears in Hurwitz under the name "The Value of a Good Wife." He cites the source of the tale as *Yalkut to Proverbs*, XXXI; §964.[37] The tale belongs to a class of rabbi tales in which the wife figures into the lesson or moral of the tale by giving good advice to the rabbi.[38] The wife in this story, Beruriah, is one of the few women mentioned in the Talmud. Other such tales in Hurwitz are "Liberality Grounded on Religion not to be Conquered by Reverse of Fortune—Exemplified in Abba Judan," "Destruction of Wickedness, the Best Way of Destroying Wicked Men," and "Compassion Toward the Unhappy: or, Rabbi Jose and His Repudiated Wife."[39]

While Rabbi Meir is out instructing the people, his two sons, "both of unusual beauty and deeply versed in the law," die in the house.[40] The rabbi's wife lays them on the nuptial bed and covers them with a white cloth. When Rabbi Meir comes home, he asks to see his sons so that he might "give them the blessing."[41] The wife answers,

"They have gone to God's house."[42] The oblivious rabbi replies that he looked around there (that is, the temple) but could not see them there.

In the meantime the wife brings "the light and the goblet with wine."[43] The rabbi drinks and then again asks where his sons are so that they might drink from a "consecrated cup."[44] At this point, the wife puts a question to the rabbi: "Some time since, one of our neighbours gave me some jewels to take care of; now he claims them back—shall I give them up?" Rabbi Meir replies with a tone of annoyance, "Not only must you give the property back, but you must give it willingly and cheerfully."[45] The wife then takes Rabbi Meir back into the bedroom and shows him the two dead bodies. The rabbi begins to cry and lament at which the wife reminds him of the lesson he had just so wisely clarified for her. The story ends in the blessed name of the Lord, "Blessed be He who giveth and taketh away!"[46]

At this point in the narrative, the Hurwitz version ends as a reflection on Proverbs 31:10 and 26, "He that has found a virtuous woman, has a greater treasure than costly pearls. She openeth her mouth with wisdom, and on her tongue is the instruction of kindness."[47] By cleverly playing with the phrase "gone to God's house," Goldschmidt's English tale highlights the virtue and wisdom of the rabbi's wife, while slightly mocking the rabbi's oblivious nature. Goldschmidt provides more than a simple lexical refinement of the Hurwitz version. He stiches an entirely new episode to the end of his version of the tale.

> And blessed and praised by Thou, my Father, my King, ruler of the universe! Amen.
>
> Rabbi Meir and his wife, when soon afterwards sailing from Africa to Spain, were taken prisoners by pirates, and the rabbi's wife, although not young, was still so handsome that she excited the illicit desires of the corsair chief.
>
> She said to her husband: "Rabbi, is a woman permitted to die by her own act to save her honour?"
>
> "It is," replied the rabbi, and he hid his face.
>
> Upon this she leaped into the sea.[48]

The tale should end on the "Amen" that occurs right before "Rabbi Meir and his wife. . . ." The new material is indexed by the adverbial "when soon afterwards." This alternative ending is somewhat reminiscent of Rashi's reading that Beruriah committed suicide. Instead of being shamed by her infidelity, Goldschmidt reassigns the act of suicide here as further testimony to her honor, one that again burdens the rabbi's authority. In typical Goldschmidt fashion, the tale is converted into a tragic love story while simultaneously performing a midrash of scripture and tradition.[49] Rabbi Meir is not a rebuking figure as he is in Rashi's version of the story. He has learned to let his sons go willingly and now he is faced with the dilemma of either having the pirate captain take his wife or letting her take her own life in order to save her virtue. Goldschmidt's Rabbi Meir is not interested in testing his wife's fidelity, only in preserving her honor though at the cost of her death. The alternative ending amplifies the affliction cast on to Rabbi Meir and positions him in a state of unavoidable shame and sorrow.

Craftily, this alternative ending only appears in Goldschmidt's English version of the tale, suggesting the play with both Hurwitz and Coleridge. The Danish version, which first appeared in *North and South* in 1852 ("Rabbi Meirs Hustru"), ends in the same fashion as the Hurwitz version. Although there are slight stylistic variations and some lexical adjustments, all three tales (the Hurwitz, Goldschmidt's Danish, and Goldschmidt's English versions) are essentially the same. This is undoubtedly what Goldschmidt did not mean by "the *spirit* of the old Hebrew tales is scrupulously maintained." The only marked difference is the alternative ending Goldschmidt tacks on to the end in the English version, and the spirit seems to be referring to the livelier, allegorical nature of Goldschmidt's that is both similar to the English versions but in essence closer to rabbinic modes of storytelling.

"A Greek Philosopher and a Rabbi"

The second of Coleridge's contributions to Hurwitz's collection, "Conversation of a Philosopher with a Rabbi," features a rabbi debating with an Athenian philosopher over the nature of God. The rabbi displays the typical midrashic line of questioning that was visible in the dialogue of "Rabbi Meir's Wife." We can see right away why Goldschmidt is attracted to such a tale, because it champions the learnedness of the rabbinical method over the Socratic, the root of European humanistic thought. Time and time again the sophistry of the West proves to be no real competition for the sagacity of the rabbi.

The Athenian poses the question to the rabbi, "why does your God so greatly abhor false gods and polytheism, yet threatens the worshipers of these gods more than the gods themselves?" Cleverly, the rabbi answers, "A King had a disobedient son, who, among other tricks, gave his dogs his father's name and titles. Should the father, then, punish the son or the dogs?" The Athenian sees the twisty questioning of the rabbi (or thinks he does) and responds that it "is only an evasive answer."[50] He refines his argument by insisting that if the rabbi's God destroyed all the other Gods, then the "root of polytheism" would likewise be destroyed. At this response, the rabbi has lured the Athenian into his rhetorical trap and retorts,

> "Should He, because there are fools worshipping the sun as god, destroy the sun? Or should He extinguish the fire, empty the sea, take away the air, and everything else in nature which they contrive to set up as a god? Should He, for the sake of the blind, repeal the law according to which the effects of light and colours are regulated? Our God is a God of freedom. If a man chooses to steal his neighbor's corn, our Lord does not make the corn unproductive, but permits it to grow when sown, according to general laws. But at the same time the theft is sown in the house of the thief, and it grows, and with its secret poison weakens the shafts upon which rests the roof of the thief."[51]

Goldschmidt's English version departs from his earlier Danish version, which is more soundly based on the Hurwitz. The moral of the tale is that human actions, specifically sin, are like the seed corn and will sprout unavoidable consequences and dangers. Goldschmidt takes it one step further by suggesting that these actions poison the very foundation of our lives and well-being. Hurwitz's version and

Goldschmidt's Danish version all end on this seed-corn metaphor; however, the statements about free will and the house of the thief are innovative to the English tale. Goldschmidt again sees fit to continue the narration a bit in his English version. That tale ends with two more rounds of quotation started by the ill tone of the philosopher. "'Who sowed the theft in the thief's house?' asked the philosopher sarcastically. The rabbi answered: 'The thief himself. Go and inquire. Behold the fate of those houses where mischief has been done.' 'That we call Nemesis, one of our goddesses.' 'And we call it justice, one of the qualities of our God.'"[52]

Goldschmidt stretches the morality of the tale more into the individual realm by bringing the consequences to the house of the thief. The rabbi's God lets the stolen corn grow as per the laws of nature, but because it is contraband it poisons the foundation of the thief's home. Goldschmidt is insistent on the individual being responsible for his actions and the divine repercussions of these actions. "Go and inquire," the rabbi tells the Greek. The philosopher who was at first sarcastic now replies with a smugness as if he has put the rabbi in check: "That we call Nemesis, one of our goddesses." The rabbi is not thrown off even for a second and delivers the knockout blow: "And we call it justice, one of the qualities of our God."[53]

The recasting here is rather sophisticated. Goldschmidt's English version weaves into the narrative an extra rhetorical victory for the rabbi. As in the original, the rabbi outfoxes the philosopher by turning the argument on the simple yes/no answer, a common Socratic maneuver. But the thief gets two more chances to have the last word until the rabbi is finally able to defeat him by making nemesis a facet of the Jewish God. It is a simple delivery; the rabbi's God supersedes the gods of the philosopher because he contains everything "in nature," including the forces and laws that are personified by the Greek pantheon. The alternative ending here also gives voice to Goldschmidt's idea that nemesis, although enjoying a rich tradition in the Western world, is originally a Semitic notion of existence.

Like the tale above, "Rabbi Meir's Wife," there is a notion of violation and robbery that drives the tale into a darker allegory. Since this tale was one of the tales that appeared in Coleridge's periodical, Goldschmidt's reshaping also concerns the European stealing of Jewish tradition and the repackaging of it as its own. Time and time again, the politic unfolds in Goldschmidt's work that what is too often considered canonically European, whether Greek philosophy or modern European fiction, is genetically Semitic. The material itself is still equally as powerful and artistic, but the house of European Bildung is contaminated, weakened, built upon the treachery of its colonization of thought.

"Rabbi Raschi"

The figure of the great rabbi plays an important yet fluid role in Goldschmidt's legends. As opposed to the four tales that are stable throughout Goldschmidt's editions, the tale of Maimonides and the three versions of the Rashi legend rotate throughout the editions. It seems to be Rashi's contemplation of the Talmud that most impresses upon Goldschmidt a sense of greatness. "Rabbi Jarchi, commonly called Rabbi Raschi, lived in the 11th and 12th centuries (1040–1105 AD), and was born at Troyes, in France. His name is still mentioned with reverence next to that of Maimonides. He wrote a commentary on some of the prophets, and likewise an explanation of the Talmud, a gigantic work, without which that obscure book would be almost unintelligible. He was, besides, a great mathematician, and a very religious man."[54]

"Rabbi Raschi" should be considered one of Goldschmidt's most stylistically important stories, although it has received next to no attention in the scholarship.[55] This tale represents the culmination of the rabbi tale in Goldschmidt's corpus. "Rabbi Raschi" also represents a departure from the rabbi tales that appear in Hurwitz's edition. Along with two other rabbi tales, "Maimonides" and "Rabbi Akiva," this story manufactures and perfects the quintessence of Goldschmidt's rabbinical figure. It is specifically the figure of Rashi that Goldschmidt uses to complete his rehabilitation of the rabbi. Akiva and Maimonides are already figures employed by Hurwitz. Who better to conscript for his cause than Rashi, the greatest of biblical commentators.

Goldschmidt published three versions of the Rashi tale. The first was the version published in *North and South* in 1852 (which is the version reprinted in *Blandede skrifter*). The second is the English translation that appeared in *Chambers's Journal* in 1862. The third was published in 1869 in the English journal *Once a Week* under the title "Rabbi Raschi: A Jewish Legend."[56] I am mostly concerned with the two English texts in my following analysis. It is important to read these two English texts alongside one another as they show Goldschmidt's dynamic process of recasting and his creative reshaping of these "living" texts. The 1869 text shows several innovative features over the earlier versions and represents the culmination of Goldschmidt's interest in the Jewish tale and the figure of the rabbi. For example, instead of beginning the tale with a historical account of Rashi's life, the 1869 text inserts a short proem about the life of Rashi's mother while she was pregnant with Rashi.

> Among the most learned and pious Jews of the twelfth century, next to the great Maimou, or Maimonides, of European fame, stands Raschi, or, as he was more properly called, Schlomo ben Isaac. He wrote a commentary on Thora and on several books of the Prophets, and also one on the Talmud. He was a great mathematician, and among his own people was reverenced for his sanctity and asceticism.
>
> His parents lived in Toulon, but Raschi was born in Troyes, and this is the reason why his father Isaac and his mother left Toulon. Shortly before the birth of the child the good woman walked down a narrow street. A cumbrous wagon was being drawn along it by four stout horses, and the wagon filled the street so as to make it impossible to pass. Seeing this the woman turned to seek a side street, but at that moment the car of a young nobleman drove up the lane towards her. The timid woman ran from side to side in quest of a corner into which she might retreat from the two vehicles.
>
> "Look at the Jewess!" exclaimed the driver of the nobleman's car; "how frightened she is."
>
> "Whip the horses and run her down," said his master.

The two vehicles approached, and the poor creature, finding no place of retreat, with a piteous cry shrank against the wall. At that moment the huge wheel of the wagon rolled towards her almost grazing the house-wall. Then, suddenly, the wall bowed inwards and formed a little recess in which the Jewess stood secure.

"Softer and more yielding are these stones than your hearts, ye Christians!" she exclaimed.[57]

Compared with the version in *Chambers's Journal*, the 1869 introduction is much cleaner. Right away, Goldschmidt seems to be interested in separating this tale from the ones that appear in Hurwitz's *Hebrew Tales* and his own earlier *Hebrew Legends*. The tale is given a subtitle of "A Jewish Legend." This move is important for Goldschmidt because it allows the figure of the rabbi to translate the rabbis of the Talmudic age into the modern European Jew. Rashi becomes in this instance Goldschmidt's rabbi par excellence. Goldschmidt has removed the erroneous name Jarchi from the text and instead prints Rashi's actual name, "Schlomo ben Isaac."[58] Both versions mention that Rashi belongs next to Maimonides but only the second version differentiates between his Jewish name (Moshe ben) Maimoun and his more common Greek name Maimonides.[59]

The prenatal story is also innovative, not in content but by design. It is a well-known story but Goldschmidt has stitched it to the more familiar medieval tale of Rashi's companion. By relating a horrifying story about Rashi's mother, Goldschmidt prefaces the trope of persecution that fleshes out his figure of the rabbi. It also surrounds the birth of Rashi with a mystical or miraculous apparatus. Goldschmidt here could be playing with the model of the bildungsroman or using the life of Christ or the saints as his model. The latter is perhaps more plausible because we know that during this time Goldschmidt was very interested in the figure of Christ and was exiled by the Jewish community in London for such beliefs.[60] The stitching also allows Goldschmidt to create a full life narrative of Rashi, a technique that he first used in his 1867 English tale "Rabbi Akiva." This recasting of the rabbi tale into a fuller life narrative is a move to further the promotion of rabbinic literature that was instigated by Hurwitz and Deutsch, both of whom Goldschmidt explored ways to out-design.

Seminal to my overall reading of the figure of the rabbi, this tale foregrounds Goldschmidt's use of the rabbi to develop his discourse on the eternal and his notion of "soul-migration." The tale begins with the assertion that upon reaching his sixtieth year, "the pale of life," Rabbi Rashi wished to know who his companion in Paradise would be. "He, of course, did not entertain the least doubt that such a pious and learned man as he, who had never transgressed any ceremonial law, would be ushered into the Garden of Eden, and be seated on a golden chair at a golden table, with a wreath of pearls round his head, and would be allowed to feast eternally on the glory of God. But he wished to know who the pious man was that should be placed opposite to him at the same table, for the righteous sit two and two in Paradise."[61]

The figure of the rabbi here encapsulates the quality of intermediation I discussed earlier. The rabbi in Goldschmidt is always poised between the past and the approaching future. In the historical introduction at the beginning of the tale, Goldschmidt reminds us that Rashi was a great Talmudic scholar and biblical interpreter. He faces Rashi, if you will, toward the past, into the prophets and ultimately the Torah. In what is developing as the quest of the tale, however, he simultaneously faces Rashi in the opposite direction, toward eternity and the promise of Paradise regained. Because the righteous sit two by two, Rashi expects that his eternal companion will have lived as piously on Earth as he himself. As if by mathematical design, Rashi's companion will be a parallel version of himself. However, as we shall see, this is not as clear for the great rabbi as it perhaps should have been.

This state of intermediation is brought out a little more in the 1869 version. There is an elevation of Rashi's character. For instance, we are told he continually fasted, mixed his food with ash, and allowed himself to take only a little water once a day. One day when he was "an old man" he overheard two Jews in the street talking about the greatness of the man who would be Rashi's table companion in Paradise, and Rashi "fell to musing. . . ." The tales are similar, but in the 1869 version Rashi has a vision of eternity. The narrative at this point in the text becomes much more poetic, expressing the grandiosity of Rashi's person and the glory of the paradisiacal.

> With his thoughts fixed on this theme, he stood long at his window gazing out over the vine-clad hills, towards the horizon where the sun had set, and where its rays shot upwards, kindling the finely attenuated vapour which hung in the air, and making the blue of heaven green as grass. Level bars of cloud burned like gold in a furnace, and small misty fragments glowed scarlet, like fiery lilies growing in a field of sunlit grass between strips of yellow crocuses.
>
> As the old man stood with his eyes fixed on the west, and his mind revolving the thoughts suggested by the speakers, he saw the western sky undergo a sudden transformation; the golden clouds became steps of light in a pavement of amethyst, and on these platforms were placed pairs of golden thrones with gorgeous robes of ruby tissue cast over them, and in these robes diamonds were set, and as the light changed they twinkled like sparks that wander about the ashes of consumed paper. Upon each throne a name was written with lightning brilliancy.[62]

This is perhaps the most stylistically beautiful moment in Goldschmidt's English writings. Rashi in his infinite wisdom stares out his window into the western horizon and beholds a vision of Paradise. Earlier we noticed how Goldschmidt's vivid descriptions of stars created a rhetoric of the infinite, but here its radiance is dressed in the liminal light of the setting sun. In an almost Stevens-esque delivery Goldschmidt transforms the narrative through a synesthesia of color-patterned similes. The "blue of heaven" transforms into the lyrically loaded "green as grass"; gold, scarlet, and yellow overwhelm. Rashi becomes a figure frozen in between. He stares westward into the dying sun, the crepuscule of his life, into a visionary land, igniting in light and solar imagery. Through this "sudden transformation," Rashi is also a figure facing east, toward the trail of texts that lead from the earthly garden. The image of the consuming paper calls forth the illumination of the text, including Rashi's own texts "without which that obscure book would be almost unintelligible."[63]

It is in this state of ecstatic stasis that Rashi learns the name of his companion, "Abraham-ben-Gerson, called the Zadik, at Barcelona."[64] With such a name as Zadik, "the righteous," Rashi, childlike, becomes anxious to meet his "Paradise-friend" whom he imagines as pale and as thin as himself. Arriving in Barcelona, Rashi is surprised to learn that the Zadik is called "Don Abraham the Wealthy" by the locals. To his dismay, he is the antithesis of Rashi's expectation, "never seen at synagogue the whole year round, nay, who eats meat prepared by Christians!"[65]

When Rashi, despite the local rabbis' better wishes, finds himself in front of Don Abraham's residence, he is astonished by its lavishness. "It was a real palace, splendid, replete with beauty and taste, so that it even moved the heart of the old rabbi, who could only find this fault with it, that it did not behoove a son of Israel to live in such splendour, whilst so many of his brethren were doomed to be in poverty and filth."[66] The luxuries of Don Abraham's palace mirror the radiant vision of Paradise that Rashi had in the beginning of the tale. Although Rashi is moved by the scene, he is not drawn into its comfort. Acting as an "instrument of God," Rashi is unable to suspend his connection to the plight and persecution of the Jewish people. How could a Jew live in such splendor while so many Jews suffer the realities and hardships of the European ghetto?

The contrast between the figure of Rashi and the liveries of Don Abraham's estate is more elaborate in the 1869 version. In general, Goldschmidt is more concerned with the actual physicality of Rashi in this text. This is what renders this particular text's uniqueness. We were told earlier of his rather Spartan eating habits and daily schedule of meditation. In such a refined environment as a European palace, the macerated figure of the rabbi is out of place, reduced to a frozen image of Jewish antiquity. Even the "rude staff" invokes images of the Mosaic past and all the sense of wandering that is associated with

European Jewry. There is even a bit of comic relief in the exaggerated contrast.

> Noblemen waited there, lounging on velvet sofas, till the master of the house could attend to them. Servants glittering with gold lace hurried about, bearing salvers of the most precious metal, on which were goblets full of iced wines, and plates with delicious confections, which they handed to the illustrious visitors.
>
> Travel-stained, dust begrimed, leaning on his rude staff, his gabardine in tatters, his long white beard untrimmed, and the white hair of his head in tangled locks, unattended to, the wondering Raschi stood entranced. A servant approached him with a golden salver, on which were wines. The old man raised his staff, and with flashing eyes indignantly signed him to retire.[67]

Goldschmidt's employment of the English language reaches a pinnacle in this description of Rashi "travel-stained" and "dust begrimed" among the "velvet sofas" and "iced wines" of Don Abraham's entourage, the sofas themselves a clear critique of embourgeoisement. The old sage waving his staff at the servant who offers him "a golden salver, on which were wines" is surely one of the finer comic ironies in all of Goldschmidt.

This contrast between Rashi's hollowed physicality and the luxuries and temptations of European aristocracy comes to full head when Don Abraham appears and meets with Rashi face to face. In *Hebrew Legends*, the man is simply described as "a tall, handsome man, of about thirty."[68] This description is, of course, more stylized in the 1869 version where Don Abraham is described as "a noble-looking Jew, in a crimson velvet dress, with gold chains about his neck. . . ."[69]

When Rashi sees Don Abraham he advances toward him. "'Make way,' said Rabbi Raschi, thrusting his staff betwixt two of the liveried servants, 'make way for me.'"[70] Again we see the figure of Rashi wielding his staff. This image of the skeletal rabbi confronting the decadence of the European court, although perhaps not Goldschmidt's own invention, is nonetheless fine for its contrasted style and simple comedy. Behind all these images is the rabbi's expectation that the man who will share his table in Paradise should be his equal in piety. "I hoped to have found one fasting and praying; I find one eating and trafficking. I thought to have found one the favourite of God, and I find one the courted of princes and nobles. Is this a house for a Jew—a child of a despised and outcast race? The temple lieth waste, and shall we live in luxury and splendour?"[71]

To Rashi's dismay, Don Abraham is engaged in a slew of activities unbefitting a pious Jew. These activities are described in opposite pairings, again rekindling the two-by-two formula of Rashi's expectation. Instead of "fasting and praying," Don Abraham partakes of nonkosher meats and "the accursed flesh of the swine." Contrary to a pious Jew, a "favourite of God," Don Abraham's attendance at synagogue, which "has been irregular," is traded for the company of "a Spanish prince of royal blood" and "the courted of princes and nobles." While looking into the hereafter and finding room to berate his eternal table companion, Rashi's thoughts are still turned backward, as his rebuke of Don Abraham is framed in the past, toward the destruction of the Temple and the subjugation of the Jewish people. There is perhaps a moment of weakness folded into Rashi's otherwise perfect countenance. As if to ward off the possibility of elevating Rashi into fairy-tale heroics, Goldschmidt gives him a human quality: despite his infinite wisdom and earthly restraint, Rashi has judged Don Abraham and conditioned the vision he was given with a projection of himself. Goldschmidt has teased out of the pious rabbi a frailty of character, vanity.

> "Alas, alas!" cried Raschi, throwing down his staff and raising his hands to heaven. "Surely there is injustice in paradise as well as on earth. Here lives a wicked Jew, a breaker of the law, in splendour, as a king; in another place is a pious man, fearing god, macerating his body, in want and nakedness, crushed by poverty, and the kingdom of Heaven receives both, and sets both on a level. Woe is me!" and he would have rushed from the chamber, had not the merchant stayed him.

> "Rabbi," he said; "I know my duty to God and man, and I practice it as best I can."
>
> "Profane one!" exclaimed the old man. "Trust not your own strength. When the ungodly are green as the grass, and when all the workers of wickedness do flourish, then shall they be destroyed—" But just then there flashed before the Rabbi's eyes that golden throne beside his own, on which was written the name of the merchant.[72]

Goldschmidt's Rashi moves beyond the generic rabbi of medieval lore. Here we see a Rashi overcome by human emotion. Frustrated, Rashi throws down his staff, the metonym for his sagacity, and questions the soundness of God's justice. He calls Don Abraham a "wicked Jew" and compares his lifestyle to that of a "king," while Rashi depicts himself as flawlessly devoted. Don Abraham tries to appease the honored rabbi, but Rashi continues to rebuke him, calling him the "profane one!"

All this reprimanding leads to the rabbi's preaching in parables on the weakness of mankind and transgression. The lyrical phrase "green as grass" appears again as the words of the rabbi slide into the visionary language of Paradise. His accosting talk of wickedness and destruction is interrupted as Rashi recalls, as if flashing "before the Rabbi's eyes," the hall of golden thrones. "Upon each throne a name was written with lightning brilliancy. And the Rabbi saw on two of the highest—Raschi ben Isaac, of Regensburg, and Abraham ben Gerson, of Barcelona."[73] The mental radiation of that vision is enough to give Rashi insight into his own behavior. Either he is as poor a Jew as he is accusing Don Abraham of being or Don Abraham is really as pious a Jew as Rashi. Either way, their names are written together in Paradise on "two of the highest" thrones. It is written; it is epigram. Heaven "sets both on a level."

At this point in the tale, the 1869 version departs from the version in *Hebrew Legends* and reverts to the narrative structure of Goldschmidt's original Danish. "Rabbi Raschi" exhibits a revised version of the marriage episode that is at the heart of the story. Why Goldschmidt chose to return to the marriage of Don Abraham's daughter after he had reassigned the nuptial motif to Don Abraham is puzzling. However, in his attempt to rehabilitate the figure of the rabbi, I suspect Goldschmidt's eroticization of Don Abraham goes a little too far. Also pushed aside in the 1869 version is the playboy image of the thirty-year-old Don Abraham, a man half Rashi's age. In this version, his features are more backgrounded, and he is described only as "noble-looking" and "master of the house."[74]

In *Hebrew Legends* and the Danish version, Don Abraham, attempting to appease Rashi, asks him to be a guest at his wedding. To Rashi's astonishment, he is to marry "a daughter of Israel, a lovely, amiable, kind-hearted girl."[75] Rashi is skeptical of the union and worries for the girl, but concedes that "it may be a *mitzwa*."[76] The use of glossed Hebrew in these tales is rare and only occurs three times.[77] The by now familiar move of glossing Hebrew at the foot of the page stands out in this text and is a feature of the narrative from which the characters of the two rabbis duel.

The discussion of the rabbis is interrupted by a poor woman, who has come to ask Don Abraham's advice. It turns out that her son is sick, "ill through love, disappointed love."[78] The eighteen-year-old was to marry "a young girl, poor and honest like himself. . . . but now the poor girl is forced by her parents to marry another, a rich man."[79] Don Abraham listens intently to the old woman's story, then asks her the name of her son. She replies, "Abraham-ben-Manuel."[80] After she leaves, Don Abraham is visibly shaken; he is "deadly pale, with large drops of sweat on his brow."[81] The good guest that he is, Rashi tries to console him by saying three times that the boy will surely not die from a broken heart. "'You may be quite sure that young fellow is not going to die. Young folks sometimes make a great noise about their love. After some time, he will find another woman quite as handsome.' 'There is no other beneath the sun!' Don Abraham exclaimed passionately: 'there is but one sun in the heavens. Take it away, and all is dark—the air is chilly, the meadow has no verdure, the garden no flower! Take it away, and you take life away! Life without love is nothing! Oh, the woman was right!'"[82]

Once again the rabbi is humanized, for Rashi cannot see as clearly as the reader can that it is Don Abraham's teenage bride with whom the poor woman's son is desperately in love. Even when Don Abraham resorts to the language of lament, Rashi, ever the mathematician, does not understand the depth of his despair for a boy he does not even know. But, behind the swell of his sorrow, Don Abraham renounces his earthly garden. "'Take it all away, and all is dark,'" he utters. Again Rashi naïvely tries to allay his fears,

> "Such sorrows may be overcome; but, of course, something must be done for the family, something of consequence even." "You are right, Rabbi Raschi; I hope I shall have something arranged by to-morrow. Do not forget to come to mincha."[83]

Unbeknownst to Rashi, he hits upon a very sensible idea. Don Abraham will do something for the poor family. In a reversal of portraits, it is Don Abraham who reminds Rashi to come to *mincha*.[84] Again Goldschmidt uses the gloss at the foot of the page to disrupt the reading of the text; whereas before it was a way of asserting Rashi's devotion, here it signals a breaking out of character. Don Abraham is moved by the sorrow of the boy whom Goldschmidt so transparently names Abraham. Rehabilitating back into the rabbinic life, his language also bends back into Ashkenazi Hebrew. The narrator is also prone to this rehabilitation. When the canopy under which the marriage is to take place is described, it is called "The hruppa or baldachin."[85] One knows there is a crisis astir in Goldschmidt when one "oriental" word is glossed with another.[86]

As promised, Rashi arrives to the ceremony on time. After the *mincha*, the bride is led in by "a band of music and torches" and the notary begins to "read the marriage-contract, upon which Don Abraham said: 'There is but one little thing to be corrected: the name of the bridegroom is not Abraham-ben-Gerson, but Abraham-ben-Manuel; I have only been the *schatchan*.'"[87] Rashi's idea of doing something good for the family has been transformed into an act of such selflessness and devotion that it cancels or corrects his amorous past, affirming the rehabilitation of Don Abraham. Again, the gloss is used to testify to Don Abraham's piety. And if that first attestation put him back in line with a life of righteousness, then this one lifts him to the status of being Rashi's companion. "'Oh,' cried Rabbi Raschi, 'thou art worthy, indeed, to be my companion in Paradise! At first, the rabbi's exclamation was unheeded; but he afterward related his dream to Don Abraham, who replied good-humouredly, 'I am glad to hear it; it is so pleasant to have a good neighbor; and, besides,' he added with quivering lips, 'I shall come single.' Since then, eight hundred years have elapsed. We may all see, in a short time, if they are seated together."

Rashi has finally accepted Don Abraham as his Paradise-friend. Harmony is restored to both the macerated, pious rabbi and the rabbi who has strayed from the radiant light of Paradise. However, Don Abraham has not lost his sense of humor and manages to close with a slim and teasing joke about the absence of the rabbi's wife, "I shall come single." An alternative to the pious tone used to complete the figure of the wife in my earlier discussion, she is made here into a comic figure of domestic irritation, although Don Abraham's "quivering lips" allow the joke a spot of grace. The intent rests somewhere on Rashi's shoulder, a testimony to the quality of his companionship. The story ends with a short sentiment about the reader's own providence, completing the historical framing that began the tale. The narrative eye is adjusted along the metaleptic parameters of the rabbinic figure, from the past along the present and into the eternal.

The 1869 version ends slightly differently and should be mentioned here. Don Abraham, after swapping his daughter with the poor girl Miriam, oversees the marriage and gives the poor widow's son the same position in his business as if he had married his daughter. There is great applause and merriment at the revelation. Goldschmidt's Rashi has the last words and closes Goldschmidt's rehabilitation of the rabbi in perfect form.

> Then Raschi, laying about him with his staff, beat himself a way through the multitude, and pressing up to the merchant, he burst

> into tears, and throwing himself on his neck embraced him, and raising his hands, cried: "Yes! You are worthy to reach Gan Eden! [Paradise]. Glory be to God, who has give me such a man as thou, to be my companion for eternity! Glory be to God, who has not made one rough road alone to Paradise, but has made many roads besides; who has prepared a throne, not for the fasting ascetic and contemplative alone, but also for him who can do what is right and just freely!"[88]

Although the rabbi here is still wielding a heavy staff toward Don Abraham's entourage, Goldschmidt has sculpted a Rashi that is capable of learning and being humbled by his relationship with Don Abraham. The old rules of attaining Paradise that allowed only "for the fasting ascetic and contemplative alone" have been effectively changed. Rashi now sees that it is the journey, not the path, that sets each man straight with the Lord. As the rabbi told the Greek philosopher, "Our God is a God of freedom."[89]

Goldschmidt's project of rehabilitating the figure of the rabbi is the culmination of a powerful construction of authority that spans some thirty-two years. It is an experiment that commences in the opening pages of *A Jew*, finds form in the columns of *North and South*, is perfected in the English tales of the sixties, and arrives in his memoirs as a genealogy of writing and the self. There is no doubt in my mind that Goldschmidt saw himself as a kind of rabbinical figure, a secular rabbi. Perhaps it is no coincidence that the first of his *Hebrew Legends* is entitled "Rabbi Meir's Wife."

There is an important intersection with the story I quoted in the opening of this chapter. The tale is a touchstone for Goldschmidt. When Moses asked God to see Rabbi Akiva, the Lord said, "Turn around." As I demonstrated, this act of turning is seminal for Goldschmidt's projection and figuring of the rabbi. Constantly turning from the past and tradition to the future and eternity, the rabbi is a narrative vehicle through which Goldschmidt accesses a profound and mystical narrative art. On the shoulders of the great Jewish sages, Goldschmidt is able to enter a rabbinical discourse and create a new format for expressing Jewishness. This is not only a turning around but a turning over, a recasting of traditional shapes and shadows into a new literature. Robert Chambers had told Goldschmidt that he had "broken a new path in English literature."[90] My analysis has attempted to confirm this claim.

Why Goldschmidt was more active in promulgating these tales in English than he was in Danish is perhaps the most interesting question at hand. Certainly the Jewish population in London was much larger than in Denmark and enjoyed a more functional level of literary activity, as illustrated by writers such as Hurwitz and Deutsch, and the popularity of Grace Aguilar's (1816–1847) and Goldschmidt's tales.[91] In Denmark Goldschmidt had a predominately gentile readership, but in England he enjoyed something not available to him back at home, a Jewish audience. Perhaps the most telling sign of Goldschmidt's success as an English writer should be measured by a little book that appeared sometime in the first decade of the twentieth century.

The book was entitled *Jewish Legends of the Middle Ages* and was translated by Claud Field (1863–1941).[92] The book contains twelve tales, although the term "Middle Ages" is misleading. In actuality, the first four tales of that volume are Goldschmidt's stories from *Chambers's Journal.* There are some minor editorial changes, but "The Bird that Sang to a Bridegroom," "The Witnesses," "The Kamzan," and "Rabbi Rashi's Companion" are all modern reappropriations of Goldschmidt's English tales. From beyond the grave, Goldschmidt has seen the rehabilitation of the rabbi continue into the twentieth century; turning around, his soul-migration continues. The figure of the rabbi, bathed in the light of stars, haunted by the words of the past, persecuted and emaciated, his eye always on the hereafter, becomes again a model for the human condition. He is rescued from obscurity, placed into the role of harmonious companion, and rehabilitated into a modern milieu.

Epilogue

The Wandering Jew as Possibility

The Danish critic Georg Brandes, concerning that elusive question of style, wrote these telling lines about the Jewish writer Meïr Aaron Goldschmidt:

> To portray the good stylist is already to portray Goldschmidt. His language is first and foremost genuine prose. . . . The characteristic of good prose is namely that although it is composed of sheer rhythms that could be verse, at each moment it breaks them all down, crashing them against one another and thus generating a calm, always restrained progress. Prose is language's trot, verse its gallop. Every rider knows that although the gallop appears more beautiful than the trot, it is the steady trot that is often the most difficult to hold, as the horse's impulse is to spring into a gallop and it will do just that if it is not reined in from doing so.[1]

The central premise of Brandes's critique of Goldschmidt seems to be that he was able to restrain his prose from getting away from him and thus becoming too lyrical, something Brandes was critical of Kierkegaard for doing. Goldschmidt held the center, the midpoint; always in control, he could tease out of the narrative a semblance of galloping without ever leaving the surefootedness of the trot.[2] The best prose is a narrative movement that is somehow suspended between the methodical and the enchanted, between the trot and the gallop.

I do not profess to fully understand Brandes's ubiquitous notion of style especially with regard to Goldschmidt, but I find this metaphor of the horse and rider to be an incredible image for Goldschmidt's craft. The image of the riding master magnificently controlling the engine of the horse is the very portrait of Goldschmidt, the master of Danish prose. It is difficult to reconcile these statements in Brandes with the ones that debase Goldschmidt for his overt Jewishness and portrayal of Jewish characters and language. Brandes found Goldschmidt's understated characters and their indirect and tribal speech patterns particularly irritating. Perhaps what Brandes disliked most about Goldschmidt was that he could not quite separate his stylistics from his narrative art. As much as he pronounced Goldschmidt's stylistic virtuosity, Brandes detested the very poetics I have discussed in this book: poetics that are intrinsically Jewish, this Goldschmidtian world of midrash and biblical allusion, Talmudic underdogs and emaciated rabbis, this narrative experience of soul-migration and the mystical metaleptic eye of the universe.

For Brandes, it was Goldschmidt's poetics that robbed his work of the certain mode of aesthetics Brandes would subjectively label the Modern Breakthrough. And it was Goldschmidt's religiosity, indeed his "*jødiske Religiøsitet*" (Jewish religiosity) that was his "*Svaghed*" (weakness).[3] As a reader Brandes did not like to feel suspended in a poetics that looked backward, as he did when he read Goldschmidt's Jewish narratives. He did not want to be reminded of orthodoxy or reactivate any simulation of the Jewish past. Brandes wanted to feel as if when he galloped, his horse's feet still touched the ground, as he did when he read Goldschmidt's less demanding and more culturally neutral material, pieces like "Min onkels tømmerplads" ("My Uncle's Lumberyard"), "Bjergtagen Nr. 1" ("Bewitched No. 1"), and the preface to *Kjærlighedshistorier fra mange lande* (Love Stories from Many Lands).[4] However, Brandes failed to see, or perhaps refused to see, that even these seemingly acculturated texts were already a translation of the Jewish experience, a poetics borne beyond Denmark's borders, and echoing with dissimilarity.

The fascinating thing about Brandes's equestrian metaphor for me is how it posits Goldschmidt at the forefront of a new modern world. For ages humankind debated the question of whether all the hooves of a horse left the ground when it galloped. Legend has it that the infamous horse-breeder and former California governor Leland Stanford offered twenty-five thousand dollars to anybody who could definitively prove or disprove his theory of equine locomotion or suspended transit. In 1877, the same year that Goldschmidt published his memoirs, the English–American photographer Eadward Muybridge (1830–1904) answered this question. With his innovations in rapid-movement photography, an apparatus that he would call the zoopraxiscope, Muybridge projected for all the world to see the horse during gallop, with all four hooves afloat. This now iconic image of the horse suspended in mid-air is a seminal node in the modern history of humankind, the birth of the cinematic, the capturing of motion.

Brandes's image of Goldschmidt as the master-rider holding that delicate midpoint between trot and gallop, giving the semblance of always having one foot on the ground, is actuated by Muybridge's rapid-movement photography, the crystallization of suspended transit. One of the main arguments in this book has been that Goldschmidt is a precursor to Modernism, a prefiguring of Kafka and the iconoclasm that defines that movement so well. This argument is certainly contrary to Brandes and most scholars, who are content to configure Goldschmidt comfortably within the parameters of Romanticism, as an early innovator of the psychological novel, the master of Danish prose, and a heirloom of national identity. Goldschmidt's reception is fraught with problems and tempered by a nationalistic aesthetics that has denied him not only citizenry but a specifically Jewish art.

In the postscript to *Zakhor*, Yerushalmi writes of the possibility that "the antonym of 'forgetting' is not 'remembering,' but *justice*."[5] I take this to mean that memory must give way to action in order to ward off the Angel of Forgetfulness. Memory alone is too fragile; we must read Goldschmidt for ourselves. There we will find, teetering on the edge of oblivion, a far better Goldschmidt, a Goldschmidt suspended out of time, like Stanford's horse, a relic of things to happen.

In his innovative and, in my opinion, most Kafkaesque tale "The Wandering Jew," Goldschmidt tells of a wealthy, ill-tempered Jewish merchant who fell and broke his leg when he tried to kick a poor beggar woman and her infant child. The break was so severe that the leg had to be amputated. Not content with the ordinary wooden leg he was issued, the merchant hired one of the neighborhood mechanicians, a pious and gentle Jew, to construct a mechanical leg that functioned "like a natural one."[6] The leg was so ingeniously built and moved so naturally, that even the merchant felt as if "he had two sound natural legs."[7]

Although the merchant was thankful, he became even more ill-tempered and sought revenge on the poor beggar-woman by having her evicted from the town. Returning home at a brisk pace after he had successfully driven the woman away, he realized how unsatisfied he was with the artificial leg and sought out the mechanician to fix the fault in the leg. The mechanician replied that he could not do so on the Sabbath. But the merchant insisted.

Giving in to his harsh words, the mechanician instructed the merchant to set his leg upon a stone so that he could examine it. "In so doing, the merchant, in his impatience, knocked the leg against the stone in such a manner that the wheels, receiving a sudden impulse, pushed him on at a terribly quick rate. Against his will, he now ran off along the street, out of the town, into the mountains, where he wanders to this day, and where he is sometimes met with, and is heard to cry, 'Stop my leg!' But whether he means the artificial leg, or that which was lifted against the poor woman, is uncertain."[8]

Thus the story runs. The Jew wanders into time against his will, his every movement mechanized by the leg that will not stop, pressed on by the myriad of legends that record and rerecord his journey.[9] But what of the mechanician? He fades so effortlessly into obscurity. Yet it was from his design that the story sprang; it was he who created the leg "so contrived with springs and wheels." And it was he who attached it to an impatient man. Here is the Goldschmidtian metaphor. Not the amphibian or the criss-crossed grave, not the "cross-eyed hunchback" or an elusive grandmother's spicy sauce.[10] Goldschmidt is the master mechanician; he who tinkers with the story, winds it up and sets it in motion, letting it get away from him, "off along the street, out of the town, into the mountains, where [it] wanders to this day." By attaching the right prosthetic to the right narrative host (perhaps this is what Goldschmidt means by recasting), Goldschmidt continues the legend by writing himself into it. By metonymy Goldschmidt becomes the Wandering Jew, or as Jan Schwarz has put it, "the quintessential Jew."[11]

The tale is reminiscent of Kafka's golem fragment.[12] Like Goldschmidt, Kafka's reception as a Jewish writer has been suppressed by privileging the quality of his linguistic craft: Goldschmidt as the exemplary Danish stylist and Kafka as the writer of a pure German tongue. In the rare case in which Kafka overtly engages with Jewish legend, we see a turning away from the traditional mechanics of the golem tale. Kafka's rabbi does not forget to deanimate the golem for the Sabbath, which is very much the usual case; instead he fails at creating it in the first place and turns himself into a furious and confused figure who simulates the golem. Likewise, in Goldschmidt's "The Wandering Jew" we witness the possibility of writing into the future through a breaking with the mechanics of tradition and the elided subjectivity that occurs in the transaction between tradition and contemporary Jewish experience, what Buber described in 1934 as "*galut*" (exile).[13] This narrative play of being a Jew in the modern world is more than a subversion or simple inversion of tradition; it creates a politics of appropriation that comments on how modern literature creates meaning by recasting tradition. For both writers this act is problematic and tensioned by a narrative that tries to incorporate the many strands of the past but ends up only creating more dissonance in the symbolical fabric of the present. This dissonance and destabilization is what Deleuze and Guattari refer to when they discuss the notion of a "minor literature."[14] Yet this dissonant cloth is also something that engenders the act of writing itself. Goldschmidt's rewiring of the medieval Christian legend of the eternal wanderer and Kafka's transfiguring of the Kabbalistic practice of golem-making are contiguous moments, narratives deeply in flux, expressing a mobility of thought that is indicative of the many categories and borders occupied by modern Jewish fiction.[15]

Goldschmidt's writings are not to be found among the literary anthologies of Modernism or even within the circles of the Modern

Breakthrough, and there is hardly a mention of him in our contemporary anthologies of modern Jewish literature. Rather, it is in the texture of modern writing where strands of Goldschmidt's art can be found—in the rebirth of Hebrew prose and the advent of Yiddish literature, in the early politics of Zionism and the discourse of nationalism, in the horror and crime of the Holocaust and the failure of the artist, in Kafka's dying obsession with Kabbalah, in the tales of Buber and the mysticism of Scholem, in the fashion of Egyptomania and the conception of macrofamily linguistics.

Brandes's image of Goldschmidt, the harmoniously suspended riding-master, speaks to the grace and precision of Goldschmidt's thought and craft. Goldschmidt's mechanician, however, operates beneath the surface, in the nuts and bolts, "so contrived with springs and wheels," of our literary present. Goldschmidt was one of the great innovators of an early, vernacular Jewish fiction that gave voice to the textual and spiritual universe of the Jewish experience in Europe. Whether we read him or not, Goldschmidt created Jewish literature and made his mark deep into the nineteenth century. When the advent of modern Jewish literature occurs in the 1890s, it did not stand on its own shoulders, but on the shoulders of giants: Perl, Heine, Kompert, and Meïr Aaron Goldschmidt. Goldschmidt's vernacular poetics of midrash, biblical, and Talmudic allusion, and the abstruse figure of the rabbi, are iconoclastic gestures toward the modern and form the fabric of the Modernism that impends. It is true that we must change the way we read Goldschmidt in order to see a more lucid and specifically Jewish craft, one that speaks to and informs us of what follows. First, however, we must begin to read Goldschmidt again; it is after all the only just thing to do. Goldschmidt deserves to be rehabilitated into a modern, global literature so that we all may enjoy and learn from his particular style of telling stories, legs suspended and running quite amok.

Notes

◆

Bibliography

◆

Index

◆ ◆ ◆

Notes

Prologue

1. The authoritative text on Goldschmidt's life is the author's own set of memoirs, *Livs Erindringer og Resultater* (Life's Memories and Results, hereafter cited in text as *LER*), which originally appeared in installments beginning in October 1876 and was completed in February 1877. *LER* is the main source of our knowledge of Goldschmidt's life. However, *LER* is a complicated narrative, autofictive in nature, bound between memory and story, and shifting midway from a biographical to a linguistic perspective. The critical edition is Meïr Goldschmidt, *Livs Erindringer og Resultater*, ed. Morton Borup, 2 vols. (Copenhagen: Rosenkilde og Bagger, 1965). The standard and most thorough biography of Goldschmidt is Hans Kyrre, *M. Goldschmidt*, 2 vols. (Copenhagen: H. Hagerup Forlag, 1919). A more recent biography is Mogens Brøndsted, *Meïr Goldschmidt* (Copenhagen: Gyldendals Uglebøger, 1965). For a briefer biography in Danish, but one particularly rich in information about Goldschmidt's travels, see Morton Borup, *Meir Goldschmidts breve til hans familie* (Copenhagen: Rosenkilde og Bagger, 1964), 1:9–108. In English, the only book-length survey of Goldschmidt's life and work is Kenneth H. Ober, *Meïr Goldschmidt* (Boston: Twayne, 1976). A brief biography can also be found in the entry on Goldschmidt in Isidore Singer's *Jewish Encyclopedia: A Descriptive Record of the History, Religion, Literature, and Customs of the Jewish People from the Earliest Times to the Present Day*, s.v. "Goldschmidt, Meïr Aaron." For a recent biographical sketch of Goldschmidt in English, see Johnny Kondrup, "Meïr Goldschmidt: The Cross-Eyed Hunchback," in *Kierkegaard and His Danish Contemporaries: Literature, Drama, and Aesthetics*, ed. Jon Stewart (Farnham, UK: Ashgate, 2009), 105–47. Ober also coedited an edition of Goldschmidt's journals: Kenneth H. Ober, Uffe Andreasen, and Merete K. Jørgensen, eds., *M. A. Goldschmidts Dagbøger*, 2 vols. (Copenhagen: Det Danske sprog- og litteraturselskab, 1987). There are also two collections of Goldschmidt's letters, both edited by Borup: Morten Borup, ed., *Breve fra og til Meir Goldschmidt*, 3 vols. (Copenhagen: Rosenkilde og Bagger, 1963); and Morten Borup, ed., *Meir Goldschmidts breve til hans familie*, 2 vols. (Copenhagen: Rosenkilde og Bagger, 1964).

2. See Johan Fjord Jensen et al., *Danske litteraturhistorie*, vol. 4, *Patriotismens tid 1746–1807* (Copenhagen: Gyldendal, 1983), 607–38; and Steffen Auring et al., *Danske litteraturhistorie*, vol. 5, *Borgerlig enhedskultur 1807–48* (Copenhagen: Gyldendal, 1984). This latter volume covers the social, political, and literary history of the Golden Age in a very detailed manner. For a concise literary history of the Golden Age, see P. M. Mitchell, *A History of Danish Literature* (Copenhagen: Gyldendal, 1957), 105–72.

3. Bruce H. Kirmmse, *Kierkegaard in Golden Age Denmark* (Bloomington: Indiana Univ. Press, 1990), 1.

4. For example, cf. Jonathan M. Hess, *Middlebrow Literature and the Making of German-Jewish Identity* (Stanford, CA: Stanford Univ. Press, 2010); Maurice Samuels, *Inventing the Israelite: Jewish Fiction in Nineteenth-Century France* (Stanford, CA: Stanford Univ. Press, 2009); and Jonathan Skolnik, *Jewish Pasts, German Fictions: History, Memory, and Minority Culture in Germany, 1824–1955* (Stanford, CA: Stanford Univ. Press, 2014). In these three texts, the only mention of Meïr Goldschmidt is in a footnote concerning Leopold Kompert: see Hess, *Middlebrow Literature*, 232n77.

5. Jonathan Hess, Maurice Samuels, and Nadia Valman, eds., *Nineteenth-Century Jewish Literature: A Reader* (Stanford, CA: Stanford Univ. Press, 2013), 5. No doubt the erroneous date is a typographic error but it still serves to illustrate my point as it demonstrates the fragility of Goldschmidt's work in contemporary Jewish Studies.

6. Meïr Goldschmidt [Adolph Meyer, pseud.], *En Jøde: Novelle af Adolph Meyer* (Copenhagen: published by the author, 1845, hereafter cited in text as *En Jøde*).

7. There are several brief references to Goldschmidt in a recent and important two-volume set that hint at a contextualization of his Jewish writings in terms of early Jewish literature and writers in German. Although it is promising to see Goldschmidt mentioned among those writers, it is always in tandem with Leopold Kompert. It is possible that if Kompert had never written about Goldschmidt, there would be even less discussion of him among German scholars of ghetto narratives. See Gabriele von Glasenapp and Hans Otto Horch, *Ghettoliteratur: eine Dokumentation zur deutsch-jüdischen Literaturgeschichte des 19. und frühen 20. Jahrhunderts*, 2 vols. in 3 bks. (Tubingen, Germany: Niemeyer, 2005). For the sections on Goldschmidt, see Glasenapp and Horch, *Ghettoliteratur* 1.1:152 and 340; 1.2:697, 704, 730, and 792. Since Glasenapp and Horch's work appeared, there appears to be some interest in Goldschmidt in German. See, for example, Florian Brandenburg, "'At Orientaleren skal tale som Orientaler . . . ' Zur Problematik von Form und Funktion 'Jüdishen Sprechens' in M. A. Goldschmidt's *En Jøde* (1845/52)," *EJSS* 44, no. 1 (2014): 103–26. Brandenburg is also working on an exciting project that deals with Goldschmidt's memoirs and the construction of modern Jewish-Danish identity.

8. Jan Schwarz, "'Serving Up His Grandmother in a Spicy Sauce': Conflicting Views on Jewish Literature in Nineteenth-Century Denmark," in *Speaking Jewish—Jewish Speak: Multilingualism in Western Ashkenazic Culture*, ed. Shlomo Berger et al. (Leuven, Belgium: Peeters, 2002–3), 201.

9. It should be noted that Goldschmidt's first novel, *En Jøde* (1845), debuted in English in 1852 in two separate translations. In 1856 the first German translation appeared. In the twentieth century both a Yiddish and a Russian translation appeared in 1919.

10. For a recent and very rich discussion of each of these writers and their Jewish fiction, see Skolnik, *Jewish Pasts*, 23–66.

11. Notable exceptions are Tine Bach, *Exodus: Om Den Hjemløse Erfaring i Jødisk Litteratur* (Hellerup, Denmark: Spring, 2004); Tine Bach, *Nu bor vi her: jødiske livshistorier fortalt af tolv kvinder* (Copenhagen: Tiderne Skrifter, 2012); and Lars Kruse-Blinkenberg, *Assimilationens (u)mulighed i M. Goldschmidts roman En Jøde: ein religionshistorisk skitse* (Copenhagen: C. A. Reitzel, 2000). See also Edan Dekel and Gantt Gurley, "How the Golem Came to Prague," *JQR* 103, no. 2 (2013): 241–58; Schwarz, "Conflicting Views"; and Lisa Rainwater van Suntum, "Creating Jewish Identity through Storytelling: The Tragedy of Jacob Bendixen," *Scandinavian Studies* 73, no. 3 (2001): 375–98.

12. See, for example, Elisabeth Oxfeldt, *Nordic Orientalism: Paris and the Cosmopolitan Imagination, 1800–1900* (Copenhagen: Tusculanum, 2005), 66; and Kondrup, "Meïr Goldschmidt," 106. The notions that Goldschmidt was somehow not Jewish because he was not Orthodox or that he was, in fact, anti-Semitic are part and parcel of the suppression that has clouded Goldschmidt's place in contemporary literary criticism.

13. See Peter Tudvad, *Stadier på Antisemitismens vej: Søren Kierkegaard og Jøderne* (Copenhagen: Rosinante, 2010), 36–51. For an interesting discussion in English of this book and its reception in Danish scholarship, see M. G. Piety, "Piety on Kierkegaard," Dec. 26, 2011, https://pietyonkierkegaard.com/.

14. The debate over whether to incorporate the duchies of Schleswig and Holstein into the Danish Kingdom intensified in the 1840s and 1850s. The relationship of the Elbe duchies to the German Federation was worrisome to a Denmark intent on consolidating its borders. After King Frederik VII died in November 1863, the historical claim to the duchies expired, and by February 1864 Denmark was invaded by Austrian and Prussian units.

15. Ober, *Meïr Goldschmidt*, 34.

16. *LER*, 1:310. All translations of Goldschmidt and other Danish writers are my own except when noted.

17. Meïr Goldschmidt, "Svar til Hr. Pastor Grundtvig," *Nord og Syd* (1849): 1:336.

18. Ibid., 1:333–45. Goldschmidt had already responded to Grundtvig's attacks but not in a feature article. The second volume of Goldschmidt's journal *Nord og Syd* (North and South) contains two columns that begin "Old Grundtvig . . ." dated March 16, 1848, and April 1, 1848. There he positions Grundtvig in the old order and asks the new political question, "Who is originally Danish?" See Meïr Goldschmidt, "Dagbog," *Nord og Syd* (1848): 2:111, 224. There is a third entry on Grundtvig and his journal *Danskeren* (The Danish) that is dated April 5, 1848: *Nord og Syd*, 2:231–32. The subjects of *Nord og Syd*'s journal section (Danish: *Dagbog*) during this time was varied but the Schleswig-Holstein question dominates many of the entries. Goldschmidt's radical stance on the matter is confirmed in a piece from the same volume, "Borgerforsamlingerne," in which he concludes, "Schleswig does not belong to Germany, nor is it unified in the idea of being incorporated into Denmark." Goldschmidt, "Borgerforsamlingerne," *Nord og Syd* (1848): 2:94. Contrary to much that has been written on Goldschmidt, there is a strong argument to be made that *Nord og Syd* was the real, radical organ of Goldschmidt's literary politics, not *Corsaren*.

19. Ober, *Meïr Goldschmidt*, 56.

20. Ibid.

21. Kyrre, *M. Goldschmidt*, 2:166.

22. Ibid.

23. For an alternative look at Goldschmidt's idea of nemesis, see Paul V. Rubow, *Goldschmidt og Nemesis* (Copenhagen: E. Munksgaard, 1968).

24. Given the date of Goldschmidt's work on this matter, it is useful to think of the context. Eighteen seventy-six was a vibrant year in European linguistics. Goldschmidt's notion of protolanguage should be seen in conversation with the development of proto-Germanic that is reignited in Karl Verner's 1876 essay (what is now called Verner's Law) and the beginning of what would become Neogrammarianism through the work of August Leskien. See respectively Karl Verner, "Eine Ausnahme der ersten lautverschiebung," *Zeitschrift für vergleichende Sprachforschung auf dem Gebiete der indogermanischen Sprachen* (1876): 97–130; and August Leskien, *Die Deklination im Slawisch-Litauischen und Germanischen* (Leipzig: Hirzel, 1876).

25. *LER*, 2:132.

26. See Gustav Albeck, Oluf Friis, and Peter P. Rohde, *Dansk litteraturhistorie*, vol. 2, *Fra Oehlenschläger til Kierkegaard* (ca. 1800–ca. 1870) (Copenhagen: Politikens Forlag, 1976), 686–92, where the subtitle reads, "*Goldschmidt dominerer Tressernes Prosa*" (Goldschmidt dominates the prose of the sixties). See also Lise Busk-Jensen et al., *Dansk litteraturhistorie*, vol. 6, *Dannelse, folkelighed, individualisme 1848–1901* (Copenhagen: Gyldendal, 1985), 154–55; and Sven H. Rossel, ed., *A History of Danish Literature* (Lincoln: Univ. of Nebraska Press, 1992), 254.

27. Kyrre, *M. Goldschmidt*, 2:167. The mark referred to is clearly the mark of Cain, and it is unfortunate that Kyrre's uses of the motif here is so easily uncritical.

28. The critic Georg Brandes is the most influential Danish literary scholar in history. He was, however, an atheist and had little empathy for religion or spirituality of any kind, including Judaism. His notion of modern Jewry demanded assimilation into the atmosphere of a contemporary national setting. He detested Goldschmidt's mysticism and spirituality, all the more because they were of Jewish origin. See Georg Brandes, "M. Goldschmidt," *Samlede Skrifter* (Copenhagen, 1899), 2:447–68. For a recent portrait of Brandes and specific Jewish themes in Danish, see Bach, *Exodus*, 177–213. For one in English, see the excellent monograph by Julie K. Allen, *Icons of Danish Modernity: Georg Brandes and Asta Nielsen* (Seattle: Univ. of Washington Press, 2012).

29. The term "Modern Breakthrough" was coined by Georg Brandes in his 1883 collection of essays *Det moderne Gennembruds Mænd* (The Men of the Modern Breakthrough) (Copenhagen: Gyldendal, 1883), although the philosophic ideas in that work had been present in Brandes's thinking since a series of lectures in 1871. In this work Brandes lists the writers who in the 1870s and 1880s had rebelliously attacked the Biedermeier culture of Danish Romanticism. Brandes called for a reorientation of Scandinavian culture and the rise of a realistic literature that demanded social change. As a movement the Modern Breakthrough and Brandes's writings had a vast effect on writers from Scandinavia to Europe to America. It is a fault of Brandes that Goldschmidt, even though he was the forerunner, was left out of this charged movement. For a brief historical account of the Modern Breakthrough, see Rossel, *History*, 261–68. For an in-depth literary and political discussion, see Leonardo Lisi, "Scandinavia," in *The Cambridge Companion to European Modernism*, ed. Pericles Lewis (Cambridge, UK: Cambridge Univ. Press, 2011), 191–203; and the important monograph Leonardo Lisi, *Marginal Modernity: The Aesthetics of Dependency from Kierkegaard to Joyce* (New York: Fordham Univ. Press, 2013).

30. Brandes, "M. Goldschmidt," 447.

31. Ibid., 466.

32. Ibid., 467.

33. Ibid., 453. Brandes uses the word *Mundart* (jargon) in referring to Goldschmidt's use of Jewish language. In his story "Maser," Goldschmidt calls this "Jargon, the mixture of German and Hebraic, which is known as *Mauscheln*." See Meïr Goldschmidt, *Noveller og andre fortællinger* (Copenhagen: Det danske sprog- og litteraturselskab, Borgen, 1994), 236. In "Avrohmche Nattergal" the term "Tydsk-Hebraisk" is also used as the mystical jargon of the rabbis. See Goldschmidt, *Noveller*, 126. In these two instances we get a glimpse into the pejorative nature of Brandes's claim, given that the German *Maschel* is equivalent to the English slur "kike" and thus *Mauscheln* would mean "to speak like a kike."

34. Schwarz, "Conflicting Views," 205.

35. Brandes, "M. Goldschmidt," 453.

36. Ober, *Meïr Goldschmidt*, 58–60.

37. Ibid., 58.

38. Mogens Brøndsted, *Goldschmidts Fortællekunst* (Copenhagen: Gyldendal, 1967).

39. See also Thomas Bredsdorff, "Efterskrift og Noter" to *Noveller og andre fortællinger*, by Meïr Goldschmidt (Copenhagen: Det danske sprog- og litteraturselskab, 1994), 301–2; Knut Wentzel, "Fremmed indflydelse på Goldschmidts forfatterskab" (PhD diss., Univ. of Copenhagen, 1966); Anja Nathan, "En kulturhistorisk efterprøvning af de jødiske skildringer i Goldschmidts fortællinger" (master's thesis, Univ. of Copenhagen, 1959); Rubow, *Goldschmidt*, 5; and Albeck et al., *Dansk litteraturhistorie*, 2:691–92. Tine Bach explores Goldschmidt's relationship to Brandes, Henri Nathansen (1868–1944), and Franz Kafka (1883–1924) by tracing the notion of homelessness in their respective writings. See Bach, *Exodus.*

40. Ober, *Meïr Goldschmidt*, 130.

41. See, respectively, Meïr Goldschmidt, *A Jew*, trans. Kenneth Ober (New York: Garland, 1990); and Ober, *Meïr Goldschmidt.*

42. Julius Salomon has written an article that deals specifically with Goldschmidt's treatment of Jewish themes, and Tine Bach has more recently contributed greatly to this area by reading the motif of homelessness in Goldschmidt as well as in Henri Nathansen, Georg Brandes, and Franz Kafka. See, respectively, Julius Salomon, "I anledning af Hundredaarsdagen for M. Goldschmidts Fødsel," *Tidsskrift for jødiske Historie og Litteratur* (1919–21): 11–35; Bach, *Exodus*; and Bach, "Jøder i dansk litteratur," *Alef. Tidsskrift for jødiske kultur* 12/13 (1995): 19–26.

43. Dan Miron, *From Continuity to Contiguity: Toward a New Jewish Literary Thinking* (Stanford, CA: Stanford Univ. Press, 2010), 306–7, 351, and 361–62.

44. Ibid., 307–8.

45. Hess et al., *Nineteenth-Century Jewish Literature*, 3.

46. Ibid., 6.

47. Hess, *Middlebrow Literature*, 28.

48. My discussion leaves out the enigmatic *Megalleh Temirim* (Revealer of secrets) published in Hebrew in 1819 by Joseph Perl. *Megalleh Temirim* is in actuality the first Jewish novel, although it was not written in a European vernacular. In 1838 Perl wrote a second epistolary work, *Bohen Zaddik*. Because his work was published in Hebrew and then translated into Yiddish, it is worth noting but beyond the scope of my project. See Ken Frieden, "Joseph Perl's Escape from Biblical Epigonism through Parody of Hasidic Writing," *AJS Review* 29 (2005): 265–82. For a recent discussion of the language of Perl's original work, see Jonathan Meir, "The Discovery and Publication of Joseph Perl's Yiddish Writings," *Zutot* 13 (2016): 55–69, but especially 67n41.

49. See Samuels, *Inventing the Israelite*, 42–50.

50. Hess, *Middlebrow Literature*, 120.

51. Skolnik, *Jewish Pasts*, 45–66; and Nitsa Ben-Ari, *Romanze mit der Vergangenheit. Der deutsch-jüdische historiche Roman des 19. Jahrhunderts und seine Bedeuntung für die Entstehung einer jüdischer Nationalliteratur* (Tubingen, Germany: Neimeyer, 2006), 17–34.

52. Hess, *Middlebrow Literature*, 124–26.

53. Michael Galchinsky, *The Origins of the Modern Jewish Woman Writer: Romance and Reform in Victorian English* (Detroit: Wayne State Univ. Press, 1996), 57–58.

54. Skolnik, *Jewish Pasts*, 7–21.

55. Ibid., 1.

56. *LER*, 2:105.

57. Hermann J. Weigand, "Heine's Return to God," *Modern Philology* 18, no. 6 (1920): 320.

58. *LER*, 2:105.

59. Ibid., 90. The Egyptian god Nun was the father of all the gods and was associated with the primordial waters. Goldschmidt reads him as "the waters of heaven," and interprets his name ('Num) as "the breath or spirit over the waters." Goldschmidt pays particular attention to several ideograms in the name, including the vessel (*'nu*) and the sail (*'nef*), which for him connect water and spirit. *LER*, 2:89–91.

60. Ibid., 2:101.

61. Sigmund Freud, *Moses and Monotheism*, trans. Katherine Jones (New York: Vintage Books, 1967), 21. Italics by the author.

62. Goldschmidt is a Levite name, a Jewish surname that shows lineage from Levi, the son of Jakob and Rachel. Moses was a descendant of Levi, as were Isaiah and Samuel. The Levites were temple servants and officers. See Exodus 28:11 *et seq*. In a note to volume 1 of *LER*, Goldschmidt writes that "not all Levites are named Goldschmidt, although Jews named Goldschmidt but who are not Levite are a rarity. Perhaps there is some connection between this and the temple vessels, between Levites and the art of goldsmithing." See *LER*, 1:231. This resonates with his reading of the vessel ideogram in the name of 'Num. For Goldschmidt, the Levite tradition was destined to both carry the vessel of spirit that was 'Num and by doing so be the site of a life of concatenating poetry and nemesis.

63. For a recent scholarly discussion of Freud's Moses as Egyptian, see Jeffrey S. Librett, *Orientalism and the Figure of the Jew* (New York: Fordham Univ. Press, 2015), 235–64. Goldschmidt too gestures to a disruption of "the religiocultural identities on which Judaeo-Christian typology is based. . . . Judaism ceases here to be even the site of the prefigurative invention of the monotheism" (Librett, *Orientalism*, 237). A major difference in their respective reading of the Egyptian is that

Freud was more interested in the historical figure of Amenhotep IV or Ikhnaton, and Goldschmidt was more interested in the primordial creator figure of 'Num. It is interesting, however, that both men signal a prefiguration of the Jewish religion through radical readings of the figure of Moses.

64. For an overview of the primary writings of this event translated in English, see Howard Vincent Hong and Edna Hatlestad Hong, eds., *The Corsair Affair and Articles Related to the Writings* (Princeton, NJ: Princeton Univ. Press, 1982). For an overview in Danish, see Elias Bredsdorff, *Corsaren, Goldschmidt og Kierkegaard* (Copenhagen: Corsarens Forlag, 1977).

65. Ramón Grosfoguel, "The Structure of Knowledge in Westernized Universities: Epistemic Racism/Sexism and the Four Genocides/Epistemicides of the Long 16th Century," *Human Architecture: Journal of the Sociology of Self-Knowledge* 11 (2013): 73–89.

66. Schwarz, "Conflicting Views," 208–9.

67. Ibid., 89.

68. This brief, introductory account follows the general trajectory of that found in Ober, *Meïr Goldschmidt*, and in a letter Goldschmidt wrote to Kristian Arentzen in May 1864 in which he outlined his biography. See Borup, *Breve fra og til Meir Goldschmidt*, 2:100–101.

69. He was the founding editor of the *Næstved Ugeblad eller Præstø Tidende*, which ran under his direction from October 3, 1837, to December 28, 1839. In January 1839, the paper merged with the *Callundborg Ugeblad* and became *Sjællandsposten eller Nestved- og Callundborg Ugeblad* before Goldschmidt sold it at the end of that same year. He would remain as the editor until April 7, 1840. See Ober, *Meïr Goldschmidt*, 21–22.

70. *Corsaren*, ed. M. A. Goldschmidt, nos. 1–327 (Copenhagen, 1840–46). See reprint, *Corsaren 1840–46*, ed. Uffe Andreasen, 7 vols. (Copenhagen: Det Danske Sprog- og Literaturselskab and C. A. Reitzel, 1977–81). Including extra numbers and inserts, Goldschmidt published 342 issues of *Corsaren*; cf. Uffe Andreasen, "Efterskrift," in Andreasen, *Corsaren 1840–46*, 7:53. See also E. Bredsdorff, *Corsaren*; Otto Borchesenius, *Fra Fyrrerne. Literære Skizzer*, vol. 2 (Copenhagen, 1880), 231–325; and Hong and Hong, *Corsair.*

71. *Nord og Syd: et Maanedskrift*, vols. 1–6 (Copenhagen, 1848–49); *Nord og Syd: et Ugeskrift*, vols. 1–6 (Copenhagen, 1849–51); *Nord og Syd*, vol. 7 (Copenhagen, 1851); *Nord og Syd: ny Række*, vols. 1–11 (Copenhagen, 1852–57); *Nord og Syd: et Ugeskrift*, vols. 1–4 (Copenhagen, 1856); *Nord og Syd: et Ugeskrift: ny Række*, vols. 1–4 (Copenhagen, 1857); *Nord og Syd: et Ugeskrift: ny Række*, vols. 1–3 (Copenhagen, 1858); *Nord og Syd: et Ugeskrift: ny Række*, vols. 1–2 (Copenhagen, 1859).

72. Goldschmidt's slang for prison on account of prisoners being fed only bread and water.

73. See Borup, *Breve fra og til Meir Goldschmidt*, 1:35–36. Note a pair of letters to P. L. Møller that Goldschmidt wrote from prison, the tone of which teeters between destituteness and the absurd. It is clear from these letters that Goldschmidt has progressed as a writer and as an activist.

74. Not only a fierce advocate for a new constitution and minority rights, Goldschmidt also influenced policy concerning publication laws and authors' rights. See Ober, *Meïr Goldschmidt*, 55. In Goldschmidt's editorships, we are able to recognize without doubt the mobilization and access of a modern liberal, free press.

75. Kondrup, "Meïr Goldschmidt," 105.

76. See Ober, *Meïr Goldschmidt*, 32. Ober seems ambivalent as to whether these relationships were sexual or not, but I am of the opinion that they were all consummated friendships.

77. Ibid., 25.

78. Hester is an intriguing figure in Goldschmidt's letters. Upon first meeting her in 1851 he described Hester to his family as "so educated, so enlightened and smart that I learn from her every moment." See Borup, *Meir Goldschmidts breve til hans familie*, 1:163. He respected her linguistic skills and Jewish education very much, which is fitting because Hester is best known for her 1866 English translation of the French traditional prayer book *Prières D'un Cœur Israélite*. For the role Benjamin and Hester Rothschild played in Goldschmidt's personal and literary life, see Kenneth Ober, "A Forgotten Translation and a Forgotten Translator: Meïr Goldschmidt's 'Maser' in French," *Scandinavica* 32 (1993): 25–45.

79. Kenneth H. Ober, *Die Ghettogeschichte: Entstehung und Entwicklung einer Gattung* (Gottingen, Germany: Wallstein, 2001), 30–35. For a discussion of Goldschmidt's literary relation to Frankl, see Dekel and Gurley, "How the Golem Came to Prague." Auerbach wrote Goldschmidt a touching letter in April 1873 that speaks to his relevance to the German Jewish writers of the period. See Borup, *Breve fra og til Meir Goldschmidt*, 2:177.

80. Immanuel Deutsch, "The Talmud," *Quarterly Review for October, 1867*, 123, no. 246 (1867): 417–64; and [Meïr Goldschmidt], *Talmud* (Copenhagen, 1868). The assertion of Goldschmidt's authorship is also supported by Brøndsted, *Meïr Goldschmidt*, 166.

81. Note a letter to Goldschmidt from Professor of Philosophy Marcus Jacob Monrad (1816–1897), who is confused as to whether to address Goldschmidt as "Professor" or "Rabbi Meïr." The letter is particularly playful because Monrad writes "Rabbi Meïr" in Hebrew. See Borup, *Breve fra og til Meir Goldschmidt*, 2:193.

82. Robert Alter, *Canon and Creativity: Modern Writing and the Authority of Scripture* (New Haven: Yale Univ. Press, 2000), 8. I discuss this notion of Alter's reading of modernity in the beginning of chapter 1, and it is the crux of my argument that Goldschmidt was a protomodernist. Alter's book is also discussed in Schwarz's

article, and there Schwarz points to the earliness of the tension between emancipation and tradition, between the universal and the Jewish attested in Goldschmidt's writings. See Schwarz, "Conflicting Views," 200–206.

83. Superfamily linguistics is the notion that families of languages, such as Indo-European, Altaic, Sino-Tibetan, and Afro-Semitic, are genetically related and that this relation is identifiable and classifiable. See, for example, Aharon Dolgopolsky and Colin Renfrew, *The Nostratic Macrofamily and Linguistic Palaeontology* (Oxford, UK: McDonald Institute for Archaeological Research, 1998); and Allan R. Bomhard and John C. Kerns, *The Nostratic Macrofamily: A Study in Distant Linguistic Relationship* (Berlin: Mouton de Gruyter, 1994).

84. For an example of Ragnhild's work, see [Ragnhild Goldschmidt], "En Kvindehistorie" (Copenhagen, 1875). This story can be found in Pil Dahlerup's seminal work *Det moderne gennembruds kvinder* (Copenhagen: Gyldendal, 1983), 176–83. It sheds light on the writer's influence in women's literature at the turn of the century. For a historical treatment of the elegy in Danish letters, see Sune Auken, *Eftermæle: en studie i den danske dødedigtning fra Anders Arrebo til Søren Ulrik Thomsen* (Copenhagen: Museum Tusculanums forlag, 1998).

85. The entire poem is cited in Borup, *Breve fra og til Meir Goldschmidt*, 1:14–15.

86. Borup, *Breve fra og til Meir Goldschmidt*, 1:15.

87. For an understanding of Goldschmidt's mobility in nineteenth-century Europe, see Kenneth Ober, "Meïr Goldschmidt and the Main Currents in 19th-century Judaism," *Nordisk Judaistik* 22, no. 1 (2001): 7–45.

88. Meïr Goldschmidt, "Ghetto," *Fortællinger og Skilldringer*, vol. 2 (Copenhagen, 1865), 129–74. Apparently, there was an earlier English version of this story that has never materialized. In a letter to Hester on May 3, 1864, first published by Ober, Goldschmidt reported, "'The Ghetto' is progressing in English—but, pray, do not say a word of my poor English!" See Ober, "Meïr Goldschmidt's 'Maser,'" 37.

89. Goldschmidt, "Ghetto," 2:154–55.

90. Skolnik, *Jewish Pasts*, 1–8.

91. Goldschmidt, "Ghetto," 2:137.

92. For an interesting twentieth-century debate on this very topic, see the numerous books and articles surrounding the "Black Athena" debate. Martin Bernal, *Black Athena: The Afroasiatic Roots of Classical Civilization*, vol. 1 (New Brunswick, NJ: Rutgers Univ. Press, 1987); Martin Bernal, *Black Athena: Afro-Asiatic Roots of Classical Civilization: The Archaeological and Documentary Evidence*, vol. 2 (New Brunswick, NJ: Rutgers Univ. Press, 1991); Martin Bernal, *Black Athena: Afro-Asiatic Roots of Classical Civilization: The Linguistic Evidence*, vol. 3 (New Brunswick, NJ: Rutgers Univ. Press, 2006); and Martin Bernal, *Black Athena Writes Back: Martin Bernal Responds to His Critics* (Durham, NC: Duke Univ. Press, 2001).

93. Schwarz, "Conflicting Views," 197.

1. "I Am of the Tribe of Levi"

1. For a history of the period covered in this book, see Jens Vibæk, *Reform og Fallit 1784–1830*, vol. 10 of *Danmarks Historie*, ed. John Danstrup and Hal Koch (Copenhagen: Politikens Forlag, 1964); and Roar Skovmand, *Folkestyrets Fødsel 1830–1870*, vol. 11 of *Danmarks Historie*, ed. John Danstrup and Hal Koch (Copenhagen: Politikens Forlag, 1964). For a concise history of Denmark in English, see John Danstrup, *A History of Denmark* (Copenhagen: Wivel, 1947).

2. For a strong overview of the political and social complexities of the Danish Golden Age, see Kirmmse, *Kierkegaard in Golden Age Denmark*, 1–258.

3. Ibid., 23–24.

4. The Golden Horns date back to the early fifth century. They were found in 1639 and 1734 around Gallehus in what is modern southwest Jutland. One of the horns contained a Runic inscription. Both Horns were stolen and melted down in 1802. For a description of the artifacts themselves, see Ottar Grønvik, "Runeinnskriften på gullhornet fra Gallehus," *Maal og Minne* 1 (1999): 1–18.

5. For a discussion on Oehlenschläger's poem "The Golden Horns" and Danish Romanticism, see John L. Greenway, *The Golden Horns: Mythic Imagination and the Nordic Past* (Athens: Univ. of Georgia Press, 1977).

6. See Vibæk, *Reform og Fallit*, 488.

7. For a short history of the "awakening movement" (*Vækkelsesbevægelse*) and the agrarian reforms of the early nineteenth century, see Kirmmse, *Kierkegaard in Golden Age Denmark*, 40–44; and H. Arnold Barton, *Essays on Scandinavian History* (Carbondale: Southern Illinois Univ. Press, 2009), 190–93.

8. Kirmmse, *Kierkegaard in Golden Age Denmark*, 11.

9. Ibid., 25–26.

10. Bent Blüdnikow, "Jews in Denmark: A Historical Review," in *Danish Jewish Art*, ed. Mirjam Gelfer-Jørgensen, trans. W. Glyn Jones (Copenhagen: Rhodos, 1999), 27. This is an excellent and concise history of Danish Jewry in English. For a more general discussion, see Ib Nathan Bamberger, *The Viking Jews: A History of the Jews of Denmark* (New York: Shengold, 1983), and *Kings and Citizens: The History of the Jews in Denmark, 1622–1983*, 2 vols. (New York: Jewish Museum, 1983). For a history in Danish, see Harald Jørgensen, ed., *Indenfor murene. Jødisk liv i Danmark 1684–1984* (Copenhagen: Reitzel, 1984). For a recent and elaborate view of Danish Jewry in English, see Martin Schwarz Lausten, *Jews and Christians in Denmark: From the Middle Ages* to Recent Times, ca. 1100–1948, trans. Margaret Ryan Hellman (Leiden: Brill, 2015). For Danish Jewry in the early nineteenth century, see Julius Salomon and Josef Fischer, eds., *Mindeskrift i Anledning af Hundredaardagen for Anordningen af 29. Marts 1814: en Fremstilling af Jødiske Rets-og Livsforhold i Udland og Indland navnlig i Tiden omkring Aar 1800: med en Samling Arkivalia*

(Copenhagen: Danmarks Loge, 1914); and Julius Margolinsky and Poul Meyer, eds., *Ved 150 Aars-Dagen for Anordningen Af 29. Marts 1814. Nogle Bidrag til Dansk-Jødisk Historie* (Copenhagen: Det Mosaiske Troessamfund, 1964).

11. For a history of the Jews in Denmark in the seventeenth and eighteenth centuries, see Bent Blüdnikow and Harald Jørgensen, "Den lange vandring til borgerlig ligestilling i 1814," in *Indenfor murene. Jødisk liv i Danmark 1684–1984*, ed. Harald Jørgensen (Copenhagen: Reitzel, 1984), 13–71.

12. Blüdnikow, "Jews in Denmark," 27–28. See also Per Katz, *Jøderne i Danmark i det 17. århundrede* (Copenhagen: Reitzel, 1981).

13. Blüdnikow, "Jews in Denmark," 30.

14. Ibid., 30. This figure is based on M. L. Nathanson's 1860 book *Historisk Fremstilling af Jødernes Forhold og Stilling i Danmark, navnlig i Kjøbenhavn.*

15. Blüdnikow and Jørgensen, "Den lange vandring," 72.

16. The chief of police, Claus Rasch, proposed the plan for a ghetto in Copenhagen but found no favor with the king's administrators. See Blüdnikow, "Jews in Denmark," 29. See also K. Carøe, "Da Claus Rash vilde lave Ghetto paa Kristianshavn," *Tidsskrift for jødiske historie og Literature* (1919–21): 103–16; and Carøe, "Ghetto i Teglgaardsstræde. Et forslag fra 1730," *Tidsskrift for jødiske historie og Literature* (1919–21): 182–84.

17. Blüdnikow and Jørgensen, "Den lange vandring," 72.

18. Jonathan Marks, "Rousseau's Use of the Jewish Example," *Review of Politics* 72 (2010): 463–81. For the possibility of another early piece of Jewish fiction and an important view on Danish imperialism in the West Indies, see Henrik Hertz's novel *Die Friefarvede* (Copenhagen, 1836).

19. H. Arnold Barton, *Scandinavia in the Revolutionary Era, 1760–1815* (Minneapolis: Univ. of Minnesota Press, 1986), 215.

20. For a comprehensive view of Struensee's political activity in Denmark, see Balthasar Münter, *Bekehrungsgeschichte des vormaligen Grafen und Königlichen Dänischen Geheimen Cabinetsministers Johann Friederich Struensee* (Copenhagen: Rothens Erben und Prost, 1772).

21. John Christian Laursen, "Spinoza in Denmark and the Fall of Struensee, 1770–1772," *Journal of the History of Ideas* 61 (2000): 190.

22. Ibid., 190–91.

23. Andrew Buckser, *After the Rescue: Jewish Identity and Community in Contemporary Denmark* (New York: Palgrave, 2003), 27. All translations from this text are Buckser's.

24. Blüdnikow, "Jews in Denmark," 34. See also Gordon Norrie, "Jødernes kamp for adgangen til Universitetet og den medicinske Docktorgrad i Danmark," in *Bibliotek for Lager* (Copenhagen: Fr. Bagges Bogtrykkeri, 1982), 3:117–38.

25. Blüdnikow, "Jews in Denmark," 32.

26. Ibid., 33.

27. Schwarz, "Conflicting Views," 200.

28. *LER*, 1:100–102.

29. For a short biographical study of Nathanson, see Gottlieg Siesby, *Mendel Levin Nathanson. En biografisk Skizze* (Copenhagen, 1845).

30. Blüdnikow, "Jews in Denmark," 34.

31. Buckser, *After the Rescue*, 28–29. See also *Jewish Encyclopedia*, s.v. "Nathanson, Mendel Levin." For a study of the Karoline-Skolen, see Carol Gold, *Educating Middle Class Daughters: Private Girls Schools in Copenhagen, 1790–1820* (Copenhagen: Royal Library, 1996), 149–50.

32. Blüdnikow, "Jews in Denmark," 34.

33. Buckser, *After the Rescue*, 30–31. See also *Jewish Encyclopedia*, "Nathanson, Mendel Levin."

34. *Jewish Encyclopedia*, "Nathanson, Mendel Levin."

35. Buckser, *After the Rescue*, 29.

36. This debate is known as the Wig War and is a very colorful story of the dismantling of rabbinic authority. See Blüdnikow and Jørgensen, "Den lange vandring," 75–77.

37. See Carol Herselle Krinsky, *Synagogues of Europe: Architecture, History, Meaning* (New York: Dover Publications, 1996), 403–4. The Great Synagogue of Copenhagen is a magnificent building, designed by the architect G. F. Hetsch (1788–1864). When Hetsch was commissioned in 1829, we see the collapse of the archaic authority of the rabbinical elite and the rise of a congregation interested in contemporary aesthetics and culture. The significance of the synagogue to my project lies in its Near Eastern aesthetic. It is one of the few synagogues from this period that has Egyptian details and style. For example, there are Egyptian details in the Thorvaldson Museum designed by M. G. B. Bindesbøll, who consulted with synagogue officials in 1829. The synagogue in Munich, completed in 1826, also displays Egyptian details and may have been a model. This aesthetic is a reproduction of the façade of Solomon's Temple. See Krinsky, *Synagogues*, 9. See also Hetsch's "Egyptian Fantasy" and other drawings in Joachim Meyer, "The Danish Synagogues," in *Danish Jewish Art*, ed. Mirjam Gelfer-Jørgensen, trans. W. Glyn Jones (Copenhagen: Rhodos, 1999), 179–205, but especially 189.

38. Buckser, *After the Rescue*, 31.

39. Ibid.

40. Martin Schwarz Lausten, *Frie jøder? Forholdet mellem kristne og jøder i Danmark fra Frihedsbrevet 1814 til Grundlove 1849* (Copenhagen: ANIS, 2005), 10–16.

41. Kondrup, "Meïr Goldschmidt," 106.

42. Buckser, *After the Rescue*, 33.

43. For a privately published study of the literary pogrom, including a good historical bibliography by Bent W. Dahlstrøm, see Lief Ludwig Albertsen, *Engelen mi: En bog om den danske jødefejde* (Copenhagen, 1984). Also see Nathanson, *Historisk Fremstilling*; *Steen Steensen Blicher*, "*Bør Jøderne taales i Staaten*" (Århus, 1813); and Jacob Davidsen, *Jødefeiden i Danmark. Den litterære jødefeide i 1813. Opløbet med Jøderne i Kjøbenhavn og flere Provinsbyer i Danmark 1819–20, Dags-Telegrafens Feuilleton* (Copenhagen, 1869).

44. The text in question is Friedrich Buchholz, *Moses und Jesus, oder über das intellektuelle und moralische Verhältniß der Juden und Christen eine historisch-politische Abhandlung* (Berlin, 1803). See Steen Steensen Blicher, "Bedømmelse over Skrivtet Moses og Jesus" (Århus, 1813); and Jonathon Hess, *Germans, Jews and the Claims of Modernity* (New Haven: Yale Univ. Press, 2002), 198–200.

45. Blüdnikow, "Jews in Denmark," 35–36.

46. Buckser, *After the Rescue*, 34.

47. Albertsen, *Engelen mi*, 9.

48. Børsen is a seventeenth-century building in central Copenhagen built by Christian IV. It was at the center of Danish finances in the nineteenth century and housed the stock exchange until 1974. It seems to have also served as a public platform for a Denmark in deep financial woes.

49. J. Davidsen, *Fra det gamle Kongens Kjøbenhavn* (Copenhagen, 1880–81), 2:258; and Blüdnikow and Jørgensen, "Den lange vandring," 90.

50. "There exist a variety of speculative explanations of the meaning of 'Hep-Hep' ranging from '*Hierosolyma est perdita*' (Jerusalem is lost) to a call for goats with which the Jews were associated because of their beards. See Rohrbacher, *Gewalt*, 94ff." Sonja Weinberg, *Pogroms and Riots: German Press Responses to Anti-Jewish Violence in Germany* (Frankfurt am Main: Peter Lang, 2010), 264n74.

51. Blüdnikow, "Jews in Denmark," 36.

52. Ibid.

53. The Danish pogrom (Danish *jødefejden*) was an offshoot of the Hep-Hep riots that spread out of Germany in the early fall of 1819. In September 1819, riots against the Jews broke out in Copenhagen, Odense, and other towns across the provinces. Historians have been in consensus that this period of "physical Jewish conflict" ended in January 1820, but a 2010 article by Jens Rasmussen argues that the pogrom lasted until the end of 1820. His argument is based on evidence from recently discovered documents belonging to A. S. Ørsted, the deputy of the Danish Chancellery. See Jens Rasmussen, "Jødefejden og de besægtede uroligheder, 1819–20, 'Indledning til den store Scene?'" in *Kirkehistoriske Samling 2010*, ed. Carsten Bach-Nielsen et al. (Copenhagen: Univ. of Copenhagen, 2010), 131–65.

54. *LER*, 1:48–49.

55. The other children were Moritz (1822–1888), Esther (1824–1898), Julius (1827–1917), and Ragnhild (1828–1890).

56. *LER*, 1:41. The Hebrew word מאיר (*meïr*) means "giving light." Interesting to note the following: In an 1844 letter to Orla Lehman, Goldschmidt signed the name "Meyer." In 1849, in a letter to his mother and sister, Ragnhild, he signed his name Meyer. In two letters to Ragnhild in 1855, he also signs his name Meyer. Kyrre also points out that his mother in her letters still referred to him as "Meyer." His usual signature was "M. Goldschmidt." Around 1876, however, he begins to use the signature "Meïr." This is probably owing to his translation of Deutsch's *Talmud*. When Goldschmidt's first novel, *En Jøde*, came out in 1845, he used the pseudonym "Adolph Meyer." Goldschmidt also had two paternal ancestors named Meyer. His grandfather who died in 1798 and his great-great-grandfather who was the king's head jeweler. This Meyer, as Goldschmidt mentions, immigrated to Copenhagen in 1684.

57. *LER*, 1:41.

58. A notable exception is Bach, *Exodus*.

59. Harold Bloom, foreword to *Zakhor: Jewish History and Jewish Memory*, by Yosef Hayim Yerushalmi (Seattle: Univ. of Washington Press, 1996), xiii–xiv.

60. *LER*, 1:41–42. The London Banker Abraham Goldschmidt (c. 1756–1810) actually committed suicide in 1810. See J. Smith Homans, ed., *The Bankers' Magazine and Statistical Register* (New York: W. Crosby and H. P. Nicholes, 1857–58), 12:911.

61. Yerushalmi, *Zakhor: Jewish History and Jewish Memory*, 93.

62. Skolnik, *Jewish Pasts*, 57.

63. Ibid., 56. This use of the narrative mode as a prophetic way of creating meaning suggests a relationship with Leopold Zunz and his 1818 essay "Etwas über die rabbinische Literatur," which was deeply concerned with engendering a contemplation of rabbinic tradition in modern Judaism. See Leopold Zunz, *Gesammelte Schriften* (Berlin, 1875), 1:1–31. Zunz called for a holistic and inclusive view of Jewish history, one that would posit a historical consciousness with the possibility of revitalization. See Skolnik, *Jewish Pasts*, 61.

64. *LER*, 1:42.

65. Harold Bloom, foreword to *Zakhor*, xii–xiv.

66. Ibid., xiv.

67. *LER*, 1:42.

68. Ibid.

69. Ibid. Goldschmidt is poking fun here at the English side of the family as clearly the baroness meant Roskilde. But it allows Goldschmidt to create a story around folk etymology. The Rothschilds to whom Goldschmidt was related had no known tie to the dynasty from Frankfurt. See Ober, "Meïr Goldschmidt's 'Maser,'" 26.

70. *LER*, 1:42.

71. Ibid. The following quotations are from *LER*, 1:42–43.

72. See *LER*, 1:42 and 52. The phrase also finds its way into Goldschmidt's novels and is a powerful attribute for certain Jewish characters. See, for example, Goldschmidt, *En Jøde*, 35–36. The very concept also seems to underlie many of the images in Ploug's elegy discussed above.

73. *LER*, 1:46.

74. For a history of Goldschmidt's paternal family and his great-great-grandfather Meyer, see Josef Fisher, "Meïr Goldschmidts Stamfædre," *Tidsskrift for jødiske historie og Literatur* (1919–21): 35–52. Goldschmidt also had a grandfather named Meyer. This part of the Goldschmidt line immigrated to Denmark from Hamburg via Hannover in the early eighteenth century when the merchant Aaron Bendix moved to Copenhagen in 1817. Aaron married his cousin Regine Fürst, who was the granddaughter of Goldschmidt's great-great-grandfather Meyer, who had come to Denmark in 1684. Their son was named Meyer and this was Goldschmidt's grandfather. Through Aaron and Regine, Goldschmidt was related to Levin Goldschmidt of Hannover who in 1688 built the city's first synagogue. See Brøndsted, *Meïr Goldschmidt*, 26–27.

75. Blüdnikow, "Jews in Denmark," 27.

76. *LER*, 1:41–95.

77. Ibid., 1:50.

78. Ibid.

79. Ibid. *Guldregn* or *Guldranke* is the Laburnum tree.

80. Ibid., 1:47. The parenthetical page numbers in the following paragraphs are from the same source.

81. Ober, *Meïr Goldschmidt*, 19.

82. This uncle, one of his father's older brothers, and his lumberyard provide the setting for one of Goldschmidt's more popular short story cycles, "Erindringer fra min Onkels Hus" (Memories from My Uncle's House), which appeared in his 1846 *Fortællinger. Af Adolph Meyer.* His classic story "Min Onkels Tømmerplads" (My Uncle's Lumberyard) was one of the stories in the cycle. It first appeared in P. L. Møller's *Gæa 1846*, published in December 1845.

83. The Schoubo School was a prestigious school in Copenhagen. N. F. S. Grundtvig was a teacher there from 1808 to 1811. See Frederick Nygård, *Det Schouboeske Institut og N.F.S. Grundtvigs Lærervirksomhed sammesteds* (Copenhagen, 1880).

84. *LER*, 1:91.

85. Ibid. Following Ober's lead, I choose to translate the Danish word *jødesmaus* as "kike." Danish *smaus* or *smovs* meant "Ashkenazi Jew" as compared to Danish *portugisiske Jøder*, *spanske Jøder*, or *Portugiser-Jude*, which meant "Sephardic

Jew." The word is perhaps of Dutch origin. Sometimes spelled *jødeschmaus*. See Goldschmidt, *A Jew*, 12.

86. *LER*, 1:92.

87. Ibid.

88. Ibid., 101.

89. Ibid., 102.

90. Brøndsted, *Meïr Goldschmidt*, 40–41.

91. Kyrre, *M. Goldschmidt*, 1:17–19.

92. Det von Westenske Institut, a gymnasium in the center of the old city, was open from 1799 to 1893. It was named for the educator and translator Johan Christopher von Westen (1769–1841). See V. A Borgen, *Efterretninger om det von Westenske Institut fra dets Stiftelse til nærværende Tid: Indbydelsesskrift til den offentlige Examen i Juli 1840* (Copenhagen, 1840).

93. Kyrre, *M. Goldschmidt*, 1:33–34.

94. *LER*, 1:109.

95. Ibid., 107. The *tefillin* (prayers) or *phylacteries* (to protect) are small leather boxes with straps worn during morning prayers. In the boxes are inscriptions from the Torah. They are wrapped around the arms and hands as a remembrance of the exodus. The Greek name points to the apotropaic nature of the tefillin. The *arba' kanfot* (lit. four corners) is a rectangular piece of cloth with an opening in the middle that passes over the head so that equal parts fall in front and in back of the wearer. It is worn under the upper garments throughout the day.

96. Ibid. Kyrre sees this search as a crisis that delivers the young Goldschmidt from the religious into his greatest victory, the aesthetic. Goldschmidt, however, he is keen to point out, had not yet read Empedocles and traced the nature of his thinking to Spinoza instead. See Kyrre, *M. Goldschmidt*, 1:36.

97. Vor Frue Kirke (The Church of Our Lady) is the national cathedral of Denmark and sits next to the university. The building was redesigned after the English destroyed it in the 1807 bombardment. The Great Danish sculptor Bertel Thorvaldsen decorated the interior of the church with among others his *Christus*, completed in 1821.

98. There is a reproduction of the report in Kyrre, *M. Goldschmidt*, 1:43.

99. Ober, *Meïr Goldschmidt*, 20.

100. *LER*, 1:123.

101. Ibid.

102. A. P. Liunge (1798–1879) was a writer and, more important, the founder of *Kjøbenhavnsposten*, one of the more prominent periodicals in Golden Age Denmark. See Ole Stender-Petersen, *Kjøbenhavnsposten, organ for "det extreme Democrati" 1827–1848* (Odense: Odense Univ. Press, 1978).

103. *LER*, 1:126. "Swill" for Danish *Pøjt*; "plonk" in British slang. Perhaps a corruption of Fr. *vin blanc*. This word is still used in current wine industry–speak. Ober translated it as "garbage," which loses some of the force of Liunge's aesthetical insult. Liunge's criticism of Goldschmidt is that his storytelling craft is poor. It is, in fact, like poorly made wine, which also "should not be offered to decent-minded folk."

104. Ibid., 127.

105. Ibid.

106. Kyrre gives a very good, concise survey of the kinds of writing that appeared in the weekly under Goldschmidt's ownership, including the first story, "Freedom and Women (Original Short Story)," and the last piece, "The Young Denmark." See Kyrre, *M. Goldschmidt*, 1:49–59. The latter was influenced by his reading of Henrik Hertz's novel *Stemninger og Tilstand* (Copenhagen, 1839), a work that articulated the polemical crossing of swords between the old and new Danish literary aesthetic. Goldschmidt reviewed the piece in *Sjællandsposten* no. 58. Kyrre, *M. Goldschmidt*, 1:55–59. Goldschmidt reports that his story "Slaget ved Marengo" (the battle of Marengo) was also composed during this time. See *LER*, 1:132–37.

107. Ibid., 1:128.

108. Liunge had retired as editor of the journal in April 1837.

109. *LER*, 1:128.

110. Ober, *Meïr Goldschmidt*, 21–22.

111. Ibid.

112. Ibid.

113. *LER*, 1:131.

114. Kyrre, *M. Goldschmidt*, 1:55–59.

115. I point out that this political dimension of Goldschmidt's journalistic style was present from the beginning of his time at *Sjællandsposten*. There are a few lines in a rare poem Goldschmidt had written for issue number 9 that illustrate my point. The poem was called "The Old and the New Denmark" and the lines draw attention to Goldschmidt's contemporary fascination with the past: "Freedom is the country on Denmark's isles / The old Denmark will never die." The poem is quoted from Kyrre, *M. Goldschmidt*, 1:50. Goldschmidt saw not only an idealism in early Romanticism but an aesthetic of contestableness, a spirit of resistance and revolution. For Goldschmidt it was the modern Danish press where the fight could be fiercest. He had understood that the press was the strongest defense the government had against the feeling "that the stream could wash over its head." Ibid., 1:58. The heroes of old were not content; they went "With broad, strong swords swinging at the belt / With strong armor and with bright shields." Ibid., 1:50. Not only would he attack conservatives, but also liberals whose ideas did not manifest action.

116. *LER*, 1:131.

117. Ibid., 1:140. As I have suggested in a recent article, Goldschmidt was one of the great Danish readers of Byron. See David Gantt Gurley, "The Concept of Byrony," *Konturen* 7 (2015): 14–41. The name Corsair also had Byronic resonances for Goldschmidt although he does not mention this in *LER*. The motto of the journal was an anthem of sorts for Goldschmidt's political agenda during this period, and spoke to his fascination with the Byronic. There is no doubt that given Goldschmidt's deep appreciation for Byron and the popularity of Byron in Denmark, the name Corsair had Byronic undertones for Goldschmidt.

118. The other two men initially involved were Ludvig Bisserup and Arboe Mahler.

119. *LER*, 1:142.

120. Ibid., 1:140. For a list of the fake editors, see Andreasen, "Efterskrift," 7:45–46. The strawmen that Goldschmidt set up behind the publication of *The Corsair* formed a masquerade of sorts, a game, and I read it as parallel to Kierkegaard's use of pseudonyms.

121. *LER*, 1:144.

122. Ibid.

123. Ibid., 1:155. The quote is from Gen. 16:12. The words do not appear in the journal until no. 10 in an article that bears that exact title. Starting with no. 27, the French phrase "Ça ira, ça ira" appears on the cover. The phrase translates to something like "We will win, we will win!" This is both the name of a popular song during the French Revolution and the name for a series of late-eighteenth-century French gunboats and vessels.

124. Ober, *Meïr Goldschmidt*, 23.

125. Kondrup, "Meïr Goldschmidt," 109.

126. Goldschmidt reports (in *LER*, 1:152) that the initial figure was three thousand; however, in *Corsaren*, Nov. 21, 1845, no. 270, 14, he claims his subscription number is nearing five thousand. Regardless, it was a very large subscription list for this time in the Danish press. See Borup's commentary in *LER*, 1:299.

127. Ober, *Meïr Goldschmidt*, 23. The criticism of *The Corsair* as a lowbrow publication is misleading and unfairly stated. Perhaps Goldschmidt's tactics were guerilla-like, and it is undeniable that he targeted individuals and did not hesitate to hit below the belt, but the publication was not anarchistic or even off base; it did, however, become more and more sensational as political change became inevitable. Goldschmidt was adamant about a new constitution, and the journal fed the desire of the Danish public, who were too uncompromising about a new constitution. Ober is correct in insinuating that Goldschmidt's place in Danish literary history is too easily reduced by the labels that were levied against him during *The Corsair* period. They were given to him by the political establishment who had nothing to gain from equality, the redistribution of Danish institutions, and a redefining of Danish values.

Goldschmidt was on the right side of change even if his tactics seem to our modern sensibility unappetizing. We must also keep in mind that Goldschmidt was not calling for a literal revolution with blood in the streets. The battlefield was the court of public opinion; the press was his armament.

128. Kondrup, "Meïr Goldschmidt," 108.

129. Andreasen, "Efterskrift," 7:31.

130. Ibid., 7:53.

131. Ibid., 7:45–46.

132. Ober, *Meïr Goldschmidt*, 25–26.

133. Along with Carl Ploug, Møller is the most important figure in Goldschmidt's life. Goldschmidt can be quite lyrical in his memories of these men, but he also projects that he had a somewhat cantankerous relationship with both men. For a summary of Goldschmidt's association with Møller, see Borup, *Breve fra og til Meir Goldschmidt*, 1:9–12. For an account of Møller's literary activity, see Niels Egebak, *Mellem Heiberg og Brandes. P. L. Møllers plads i dansk kritiks historie* (Aarhus: Modtrykt, 1992); and Hans Hertel, "P. L. Møller and Romanticism in Danish Literature," in *Kierkegaard and His Contemporaries: The Culture of Golden Age Denmark*, ed. Jon Stewart (Berlin: Walter de Gruyter, 2003), 356–72.

134. *LER*, 1:166.

135. Ibid., 1:169.

136. Ibid., 1:170.

137. Rossel, *A History*, 251.

138. Ibid.

139. *LER*, 1:188–89.

140. John L. Campbell, John A. Hall, and Ove Kaj Pedersen, eds., *National Identity and the Varieties of Capitalism: The Danish Experience* (Montreal: McGill-Queen's Univ. Press, 2006), 135. Goldschmidt's notion of a federation of states was modeled on the Swiss constitution adopted in 1848 after the *Sonderbundskrieg*. In a brilliant article entitled "Føderativstaten," Goldschmidt compares the Danish Crown's policy of incorporation as a "Sisyphus-stone" and calls for a "moral interior" to Danish "point of view" in order to ensure the health and freedom of the federation. See Meïr Goldschmidt, "Føderativstaten," *Nord og Syd* 2 (1849): 1, 7, and 9.

141. See Meïr Goldschmidt, "Planen til Slesvigs Deling," *Nord og Syd* 1 (1849): 1–8; and Goldschmidt, "Føderativstaten," 1–14. This moral objection to the monarchy and its dominion is a consistent belief Goldschmidt held throughout his political career, and his call for a federation of states positioned him at the extreme edge of Danish politics.

142. *LER*, 1:186.

143. Ibid., 1:187.

144. Ibid., 1:188.

145. Ober, *Meïr Goldschmidt*, 25.

146. All in all, Goldschmidt made thirty-five trips abroad to eight different countries and was fluent in Italian and French as well. For a list, see Borup, *Meïr Goldschmidts breve til hans familie*, 1:109.

147. See Hannah Machnin, "The Grisette as a Female Bohemian" (PhD diss., Brown Univ., 2000).

148. *LER*, 1:192.

149. Borup, *Breve fra og til Meir Goldschmidt*, 1:37.

150. For an insightful look at Goldschmidt's views on women, see Stefanie von Schnurbein, "Kampf um Subjektivität—Nation, Religion und Geschlecht in zwei dänischen Romanen um 1850," in *Bildung und Anderes. Alterität in Bildungsdiskursen in den skandinavischen Literaturen, ed. Christiane Barz and Wolfgang Behschnitt* (Wurzburg, Germany: Ergon, 2007), 111–29.

151. *LER*, 1:192.

152. Ibid., 1:193.

153. Goldschmidt mentions that he attended the festival in May 1844. He must have conflated the first meeting in May 1843 with the one at which he spoke on July 4, 1844. It is very likely he was at several of the meetings that took place between 1843 and 1859. See *LER*, 1:310.

154. The speech appeared in *Dansk Folkeblad* Tillæg til Nr. 15–16 (1844), and is reprinted in full in *LER*, 1:310.

155. Oxfeldt suggests that the figure was as high as ten thousand. See Oxfeldt, *Nordic Orientalism*, 62.

156. *LER*, 1:194.

157. Ibid., 1:196.

158. Ibid.

159. *A Jew* came out in a second edition in 1852, the same year it was translated into English. In 1856 it was translated into German and in 1919 the book appeared in both Yiddish and Russian. There was a new Danish edition in 1968, and Ober's English translation appeared in 1990.

2. Midrash and Metaphor

1. David Stern, *Midrash and Theory: Ancient Jewish Exegesis and Contemporary Literary Studies* (Evanston, IL: Northwestern Univ. Press, 1996), 3. For a general orientation of midrash proper in critical studies, see also Jacob Neusner, *Midrash in Context: Exegesis in Formative Judaism* (Philadelphia: Fortress Press, 1983); Jacob Neusner, *What Is Midrash?* (Philadelphia: Fortress Press, 1994); Michael Fishbane, *Biblical Interpretation in Ancient Israel* (Oxford, UK: Clarendon Press, 1985); and Michael Fishbane, *The Exegetical Imagination: On Jewish Thought and Theology* (Cambridge, MA: Harvard Univ. Press, 1998). To be clear, I do not mean to

use the term *midrash* in its technical sense in the taxonomy of rabbinic literature. Jacob Neusner has pointed to three types of "Midrash-processes" that are found in late antiquity: paraphrase, prophecy, and parable. These processes are particular to religious communities; modern writers such as Goldschmidt have adopted these processes, especially the latter, into the way they create fiction. See Neusner, *What Is Midrash?*, 1–3; and Irving Jacobs, *The Midrashic Process: Tradition and Interpretation in Rabbinic Judaism* (Cambridge, UK: Cambridge Univ. Press, 1995). David Biale uses the term "secular kabbalists" to refer to the writers who were influenced by medieval Jewish mysticism and whose writings were haunted by the divine shadow in existence. See David Biale, *Not in the Heavens: The Tradition of Jewish Secular Thought* (Princeton, NJ: Princeton Univ. Press, 2011), 15.

2. Some important examples are the *Bereshit Rabbah*, a commentary on the book of Genesis redacted sometime in the fifth century; the *Pirke de Rabbi Eliezer*, a midrashic narrative of the more important events of the Pentateuch probably dating from the ninth century; and the *Mekhilta de Rabbi Ishmael*, an exegetical and homiletic reading of the book of Exodus dating from the fifth or sixth century.

3. The system of Hebrew transliteration I have adopted is the one suggested by the *Encyclopaedia Judaica*, vol. 1 (Jerusalem: Keter Publishing, 1972), 90.

4. There are various studies of midrash in contemporary literary critical studies today that move past the bounds of midrash proper, that is, the concept as applied to secular discourses and text. For my purposes here, they are either interested only in non-Jewish writers, focusing on a narrow set of authors with Daniel Defoe (1660–1731), Henry Fielding (1707–1754), Laurence Sterne (1713–1768), George Eliot (1819–1880), and Thomas Hardy (1840–1928) being mentioned most, or they are interested only in twentieth-century Hebrew authors. Goldschmidt must be taken as extraordinary here; for he is an author, not a rabbi (just like Melville and Sterne), and he is a Jew (exactly unlike Melville and Sterne). For discussion of midrash and the middle-class Protestant novel, see Harold Fisch, *New Stories for Old: Biblical Patterns in the Novel* (New York: St. Martin's Press, 1998); Robert Alter, *Fielding and the Nature of the Novel* (Cambridge, MA: Harvard Univ. Press, 1968); Hebert N. Schneidau, *Sacred Discontent: The Bible and Western Tradition* (Berkeley: Univ. of California Press, 1976). For discussion of midrash and modern Jewish writers, see David C. Jacobson, *Modern Midrash: The Retelling of Traditional Jewish Narratives by Twentieth-Century Hebrew Writers* (Albany: State Univ. of New York Press, 1987); and Alter, *Canon and Creativity.*

5. *Pirke Avot* [The Sayings of the Fathers] 5.22, quoted in Alter, *Canon and Creativity*, 76.

6. The locus classicus for the term "parabiblical" and the first occurrence of the term is found in H. L. Ginsberg, Review of Joseph A. Fitzmyer's *The Genesis Apocryphon of Qumran Cave 1: A Commentary, Theological Studies* 28 (1967): 574: "I . . .

approve of his rejection of such labels as 'targum' and 'midrash.' . . . To the question of literary genre, I should like to contribute a proposal for a term to cover works, like *GA*, Pseudo-Philo, and the *Book of Jubilees*, which paraphrase and/or supplement the canonical Scriptures: parabiblical literature. The motivation of such literature—like that of midrash—may be more doctrinal, as in the case of the *Book of Jubilees*, or more artistic, as in at least the preserved parts of *GA*, but it differs from midrashic literature by not directly quoting and (with more or less arbitrariness) interpreting canonical Scripture."

7. Alter, *Canon and Creativity*, 63–96. Also see Robert Alter, *Necessary Angels: Tradition and Modernity in Kafka, Benjamin, and Scholem*; aphorism 10 in Gershom Scholem, "Zehn unhistorische Sätze über Kabbala," in *Geist und Werk aus der Werkstatt unserer Autoren: zum 75. Geburtstag von Dr. Daniel Brody* (Zurich: Rhein-Verlag, 1958), 215; Karl Erich Grözinger, *Kafka und die Kabbala: Das Jüdische im Werk und Denken von Franz Kafka* (Frankfurt: Eichborn, 1992); Walter Benjamin, "Franz Kafka: On the Tenth Anniversary of His Death," in *Illuminations*, ed. Hannah Arendt, trans. Harry Zohn (New York: Schocken Books, 1969), 111–40; Martin Buber, *Two Types of Faith*, trans. Norman P. Goldhawk (New York: Harper, 1961); Heinz Politzer, *Franz Kafka: Parable and Paradox* (Ithaca, NY: Cornell Univ. Press, 1962); Fish, *New Stories*, 81–99; and Jill Robbins, "Kafka's Parables," in *Midrash and Literature*, ed. Geoffrey H. Hartman and Sanford Budick (New Haven: Yale Univ. Press, 1986), 265–84. Northrop Frye also saw in *The Trial* "a kind of *midrash* on the book of Job." See Northrop Frye, *The Great Code: The Bible and Literature* (New York: Harcourt Brace Jovanovich, 1982), 95.

8. Alter, *Canon and Creativity*, 8. See also Chana Kronfeld, "Theories of Allusion and Imagist Intertextuality: When Iconoclasts Evoke the Bible," *On the Margins of Modernism: Decentering Literary Dynamics* (Berkeley: Univ. of California Press, 1996), 114–40.

9. Ibid., 66–67.

10. Ibid., 68–69.

11. There is an inherent confusion for (American) English speakers in discussing the poetical nature of a Danish writer and the Danish usage of descriptors such as *poetisk* (poetical) and *digter* (poet), both of which are ascribed to Goldschmidt. (It would be very odd to speak of the poetical writings of John Steinbeck.) For example, one of Goldschmidt's collected works is entitled *Poetiske skrifter* (1896–98) (Poetical Writings) and a fairly recent anthology is called *Meïr Goldschmidt. Digteren og journalisten: En mosaik af tekster* (1974) (Meïr Goldschmidt. Poet and Journalist: A Mosaic of Texts). An English reader might be surprised to note that both the 1896–98 collection and the 1974 anthology contain not one single poem and likewise offer no analysis of the poetical nature of the writings therein. Rather, these terms are common descriptors for Danish and Scandinavian writers, regardless of form or

medium, who compose at the highest level of artistic ability. Although there is no direct English equivalent, the terms "artistic" and "artist" would suffice.

12. Meïr Goldschmidt, *Hjemløs* (Copenhagen: Det danske sprog- og litteraturselskab, 1999), 1:9.

13. All references to the Hebrew Bible are taken from Robert Alter, trans., *The Five Books of Moses: A Translation with Commentary* (New York: W. W. Norton, 2004).

14. See Annemette Hoppe, "Syndefaldet: et hovedmotiv i dansk og europæisk digtning" (master's thesis, Univ. of Copenhagen, 1976).

15. Alter describes this process of readership exquisitely: "There is something almost uncanny about Kafka as a reader of the Bible. Midrash, Talmud, and Kabbalah were certainly not part of his formative cultural experience, and even his late acquaintance with them was rather marginal. Yet the way he read the bible reflected a spiritual kinship with these classical vehicles of Jewish exegesis. Such kinship, which may look like a kind of spontaneous intellectual atavism, defies any simple causal explanation. My guess is that it has a good deal to do with Kafka's habitual concentration on the idea of revelation, and on the notion of the Law that in the Jewish view is the principal consequence of revelation for human praxis. That is to say, if you begin with the working assumption that this particular text, which as a canonical text is compact, enigmatic, and charged with a sense of authority, may be divinely revealed, you then proceed to exert terrific interpretive pressure on the text in order to unlock the truth, or multiple truths, it holds for you." Alter, *Canon and Creativity*, 64–65.

16. The fact that scholars are unaware of Goldschmidt and blind to this Jewish phenomenon in the nineteenth century is exemplified in the emphatic opening words and title of David Jacobson's *Modern Midrash*: "Since the turn of the twentieth century, Hebrew writers have persisted in publishing retold versions of traditional Jewish narratives." Jacobson, *Modern Midrash*, 1.

17. For a historical understanding of Luther's influence on the way the Bible is read, see Jean-François Gilmont, "Protestant Reformations and Reading," in *A History of Reading in the West*, ed. Guglielmo Cavallo and Roger Chartier, trans. Lydia G. Cochrane (Amherst: Univ. of Massachusetts Press, 1999), 213–37. Also pertinent to this matter is Dominique Julia, "Reading and the Counter-Reformation," in *History of Reading*, 238–68.

18. *Dannelse* is difficult to translate into English; it means "formation," both "education" and "culture," and in the plural a broader sense of "good manners" or "good breeding." The broad parameters of the genre *dannelsesroman* are emphasized in the alternative generic term in Danish, *udviklingsroman* or developmental novel.

19. For this project I have chosen to work with the novel's seventh edition, which was published by Gyldendal in 1927. Meïr Aaron Goldschmidt, *En Jøde* (Copenhagen: Gyldendal, 1927).

20. The German bildungsroman is founded in the *Goethezeit* with Christoph Martin Wieland's *Die Geschichte des Agathon* (1767) and Goethe's *Wilhelm Meisters Lehrjahre* (1795–96), usually considered the foundational texts. For this point see François Jost, "Variations on a Species: The *Bildungsroman*," *Symposium*, 1983:125–46. For the genre itself, see Jürgen Jacobs and Markus Krause, *Der Deutsche Bildungsroman: Gattungsgeschichte vom 18. bis zum 20. Jahrhundert* (Munich: C. H. Beck, 1989); and Michael Minden, *The German Bildungsroman: Incest and Inheritance* (Cambridge, UK: Cambridge Univ. Press, 1997). For Goldschmidt's role in the nineteenth century, see Søren Frank Martin Jakobsen, "Dannelsesromanen i en overgangstid—1850'erne" (master's thesis, Univ. of Copenhagen, 1983). Other classic Danish examples of this genre are B. S. Ingemann's *Landsbybørnene* (Copenhagen, 1852); H. C. Andersen's *Improvisatoren* (Copenhagen, 1835); and Hans Egede Schack's *Phantasterne* (Copenhagen, 1857), as well as Goldschmidt's third novel, *Arvingen* (Copenhagen, 1865).

21. Note that the title in Danish is suspiciously arbitrary; one could just as well read it as "One Jew." The multiplicity here is important to note as the reader also is ambivalent as to how Jacob functions on a metonymic level. In short, is Jacob representative of his tribe by means of his indefiniteness or dissimilar owing to his uniqueness?

22. Minden, *German Bildungsroman*, 246.

23. Brøndsted, *Meïr Goldschmidt*, 69.

24. *En Jøde*, 10. Page numbers from the Danish edition of this novel are provided in parentheses in the text.

25. Ober suggests this conflict between the Byronic hero that European readers were accustomed to and the "first Jewish hero with Byronic overtones." See Ober, "Afterword," 324. The conflict here is imminent. And when Jacob begins to translate the *Gemara* into Danish instead of German, the tension between the Jewish and the Romantic is annunciated more clearly than the usual suspect of the Jewish versus the Christian. This is not to say that the novel, as a whole, is not a critique of assimilation; however, I believe there is an even deeper connotation to Jacob's failure in the world around him, namely that the Romantic mode (personified by his mother and his friend, doctor, and confidant Martin Levy) is disrupted by the notion of a Jewish education.

26. Here I draw attention to the work of Tamar Yacobi on the dynamics between the reader and the narrator. Goldschmidt not only constructs peculiarities in his characters that seem to create meaning out of "discordant elements," but he baits these constructions in order to lure readers into certain positions of mediation. Thus the (un)reliable narrator is also a construction of the text itself and can have substantial influence over the way the reader then constructs his portrait of the narrator. See Tamar Yacobi, "Package Deals in Fictional Narrative: The Case of the Narrator's

(Un)Reliability," *Narrative* 9 (2001): 223–29; Tamar Yacobi, "Narrative Structure and Fictional Mediation," *Poetics Today* 8 (1987): 335–72; and Tamar Yacobi, "Fictional Reliability as a Communicative Problem," *Poetics Today* 2 (1981): 113–26.

27. Georg Brandes, "M. Goldschmidt," 453.

28. Ober, *Ghettogeschichte*, 31–32.

29. The use of footnotes in the novel, which clearly addresses the "you" of the readership, was not Goldschmidt's invention. In Danish, H. C. Andersen used them in *Improvisatoren* (Copenhagen, 1835), although they seem to have no political role in terms of Bildung. In German, Josef Seligman Kohn used them in his 1834 picaresque novel *Der Jüdische Gil Blas.* It also should be noted that Wolf Pascheles glossed Hebrew words in German in his 1847 anthology and used footnotes to explain Jewish religion and historical figures; see Wolf Pascheles, *Gallerie der Sipurim: eine Sammlung jüdischer Sagen, Märchen, und Geschichten, als ein Beitrag zur Völkerkunde* (Prague, 1847). What is unique to Goldschmidt is how the glosses perform a subversive role to undermine the readability of the text proper. There is some similarity with Kohn's work, particularly in terms of how Jewish folktale is represented, but again Kohn's work does not seem to have the same politics of identity as Goldschmidt's.

30. Goldschmidt's note, *En Jøde*, 46: "Hanukkah: The festival of lights that is celebrated yearly for eight days in remembrance of that Lamp with Oil that after the Temple's destruction was found in the ruins by Antiochus Epiphanes, and who tended the Lamp for eight days, although there was oil but for one."

31. Goldschmidt's note, *En Jøde*, 55: "Rosh-hashana: The year's head, New Year's."

32. The politics of the glosses are in the way in which they control the translation of Jewishness in the novel. Even in their assumption to be there at all, the reader hands over control of meaning and is forced to read them as pure source. But what is exactly manipulated away from the reader if such a dynamic occurs? If the reader has neither the ability nor the authority to consider the verisimilitude of the glosses, what does he forfeit in proxy when Goldschmidt's narrator omits information or fast-forwards through it? Surely Jewishness cannot be thoroughly exposed in a mere 210 glosses. Behind all this pseudo-myth and cheap anthropology there must be another agenda than thick description. For example, compare Goldschmidt's two-page gloss on *Gelilo*, *En Jøde*, 55, to the rather meager one for Yom Kippur, *En Jøde*, 25: "Yom Kippur: The great festival of atonement."

33. See Yacobi, "Package Deals."

34. I might add here that Goldschmidt in high ironic fashion has a great affinity for Jewish stereotypes. His character Simon Levi in his later works is an excellent example of this ironic layering of the stereotype in Goldschmidt. Lars Kruse-Blinkenberg, *Jøden Simon Levi i M. Goldschmidts roman* Ravnen: *en religionhistorisk studie*

(Copenhagen: C. A. Reitzel, 1998). This play with the Jewish stereotype, which is also play on the self, is found all over *The Corsair* and in the piece discussed above, "Ghetto," as well as in the autobiographic allusions in *A Jew*.

35. Note the Avestan word *pairidaēza* (enclosure, park, [that which is] surrounded by walls).

36. Rambám is the acronym for Rabbi Mosche Ben Maimon (1135–1204), also known as Maimonides. I discuss the figure of the rabbi in Goldschmidt in depth in chapter 3.

37. There is also the delightful possibility that Goldschmidt here is alluding to the strange tale that Jesus was the son of a panther. This is already represented in the Talmud through the appellation Yeshu'a ben Panthera but the classical source is Origen *Contra Celsum*, 1.21. The ben Panthera legend was also reported by St. Epiphanius in his *Heresies* lxxvii, 7. The tale is likely based on a metathesis of the /r/ and the /n/ in the Greek word for virgin, *parthéna*, into the word for panther, *pánthera*.

38. Whereas Abraham had the ethical dexterity to notice the ram and thereby avoid transgression, Goldschmidt's Jacob is rather "straightjacketed" for prophecy.

39. The eating of pork and many other foods and combinations of food is forbidden in Orthodox Judaism.

40. Kaddish is a prayer said by mourners, and sons are required to say Kaddish over their fathers' graves. For such a large moment in the text, the gloss here appears quite thin. Goldschmidt's note, p. 12: *Kadisch: Sjælemesse* (elegy). One can also see the same rhetorical maneuver as described above in Goldschmidt's gloss for Yom Kippur. Although the Kaddish is central to the story line, the redacted gloss suggests the very opposite when compared to more detailed entries.

41. Goldschmidt's note, *En Jøde*, 293: *Schikse: Kristenpige* (Christian girl).

42. The scene here should be carefully read beside the suspicious scene in Goldschmidt's memoirs in which the Danish teacher steps away from the grammar curriculum and instead reads aloud from Oehlenschläger's *St. Hansaftenspil*. Here the poetics of young Goldschmidt is born, not exactly from hearing the "music" of Oehlenschläger but from the resulting process of imitating him. See *LER*, 1:112. This is the only mention in the memoirs that clearly describes Oehlenschläger as playing a role in the development of Goldschmidt's poetic sensibility. The six following mentions are in passing or concern P. L. Møller and the Corsair Affair. See *LER*, 1:154, 179, 183, 215, and 217–18.

43. *En Jøde*, 113.

44. At his bar mitzvah, Jacob reads a passage from the Torah "which chance had chosen for him." The narrator tells us that many Jews believe that the verse that one reads on this day is a prophecy for one's entire life. The failed relation with Thora Fangel is announced in this passage years before Jacob meets the girl, superseding the songs of his mother that bore her name. The passage selected, Genesis 3:14–15,

also echoes the Hebrew epigraph of the novel: "The Lord God said to the serpent, 'Cursed are you above all cattle, and above all wild animals; upon your belly you shall go, and dust you shall eat all the days of your life. I will put enmity between you and the woman, and between your seed and her seed; he shall bruise your head, and you shall bruise his heel.'" See *En Jøde*, 76.

45. Coleridge used the term in his 1817 *Biographical Sketches* to refer to a passage in Milton's *Paradise Lost*:

On the imagination, or esemplastic power.

O Adam! one Almighty is, from whom
All things proceed, and up to him return
If not depraved from good: created all
Such to perfection, one first nature all
Indued with various forms, various degrees.

In Samuel Taylor Coleridge, *Biographia Literaria or Biographical Sketches of My Literary Life and Opinions*, vol. 1, ch. 13 (London, 1817). The Milton is from *Paradise Lost*, book 5, lines 468–72.

46. Adam Oehlenschläger, *Aladdin eller den Forunderlige Lampe: et Lystspil, Poetiske Skrifter* (Copenhagen, 1805), 2:61–379. The play is one of the early hallmarks of Danish Romanticism. For a discussion of *Aladdin* focusing on Goldschmidt's call for a national cultural identity and the politics of reading in an imagined community, see Oxfeldt, *Nordic Orientalism*, 58–64.

47. See the second volume of *LER* for the fullest explanation and treatment of Goldschmidt's language project, including his insistence on an Afro-Semitic category based on Ancient Egyptian hieroglyphs.

48. Oddly Jacob's absorption into the tone and timbre of the office clerk's reading is not because of his aesthetic instinct, but rather predicated by his need to please others, in this case the older and more established company present. It is his innate compulsion to comply with proper etiquette: he is a guest in a prominent man's house, which causes him to find beauty in the lyric. These pretenses are contrasted with the students in the back who are mocking the office clerk's approach to Oehlenschläger. To Jacob this setting is more easily absorbed because the accent must be profoundly familiar. In these settings (here and at the ball in chapter 4) where there are wealthy urban Jews, we must never forget that Jacob is somewhat of a "country mouse."

49. Oxfeldt, *Nordic Orientalism*, 228.

50. T. S. Eliot, *Four Quartets* (New York: Harcourt and Brace, 1943), 27. For a discussion of lyric and the nature of performance, see Greg Nagy, *Poetry and Performance: Homer and Beyond* (Cambridge, UK: Cambridge Univ. Press, 1996).

51. Oehlenschläger, *Aladdin*, 136.

52. Also known as Ahusueras or Ahasverus, the Jewish man who drove Christ away from his shop door when he stopped to rest on his way to the Crucifixion and was subsequently cursed to roam the earth until the Advent. For a detailed history of the figure in literature, see George K. Andersen, *The Legend of the Wandering Jew* (Providence, RI: Brown Univ. Press, 1965). An entire monograph could be written on Goldschmidt's use of the figure, especially in his English tale "The Wandering Jew," which appeared in 1862 and is discussed below in closing. Many a Jewish character in Goldschmidt's repertoire displays these strong undertones of Jerusalem's Shoemaker.

53. The one time Jacob speaks more than two words of Hebrew is the false elegy he speaks upon learning of his father's death, "*Jisgadal vejiskadisch schemei rabo.*" Goldschmidt's note, *En Jøde*, 231: "*Velsignet være den Højestes Navn*" (Blessed be the name of the Highest).

54. I have chosen, following Ober, to translate Danish *Aand* in the passage as "intellect" rather than "spirit" as Oxfeldt has done. See Oxfeldt. *Nordic Orientalism*, 65. Taken out of context the quote certainly seems to make the most of the enmity of Jacob's Jewish ethnicity and his desire for a Christian providence. However, as his speech to Levy continues, it is evident that this could not be the case.

55. Goldschmidt's powerfully ethnic remark that opens the story of his life. *LER*, 1:41. The twelve tribes of Israel are historically descended from the twelve sons of Jacob. Levi was one of the sons of Jacob and Leah. The Tribe of Levi was not included in the tribes who were given allotments of land during the conquest of Canaan. Instead, Moses singled out the Tribe of Levi to serve as Israel's priests. Instead of a land allotment, Joshua, who led the conquest of Canaan, gave forty-eight towns, scattered throughout the land of Israel, to the Tribe of Levi. The descendants of Levi played a role in guarding and serving the tabernacle (Numbers 3:21–37). More important for Goldschmidt, Moses and his brother, Aaron, were descendants of Levi, and this helps him establish narrative authenticity. Also, Levites are the only Jewish lineage traced from both the mother and the father. That is, one's mother must be Jewish and one's father must be a Levite. With this statement, Goldschmidt is figuring himself as pure Jewish, clean from Scandinavian blood.

56. For example, "*talte mærkelig rent Dansk*" (spoke remarkably clean Danish). See *LER*, 1:42.

57. For a discussion of the mark in literature and the arts, see Ruth Mellinkoff, *The Mark of Cain* (Berkeley: Univ. of California Press, 1981).

58. Thora's last name is Fangel, and this too adds to the metaphorical constraint of Jacob's environment. The Danish verb *fange* means "to catch, capture, trap" and its substantive means "prisoner, captive." Note also *fangarm* (tentacle) and *fangelejr* (prison camp).

59. Minden, *German Bildungsroman*, 246.

60. Given Goldschmidt's name games in the novel, there is a tendency to read a false harmony in Martin Levy. On the one hand, "Martin" is a not just any Protestant name, it is Luther's name. And on the other hand, "Levy" should be equivalent to Goldschmidt's perception of Jewish "nobility." Despite the thinness of Martin's character, we are given insight into his genealogy, and his Levite heritage is suspect among the elders. He is mistaken for the son of Leibche Levy when his real father's name is Leib Schächter. See *En Jøde*, 292–93.

61. H. C. Andersen, *Improvisatoren* (Copenhagen: Gyldendal, 2015), 102.

62. The phrase is Alter's; see Alter, *Canon and Creativity*, 66–67.

63. Cf. Genesis 9:26–27. For a historical study of the curse of Ham, see David B. Goldenberg, *The Curse of Ham: Race and Slavery in Early Judaism, Christianity, and Islam* (Princeton, NJ: Princeton Univ. Press, 2003).

64. Here, I suspect reverberations of the Moses narrative at play.

65. Genesis 9:25.

66. The November Uprising or Cadet Revolution (1830–31) took place when a group of military cadets at a Warsaw military academy gained support among the Polish people and attempted to overthrow their Russian occupiers. The fight for the Polish homeland is seen as more heroic because it is about overthrowing the occupier, whereas the Algerian campaign is about occupation. Although Jacob's only companion in Algeria, Josinski, jokes about the possibility of Jacob's defection, it is precisely the move he should make: "'Gaa blot ikke over til Beduinerne!' sagde Josinski spøgende. 'O, nej! Vi Europæere ere lænkede til hinanden ved Civilisationen. . . . '" ("'Don't go over to the Bedouins!' said Josinkski jokingly. 'O, no! We Europeans are linked to one another by civilization'"). See *En Jøde*, 238.

67. Goldschmidt's note: *Schikse: Kristenpige* (Christian girl).

68. The lines were at Keats's request carved on his tombstone. See Brendan Corcoran, "Keats's Death: Towards a Posthumous Poetics," *Studies in Romanticism* 4, no. 2 (2009): 332.

69. See Bruce H. Kirmmse, "Kierkegaard, Jews, and Judaism," *Kierkegaardiana* 17 (1994): 83–97.

3. The World of Allusion

1. Recent investigations into intertextuality, influence, and intent have produced myriad descriptions and definitions of allusion. For a theoretical overview, see Robert Alter, *The Pleasures of Reading in an Ideological Age* (New York: Simon and Schuster, 1989); Ziva Ben-Porat, "The Poetics of Literary Allusion," *PTL: A Journal for Descriptive Poetics and Theory of Literature* 1 (1976): 105–28; John Hollander, *The Figure of Echo: A Mode of Allusion in Milton and After* (Berkeley: Univ. of California Press, 1981); Carmela Perri, "On Alluding," *Poetics* 7 (1978): 289–307;

Leonard Diepeveen, *Changing Voices: The Modern Quoting Poem* (Ann Arbor: Univ. of Michigan Press, 1993); and Stephen Greenblatt, *Renaissance Self-Fashioning: From More to Shakespeare* (Chicago: Univ. of Chicago Press, 1980).

2. William Wordsworth, *The Prelude or Growth of a Poet's Mind*, ed. Ernest De Selincourt (Oxford, UK: Oxford Univ. Press, 1926), 357–72.

3. See J. Paul Hunter, "Steinbeck's Wine of Affirmation in *The Grapes of Wrath*," in *Essays in Modern American Literature*, ed. Richard E. Langord (DeLand, FL: Stetson Univ. Press, 1963), 76–89; Tamara Rombold, "Biblical Inversion in *The Grapes of Wrath*," *College Literature* 14, no. 2 (1987): 146–66; Louis Owens, *The Grapes of Wrath: Trouble in the Promised Land* (Boston: Twayne, 1989).

4. Genesis 10.

5. John Steinbeck, *The Grapes of Wrath* (New York: Penguin Books, 2006), 113.

6. In fact there is no scene in Genesis in which Noah looks up at the ark after it had been loaded, so it cannot be pure allusion. Rather, this is heretical midrash. We are perhaps being invited by the narrator to imagine a point at which Noah looked up at the great ark fully packed with all the earth's winged and crawling things and felt something profound, but what that something was is left in the background of the narrative. This brings us to an important conclusion: that midrash must always allude to an antecedent text in order to explain or fill in the gaps. Because of this the two are related; however, allusion works independently of any narrative gaps in the original text.

7. The curse of Ham that I discussed above is also active in the text, as Noah Joad was delivered by his father when the midwife was not there, and the boy was thus deformed. This curse follows the family west.

8. Steinbeck, *Grapes of Wrath*, 113.

9. See Bloom, *Anxiety*.

10. Quoted in Mary Carruthers, *The Book of Memory: A Study of Memory in Medieval Culture* (Cambridge, UK: Cambridge Univ. Press, 1990), 219.

11. Robert Alter, *The World of Biblical Literature* (New York: BasicBooks, 1992), 110.

12. Alter, *Pleasures of Reading*, 113.

13. Ibid., 132.

14. Alter, *Biblical Literature*, 108.

15. By ecology, I mean to mark an entire system of metonymic narration, of the Hebrew Bible, midrash, parabiblical narrative, and Jewish folklore. This is a living and breathing system for Goldschmidt, at once organic and hermeneutic. Ecology marks the root and canopy of this system.

16. *LER*, 1:69.

17. There is, of course, no one-to-one correspondence between any of Goldschmidt's characters and the biblical figure of Moses. I am not suggesting that

Goldschmidt's "play" with this figure is even obvious. Rather, his construction of the Mosaic figure is complicated by its embedded and often covert construction. In addition, a character like Jacob Bendixen from *A Jew* is skeletally designed around the Mosaic pattern, but is fleshed out with other biblical characters, specifically the figures of Jacob and David.

18. Goldschmidt's powerfully ethnic remark that opens the story of his life. *LER*, 1:41. The phrase occurs elsewhere, used to characterize a Jewish figure with deep Talmudic understanding; cf. *The Raven*, in *Udvalgte skrifter: romaner, fortaellinger og skildringer* (Copenhagen: Gyldendal, 1916), 4:158.

19. The life of Moses unfolds across four books of the Hebrew Bible. The problem for modern readers is that it is heavily interlaced with legal and cultic procedures, from a time when epic and the code of law were not entirely separate categories of narrative. The narrative is meant to be continuous and interlaced, and reveals a highly stylized notion of the art of compilation even though it evolved over time as a project of generational aesthetics. For an understanding of the narrative continuity and compositional unity of the Torah, see Alter, *Five Books of Moses*, ix–xlviii.

20. Goldschmidt even contends that his Jewish heritage should be put on a par with the royal house of Denmark, although the Christians would not give recognition to his bloodline. This is something that separates Goldschmidt from his Jewish contemporaries in Copenhagen. Whereas Henrik Hertz, Johanna Louise Heiberg, and Georg Brandes relished their assimilation, Goldschmidt, despite what some scholars have insinuated, never turned from his Jewishness. (It is not discussed here, but Henrik Hertz's 1836 novel *De Frifarvede* might also prove fruitful as parabiblical narrative.) Because his ethnicity is mitigated by this genetic trope of blood, Jewishness to Goldschmidt is fixed and immutable. This tone of the passage is reminiscent of what Henri Nathansen wrote about Brandes: "But a stranger he was—of course, he was a stranger. In nature and spirit, in thought and feeling, in instinct and temperament. His blood and nerves were Jewish." Henri Nathansen, *Georg Brandes—Et Portræt* (Copenhagen: Nyt Nordisk Forlag, 1929), 99.

21. *LER*, 1:69–70.

22. Nemesis in Greek mythology was the goddess of divine retribution. It is a term originally used by Aristotle to describe a system of retributive (or "poetic") justice, "righteous indignation," in which characters receive punishments appropriate to their particular actions and dispositions. For Goldschmidt it is a way to explain balancing the relationships between experiences during the course of a life and is a type of retrospective mysticism.

23. Alter, *Canon and Creativity*, 170.

24. Deut. 34:6.

25. Bredsdorff, "Efterskrift," 289 and 293.

26. "Mendel Hertz" was one of the last short stories Goldschmidt wrote; it appeared in his 1883 *Fortællinger og Virkelighedsbilleder. Ny Samling*. The version used here is from M. A. Goldschmidt, *Noveller og andre fortællinger* (Copenhagen: Det danske sprog- og litteraturselskab, 1994), 7–13.

27. According to later traditions, the stepdaughter of Herod Antipas who asked for the head of John the Baptist; cf. Mark 6:21–29 and Matthew 14:3–12.

28. Brøndsted talks about the "*tre spejlfigurer*" (three glass figures) but does not develop any sense of their being in competition for the emotional center of the text. See Brøndsted, *Goldschmidts Fortællekunst*, 303–4.

29. "Mendel Hertz," 8.

30. Ibid.

31. Ibid.

32. Ibid.

33. See Mogens Brøndsted, *Ahasverus: jødiske elementer i dansk litteratur* (Odense: Syddansk Universitetsforlag, 2007).

34. *En Jøde*, 15.

35. Ibid., 64–65.

36. He uses language that entails an intimate knowledge of Jewish households and customs, namely, "which belongs to Orthodox Jews." See Goldschmidt, "Mendel Hertz," 7. The narrator also quotes in Yiddish three times and supplies glosses at the foot of the page, showing that this technique of using glosses was used by Goldschmidt during the whole of his literary career. Ibid., 13.

37. Ibid., 8.

38. For a short discussion of this complex text, see Zunz's 1832 essay: Leopold Zunz, "Die gottesdienstlichen Vorträge der Juden historisch entwickelt; ein Beitrag zur Alterthumskunde und biblischen Kritik, zur Literatur- und Religionsgeschichte," in *Gesammelte Schriften* (Berlin, 1875), 1:32–40.

39. For the Noachic tradition in literature, see Ruth Mellinkoff, "Cain's Monstrous Progeny in Beowulf: Part I, Noachic Tradition," *Anglo-Saxon England* 8 (1979): 143–62.

40. The figure of Moses, which more than any other determined the character of Jewish identity and the beginning of monotheism and which straddles four of the five books of the Torah, has drawn the attention of thinkers, writers, and poets. Freud's last book, *Moses and Monotheism* (1939); Martin Buber's *Moses* (1946); and the Yiddish novel *Moses* by Shalom Asch (1951) attest to the interest that the figure and activity of Moses stirred among twentieth-century scholars and authors.

41. "Mendel Hertz," 8.

42. Cf. Gen. 5:22.

43. Num. 20:8.

44. Ibid., 20:10–12.

45. Ibid., 20:12–13.

46. Alter, *Books of Moses*, 784n13.

47. Deut. 1:37.

48. Cf. Deut. 3:26 and 4:21.

49. Deut. 34:4–6.

50. "Mendel Hertz," 9.

51. Henri Gratien, Comte Bertrand (1773–1844), was a French general who accompanied Napoleon at Longwood House during his exile on St. Helena from 1815 until his death in 1821. In 1840 he was chosen to accompany the prince of Joinville to St. Helena to retrieve and bring Napoleon's remains to France. His fidelity and trustworthiness are the topic of legendary and heroic song. See Goldschmidt, *Noveller*, 315–16.

52. "Mendel Hertz," 9.

53. Ibid. Italics mine.

54. Meïr Goldschmidt, "Keiser Napoleon: et Eventyr for Børn," in *Udvalgte skrifter*, ed. Julius Salomon (Copenhagen: Gyldendal, 1908), 1:432–47. There are, however, some sixteen mentions in *LER* of Napoleon, and many essays and reflections on Napoleon in Goldschmidt's journalistic writings.

55. Ibid., 447.

56. "Mendel Hertz," 8.

57. Ibid., 9.

58. Ibid.

59. Adam Oehlenschläger, *Axel og Valborg in Oehlenschlägers Tragødier* (Copenhagen, 1849), 5:4–111. The lovers Axel and Valborg were related and their union was deemed forbidden by the Church unless they could acquire a papal dispensation. This was further hindered by the discovery that they were baptismal siblings. *Axel og Valborg* is also a *riddervise* (chivalrous ballad) known from the *visebøger* (balladbooks) of Anders Sørensen Vedel and Peter Syv from the late sixteenth and early seventeenth centuries. It later spread by broadsheet across Scandinavia and enjoyed great popularity in the nineteenth century as shown by Oehlenschläger's staging of the song.

60. "Mendel Hertz," 9.

61. Ibid., 10.

62. I should comment on the relation between Salome and Mendel here. The text is explicit. Salome "was *like* her own daughter and Mendel's niece by blood" (italics mine). See "Mendel Hertz," 10. Brøndsted writes, "The young cousin Salome grew up and grew in to Mendel's heart, just like Valborg." Brøndsted is being too loose here with his terminology. Salome is not Mendel's *kusine* or *søskendebarn* (both words meaning "cousin") as was Valborg to Axel. She is his aunt's stepdaughter and

any relation between them is fictive or metaphoric. Brøndsted, *Goldschmidts Fortællekunst*, 304.

63. "Mendel Hertz," 12.

64. Ibid., 13.

65. Salome is traditionally the name given to the unnamed dancing girl in the gospels that causes the death of John the Baptist. For a discussion on the role of the biblical Salome in literature, see Paul-André Claudel, *Salomé: destinées imaginaires d'une figure biblique* (Paris: Ellipses, 2013).

66. Goldschmidt's note, "Mendel Hertz," 13: *Frisch und gesund und meschugge: Fejler Intet uden paa Forstanden* (Nothing wrong except the intellect).

67. Goldschmidt's note, "Mendel Hertz," 13: *Du gaar verstellt: Maskeret. Du spiller en Rolle for at lykønske* (Disguised. You are putting on an act in order to be congratulated).

68. Ibid.

69. Brøndsted, *Goldschmidts Fortællekunst*, 304.

70. There is a possible reading that would make Salome and Mendel actually related, but I think it is only there for obfuscatory effect. The line reads, "Mendel havde en Moster, og hun havde en Steddatter, der forresten Ganske var som hendes egen Datter og Mendels kjødelige Søskendebarn" (Mendel had a maternal aunt, and she had a stepdaughter who was for the most part like her own daughter and Mendel's niece by flesh). See "Mendel Hertz," 10. Depending on whether one continues reading the simile to Mendel, the meaning could change. It could mean that Salome was like a daughter to the aunt but was actually Mendel's real niece. For example, Salome could be the daughter of a deceased brother or sister of Mendel's.

71. The untrained musician who plays by ear is a metaphor Goldschmidt also used to describe Jacob Bendixen's "Talmudic adroitness" when he arrives at the Latin school without any formal training. It is a topic of some discussion in the following section.

72. The quote is actually from *The Raven* to describe Simon Levi but I use it here to show this global character trait of Goldschmidt's heroes. This could also be compared to Jacob's "Talmudic adroitness" and the way characters such as Mendel Hertz speak in Gnostic pitches. *Ravnen*, 158.

73. "Mendel Hertz," 13. Goldschmidt's note, 13: *den guten Ort: Kirkegaarden* (graveyard).

74. There is no doubt that Goldschmidt was an admirer of Leopold Kompert (1822–1886). In 1869 he translated Kompert's 1865 novel *Christian og Lea*, labeled number 2275 in Erland Much-Petersen, *Bibliografi over oversættelser til dansk 1800–1900 af prosafiktion fra de germanske og romanske sprog* (Copenhagen: Rosenkilde og Bagger, 1976). There was also a translation of three of Kompert's short stories into Danish in 1872 under the title *Fra Gaden 1–2: tre jødiske fortællinger*. I have little

doubt Goldschmidt was also involved in this translation if not the translator himself. It appeared in a volume with Aaron Bernstein's *Mendel Gibbor (en jødisk fortælling)*, trans. Frederik Levy (1851–1924), and is labeled 2276 in the Munch-Petersen.

75. Deut. 34:5.

76. Alter, *Books of Moses*, 1058n5.

77. "Mendel Hertz," 8.

78. Ibid., 13.

79. Hebrew for "learning," "study"; the Talmud consists of the oral law, the Mishnah, which was developed on the basis of the laws in the Pentateuch together with the commentaries for the Mishnah, the Gemara. The term "Talmud," as used here, refers to the Babylonian Talmud, written down about 500 CE.

80. See Gérard Genette, *Narrative Discourse: An Essay in Method*, trans. Jane E. Lewin (Ithaca, NY: Cornell Univ. Press, 1980), 229–31.

81. Lazarus Goldschmidt's translation into German was begun in 1897 and was finished in 1909. See Sharon Liberman Mintz and Gabriel M. Goldstein, eds., *Printing the Talmud: From Bomberg to Schottenstein* (New York: Yeshiva Univ. Museum, 2005), 308. In English, the project was initiated by Michael Levi Rodkinson, a controversial figure, in 1896 and finished in 1901. See Marvin J. Heller, *Further Studies in the Making of the Early Hebrew Book* (Leiden: Brill, 2013), 217–50.

82. First published in *Quarterly Review* 123, no. 246 (Oct. 1867). (Note: Goldschmidt's translation was published in 1868.) Deutsch's monograph attempted to bring the Talmud to an English-speaking audience by positioning it vis-à-vis classic Indo-European texts, such as the Vedas and Homer, and with other ancient wisdom texts such as the *Avesta*, the Egyptian *Book of the Dead*, accounts of the Oracle at Delphi, and so forth.

83. Borup, *Breve fra og til Meir Goldschmidt*, 2:134.

84. Ibid.

85. Ibid.

86. Ibid., 136.

87. Note that these very same articles were also cast aside by Jacob Bendixen in *A Jew*.

88. Ibid., 137.

89. Ibid.

90. Ibid.

91. Ibid., 138.

92. Ibid.

93. Ibid., 139.

94. Ibid., 138.

95. Brandes, "M. Goldschmidt," 467.

96. Borup, *Breve fra og til Meir Goldschmidt*, 2:139.

97. Ibid.

98. *LER*, 1:98–99.

99. *En Jøde*, 81.

100. The novel is second only to *A Jew* and is deserving of an English translation and commentary.

101. *Ravnen*, 157–58.

102. Ober, *Meïr Goldschmidt*, 109.

103. Surprisingly, the popularity the novel has enjoyed in Denmark suggests that this Talmudic mode of discourse and characterization is not beyond the aesthetics of Goldschmidt's Christian readers, another sophisticated mark of Goldschmidt's poetical eye.

104. Meir Goldschmidt, "Anmærkninger" to *Kjærlighedshistorier fra mange lande*, in *Udvalgte skrifter*, 5:113.

105. In fact, contrary to Goldschmidt's statement, the tale is not Talmudic. The spuriousness of his claim suggests that his power of authenticity has become so great that he can label things Jewish or prior just by asserting they are Talmudic. To take the matter one step further, it is possible Goldschmidt obtained the tale from a German source. See Kenneth H. Ober, "Meïr Goldschmidt's 'Hebrew Legends': The Writer as Plagiarist?" *Scandinavica* 22 (1983), 20–21. For a contrary opinion, see Brøndsted, *Goldschmidts Fortællekunst*, 362.

106. The first complete edition of this little known work is Carl von Linné, *Nemesis divina*, ed. Elis Malmeström and Telemak Fredbärj (Stockholm: Bonniers, 1968). For the version Goldschmidt knew, see Elias Fries, "Carl von Linnés Anteckningar öfver Nemesis divina, Indbjudningsskrift til filosofiska Promotionen vid Upsala Universitetet 1848," in *Botaniska Utflygter: en samling af strödda tillfällighets-skrifter*, ed. Elias Fries (Uppsala, Sweden, 1848), 2:299–344. See also Wolf Lepenies, "Linnaeus's *Nemesis divina* and the Concept of Divine Retaliation," *Isis* 73, no. 1 (1982): 11–27.

107. *LER*, 2:17.

108. For the most detailed description of these philosophical and linguistic underpinnings in Goldschmidt's thinking, see *LER*, 2:79–135. Goldschmidt is clear that the task of tracing the notion of nemesis ends where it begins, in Egypt; cf. *LER*, 2:79: "But the journey we shall make is not the common one, by train or steamship over to the country Egypt, which has always been there; our way is an historic way through the ages to the land lost and found again." Again we see an echo of Zunz's notion of a renewal in the present through the past.

109. He is dissimilar not only from writers such as Heine and Hertz, but also from those early writers in Eastern Europe such as Avraham Mapu, author of the 1853 novel *'Ahavat Tsiyon* (*The Love of Zion*), who are inventing the Hebrew novel at roughly the same time Goldschmidt is writing. For a scholarly discussion of the very

first Hebrew fiction writers, see Robert Alter, *The Invention of Hebrew Prose: Modern Fiction and the Language of Realism* (Seattle: Univ. of Washington Press, 1988).

4. The Figure of the Rabbi

1. BT Menahot 29b, trans. Eli Cashdan (London: Soncino, 1948).

2. Brandes, "M. Goldschmidt," 455.

3. The name of a rabbi occurs a dozen times in *LER*. In volume 1 of *LER*, Rabbi Manasse is mentioned at 42.6; Josef Albo at 45.5; Maimonides at 45.5 and 122.35; Rabbi Eliezer at 96.40; Rabbi Schachno at 100.1, 100.2, 100.26, and 100.37. In vol. 2, Rabbi Eliezer at 41.40; Maimonides at 95.15; and "*den fromme Rabbi*" (the pious rabbi) Rabbi Judah Loew, the Maharal of Prague, at 123.24. For Goldschmidt and the figure of the rabbi, see Dekel and Gurley, "How the Golem Came to Prague." For a recent and scholarly portrait of Zoëga, see Karen Ascani, Paola Buzi, and Daniela Picchi, eds., *The Forgotten Scholar: Georg Zoëga (1755–1809): At the Dawn of Egyptology and Coptic Studies* (Leiden: Brill, 2015).

4. *LER*, 1:41.

5. Ibid., 1:44–45. The grandmother Goldschmidt is referring to is Sara Levin, f. Pincus (1760–1835).

6. *LER*, 1:45.

7. Take, for instance, the influence Maimonides had on Aquinas's reading of Aristotle. See David B. Burrell, "Aquinas and Islamic and Jewish Thinkers," in *The Cambridge Companion to Aquinas*, ed. Norman Kretzmann and Eleonore Stump (Cambridge, UK: Cambridge Univ. Press, 1993), 60–84.

8. Meïr Goldschmidt, "Hebrew Legends: In Two Parts," *Chambers's Journal of Popular Literature, Science and Arts*, July–Dec. 1862:212–14 and 232–37. The first four tales had already appeared in Danish in *Nord og Syd* in 1852 along with a fifth tale, "Maimonides." See Meïr Goldschmidt, "Jødiske Sagn," *Nord og Syd* 2 (1852): 80–85. They were reprinted in his 1860 *Blandede Skrifter*, 4:51–72, along with three additional tales, "Kongens Hjerneskal," "Rabbi Raschi," and "Den Gjerrige" (The miser), which is the first story in part 2 of *Hebrew Legends* and is entitled "The Kamzan." Note that the story called "Rabbi Raschi" in *Blandede Skrifter* is much different from the one printed in *Chambers's Journal*. This difference is discussed at length below.

9. These stories are "The Kamzan," "The Bird that Sang to a Bridegroom" (which appeared in *Kjærlighedshistorier fra mange Lande* in 1867 and is discussed in chapter 2); "David's Death"; "The Witnesses" (reprinted in *The Jewish Chronicle and Hebrew Observer*, Oct. 17, 1862, 7; the Danish version was included in Goldschmidt's 1865 piece "Ghetto," 170–74); "The Drunkard and his Sons"; "Our Pledges"; "The Ram"; "Isaac"; "Ambition"; "Reward–Chastity"; "The Wandering Jew"; "Tolerance"; "Solidarity of Sin"; and "Martyrs."

10. All of these English translations were most likely edited by Hester Rothschild, the wife of Goldschmidt's cousin Benjamin Rothschild. Goldschmidt lived with them in London during the years 1861–63. For a discussion of Goldschmidt's endeavors in the English language, see Kenneth Ober, "Meïr Goldschmidt as a Writer of English," *Orbis Litterarum* 29 (1974): 231–44.

11. Goldschmidt, *Hebrew Legends*, 212–13.

12. For a contrary point of view, see Kenneth H. Ober, "Meïr Goldschmidt's 'Hebrew Legends': The Writer as Plagiarist?" *Scandinavica* 22 (1983): 15–21.

13. Hyman Hurwitz, *Hebrew Tales: Selected and Translated from the Writings of the Ancient Hebrew Sages; to which is prefixed, an essay, on the uninspired literature of the Hebrews* (London, 1826). The book was reprinted in a revised and edited edition by George Alexander Kohut, in Library of Jewish Classics, vol. 2 (New York: Bloch, 1911). This is the version I used for quotations. For a more detailed account of Hurwitz's life and works, see Leonard Hyman, "Hyman Hurwitz, the First Anglo-Jewish Professor," *Transactions—The Jewish Historical Society of England* 21 (1967): 232–42.

14. See Hyman Hurwitz, *Elements of the Hebrew Language, in Two Parts* (London, 1807); Hyman Hurwitz, *The Etymology and Syntax (in Continuation of the Elements) of the Hebrew Language* (London, 1835); and Hyman Hurwitz, *A Grammar of the Hebrew Language* (London, 1837).

15. Hurwitz, *Hebrew Tales*, 12.

16. The notion of Coleridge as a Hebraist is dubious at best. Barbara Rooke's note in *The Collected Works* makes this clear. It seems Coleridge was a better translator of German than Hebrew: "In *Friend* (1809–10) each tale is headed 'Specimens of Rabbinical Wisdom, selected from the Mishna'; and there was a fourth tale (see below, II 309). All appear, under the same title, 'Proben Rabbinischer Weisheit', in J. J. Engel *Schriften* vol. I (Berlin 1801), which is C.'s source. For this tale cf. 'Den Menschen und dem Veihe hilft der Herr' ibid. I 297–300. In 1817 John Murray offered C. £200 for an 'Octavo Volume of Specimens of Rabbinical Wisdom' (*CL* IV 656–57). C. claimed that he never went on with the tales because he lacked learning enough (of Hebrew) and therefore needed a copy of the Latin translation, *Mischna sive totius Hebraeorum juris, ritum, antiquitatum ac legum oralium systma* . . . ed. Guglielmus Surenhusius (Willem Surenhus; 6 vols Amsterdam 1698–1703), with text in Hebrew and Latin. These three tales tr by C. were included in Hyman Hurwitz *Hebrew Tales* (1826) 5–12, acknowledged with a compliment in the preface (p. v)." *The Collected Works of Samuel Taylor Coleridge*, vol. 4, *The Friend*, part 1, ed. Barbara E. Rooke (Princeton, NJ: Princeton Univ. Press, 1967), 370n2. Note: Engel's source for these *Proben* was none other than Moses Mendelssohn (1729–1786).

17. Hurwitz, *Hebrew Tales*, 13.

18. Ibid., 11. Also see Hyman, "Hyman Hurwitz, the First Anglo-Jewish Professor." This fact can be read against Goldschmidt's remarks in *LER* that I discussed earlier concerning the Talmudic grocer who could debate any "Christian Professor of Hebrew." Undoubtedly, this is a marked tribute to Hurwitz's being the first Jewish professor of Hebrew.

19. For examples of his remarkable prose style, see Hyman Hurwitz, *Vindiciae hebraicae; or, A defense of the Hebrew Scriptures, as a vehicle of revealed religion: occasioned by the recent strictures and innovations of Mr. J. Bellamy; and in confutation of his attacks on all preceding translations, and on the established version in particular* (London, 1820); Hyman Hurwitz and Solomon Hirschel, *A letter to Isaac L. Goldsmid, Esq. F.R.S.: chairman of the association for obtaining for British Jews civil rights and privileges, on certain recent mis-statements respecting the Jewish religion, reported to have been made by one of the hon. members for Oldham* (London, 1833).

20. Hurwitz, *Hebrew Tales*, 9 and 13. Editions of Hurwitz's book were published in New York in 1847 and Edinburgh in 1863.

21. David B. Ruderman, *Jewish Enlightenment in an English Key: Anglo-Jewry's Construction of Modern Jewish Thought* (Princeton, NJ: Princeton Univ. Press, 2000), 261.

22. Ibid., 267–68.

23. Ibid., 265–66.

24. Hurwitz, *Vindiciae hebraicae*, 13.

25. Hurwitz, *Hebrew Tales*, 80.

26. Deutsch, "Talmud," 417–19.

27. Hurwitz, *Hebrew Tales*, 80–81; quoted in Ruderman, *Jewish Enlightenment*, 266–67. The story referenced is from Diogenes Laertius, *Lives*, Chilo 2.

28. Hurwitz, *Hebrew Tales*, 80.

29. Ibid., 4–5.

30. Ruderman, *Jewish Enlightenment*, 268.

31. See Ober, "Meïr Goldschmidt's 'Hebrew Legends.'"

32. Goldschmidt, *Hebrew Legends*, 213.

33. Only one tale from part 2 appears in Hurwitz, "The Drunkard and His Sons."

34. Coleridge, *The Friend*. Also appearing in this publication were Hurwitz's "The Lord Helpeth Man and Beast." See Hurwitz, *Hebrew Tales*, 13.

35. Goldschmidt, *Hebrew Legends*, 212.

36. For Goldschmidt's relation to Jewish folklore, also see Dekel and Gurley, "How the Golem Came to Prague"; and van Suntum, "Creating Jewish Identity through Storytelling," 383–84.

37. Hurwitz, *Hebrew Tales*, 16–18.

38. Rabbi Meir Baal Haness (121 CE) was a student of Rabbi Akiva. There are some 335 *halachot* mentioned in the Mishnah with interpretation by Rabbi Meir. His wife was Beruriah, a wise and sagacious woman. She advised Rabbi Meir in conflict with wicked men (*Berachot* 10a), and when their two sons died she broke the news gently and comforted him. Beruriah is mentioned a handful of times in the Talmud, always in a very positive light. It is therefore surprising that Rashi, in his commentary to *Abodah Zarah* 18b, should relate a story about Beruriah in which she ends up committing suicide. There is no extant earlier source for this story and it is possibly innovative. The Gemara tells that Rabbi Meir ran away to Babylon because of an incident involving Beruriah. Rashi inserts the following: Once Beruriah criticized the Rabbinic view (*Kid.* 80b) that women are light-minded and easily persuaded, to which Rabbi Meir replied that one day she herself would testify to the truth of the rabbi's words. Rabbi Meir had one of his students test her by repeatedly trying to seduce her until she finally gave consent. Rabbi Meir thereupon proved to Beruriah the light-mindedness of women. But the plan backfired; Beruriah committed suicide and Rabbi Meir was forced to flee Palestine out of shame. There is at least one alternate version. According to Rabbi Nissim (ca. 1310–ca. 1380), Rabbi Meir and Beruriah had to flee to Babylon after the Romans executed her father and sold her mother into slavery and put her sister in a brothel. (Consequently, Rabbi Meir later rescues her from debauchery.)

39. See Hurwitz, *Hebrew Tales*, 35–39, 48–49, and 59–62, respectively.

40. Hurwitz reads "both of them of uncommon beauty and enlightened in the law" (Hurwitz, *Hebrew Tales*, 16); Goldschmidt's Danish reads "*der begge vare af usædvanlig Skjønhed og saare kyndige i Loven*" (Goldschmidt, *Blandede skrifter*, 4:56).

41. Hurwitz reads "give them my blessing" (Hurwitz, *Hebrew Tales*, 16); Goldschmidt's Danish reads "*kan give dem Velsignelsen*" (Goldschmidt, *Blandede skrifter*, 4:56).

42. Hurwitz reads "They are gone to the school" (Hurwitz, *Hebrew Tales*, 16); Goldschmidt's Danish reads "*De ere gaaede til Synagogen*" (Goldschmidt, *Blandede skrifter*, 4:56). This final lexical difference is of great importance because it marks a definite refinement in the narrative. The play with the name of the place where the sons have gone only works in Goldschmidt's English version. Neither "school" nor "*Synagogen*" has the same metonymic ability or style as "God's house," which can mean either "school," "Synagogen," or even "paradise." It also has the function of painting the rabbi's wife in a cleverer and less deceptive light. Quite simply, the game does not really work any other way and has the privilege of sounding the most folkloric. The Hebrew reads "*Bet Ha-Midrash*," literally the "house of study," which was different from both the "school" (*bet sefer*) and the synagogue (*bet knesset*). It

is interesting that Hurwitz has "school" and Goldschmidt corrects it in Danish to "synagogue." This suggests that Goldschmidt is working from a Hebrew source alongside the Hurwitz. If Goldschmidt, unlike Coleridge, read the Hebrew original in the *Yalqut*, this furthers my argument against Ober that he plagiarized from Hurwitz. It also shows how serious Goldschmidt is about his claim of kinship to source.

43. Hurwitz reads "a goblet" (Hurwitz, *Hebrew Tales*, 16); Goldschmidt's Danish reads "*Bægeret med Vin*" (Goldschmidt, *Blandede skrifter*, 4:56). Goldschmidt's English is a stylistic correction of his Danish version in which the narrator leaves out the wife bringing the light, but then right away has the rabbi bless the light; cf. "*han velsignede Vinen og Lyset og drak af Bægret.*"

44. Hurwitz reads "cup of blessing" (Hurwitz, *Hebrew Tales*, 17); Goldschmidt's Danish reads "*det indviede Bæger*" (Goldschmidt, *Blandede skrifter*, 4:56).

45. Goldschmidt, *Hebrew Legends*, 213.

46. Ibid.

47. Hurwitz, *Hebrew Tales*, 18.

48. Goldschmidt, *Hebrew Legends*, 213.

49. See Deut. 21:10–14; cf. *Ketubot* 52a. There is also the possibility of conflation with legends of Rabbi Meir of Rotenburg (1215–1293), who was seized and unjustly imprisoned by Emperor Rudolph I and held for ransom. Although the money was raised to ensure his release, Rabbi Meir himself would not allow the ransom to be paid out for fear that it would encourage the kidnapping of other Jewish leaders. He remained steadfast in his refusal and eventually died in captivity.

50. Hurwitz reads "Well turned" (Hurwitz, *Hebrew Tales*, 21); Goldschmidt's Danish reads "*Ja, det er godt nok!*" (Goldschmidt, *Blandede skrifter*, 4:60).

51. Goldschmidt, *Hebrew Legends*, 214. Goldschmidt's English is rhetorically superior here. Hurwitz reads "'Yea,' retorted the Rabbi, 'if fools worshipped such things only as were of no further use than that to which their folly applied them,—if the idols were always as worthless as the idolatry is contemptible. But they worship the sun, the moon, the host of heaven, the rivers, the sea, fire, air, and what not. Would you that the Creator, for the sake of these fools, should ruin his own works, and disturb the laws appointed to nature by his own wisdom? If a man steals grain and sows it, should the seed not shoot up out of the earth, because it was stolen? Oh, no! the wise Creator lets nature run her own course; for her course is his own appointment. And what if the children of folly abuse it to evil? The day of reckoning is not far off, and men will then learn that human actions likewise reappear in their consequences, by as certain a law as the green blade rises up out of the buried corn-seed'" (Hurwitz, *Hebrew Tales*, 21). Goldschmidt's Danish reads "Skulde han, fordi de Narre tilbede Solguden, ødelægge Solen? Eller slukke Ilden, udtørre Havet, borttage Luften og hvad Andet de falde paa at gjøre til Guder? Skulde han for de Enfoldiges Skyld tilintetgjøre sine Værker og de vise Naturlove? Sæden voxer

af Jorden, og end den, som saaede den, har stjaalet den. Men den menneskelige Udsæd voxer ogsaa ifølge uforanderlige Love, og Følgerne af hver Gjerning komme saa sikkert, som det grønne Blad kommer af Sædkornet, der blev begravet i Jorden" (Goldschmidt, *Blandede skrifter*, 4:60).

52. Goldschmidt, *Hebrew Legends*, 214.

53. Ibid.

54. Ibid.

55. The source of the tale is uncertain. It appears in Micah Joseph Berdichevsky, *Mimekor Yisrael: Classic Jewish Folktales* (Bloomington: Indiana Univ. Press, 1976), 783–84, where it is said to come from Jehiel ben Solomon Heilprin, *Seder ha-Dorot*, 1:111 (1769), which is based on Abraham Zacuto, *Sefer Yuhassin*, 5:222 (1504).

56. Meïr Goldschmidt, "Rabbi Raschi: A Jewish Legend," *Once a Week* 20 (1869): 346–49.

57. Ibid., 346.

58. Rashi is the Hebrew acronym for Rabbi Shlomo Yitzhaqi and was misread as "Jarchi" by the thirteenth-century Dominican theologian and orientalist Raymund Martin. Martin was of the opinion that the Talmudists had corrupted the Bible and was the author of two anti-Jewish treatises, so it is understandable why Goldschmidt would want to purge his text of such an error. The fact that he uses it in the *Chambers's* version (note: "Jarchi" does not appear in the Danish version) suggests that it was a common English convention at the time. See *Jewish Encyclopedia*, s.v. "Martin, Raymund."

59. Moshe ben Maimon (Arabic: *Abu Imran Mussa bin Maimun ibn Abdallah al-Qurtubi al-Israili*).

60. Ober, *Meïr Goldschmidt*, 48–49.

61. Goldschmidt, *Hebrew Legends*, 214.

62. "Rabbi Raschi: A Jewish Legend," 347.

63. Goldschmidt, *Hebrew Legends*, 214.

64. Ibid.

65. Ibid.

66. Ibid., 215.

67. "Rabbi Raschi: A Jewish Legend," 347–48.

68. Goldschmidt, *Hebrew Legends*, 215.

69. "Rabbi Raschi: A Jewish Legend," 348.

70. Ibid.

71. Ibid.

72. Ibid.

73. Ibid., 347.

74. Ibid., 348.

75. Goldschmidt, *Hebrew Legends*, 215.

76. Ibid. Goldschmidt's note, *mitzwa*: "a good action."

77. Hebrew words transliterated into the Danish alphabet according to the traditional Ashkenazi pronunciation. The Hebrew word *Mohel* is glossed in "The Kamzan" as "One who performs the ceremony prescribed in Genesis, chapter xvii, verse 13" (Goldschmidt, *Hebrew Legends*, 232); and *Masel tob* and *Gan Eden* are parenthetically glossed in "Rabbi Raschi: A Jewish Legend," 349, as "good luck" and "Paradise."

78. Goldschmidt, *Hebrew Legends*, 215.

79. Ibid.

80. Ibid.

81. Ibid.

82. Ibid.

83. Ibid.

84. Goldschmidt's note, *mincha*: "the afternoon prayer with which the marriage-ceremony commences."

85. Goldschmidt, *Hebrew Legends*, 215. Interestingly, this word is not glossed in the foot of the page. Instead it is defined in apposition by an English word that comes from the Old Italian name for Baghdad, *Baldacco*.

86. Cf. Joel 2:16 and Psalms 19:6. A similar technique is used by Ludwig August Frankl in his golem story, where he parenthetically gives an Arabic gloss for beadle or "(*Schames*, usually called *Mulassim* by the peoples of the Orient)." See Dekel and Gurley, "How the Golem Came to Prague," 248.

87. Goldschmidt, *Hebrew Legends*, 216. Goldschmidt's note, *schatchan*: "he who demands the bridge from her parents for another."

88. Goldschmidt, "Rabbi Raschi: A Jewish Legend," 349.

89. Goldschmidt, *Hebrew Legends*, 214.

90. Borup, *Meïr Goldschmidts breve til hans familie*, 2:34.

91. Concerning Aguilar and the London Jewish literary scene, see Galchinsky, *Origins*.

92. Claud Field, *Jewish Legends of the Middle Ages* (London, n.d., ca. 1910). The actual publication date of the book is uncertain, but most likely the first decade of the twentieth century.

Epilogue

1. Brandes, "M. Goldschmidt," 449.

2. Ibid.

3. Ibid., 454–55.

4. Ibid., 450–51. "My Uncle's Lumberyard" (1845) first appeared in P. L. Møller's annual *Gæa* and at Møller's request avoided any sense of a Jewish poetics. "Bewitched No. 1" is one of Goldschmidt's more popular and beloved provincial

tales that showcases his literary debt to Steen Steensen Blicher. The fact that Brandes speaks so highly of the preface to one of Goldschmidt's greatest literary achievements, *Love Stories from Many Lands*, speaks for itself.

5. Yerushalmi, *Zakhor*, 117. Italics by author.

6. Goldschmidt, *Hebrew Legends*, 236. The two tales that fall under this heading seem to be the first Jewish adaption of the medieval Christian legend in an anthology of authentic legendary material.

7. Ibid.

8. Ibid.

9. Goldschmidt claims the two tales that comprise "The Wandering Jew" to be of "recent origin." See Goldschmidt, *Hebrew Tales*, 235.

10. See Søren Kierkegaard, *Søren Kierkegaards Papirer*, ed. Peter Andreas Heiberg, Victor Kuhr, and Einter Torsting, VII-I B 49 (Copenhagen: Gyldendal, 1946), 221.

11. Schwarz, "Conflicting Views," 201.

12. For a complete discussion of this text, see Edan Dekel and Gantt Gurley, "Kafka's Golem," *AJS* (forthcoming).

13. See, for example, Martin Buber, "The Jew in the World," in *Israel and the World: Essays in a Time of Crisis*, trans. Olga Marx and Greta Hort (Syracuse, NY: Syracuse Univ. Press, 1997), 167.

14. See Gilles Deleuze and Félix Guattari, *Kafka: Pour une Littérature Mineure* (Paris: Les Éditions de Minuit, 1975). This reading of Deleuze and Guattari is shared by Yasemin Yildiz, *Beyond the Mother Tongue: The Postmonolingual Condition* (New York: Fordham Univ. Press, 2011), 34.

15. Miron, *Continuity to Contiguity*, 306–9.

◆ ◆ ◆

Bibliography

Goldschmidt's Works

Goldschmidt, Meïr. "Aaron and Esther, or, Three Days of Rabbi Nathan Clausener's Life." *Chambers's Journal of Popular Literature, Science and Arts* 473 (1863): 53–61.

———. *Arvingen* (The Heir). Copenhagen: Steen, 1865.

———. *Arvingen* (The Heir). Edited by Johnny Kondrup. Copenhagen: Danske sprog- og litteraturselskab, 1988.

———. *Avrohmche Nattergal* (Avrohmche Nightingale). Copenhagen: Steen, 1871.

———. *Blandede skrifter* (Miscellaneous Writings). 4 vols. in 3 bks. Copenhagen: Wroblewsky, 1859–60.

———. *Breve fra choleratiden, indeholdende en lille begivenhed* (Letters from the Time of Cholera, Containing a Little Incident). Copenhagen: Steen, 1865.

———. *Dagbog fra en reise paa vestkysten af Vendsyssel og Thy* (Journal from a Trip to the West Coast of Vendsyssel and Thy). Copenhagen: Forlagsbureau, 1865.

———. *Den vægelsindede paa Graahede* (The Fickle Woman of Graahede). Copenhagen: Steen, 1867.

———. "Discoveries near Rome." *Athenæum* 1859 (1863): 779.

———. *En Jøde* (*A Jew*). 7th ed. Copenhagen: Gyldendal, 1927.

———. [Adolph Meyer, pseud.]. *En Jøde: Novelle af Adolph Meyer* (A Jew: Novel by Adolph Meyer). Copenhagen: published by the author, 1845.

———. "The Elf's Ring." *Victoria Magazine*, Oct. 1864, 508–31.

———. [Adolph Meyer, pseud.]. *Fortællinger. Af Adolph Meyer* (Stories. By Adolph Meyer). Copenhagen: Reitzel, 1846.

———. *Fortællinger og skildringer* (Stories and Descriptions). 3 vols. Copenhagen: Steen, 1863–65.

———. *Fortællinger og virkelighedsbilleder, ældre og nye* (Stories and Pictures of Reality, Old and New). 2 vols. Copenhagen: Gyldendal, 1877.

———. *Fortællinger og virkelighedsbilleder: Ny Samling* (Stories and Pictures of Reality: New Collection). Copenhagen: Gyldendal, 1883.

———. *En hedereise i Viborg-Egnen* (A Trip through the Heath in the Viborg District). Copenhagen: Steen, 1867.

———. "Hebrew Legends: In Two Parts." *Chambers's Journal of Popular Literature, Science and Arts* 457 and 458 (1862): 212–14, 232–37.

———. *Hjemløs: En fortælling* (Homeless: A Story). 3 vols. Copenhagen: Høst, 1853–57.

———. *Hjemløs. En Fortælling I–II* (Homeless: A Story I–II). Edited by Mogens Brøndsted. Copenhagen: Danske sprog- og litteraturselskab, 1999.

———. *Homeless, or A Poet's Inner Life.* 3 vols. London: Hurst and Blackett, 1861.

———. *I den anden verden: Komedie i to acter* (In the Other World: Comedy in Two Acts). Copenhagen: Steen, 1869.

———. *A Jew.* Translated by Kenneth Ober. New York: Garland, 1990.

———. *Kjærlighedshistorier fra mange lande* (Love Stories from Many Lands). Copenhagen: Steen, 1867.

———. *Livs erindringer og resultater* (Life's Memories and Results). 2 vols. Copenhagen: Gyldendal, 1877.

———. *Livs erindringer og resultater* (Life's Memories and Results). 2 vols. Edited by Morten Borup. Copenhagen: Rosenkilde og Bagger, 1965.

———. *Meïr Goldschmidt i folkeudgave* (Meïr Goldschmidt in Popular Edition). 8 vols. Edited by Julius Salomon. Copenhagen: Gyldendal, 1908–10.

———. "Mendel Hertz." In *A Golden Treasury of Jewish Literature*, edited by Leo W. Schwartz, translated by J. B. C. Watkins, 150–56. New York: Farrar and Rinehart, 1937.

———. "My Uncle and His House: A Story of Danish Life." *Macmillan's Magazine* 7 (1863): 461–76.

———. "A Norwegian Musician." *Cornhill Magazine* 6 (1862): 514–27.

———. *Noveller og andre fortællinger* (Novellas and Other Stories). Edited by Thomas Bredsdorff. Copenhagen: Danske sprog- og litteraturselskab, 1994.

———. *Om physiognomiken* (On Physiognomy). Copenhagen: Wroblewsky, 1859.

———. "On the Danube, and Among the Mountains." *Chambers's Journal of Popular Literature, Science and Arts* 448 (1862): 65–70.

———. *Poetiske skrifter* (Poetical Works). 8 vols. Edited by A. Goldschmidt. Copenhagen: Gyldendal, 1896–98.

———. *Rabbi Eliezer: Dramatisk digtning* (Rabbi Eliezer: Dramatic Poem). Copenhagen: Wroblewsky, 1861.

———. *Rabbi'en og ridderen: Drama i tre Acter* (The Rabbi and the Knight: Drama in Three Acts). Copenhagen: Steen, 1869.

———. "Rabbi Raschi: A Jewish Legend." *Once a Week* 20 (1869): 346–49.

———. *Ravnen: Fortælling* (The Raven: Story). Copenhagen: Steen, 1867.

———. *En roman i breve* (A Novel in Letters). Copenhagen: Steen, 1867. (Second edition of *Breve fra choleratiden, indeholdende en lille begivenhed.*)

———. *En skavank: Skuespil i tre acter og med et forspil* (A Flaw: Play in Three Acts with a Prelude). Copenhagen: Steen, 1867.

———. *Smaa fortællinger* (Small Stories). Copenhagen: Steen, 1868.

———. *Smaa skildringer fra fantasi og fra virkelighed* (Small Descriptions from Fantasy and from Reality). Copenhagen: Gyldendal, 1887.

———. "Social Aspects of the Danish War." *Athenæum* 1907 (1864): 676–77; 1909 (1864): 741–42; 1911 (1864): 806–7; 1915 (1864): 51–52; 1916 (1864): 82–83; 1917 (1864): 116–17.

———. "The Society of Virtue at Rome: Social Sketches." *Victoria Magazine*, Jan. 1868, 216–31; Feb. 1868, 320–38; Mar. 1868, 399–422.

———. *Svedenborgs ungdom: Dramatiseret skildring* (Swedenborg's Youth: Dramatized Portrait). Copenhagen: Høst, 1863.

[———]. *Talmud.* Copenhagen: Chr. Steen and Sons, 1868.

———. *Udvalgte skrifter: romaner, fortaellinger og skildringer* (Selected Writings: Novels, Stories, and Descriptions). 6 vols. Edited by Julius Salomon. Copenhagen: Gyldendal, 1916.

Anthologies

Brandt, Jørgen Gustava, ed. *Meïr Goldschmidt. Digteren og journalisten: En mosaik af tekster.* Søborg: Danmarks Radio, 1974.

Sørensen, Knud. *Goldschmidt—en fortrolig fremmed.* Risskov, Denmark: Hovedland, 1985.

Goldschmidt Journals

Næstved Ugeblad eller Præstø Amts Tidende, edited by M. A. Goldschmidt. Oct. 3, 1837–Dec. 28, 1838; *Sjællandsposten eller Nestved- og Callundborg Ugeblad*, Jan. 1839–Apr. 7, 1840.

Corsaren, edited by M. A. Goldschmidt, nos. 1–327, Copenhagen, 1840–46.

Nord og Syd: et Maanedskrift, edited by M. A. Goldschmidt. vols. 1–6, Copenhagen, 1848–49; *Nord og Syd: et Ugeskrift*, vols. 1–6, Copenhagen, 1849–51; *Nord og Syd*, vol. 7, Copenhagen, 1851; *Nord og Syd: ny Række*, vols. 1–11, Copenhagen, 1852–57; *Nord og Syd: et Ugeskrift*, vols. 1–4, Copenhagen, 1856; *Nord og Syd: et Ugeskrift: ny Række*, vols. 1–4, Copenhagen, 1857; *Nord og Syd: et Ugeskrift: ny Række*, vols. 1–3, Copenhagen, 1858; *Nord og Syd: et Ugeskrift: ny Række*, vols. 1–2, Copenhagen, 1859.

General Bibliography

Albeck, Gustav, Oluf Friis, and Peter P. Rohde. *Fra Oehlenschläger til Kierkegaard (ca. 1800–ca. 1870)*. Vol. 2, *Dansk litteratur historie*. Copenhagen: Politikens Forlag, 1976.

Albertsen, Leif Ludwig. *Engelen mi: en bog om den danske jødefejde*. Copenhagen: Privattryk, 1984.

Alter, Robert. *The Art of Biblical Narrative*. London: Allen and Unwin, 1981.

———. *Canon and Creativity*. New Haven: Yale Univ. Press, 2000.

———. *Fielding and the Nature of the Novel*. Cambridge, MA: Harvard Univ. Press, 1968.

———, trans. *The Five Books of Moses: A Translation with Commentary*. New York: W. W. Norton, 2004.

———. *The Invention of Hebrew Prose: Modern Fiction and the Language of Realism*. Seattle: Univ. of Washington Press, 1988.

———. *The Pleasures of Reading in an Ideological Age*. New York: Simon and Schuster, 1989.

———. *The World of Biblical Literature*. London: SPCK, 1992.

Andersen, H. C. *Improvisatoren: original roman i to dele*. Copenhagen: Danske sprog- og litteraturselskab, 1987.

Andersen, Vilhelm. "Bjergtagen. Et Motiv hos Goldschmidt." *Edda* 1 (1914): 75–87.

Anderson, George Kumler. *The Legend of the Wandering Jew.* Providence, RI: Brown Univ. Press, 1965.

Andreasen, Uffe, ed. *Corsaren 1840–46.* 7 vols. Copenhagen: Det Danske Sprog- og Literaturselskab and C. A. Reitzel, 1977–81.

Ascani, Karen, Paola Buzi, and Daniela Picchi. *The Forgotten Scholar: Georg Zoëga (1755–1809): At the Dawn of Egyptology and Coptic Studies.* Leiden: Brill, 2015.

Auerbach, Erich. *Mimesis; The Representation of Reality in Western Literature.* Princeton, NJ: Princeton Univ. Press, 1953.

Auken, Sune. *Eftermæle: en studie i den danske dødedigtning fra Anders Arrebo til Søren Ulrik Thomsen.* Copenhagen: Museum Tusculanums forlag, 1998.

Auring, Steffen, Søren Baggesen, Finn Hauberg Mortensen, Søren Petersen, Marie-Louise Svane, Erik Svendsen, Poul Aaby Sørensen, Jørgen Vogelius, and Martin Zerlang. *Borgerlig enhedskultur 1807–48.* Vol. 5, *Danske litteraturhistorie.* Copenhagen: Gyldendal, 1984.

Bach, Tine. *Exodus: om den hjemløse erfaring i jødisk litteratur.* Hellerup, Denmark: Forlaget Spring, 2004.

———. "Jøder i dansk litteratur." *Alef: Tidsskrift for jødisk kultur* 12/13 (1995): 19–26.

———. *Nu bor vi her: jødiske livshistorier fortalt af tolv kvinder.* Copenhagen: Tiderne Skrifter, 2012.

Bach-Nielsen, Carsten, Jens Rasmussen, and Carsten Selch Jensen, eds. *Kirkehistoriske Samling 2010.* Copenhagen: Univ. of Copenhagen Press, 2011.

Baggesen, Søren. *Den blichereske Novelle.* Copenhagen: Gyldendal, 1965.

Bakhtin, M. M. *The Dialogic Imagination: Four Essays.* Translated by Caryl Emerson and Michael Holquist. Austin: Univ. of Texas Press, 1981.

———. *Rabelais and His World.* Translated by Hélène Iswolsky. Cambridge, MA: MIT Press, 1968.

Bamberger, Ib Nathan. *The Viking Jews: A History of the Jews of Denmark.* New York: Shengold Publishers, 1983.

Barton, H. Arnold. *Essays on Scandinavian History.* Carbondale: Southern Illinois Univ. Press, 2009.

———. *Scandinavia in the Revolutionary Era, 1760–1815.* Minneapolis: Univ. of Minnesota Press, 1986.

Ben-Ari, Nitsah. *Romanze mit der Vergangenheit: der deutsch-jüdische historische Roman des 19. Jahrhunderts und seine Bedeutung für die Entstehung einer neuen jüdischen Nationalliteratur.* Tubingen, Germany: Niemeyer, 2006.

Benjamin, Walter. *Illuminations.* Edited by Hannah Arendt. Translated by Harry Zohn. New York: Schocken Books, 1969.

Ben-Porat, Ziva. "The Poetics of Literary Allusion." *PTL: A Journal for Descriptive Poetics and Theory of Literature* 1 (1976): 105–28.

Berdichevsky, Micah Joseph. *Mimekor Yisrael: Classical Jewish Folktales.* Bloomington: Indiana Univ. Press, 1976.

Biale, David. *Not in the Heavens: The Tradition of Jewish Secular Thought.* Princeton, NJ: Princeton Univ. Press, 2011.

Bloom, Harold. *The Anxiety of Influence: A Theory of Poetry.* New York: Oxford Univ. Press, 1973.

———. Foreword to *Zakhor: Jewish History and Jewish Memory,* by Yosef Hayim Yerushalmi, xiii–xxv. Seattle: Univ. of Washington Press, 1996.

Blüdnikow, Bent. "Jews in Denmark: A Historical Review." In *Danish Jewish Art,* edited by Mirjam Gelfer-Jørgensen, translated by W. Glyn Jones, 23–49. Copenhagen: Rhodos, 1999.

Blüdnikow, Bent, and Harald Jørgensen. "Den lange vandring til borgerlig ligestilling i 1814." In *Indenfor murene: jødisk liv i Danmark 1684–1984,* edited by Harald Jørgensen, 13–90. Copenhagen: C. A. Reitzel, 1984.

Bomhard, Allan R., and John C. Kerns. *The Nostratic Macrofamily: A Study in Distant Linguistic Relationship.* Berlin: Mouton de Gruyter, 1994.

Bondebjerg, Ib. "Den hjemløse myte—en ideologikritisk analyse: Om dannelsesromanen og Goldschmidts *Hjemløs.*" *Kritik* 23 (1972): 5–24.

Borchsenius, Otto. *Fra Fyrrerne. Literære Skizzer.* Vol. 2. Copenhagen, 1880.

Borup, Morten, ed. *Breve fra og til Meir Aron Goldschmidt.* 3 vols. Copenhagen: Rosenkilde og Bagger, 1963.

———. "Goldschmidtiana." *Danske Studier* 61 (1966): 106–18.

———, ed. *Meïr Goldschmidts breve til hans familie.* 2 vols. Copenhagen: Rosenkilde og Bagger, 1964.

Brandenburg, Florian. "'At Orientaleren skal tale som Orientaler . . .' Zur Problematik von Form und Funktion 'Jüdishen Sprechens' in M. A. Goldschmidt's *En Jøde* (1845/52)." *EJSS* 44 (2014): 103–26.

Brandes, Georg Morris Cohen. *Det moderne Gennembruds Mænd.* Copenhagen, 1883.

———. *Samlede Skrifter.* Vol. 2. Copenhagen, 1899.

Bredsdorff, Elias. *Corsaren, Goldschmidt og Kierkegaard*. Copenhagen: Corsarens forlag, 1977.

———. *Goldschmidts "Corsaren": Med en udførlig redegørelse for striden mellem Søren Kierkegaard og "Corsaren."* Aarhus, Denmark: Sirius, 1962.

Bredsdorff, Morten. "Digteren Goldschmidt og Grundtvig: Et opgør om Nationalitet og Danskhed." *Grundtvig-Studier* (1974): 26–50.

Bredsdorff, Thomas. Efterskrift og Noter (afterword and notes) to *Noveller og andre fortællinger*, by M. A. Goldschmidt, 289–333. Copenhagen: Det danske sprog- og litteraturselskab, 1994.

Brøndsted, Mogens. *Ahasverus: jødiske elementer i dansk litteratur*. Odense: Syddansk Universitetsforlag, 2007.

———. *Goldschmidts Fortællekunst*. Copenhagen: Gyldendal, 1967.

———. *Meïr Goldschmidt*. Copenhagen: Gyldendal, 1965.

Buber, Martin. "The Jew in the World." In *Israel and the World: Essays in a Time of Crisis*, translated by Olga Marx and Greta Hort. Syracuse, NY: Syracuse Univ. Press, 1997.

———. *Tales of the Hasidim*. Translated by Olga Marx. New York: Schocken Books, 1947.

———. *Two Types of Faith*. Translated by Norman P. Goldhawk. New York: Macmillan Co., 1951.

Buchholz, Friedrich. *Moses und Jesus, oder über das intellektuelle und moralische Verhältniß der Juden und Christen eine historisch- politische Abhandlung*. Berlin, 1803.

Buckser, Andrew. *After the Rescue: Jewish Identity and Community in Contemporary Denmark*. New York: Palgrave Macmillan, 2003.

Busk-Jensen, Lise, Per Dahl, Anker Gemzøe, Torben Kragh Grodal, Jørgen Holmgaard, and Martin Zerlang. *Dannelse, folkelighed, individualisme 1848–1901*. Vol. 6, *Dansk litteraturhistorie*. Copenhagen: Gyldendal 1985.

Campbell, John L., John A. Hall, and Ove Kaj Pedersen, eds. *National Identity and the Varieties of Capitalism: The Danish Experience*. Montreal: McGill-Queen's Univ. Press, 2006.

Carruthers, Mary J. *The Book of Memory: A Study of Memory in Medieval Culture*. Cambridge, UK: Cambridge Univ. Press, 1990.

Carøe, K. "Da Claus Rash vilde lave Ghetto paa Kristianshavn." *Tidsskrift for jødiske historie og litteratur*, 1919–21:103–16.

———. "Ghetto i Teglgaardsstræde. Et forslag fra 1730." *Tidsskrift for jødiske historie og Literature*, 1919–21, 182–84.

Cavallo, Guglielmo, and Roger Chartier, eds. *A History of Reading in the West.* Translated by Lydia G. Cochrane. Amherst: Univ. of Massachusetts Press, 1999.

Cohen, A. D. *De mosaiske troesbekjenderes stilling i Danmark forhen og nu: historisk fremstillet i et tidsløb af næsten 200 aar, tilligemed alle lovsteder og offentlige foranstaltninger dem angaande, som ere udkomne fra 1651 til 1836.* Odense, Denmark, 1837.

Coleridge, Samuel Taylor. *Biographia Literaria or Biographical Sketches of My Literary Life and Opinions.* Vol. 1. London, 1817.

———. *The Collected Works of Samuel Taylor Coleridge, The Friend.* Vol. 4.1. Edited by Barbara E. Rooke. Princeton, NJ: Princeton Univ. Press, 1967.

Corcoran, Brendan. "Keats's Death: Towards a Posthumous Poetics." *Studies in Romanticism* 48, no. 2 (2009): 321–48.

Dahlerup, Pil. *Det moderne gennembruds kvinder.* Copenhagen: Gyldendal, 1983.

Danstrup, John. *A History of Denmark.* Copenhagen: Wivel, 1949.

Danstrup, John, and Hal Koch. *Danmarks historie.* 14 vols. Copenhagen: Politikens forlag, 1962.

Davidsen, Jacob. *Fra det gamle Kongens Kjøbenhavn.* 2 vols. Copenhagen, 1880.

———. *Jødefeiden i Danmark: Den litterære Jødefeide, begyndt i 1813: Opløbet mod Jøderne i Kjøbenhavn og flere Provindsbyer i Danmark 1819–20: Af "Dags-Telegraphens" Feuilleton.* Copenhagen, 1869.

Dekel, Edan, and David Gantt Gurley. "How the Golem Came to Prague." *Jewish Quarterly Review* 103 (2013): 241–58.

Deutsch, Emanuel Oscar Menahem. *The Talmud.* Philadelphia, 1895.

Diepeveen, Leonard. *Changing Voices: The Modern Quoting Poem.* Ann Arbor: Univ. of Michigan Press, 1993.

Dolgopolsky, Aharon, and Colin Renfrew. *The Nostratic Macrofamily and Linguistic Palaeontology.* Oxford, UK: McDonald Institute for Archaeological Research, 1998.

Dreier, Frederik. *M. A. Goldschmidt, et Litteraturbillede.* Copenhagen, 1852.

Egebak, Jørgen. "Alting og forstanden: Meïr Goldschmidt, Bjergtagen I–II." In *Analyser af danske kortprosa*, edited by Jørgen Dines Johansen. Vol. 1, 204–25. Copenhagen: Borgen, 1971.

Egebak, Niels. *Mellem Heiberg og Brandes: P.L. Møllers plads i dansk kritiks historie*. Aarhus, Denmark: Modtryk, 1992.

Eliot, T. S. *Four Quartets*. New York: Harcourt Brace, 1943.

Encyclopaedia Judaica. Jerusalem: Encyclopaedia Judaica, 1971.

Field, Claud. *Jewish Legends of the Middle Ages*. London: S. Vallentine, n.d., ca. 1910.

Fisch, Harold. *New Stores for Old: Biblical Patterns in the Novel*. New York: St. Martin's Press, 1988.

Fishbane, Michael A. *Biblical Interpretation in Ancient Israel*. Oxford, UK: Clarendon Press, 1985.

———. *The Exegetical Imagination: On Jewish Thought and Theology*. Cambridge, MA: Harvard Univ. Press, 1998.

———. *The Midrashic Imagination: Jewish Exegesis, Thought, and History*. Albany: State Univ. of New York Press, 1993.

———. *Text and Texture*. New York: Schocken Books, 1979.

Fisher, Josef. "Meïr Goldschmidts Stamfædre." *Tidsskrift for jødiske historie og Literatur*, 1919–21, 35–52.

Freud, Sigmund. *Moses and Monotheism*. Translated by Katherine Jones. New York: Vintage Books, 1967.

Frieden, Ken. "Joseph Perl's Escape from Biblical Epigonism through Parody of Hasidic Writing." *AJS Review* 29 (2005): 265–82.

Frye, Northrop. *The Great Code: The Bible and Literature*. New York: Harcourt Brace Jovanovich, 1982.

Galchinsky, Michael. *The Origins of the Modern Jewish Woman Writer: Romance and Reform in Victorian English*. Detroit: Wayne State Univ. Press, 1996.

Gelfer-Jørgensen, Mirjam, ed. *Danish Jewish Art: Jews in Danish Art*. Copenhagen: Rhodos International Science and Art Publishers, 1999.

Genette, Gérard. *Narrative Discourse: An Essay in Method*. Translated by Jane E. Lewin. Ithaca, NY: Cornell Univ. Press, 1980.

Ginsberg, H. L. "Review of Joseph A. Fitzmyer's *The Genesis Apocryphon of Qumran Cave 1: A Commentary*." *Theological Studies* 28 (1967): 574–77.

Glasenapp, Gabriele von, and Hans Otto Horch. *Ghettoliteratur: eine Dokumentation zur deutsch-jüdischen Literaturgeschichte des 19. und frühen 20. Jahrhunderts.* 3 vols. in 2 bks. Tubingen, Germany: Max Niemeyer Verlag, 2005.

Gold, Carol. *Educating Middle-Class Daughters: Private Girls Schools in Copenhagen, 1790–1820.* Copenhagen: Royal Library, 1996.

Goldenberg, David B. *The Curse of Ham: Race and Slavery in Early Judaism, Christianity, and Islam.* Princeton, NJ: Princeton Univ. Press, 2003.

Greenblatt, Stephen. *Renaissance Self-Fashioning: From More to Shakespeare.* Chicago: Univ. of Chicago Press, 1980.

Greene-Gantzberg, Vivian. "En Jøde og samtidige jødiske skildringer." In *Danske studier*, edited by Iver Kjær and Flemming Lundgreen-Nielsen, 133–43. Copenhagen: Akademisk forlag, 1980.

Greenway, John L. *The Golden Horns: Mythic Imagination and the Nordic Past.* Athens: Univ. of Georgia Press, 1977.

Grosfoguel, Ramón. "The Structure of Knowledge in Westernized Universities: Epistemic Racism/Sexism and the Four Genocides/Epistemicides of the Long 16th Century." *Human Architecture: Journal of the Sociology of Self-Knowledge* 11 (2013): 73–89.

Hammerich, Fredrik. "Jødefolket after Christus." In *Brage og Idun, et nordisk Fjærdingårsskrift.* Vol. 3, edited by Frederik Barfod, 178–211. Copenhagen, 1840.

Hartman, Geoffrey H., and Stanford Budick. *Midrash and Literature.* New Haven: Yale Univ. Press, 1986.

Heinemann, Grace Birgit Wagner. "Den ideale Stræben: Træk af M. A. Goldschmidts livssyn og æsteti-belyst via 'Nord og Syd' og *Hjemløs*." Speciale til kandidateksamen, Univ. of Copenhagen, 1984.

Heller, Marvin J. *Further Studies in the Making of the Early Hebrew Book.* Leiden: Brill, 2013.

Hess, Jonathan M. *Germans, Jews, and the Claims of Modernity.* New Haven: Yale Univ. Press, 2002.

———. *Middlebrow Literature and the Making of German Jewish Identity.* Stanford, CA: Stanford Univ. Press, 2010.

Hess, Jonathan, Maurice Samuels, and Nadia Valman, eds. *Nineteenth Century Jewish Literature: A Reader.* Stanford, CA: Stanford Univ. Press, 2013.

Hollander, John. *The Figure of Echo: A Mode of Allusion in Milton and After.* Berkeley: Univ. of California Press, 1981.

Hong, Howard Vincent, and Edna Hatlestad Hong, eds. *The Corsair Affair and Articles Related to the Writings.* Princeton, NJ: Princeton Univ. Press, 1982.

Hoppe, Annemette. "Syndefaldet: et hovedmotiv i dansk og europæisk digtning." Speciale til kandidateksamen, Univ. of Copenhagen, 1976.

Hurwitz, Heimann. *Hebrew Tales: Selected and Translated from the Writings of the Ancient Hebrew Sages, to Which Is Prefixed an Essay on the Uninspired Literature of the Hebrews.* London, 1826.

———. *An Introductory Lecture Delivered in the University of London on Tuesday, November 11, 1828.* London, 1828.

———. *A Letter to Isaac L. Goldsmid, Chairman of the Association for Obtaining for British Jews Civil Rights and Privileges, on Certain Recent Mis-Statements Respecting the Jewish Religion, Reported to Have Been Made by One of the Hon. Members for Oldham.* London, 1833.

———. *Vindiciae Hebraicae; Or, A Defence of the Hebrew Scriptures, As a Vehicle of Revealed Religion: Occasioned by the Recent Strictures and Innovations of Mr. J. Bellamy; and in Confutation of His Attacks on All Preceding Translations, and on the Established Version in Particular.* London, 1820.

Hyman, Leonard. "Hyman Hurwitz, the First Anglo-Jewish Professor." *Transactions (Jewish Historical Society of England)* 21 (1967): 232–42.

Jacobs, Irving. *The Midrashic Process: Tradition and Interpretation in Rabbinic Judaism.* Cambridge, UK: Cambridge Univ. Press, 1995.

Jacobs, Jürgen, and Markus Krause. *Der deutsche Bildungsroman: Gattungsgeschichte vom 18. bis zum 20. Jahrhundert.* Munich: Beck, 1989.

Jacobson, David C. *Modern Midrash: The Retelling of Traditional Jewish Narratives by Twentieth-Century Hebrew Writers.* Albany: State Univ. of New York Press, 1987.

Jensen, Johan Fjord, Morten Møller, Toni Nielsen, and Jørgen Stigel. *Patriotismens tid 1746–1807.* Vol. 4, *Dansk litteraturhistorie.* Copenhagen: Gyldendal, 1983.

Jørgensen, Harald. *Indenfor murene: jødisk liv i Danmark 1684–1984.* Copenhagen: C. A. Reitzel, 1984.

Jost, François. "Variations on a Species: The *Bildungsroman.*" *Symposium* 37 (1983): 125–46.

Juhl-Christiansen, Marianne. "Goldschmidts digtning i 1860'erne." Speciale til kandidateksamen, Univ. of Copenhagen, 1967.

Katz, Per. *Jøderne i Danmark i det 17. århundrede.* Copenhagen: Reitzel, 1981.

Kings and Citizens: The History of the Jews in Denmark, 1622–1983. 2 vols. New York: Jewish Museum, 1983.

Kirmmse, Bruce H. *Kierkegaard in Golden-Age Denmark.* Bloomington: Indiana Univ. Press, 1990.

———. "Kierkegaard, Jews, and Judaism." *Kierkegaardiana* 17 (1994): 83–97.

Kohut, Alexander. "Abraham's Lesson in Tolerance." *Jewish Quarterly Review* 15 (1902): 104–11.

Kondrup, Johnny. "Meïr Goldschmidt: The Cross-Eyed Hunchback." In *Kierkegaard and His Danish Contemporaries*, edited by Jon Stewart, 105–47. Farnham, England: Ashgate, 2009.

Krinsky, Carol Herselle. *Synagogues of Europe: Architecture, History, Meaning.* Mineola, NY: Dover Publications, 1996.

Kronfeld, Chana. "Theories of Allusion and Imagist Intertextuality: When Iconoclasts Evoke the Bible." In *On the Margins of Modernism: Decentering Literary Dynamics*, 114–40. Berkeley: Univ. of California Press, 1996.

Kruse-Blinkenberg, Lars. *Assimilationens (u)mulighed.* Copenhagen: C. A. Reitzels Forlag, 2000.

———. *Jøden Simon Levi i M. Goldschmidts roman Ravnen.* Copenhagen: C. A. Reitzels Forlag, 1998.

Kugel, James L. *Traditions of the Bible: A Guide to the Bible as It Was at the Start of the Common Era.* Cambridge, MA: Harvard Univ. Press, 1998.

Kyrre, Hans. *M. Goldschmidt.* 2 vols. Copenhagen: H. Hagerup, 1919.

Langford, Richard E., ed. *Essays in Modern American Literature.* DeLand, FL: Stetson Univ. Press, 1963.

Laursen, John Christian. "Spinoza in Denmark and the Fall of Struensee, 1770–1772." *Journal of the History of Ideas* 61 (2000): 189–202.

Lausten, Martin Schwarz. *Frie jøder? Forholdet mellem kristne og jøder i Danmark fra Frihedsbrevet 1814 til Grundloven 1849.* Copenhagen: ANIS, 2005.

———. *Jews and Christians in Denmark: From the Middle Ages to Recent Times, ca. 1100–1948.* Translated by Margaret Ryan Hellman. Leiden: Brill, 2015.

Librett, Jeffrey S. *Orientalism and the Figure of the Jew.* New York: Fordham Univ. Press, 2015.

Lisi, Leonardo. *Marginal Modernity: The Aesthetics of Dependency from Kierkegaard to Joyce.* New York: Fordham Univ. Press, 2013.

———. "Scandinavia." In *The Cambridge Companion to European Modernism*, edited by Pericles Lewis, 191–203. Cambridge, UK: Cambridge Univ. Press, 2011.

Margolinsky, Jul, and Poul Meyer. *Ved 150 [hundrede halvtredsindstyve] aars-dagen for anordningen af 29. marts 1814. Nogle bidrag til Dansk-Jødisk historie.* Copenhagen: Det mosaiske Troessamfund og Danmarks Loge, 1964.

Marks, Jonathan. "Rousseau's Use of the Jewish Example." *Review of Politics* 72 (2010): 463–81.

Mellinkoff, Ruth. "Cain's Monstrous Progeny in Beowulf: Part I, Noachic Tradition." *Anglo-Saxon England* 8 (1979): 143–62.

———. *The Mark of Cain.* Berkeley: Univ. of California Press, 1981.

Minden, Michael. *The German Bildungsroman: Incest and Inheritance.* Cambridge, UK: Cambridge Univ. Press, 2010.

Mintz, Sharon Liberman, and Gabriel M. Goldstein, eds. *Printing the Talmud: From Bomberg to Schottenstein.* New York: Yeshiva Univ. Museum, 2005.

Mitchell, P. M. *A History of Danish Literature.* Copenhagen: Gyldendal, 1957.

Munksgaard, Ulla. "Nemesis." Speciale til kandidateksamen, Univ. of Copenhagen, 1982.

Münter, Balthasar. *Bekehrungsgeschichte des vormaligen Grafen und Königlichen Dänischen Geheimen Cabinetministers Johann Friederich Struensee, nebst desselben eigenhändiger Nachricht von der Art, wie er zur Aenderung seiner Gesinnungen über die Religion gekommen ist.* Copenhagen: Rothens Erben und Prost, 1772.

Nagy, Gregory. *Poetry as Performance: Homer and Beyond.* Cambridge, UK: Cambridge Univ. Press, 1996.

Nathan, Anja. "En kulturhistorisk efterprøvning af de jødiske skildringer i Goldschmidts fortællinger." Speciale til kandidateksamen, Univ. of Copenhagen, 1959.

Nathansen, Henri. *Georg Brandes; et portræt.* Copenhagen: Nyt nordisk forlag, 1929.

Neusner, Jacob. *Midrash in Context: Exegesis in Formative Judaism*. Philadelphia: Fortress Press, 1983.

———. *What Is Midrash?* Philadelphia: Fortress Press, 1994.

Nielsen, Søren Ole. "M. Goldschmidt: Den problematiske idealisme." MA thesis, Univ. of Copenhagen, 1981.

Norrie, Gordon. "Jødernes kamp for adgangen til Universitetet og den medicinske Docktorgrad i Danmark." In Bibliotek for Lager. Vol. 3, 117–38. Copenhagen: Fr. Bagges Bogtrykkeri, 1982.

Ober, Kenneth H. Afterword to *A Jew*, by Meïr Goldschmidt, translated by Kenneth Ober, 323–25. New York: Garland Publishing, 1990.

———. *Die Ghettogeschichte: Entstehung und Entwicklung einer Gattung*. Gottingen, Germany: Wallstein, 2001.

———. "A Forgotten Translation and a Forgotten Translator: Meïr Goldschmidt's 'Maser' in French." *Scandinavica* 32 (1993): 25–45.

———. "Goldschmidt's English Novel *Homeless*." *Orbis Litterarum* 34 (1979): 113–23.

———. "'Jeg vil . . . leve som Poet og som Oversætter.' Meïr Goldschmidt as a Translator." *Scandinavian Studies* 66 (1994): 23–44.

———. "'Med saadane Følelser skriver man en Roman.' Origins of Meïr Goldschmidt's *En Jøde*." *Scandinavica* 30 (1991): 25–39.

———. *Meïr Goldschmidt*. Boston: Twayne Publishers, 1976.

———. "Meïr Goldschmidt as a Writer of English." *Orbis Litterarum* 29 (1974): 231–44.

———. "Meïr Goldschmidt's 'Hebrew Legends': The Writer as Plagiarist?" *Scandinavica* 22 (1983): 15–21.

———. "Meïr Goldschmidt and the Main Currents in 19th-Century Judaism." *Nordisk Judaistik* 22, no. 1 (2001): 7–45.

———. "Meïr Goldschmidt og den tysk-jødiske ghetto fortælling." *RAMBAM* 31 (1991): 82–92.

Oehlenschläger, Adam. *Aladdin eller den Forunderlige Lampe: et Lystspil*. In *Poetiske Skrifter*. Vol. 2. Copenhagen, 1805.

———. *Axel og Valborg: et sörgespil*. Copenhagen, 1810.

Owens, Louis. *The Grapes of Wrath: Trouble in the Promised Land*. Boston: Twayne, 1989.

Oxfeldt, Elisabeth. *Nordic Orientalism: Paris and the Cosmopolitan Imagination, 1800–1900*. Copenhagen: Museum Tusculanum Press, 2005.

Pascheles, Wolf. *Gallerie der Sipurim: eine Sammlung jüdischer Sagen, Märchen, und Geschichten, als ein Beitrag zur Völkerkunde.* Prague, 1847.

Perri, Carmela. "On Alluding." *Poetics* 7 (1978): 289–307.

Politzer, Heinz. *Franz Kafka, Parable and Paradox.* Ithaca, NY: Cornell Univ. Press, 1962.

Prickett, Stephen. *Origins of Narrative: The Romantic Appropriation of the Bible.* Cambridge, UK: Cambridge Univ. Press, 1996.

———. *Words and The Word: Language, Poetics, and Biblical Interpretation.* Cambridge, UK: Cambridge Univ. Press, 1986.

Rasmussen, Jens. "Jødefejden og de besægtede uroligheder, 1819–20, 'Indledning til den store Scene?'" In *Kirkehistoriske Samling 2010*, edited by Carsten Bach–Nielsen, Jens Rasmussen, and Carsten Selch, 131–65. Copenhagen: Univ. of Copenhagen Press, 2010.

Reed, Walter. *Dialogues of the Word: The Bible as Literature According to Bakhtin.* New York: Oxford Univ. Press, 1993.

Rombold, Tamara. "Biblical Inversion in *The Grapes of Wrath*." *College Literature* 14 (1987): 146–66.

Rosenkjær, Birte. "Personligheden og dens ansvar i Goldschmidts romaner." Speciale til kandidateksamen, Univ. of Copenhagen, 1969.

Rossel, Sven Hakon. *A History of Danish Literature.* Lincoln: Univ. of Nebraska Press, 1992.

Rubow, Paul V. *Goldschmidt og Kierkegaard.* Copenhagen: Gyldendal, 1952.

———. *Goldschmidt og Nemesis.* Copenhagen: E. Munksgaard, 1968.

Ruderman, David B. *Jewish Enlightenment in an English Key: Anglo Jewry's Construction of Modern Jewish Thought.* Princeton, NJ: Princeton Univ. Press, 2000.

Salomon, Julius, and Josef Fischer. *Mindeskrift i anledning af hundredaarsdagen for anordningen af 29. marts 1814; en fremstilling af jødiske rets- og livsforhold i udland og indland navnlig i tiden omkring aar 1800, med en samling arkivalia.* Copenhagen: Denmarks Loge, 1914.

Samuels, Maurice. *Inventing the Israelite Jewish Fiction in Nineteenth-Century France.* Stanford, CA: Stanford Univ. Press, 2009.

Sasson, Sarah. *Longing to Belong: The Parvenu in Nineteenth-Century French and German Literature.* New York: Palgrave Macmillan, 2012.

Schneidau, Herbert N. *Sacred Discontent: The Bible and Western Tradition.* Berkeley: Univ. of California Press, 1977.

Scholem, Gershom. "Zehn unhistorische Sätze über Kabbala." In *Geist und Werk aus der Werkstatt unserer Autoren: zum 75. Geburtstag von Dr. Daniel Brody*, 209–15. Zurich: Rhein-Verlag, 1958.

Schou, Søren. "Kærlighedens Babelstårn. Meïr A. Goldschmidt: Kjærlighedshistorier fra mange lande." In *Læsninger i dansk litteratur*. Vol. 2, edited by Povl Schmidt. Odense, Denmark: Odense Univ. Press, 2001.

Schwarz, Jan. "En kultursociologisk analyse af Meïr A. Goldschmidts roman *En Jøde* (1845)." Speciale til kandidateksamen, Univ. of Copenhagen, 1983.

———. "'Serving Up His Grandmother in a Spicy Sauce': Conflicting Views on Jewish Literature in Nineteenth-Century Denmark." In *Speaking Jewish—Jewish Speak: Multilingualism in Western Ashkenazic Culture*, edited by Shlomo Berger, Aubrey Tolerance, Andrea Schatz, and Emile Schrijver. Studia Rosenthaliana, vol. 36. Leuven, Belgium: Peeters, 2003.

Schwartz, Regina, ed. *The Book and the Text: The Bible and Literary Theory*. Oxford, UK: Basil Blackwell, 1990.

Siesby, Gottlieb. *Mendel Levin Nathanson: en biographisk Skizze*. Copenhagen, 1845.

Singer, Isidore. *The Jewish Encyclopedia; A Descriptive Record of the History, Religion, Literature, and Customs of the Jewish People from the Earliest Times to the Present Day*. New York: Funk and Wagnalls, 1901.

Skolnik, Jonathan. *Jewish Pasts German Fictions: History, Memory, and Minority Culture in Germany, 1824–1955*. Stanford, CA: Stanford Univ. Press, 2014.

Skovmand, Roar. *Folkestyrets Fødsel 1830–1870*. Vol. 11 of Danmarks Historie, edited by John Danstrup and Hal Koch. Copenhagen: Politikens Forlag, 1964.

Søholm, Ejgil. "Goldschmidts to jyske fortællinger." *Danske Studier* 67 (1968): 27–59.

Sorkin, David Jan. *The Transformation of German Jewry, 1780–1840*. New York: Oxford Univ. Press, 1987.

Steinbeck, John. *The Grapes of Wrath*. New York: Penguin Books, 2006.

Stern, David. *Midrash and Theory: Ancient Jewish Exegesis and Contemporary Literary Studies*. Evanston, IL: Northwestern Univ. Press, 1996.

Stewart, Jon, ed. *Kierkegaard and His Contemporaries The Culture of Golden Age Denmark*. New York: Walter de Gruyter, 2003.

Toldberg, Helge. "Goldschmidt og Kierkegaard." In *Festskrift til Paul V. Rubow*, edited by Henning Fenger and Henrik Nyrop-Christensen, 211–35. Copenhagen: Gyldendal, 1956.

Tudvad, Peter. *Stadier på Antisemitismens vej: Søren Kierkegaard og Jøderne.* Copenhagen: Rosinante, 2010.

Valman, Nadia. *The Jewess in Nineteenth-Century British Literary Culture.* Cambridge, UK: Cambridge Univ. Press, 2007.

van Suntum, Lisa A. Rainwater. "Creating Jewish Identity Through Storytelling: The Tragedy of Jacob Bendixen." *Scandinavian Studies* 73 (2001): 375–98.

Vibæk, Jens. *Reform og Fallit 1784–1830.* Vol. 10 of *Danmarks Historie*, edited by John Danstrup and Hal Koch. Copenhagen: Politikens Forlag, 1964.

von Schnurbein, Stefanie. "Kampf um Subjektivität—Nation, Religion und Geschlecht in zwei dänischen Romanen um 1850." In *Bildung und Anderes. Alterität in Bildungsdiskursen in den skandinavischen Literaturen*, edited by Christiane Barz and Wolfgang Behschnitt, 111–29. Wurzburg, Germany: Ergon, 2007.

Weigand, Hermann J. "Heine's Return to God." *Modern Philology* 18, no. 6 (1920): 309–42.

Weinberg, Sonja. *Pogroms and Riots: German Press Responses to Anti-Jewish Violence in Germany and Russia (1881–1882).* Frankfurt am Main: Peter Lang, 2010.

Wentzel, Knud. *Fortolkning og Skæbne: Otte danske romaner fra romantismen og naturalismen.* Copenhagen: Fremad, 1970.

———. "Fremmed indflydelse på Goldschmidts forfatterskab." PhD diss., Univ. of Copenhagen, 1966.

———. "Udvikling og på virkning. Goldschmidts vej fra korsar til skriftklog." *Kritik* 10 (1969): 52–89.

Wöhrle, Georg. *Telemachs Reise: Väter und Söhne in Ilias und Odyssee oder ein Beitrag zur Erforschung der Männlichkeitsideologie in der homerischen Welt. Hypomnemata*, no. 124. Gottingen, Germany: Vandenhoeck and Ruprecht, 1999.

Wordsworth, William. *The Prelude, or Growth of a Poet's Mind.* Edited by Ernest De Selincourt. Oxford, UK: Oxford Univ. Press, 1926.

Yacobi, Tamar. "Fictional Reliability as a Communicative Problem." *Poetics Today* 2 (1981): 113–26.

———. "Narrative Structure and Fictional Mediation." *Poetics Today* 8 (1987): 335–72.

———. "Package Deals in Fictional Narrative: The Case of the Narrator's (Un)Reliability." *Narrative* 9 (2001): 223–29.

Yerushalmi, Yosef Hayim. *Zakhor, Jewish History and Jewish Memory*. Seattle: Univ. of Washington Press, 1996.

Yildiz, Yasemin. *Beyond the Mother Tongue: The Postmonolingual Condition*. New York: Fordham Univ. Press, 2011.

Zunz, Leopold. *Gesammelte Schriften*. 3 vols. Berlin, 1875.

Index

Italic page number denotes table.

David Gantt Gurley was born in Opelousas, Louisiana. He is an assistant professor of Scandinavian at the University of Oregon. His research interests include Jewish literature, Scandinavian literature, folklore, poetry and poetics, Indo-Iranian philology, and comparative epic, saga, and romance.